Leela's Book

Non-fiction

Empires of the Indus

Leela's Book

a novel

Alice Albinia

W. W. Norton & Company
New York · London

For information about permission to reproduce selections from this book,
write to Permissions, W. W. Norton & Company, Inc.,
500 Fifth Avenue, New York, NY 10110

For information about special discounts for bulk purchases,
please contact W. W. Norton Special Sales at
specialsales@wwnorton.com or 800-233-4830

Manufacturing by Courier Westford
Production manager: Anna Oler

Library of Congress Cataloging-in-Publication Data

Albinia, Alice, 1976–
Leela's book : a novel. — 1st American ed.
p. cm.
ISBN 978-0-393-08270-8 (hardcover)
1. Weddings—Fiction. 2. Ganesa (Hindu deity)—Fiction.
3. Delhi (India)—Fiction. I. Title.
PS6101.L42L44 2012
823'.92—dc23   2011040074

W. W. Norton & Company, Inc.
500 Fifth Avenue, New York, N.Y. 10110
www.wwnorton.com

ISBN 978-0-393-34393-9

W. W. Norton & Company Ltd.
Castle House, 75/76 Wells Street, London W1T 3QT

1 2 3 4 5 6 7 8 9 0

T.S.

Part One

chapter 1

'O elephant-headed god, son of Lord Shiva and Parvati; scribe who wrote down the Mahabharata from the seer Vyasa's dictation: Lord Ganesh, look favourably on this endeavour.'

Professor Ved Vyasa Chaturvedi paused, looked out across his audience, and smiled. 'The god invoked at the start of all compositions. What better way to begin?'

A ripple of laughter, fruity and indulgent, washed pleasantly through the room – and Vyasa knew at once that the audience was going to give him an easy time. At home, in India, he was equally familiar with adulation and denigration. His work was always coming under attack – from apoplectic Hindus, jealous colleagues, upstart young students, all of whom fired darts that fell harmlessly from him, as if he was Bhishma, invincible warrior of the Mahabharata. It was just such a missile – an egg, splatting against Vyasa's shoulder, leaving its bright trickle of photogenic yellow down his starched white kurta – that had first put his face on the front of every Delhi newspaper, and first linked his name with iconoclasm and controversy.

But these people – these coiffed and pressed, impeccably opinionated, yet traumatised New Yorkers – were not going to put up their hands at the end of his talk and ask complicated questions about obscure shlokas. It was unlikely that any of them would shuffle to their feet when Vyasa had finished speaking to tell a long, rambling anecdote about the god Ganesh's popularity among the Hindus and Buddhists of Nepal. That lady at the front with the blonde curls and white linen jacket: she was not going to rant about how Professor Chaturvedi maligned the divine dictation of India's epic. The New York Public Library was too large for such tirades, the domed glass ceiling of this room too politely soaring. Here, Vyasa had the soothing sensation of being underwater, in a cave of darting fish, cosseted deep within the library's glinting heart, within the belly of the city. These people had come to hear him because his books sold well, because he had appeared on American TV, because they had heard his voice on the radio reasoning with all the assembled cranks and ignoramuses of India. He knew it was odd – how in India, and increasingly elsewhere, such arcane knowledge, such esoteric subject-matter, had worked in his favour; how the journalists and editors had come to rely on his opinion, of all the very many available to them; how his doctoral thesis was edited down into a sumptuously illustrated book (which leapt to the top of the Indian bestseller lists and stayed there from Diwali through to Holi). He smiled at himself, at his outstanding good fortune, and when he opened his mouth again, the words came out just as he intended: honeyed, practised, slow.

'It is an honour for me to address you tonight at this time of crisis for your city,' he said, bowing his head towards the faces turned piously in his direction, so that the room burst into spontaneous applause. He paused again – gave the clapping a moment to subside – allowed the silence to thicken, grow rich; and when at last his elegant, persuasive voice vibrated through the air, and licked its way around the hall, the audience seemed to tremble in collective anticipation.

'Tonight I will speak on a subject very close to my heart, on the elephant-headed god Ganesh, the most endearing deity of the voluminous Hindu pantheon. Ganesh's cheerful, rotund form is found in homes and temples the length and breadth of the subcontinent. Every endeavour – every wedding, every business, every lecture, even – must begin with an invocation to Ganesh, who removes obstacles, and imposes them, on mortals. Ganesh is renowned, too, as the scribe of India's mammoth, all-encompassing epic, the Mahabharata. Tradition has it that he alone, of the many thousands of Hindu gods, was chosen by Brahma to write down this work of literature for Vyasa, its author.' Vyasa looked up from his notes and glanced around the hall. 'Yes, this same jovial-mysterious god was employed by my namesake.' The ties between them, Vyasa thought, went deeper than history and when he spoke next, his voice was almost a whisper: 'Yet in the current political climate, when my country is being run by right-wing Hindus, it behooves me to state clearly that, contrary to popular belief, despite the agonised utterances of certain religious factions, Ganesh was not actually the Mahabharata's scribe. It is dangerous to invoke the wrath of any deity's fanbase' – he threw the room a quick, practised smile – 'particularly those of the ever-living gods of India; but I feel sure that Ganesh himself would agree with me when I state that the elephant-headed god is an impostor.'

With that, Vyasa leant back on his heels – and the audience relaxed once more into laughter.

It was simple now; he had got them on his side. All he had to do for the rest of the hour allotted to this lecture was to stand here, square his shoulders, open his mouth, and the words he had spoken so often, in so many other, less-illustrious halls, in much further-flung corners of the world, would flow out of their own accord: as if his ancient literary forefather, Vyasa himself, was dictating the narration.

A door opened at the far end of the hall, and Vyasa registered a slim figure on the periphery of his vision, clad in an intense saffron-yellow. It wasn't one of his Hindu nationalist detractors, however. It was an Indian woman in a sari, who moved quietly along the back row of chairs and sat down in the corner. The colour was unusual for this borough of New York. The smart Indians who inhabited Manhattan did not usually wear saris like that, especially not in late October. They dressed like everybody else, in blacks and blues and cool off-whites, in wool and plaid and leather. They did not want to be mistaken for more recent, more aromatic, arrivals, the type who ran grocery stores in Queens. And Vyasa supposed that in the past month, few people of a certain complexion would venture forth in ethnic attire.

He still didn't turn to look at the woman in the sari – anyway, she was too far away for him to make out the details of her face, whether she was young or middle-aged, native to Manhattan or a provincial visitor – but her presence was beatific nonetheless, and as his argument grew in pace and complexity, as he dragged his audience back in time to the riverbanks and forests of ancient India, through prehistoric dictations and modern interpolations, the idea occurred to Vyasa, with a delicious shudder, that this distant blur of saffron-coloured femininity might be the very woman for whom he had pined so long – Leela.

New York had become her home. She was one of those Indians who, having left, chose never to return. He had wondered about her so often during the intervening years, had so frequently tried to imagine her new life in America, with its inevitable parade of children and possessions, accomplishments and disappointments, that this yearning had become a part of his being. But there was no need, any more, to be haunted by phantoms of her presence because, after all this time, and despite her many efforts to the contrary, Leela and he were destined to come together. His unsuspecting son was marrying the niece of Leela's husband – and Vyasa himself had subtly encouraged the union. Every thought he had had since arriving in New York, in her city, was freighted with the knowledge of this triumph.

'The Brahmins usually outlawed their sacred texts from being committed to writing,' Vyasa said now. 'Indeed, the Mahabharata's claim to sacred status as the fifth Veda is partially predicated on the ancient oral form of its transmission. So how, we might ask, did Ganesh come to be associated with the writing of it? I would like to suggest,' and here Vyasa gave one of his disarming smiles, 'that the sections of the Mahabharata that deal with Ganesh's scripting are in fact later interpolations. Ganesh was not there in the beginning.'

And as the roomful of New Yorkers leant forward to hear his controversial argument, Vyasa, almost giddy with desire, turned his eyes at last on the woman in the corner. He was bringing Leela back into the family, and there was nothing whatsoever she could do about it.

chapter 2

Hari gave his wife a nudge. 'Look, Leela. India.' She raised her eyes
from the newspaper she had been pretending to read and looked
out of the aeroplane window. There was nothing much to see yet:
a vast brown land mass shot through with green, waterways that
looked like trickles from this distance, those paper-thin fields upon
which the country depended for nourishment. 'We'll soon be flying
over Delhi,' Hari said, trying to contain his excitement. 'Connaught
Place, Humayun's tomb, India Gate, the Yamuna River.'

'Do we really fly in over the city?' Leela asked. She doubted it.
The airport was in the south-west.

But Hari wasn't listening. 'It's changed completely since you
were here last. Beyond the river there's so much development now.
Those jungly places in the south – where it was scrubland and dust
– nothing but houses. Offices everywhere, and new roads, and cars
of all types, from all over.'

Leela nodded. She had heard this wonderful story many times
before – the tamarisk and mango groves magically transformed
into high-rise blocks; the housing colonies and markets that had
sprung up along the river; and, above all, the arrival of the flashing,
beeping icons of modernity: cellphones, cappuccino, chainstores.

'You'll see,' Hari said. 'It's not the city you left behind.'

'We'll see,' she agreed.

She looked down again at the newspaper in her lap. A smiling stewardess had placed it in her hands as they boarded the flight. It was a Delhi tabloid, the *Delhi Star*, with yesterday's date on it, Thursday 8 November 2001; a paper which Hari's money had helped to finance. For the past seven hours she had let it lie there unopened, as if by ignoring it she might be able to defer the moment of return indefinitely; just as during the past twenty years she had avoided any news from India: no stories of her aunts (she had none), of the Congress Party (she wasn't bothered), of the fate of its poets, its radicals, its rivers (she blocked out these things she loved with scrupulous, ruthless care). Hari, for his part, had always done his best to bring these chaotic noises to her door. When his work took him into Jackson Heights, he would return to their apartment near the Met tenderly bearing boxes of guavas or mangoes; she knew from the smudge of red on his forehead and a particular glassy look in his eye that he had visited the temple. It was even worse after his journeys back to Delhi: then his clothes smelt different, his speech sounded foreign, and the temple-look had taken hold of his person, so that as he unpacked brocade silk saris for her from his suitcase, and sandalwood soap, and news of his brother Shiva Prasad's latest outrage, and breathless accounts of the effects of economic liberalisation, she always knew what would follow. 'Shall we go back in the autumn?' he would plead as he placed the empty suitcase back in the closet. 'Just for a holiday? To Kerala? Or Goa?' But each time she shook her head. 'There's nothing for me now in India, you know that.' And he would nod, resigned to this empty verdict, until the next time.

As the pilot's voice came over the tannoy, warning the passengers to fasten their seatbelts for the descent into Delhi, Leela lifted the newspaper in her hands, weighing it, as if its heft might tell her something. Then she bit her lip and fixed her eyes on the front page, where there was a story about the deal Pakistan's military dictator had done with the Americans, and a photograph of India's right-wing Hindu Prime Minister: a man whose thick-set, sleepy-looking face belied his sinister, sectarian politics. A column along the bottom told of a cultural détente between the two neighbours involving the exchange of important antiquities. It was just as she had thought: under the glitter, the same old India.

'There's an article about Professor Chaturvedi's wife,' Hari observed, without looking round from the window.

'Is there?' Leela said. Her heart began to pound.

'She wrote poems,' Hari observed. 'Her husband – Professor Chaturvedi – had them published after she died.'

'Really?' She flicked quickly through the inside pages, her eyes glancing over photographs of Delhi's highlife, at the news from the provinces. She turned to the back, to the finance and cricket. 'I can't see it,' she said, trying to keep her voice steady.

'It's in the Culture section,' Hari said. 'A new poem by her has just been discovered. What a literary family my niece is marrying into. You will find it interesting to meet them at the wedding, I am sure.'

'Indeed,' Leela said. The article was by a journalist called Pablo Fernandes who explained how, for three brief years during the late 1970s, Meera Chaturvedi had spun a series of poems richly interlaced with references to India's epic culture, shot through with veiled references to the poet's own experience, and then, two years after producing twins, Ashwin and Bharati, and twelve months or so after her Muse deserted her, died when a speeding truck ran her down early one morning in Delhi while her husband was away in Bombay. A small collection of what was believed to be her life's work had been published after her death. So this poem – this new discovery – shed a 'fascinating light' on Meera's *oeuvre*. Pablo

Fernandes made much of the scoop: how the envelope received at the newspaper offices in Delhi contained just one sheet of paper – the handwritten poem itself. There was no covering note, no return address, nothing. The poem, entitled 'The Last Dictation', was a nine-shloka verse in the anustubh metre, signed by 'Lalita', the poetic persona that Meera had adopted. But 'most intriguing of all', were certain lines – *'As we write, defend our children, | This last poem is our weapon, | A sisterhood of blood and ink: | Proof of our collaboration'* – which seemed to hint that Meera was not the sole author of this work. 'It looks to be one of India's most teasing literary connundrums,' Pablo Fernandes wrote – before concluding with a description of the poet herself, a woman whom many described as a Khajuraho carving come to life. There was a black-and-white photograph of her to prove it.

Leela stared down at the picture of her sister, all long, dark hair and flirtatious eyes; the caption even called her a 'literary siren'. Meera had died so long ago that Leela had learnt to contain the catastrophe of her loss, to hide it from the world, to hide it even from Hari, who had never been told that she once had a sister. But the picture had caught her off guard, and the sadness coursed through her as if the death was still fresh. Quickly, she bent her head towards the poem, and her eyes moved along the lines, seeing but not reading the verses, tears blurring the words she knew by heart, which Meera and she had written together.

She looked up suddenly, wondering whether Hari had some-how discovered that Meera Chaturvedi was her sister, whether this surprise wedding wasn't, in fact, a clever trap, a way of bringing her back into contact with everything she had banished so successfully for the past two decades. But she could see that her husband had already forgotten about the newspaper article. He was tensing himself instead for the joy of the moment when the plane's wheels hit the runway: was already anticipating pulling off his seatbelt, pulling out their luggage from the overhead locker, pulling her by the hand into the city.

She closed the paper and leant back in her seat. Who could have sent the poem to the paper? Surely not Vyasa. She shuddered at the thought of the man, with his seductive smile, his hair pulled back behind his head, his eyes that had a habit of softening when they rested on women he favoured. For years she had put him out of her mind, had tried to forget his brusque, confident way of speaking in public, and those whispered confidences, so striking in their contrast, which he had used like a charm on Meera. But now Hari was forcing her to remember. More than that, he was forcing her to be part of Vyasa's family. As they flew onwards through the sky, ever nearer to Delhi, Leela asked herself why she had allowed Hari to persuade her to return to the land she grew up in – when for years she had worked so hard to forget it.

She remembered the moment when Hari broke the news. It had been typical of him – of his sense of efficiency, of his dread of coming face to face with her displeasure – to choose a cellphone conversation as the means of imparting something so momentous. It was half past eight in the morning; she was walking her usual circuit through Central Park. 'I've reached the office,' Hari said, and Leela knew at once that he had something important to tell her. 'I've just heard some interesting news,' he said. 'The father of my niece Sunita's fiancé, the man she is marrying just before Diwali, a huge society wedding in Delhi, is—'

'Who?' Leela interrupted.

'Professor Ved Vyasa Chaturvedi,' Hari finished at last. 'And he is speaking tonight at the New York Public Library.'

'What?' Leela stopped walking, the phone still pressed to her ear, bewildered by hearing that man's name in Hari's mouth.

'He's giving a lecture,' Hari said, confident now that he had her attention. 'On the Mahabharata. It's just the kind of thing you like, isn't it, Leela? He's a very well-known professor. And his son is marrying my niece.' He paused, evidently pleased with the effect of this revelation. In the silence that followed, Leela turned this new information over in her mind. It seemed implausible that Hari had only just found out about this wedding. What else was he plotting?

Indeed, when Hari spoke next, he sounded nervous. 'There's something more I have to tell you, Leela. My nephew, Ram – Sunita's brother. I need someone I can trust to manage the business. I am making him my heir. He is such a good boy. I know that you'll like him. You will like him, won't you? He's a hard worker, an ideal son.'

'Your heir? A son?'

'Yes,' said Hari, growing excited. 'It would make a change to fill our lives with young people, wouldn't it, Leela?'

And the old, assertive Hari returned: 'It is not so unusual for brothers to take each other's children. We could go and collect him. We could move back home. Back to India. I want to live there, Leela. We could move into your house on Kasturba Gandhi Marg. We could all move there together. You, me and Ram. We will be like a family together.'

Leela had stood looking up through the grandeur of those tall, silent trees in which she had instinctively taken comfort when she arrived in this city, remembering the deal they had done when they married: that she would emigrate with him, bringing all her culture and poise to bear on his business, and that he, in return, would never ask about the time before they were married, would never – above all – force her to return to India. Like many of their compatriots, Hari pined for the place he grew up in; yet for twenty-two years he had honoured this arrangement.

Hari was still talking. 'I would go to the lecture myself,' he said, 'but I have an important dinner this evening. Can you go instead? I'd like you to meet him.'

'Who?' she asked, still disbelieving.

'Professor Ved Vyasa Chaturvedi. We should get to know him, now that he's going to be family.'

And so the sickening feeling came back to her that, once again, Vyasa was dictating the course of her life. The mere thought of Vyasa – of everything he had done – filled her with rage. But she said nothing further to Hari; and although she still felt angry, sitting on the plane with the paper folded in her hands – while she wanted to scream that she had been doubly betrayed, to weep that she would not set foot in her motherland however much he begged her – she knew, too, that the reason why she had agreed to come back had nothing to do with her husband and everything to do with Meera. Once, long ago, she had made a promise, and she could not leave India a second time until that promise had been honoured.

chapter 3

The day Hariprasad Sharma brought his wife back to India was the sum and pinnacle of all his achievements. For the month leading up to their departure from New York he could barely sleep from excitement.

'It will be Diwali just after we arrive!' he said as he showed her the tickets.

'The wedding is two days after we land,' he explained as he unlocked her jewellery.

'I've done up your house,' he confessed a week before their departure. 'Leela? The place your father left you?'

'Leela?' he said, when she failed to respond. 'Aren't you excited?'

No, Leela was not excited. She packed a small bag. A saffron-coloured sari. A sheaf of papers. A couple of old LPs.

They were met at the airport by his driver, who took them straight into the centre of Delhi on a suitably genteel route: along the empty road that led out of the airport terminus, past multinational hotels serving visitors in the city on business, into the calm diplomats' enclave of Chanakyapuri, through India Gate's ceremonial sand-stone vistas, along the wide, bungalow-lined avenues designed by Lutyens (Hari loved the Raj incarnation best of all Delhi's avatars) and due north-west along the street once known as Curzon Road, but which, since Independence, had been renamed Kasturba Gandhi Marg after the wife of the Father of the Nation.

Finally, Hari led his wife up the path to the secluded, two-storey house with its massive garden behind, whose construction dated back to before Independence, to the time when Connaught Place was built, to the creation of New Delhi. He was aware that his hands were trembling. The last time they stood together in front of this door was in 1980, when he had just asked this beautiful, English-speaking woman to marry him. He had already learnt that she was the only one living in this spacious residence which she was borrowing from her father who lived alone in Calcutta. She had explained that she had a job teaching at a school in Delhi. He had expected to find out so much more about her. But just as she had never invited him into the house, so she had never opened her past to him. And now, here they were, two decades later, having returned in this triumphant way to India.

Hari stepped aside and allowed Leela to enter the building first. But he followed eagerly after, for he couldn't wait to show her how wonderfully her father's gift to her had been transformed. 'A very rare location,' his architect had said, when Hari told him about it. 'A house on Kasturba Gandhi Marg? Impossible! Like gold dust.' When his nephew Ram suggested they live somewhere more modern, Hari shook his head. It was the heritage he wanted; and the link to Leela's past.

Over the past year, he'd had the house renovated from top to bottom: the kitchen ripped out, new units fitted, the roof terrace whitewashed and filled with plant pots, the Burma teak woodwork stripped and waxed, the terrazzo floor polished. Chandeliers now hung from the ceilings. Works of art from their house in America were splashed across the walls. Magazines and newspapers had been splayed out in a fan on the table in the hall. In the garden, steps led straight down from the terrace to a lawn that it had taken three malis eight months to tend, as if each blade of grass was a helpless newborn baby. The old ficus tree cast some perfect shade, the raat-ki-rani provided the sweet smell of autumn, and all along the edge were bougainvillea and jasmine, a gulmohar tree and an ashoka. A brick path led through the lawn to a red sandstone bench, above which was an alcove with a small stone statue of the god Ganesh. This space, so near Connaught Place, yet peaceful and secluded! Away from all the bustle and commerce and pollution!

But the pièce de résistance – Hari took Leela into the bedroom to show her – was a wardrobe full of new saris: silks, georgettes, chiffon, Banarsi, and his favourite, Bengali tangail cotton. He had chosen them personally. Hari couldn't stop smiling. His wife, back in India. His dream had come true.

The following morning was a Saturday, and (ever the tactician) Hari took the opportunity to drive down to his office in South Delhi – supposedly to make sure everything was in order, but really to give his wife the chance to unpack and get acquainted with her new surroundings. 'Will you be all right?' he said as he left. 'Do you need anything? The driver is here. The cook will leave at seven. The maid should be done by then too. There's—'

'I'll be just fine,' she said, blowing cigarette smoke into the air and smiling.

He watched her as she stood in the middle of the garden. Smoking was a new habit; Hari had yet to voice his disapproval.

It being so near Diwali, there was a festive spirit in Delhi's exhaust-filled air, and Hari's Saturday excursion took longer than he meant it to. When he arrived home at six, the house was empty. 'Where is Mrs Sharma?' he asked the cook, who was making curd in the kitchen.

'She went out,' the cook said.

Hari walked through to the high-ceilinged drawing room, which overlooked the garden, mixed himself a gin and tonic, and settled back into one of his newly upholstered pale khadi silk chairs. The familiar warmth of alcohol would settle his nerves. He felt tense sitting here, like a shy young groom awaiting his bride.

The maid had lit only two of the silk-shaded lamps, and the light they cast in the early-evening shadow, across the faded Persian . carpets and embroidered settee, was pleasantly dappled; it reminded Hari of the sal forests outside the village he grew up in, where his father had taken him every Sunday morning, explaining about the mahua tree and how this land was sacred to its indigenous inhabitants who had lived there since time began. Hari was pleased with the effect he had created in this house, with its amalgamation of different epochs of his marriage – the paintings from their modern art-daubed apartment in New York, the Mexican ethnic artefacts gathered during a trip across the border, the bits and pieces collected from travels to London, Geneva, Venice, and transplanted to New Delhi. Things had moved on considerably since that morning three years ago in New York, when Leela revealed that her father had left her the Delhi property.

Hari had been taken aback. 'But your father died, what, in nineteen eighty-five? Almost twenty years ago.'

Leela stirred brown sugar into her porridge. 'There were tenants in the building till just now. The issue has only just been resolved.' She unfolded the crisp, lawyer's letter, and passed it over.

Leela said nothing more, and during the next fifty trips to Delhi, Hari stayed as usual in the Imperial Hotel. But it was the house that set him thinking. Does a house represent a root? he wondered, late at night, lying on his side in New York, in the enormous double bed they still shared. Was a house enough to bring his wife back home?

The night Hari met Leela he was at a crowded garden party thrown by the company he worked for. He had been in a strangely febrile mood. For the past few months he had been obsessed by the idea of setting up his own business. As he approached his boss (soon to be his rival), bearing a small box of sweets tied with a ribbon, Hari's attention was drawn to a young woman. It was Leela. Hari's boss and his wife, who was Leela's colleague, were listening attentively as she told a story. Hari took in her dark, sardonic eyes, her dignified bearing, wrapped so elegantly in a simple cotton sari, and he told himself with a defiant pang that with a woman like that at his side, he could take on the world. That evening, when Hari offered Leela a lift home, to his surprise she ended up staying at his place. They continued to see each other in the weeks that followed. Two months later, he had started his own import-export cotton clothing company, Harry Couture (he thought of calling it Dharma or Karma or even Bharata but Leela persuaded him this was more personable). Soon after that they were married, and on their way to New York. Leela's father blessed their union with his approval but not his presence. Leela explained to Hari that she was adopted, that her mother had died when she was at college, that her father loved her, but his grief kept him in Calcutta. The intimate disclosure affected Hari deeply; he promised himself that he would protect her. This feeling was reinforced some five years later, when her father died. She was all alone in the world, with nobody to look after her except Hariprasad Sharma. The sacred duty made him proud.

Happily, Leela more than made up for her negative equity in the area of family. She was an excellent investment: loving and supportive, constantly feeding his commercial instinct with money-making plans. As she set up house in New York, Hari instructed his workers back home to sew see-through frills of shiny polyester into slippery shifts and lacy slips – replicating designs Leela brought home from

Macy's. In 1982, he opened a second line, Namaste India, selling ethnic chic to American teenagers. In 1984, their wealth was assured with the purchase of a riot-stripped dried fruits shop belonging to an Old Delhi Sikh; Hari took over the ailing godown – the man was emigrating to America to run one of those 7-Elevens – expanded the line to include pistachios and Kullu apricots, Leela designed the packaging in black and gold, and he sold his product to all the smartest grocery stores in New York, cresting a wave of interest in Indian cuisine. As the eighties stretched profitably into the liberalised nineties, Hari became a gem king, making the emerald his corporation's niche. Cut in Rajasthan, designed in Karol Bagh, set by a team of Bangladeshis on the top floor of a workshop behind Chandni Chowk, destined for Manhattan, the margins were wide, the profits divine. Finally, in 1994, Hari agreed to put money into a new English-language newspaper, a tabloid jauntily named the *Delhi Star*, twenty-four per cent of which was owned by a foreign media conglomerate. It was an exciting departure for India. Hari never dreamt of the trouble that would ensue.

The 'trouble' concerned Hari's elder brother, Shiva Prasad, who threatened never to speak to him again if he persisted in this money-grabbing, foreign-funded, English-language venture. He shouted that his little brother's trade was demeaning for a Brahmin; that it was unpatriotic to promote the colonial language through his media venture; that it was wicked to do business with immoral global corporations. For Hari, whose patriotism was as mild as his personal politics were vague, Shiva Prasad's vehemence was perplexing, irritating and economically irrelevant. 'He's out of date,' Hari protested to Leela. 'And besides, even his own party is in bed with the multinationals.'

'He's jealous of your success, that's all,' she replied. Shiva Prasad had always been a bully; and Hari refused to give up his new endeavour. For a time, the brothers seemed destined to go their separate ways.

But Hari missed his brother. Though they hadn't been close as children, Shiva Prasad was part of his life. It was all right for Westerners to behave in that detached way, Hari reflected, but it wasn't possible for Indians. And he wondered, late one night, whether he had spent rather too much time in super-charged, family-lite America. Then he hit on a plan. It wasn't revenge. Far from that. It was a way of reconnecting with family.

Soon after they were married, Hari and Leela had agreed to wait a few years before having children. A few years turned to six; by now Hari was amply rich; he expected a child. They copulated scientifically. Leela turned thirty, his mother rang him from India to explain about gurus and practices, and Hari began going to the temple on the other side of town. He would enter the sanctum quietly, aware of where the idol stood, a black stone, dabbed orange at its base: Ganesh with his long curved trunk, ears alert and wide apart, listening. Hari felt comfort in this place.

But he began to see that he had wanted too much from Leela Bose. He was proud of his graceful, atheist, modern wife. But he had other expectations, too, of a kind of womanhood that came to seem impossible. Too late, he understood that he had wanted a virgin on his wedding night; that he had expected a religious wife. Hari never discussed religion with Leela. In the early years, she went through the motions of pious belief, bowing her head to the puja fire his mother lit on her visits to New York, buying the appropriate sweets for the proper people on every propitious date. But he felt there was something missing – a critical lack of fervour – and that for his wife, the fathomless space, which his mother filled with voluminous gods, remained empty. It was but a matter of time before Hari sought the solace of the supernatural.

But even that couldn't help when it came to reproduction. So in the end, Hari fell back on the resources of family.

On one of his many visits back to India, Hari arranged a secret meeting with his brother's son Ram. Uncle and nephew – united by a mutual love of capital – had always got on, and Hari, who kept a careful eye on his brother's finances (dented by a self-published book in Hindi on the 'Indigenous Origins of the Indo-Arya'), guessed that Shiva Prasad had nothing to offer the market-oriented Ram which he could possibly desire. This was Hari's moment. Like a fairy godmother in a smartly tailored Western suit, he stepped neatly into the financial breach, waving a dollar-coloured wand.

Hari was philosophical. He knew that he mustn't, under any circumstances, make it too easy for his heir. Ram would have to work, he would have to sing for his supper, he would have to prove that, despite his father's Arya posturing, he was worthy of being his uncle's heir. Ram did exactly as Hari asked. He took a degree in Economics. He studied for an MBA. He even did time on the garment-factory floor. Having done all this, he was ready to move into Hari's office as his understudy, and thence into Hari's house. But there was one major obstacle to this plan: Hari's relationship with his brother.

Shiva Prasad's beloved eldest daughter, Urvashi, meanwhile, had made an unsuitable marriage. She eloped with a Muslim, which in the context of her father's position as a pillar of Hindu society, was a near disaster. She was already twenty-three, and the Muslim boy, Hari discovered, came from an upper-middle-class family of printers, now settled in South Delhi. With rewarding prescience, Urvashi's husband had shifted the printing press from the site of his father's works near Kashmiri Gate to a modern complex in Okhla, easily accessible to the South Delhi businesses; while his father printed a respected Urdu daily, the son switched to English; and so the business boomed.

Shiva Prasad responded to his favourite daughter's Muslim marriage with characteristic zeal, banishing his Urvashi from the house. Childless himself, Hari was at pains to understand his brother's trenchant attitude to his offspring. What he did comprehend was that while the loss of a daughter was one thing (she was bound to leave in the end), the loss of a son would have been sacrilege beyond repair.

But then Sunita, Urvashi's little sister, got herself engaged – a surprise love match, all her own initiative – to the son of India's most celebrated Sanskrit scholar. The Sharmas hailed from a small town in the middle of India. The Chaturvedis belonged to Delhi's urban elite. It was a glittering alliance: far beyond the prospects of Sunita's family and friends. Her father, a sucker – like anyone with political ambitions – for celebrity, power and connections, was overwhelmed. According to Ram, Shiva Prasad considered, only briefly, the awkward fact that he, father of the bride, was ideologically opposed to him, father of the groom. He briskly set aside in his mind the hours he had spent ranting with fellow party members about Professor Ved Vyasa Chaturvedi's heinous views on Hindu mythology, the gods, the Vedas. He became amnesiac about the curses he had shouted against liberal academics, anti-national atheists, and other persons of Chaturvedi's ilk. There were, finally, greater issues at stake than national and religious morality.

But this chance for his own and his family's social promotion did not come without its worries. As Ram told Hari, Shiva Prasad was in financial despair. The expense of putting on a wedding with a guest list of politicians, TV figures and newspaper editors was astronomical. Shiva Prasad had already cashed in his Provident Fund – and that barely covered the basic catering arrangements.

It still left the venue, the invitations, the pandal, the pandit, his daughter's trousseau and a modern-era dowry of assorted electronic items.

Hari saw his chance. Without letting on to his wife what he was up to, he rang Manoj, his brother's assistant, early one morning from New York, to discuss a donation to the 'wedding account'. 'Would fifty lakhs cover some of the more vital costs?' Hari asked. And from the next room, Shiva Prasad intimated that fifty lakh rupees would just about do. So brother Hari bankrolled the wedding party. But there is no such thing as a free lunch – at least, not when it is on a wedding menu. Now that he was back in Delhi, Hari planned to visit his brother's house and suggest a revision of family affairs. But he had to do it delicately. It wasn't just that Shiva Prasad might feel inadequate for failing to provide for Ram's material ambitions; he would also object to the taint of merchants, money and foreign influence that came from associating with – profiting from – his brother Hari's world.

What Hari most wanted to achieve, however, was something that went beyond a convenient family business arrangement. He wanted a reconciliation. He wanted his brother to welcome him back, so that the Sharmas could be a family again. That was his plan.

Hari put down his gin and tonic and moved to the old record player under the garden window. Wonderful things were in the offing, and yet, despite everything, he still worried about Leela. He took one of her LPs from its torn and faded sleeve, and placed it on the turntable. 'This is my only dowry,' Leela had told him as she put the thirteen records in his arms. In the early days, she listened to them again and again – she could sing each film song by heart – and the thin sweet music still made Hari thirst for dreams of that early married time. Back then, he had imagined tiny pattering feet and plump infant limbs; he had thought he would see her dressed in a cotton sari, frying parathas for their son; or on the terrace of a Delhi barsaati, rocking their daughter in her arms. He had visions of himself, the perfect father, lighting Diwali diyas with his daughter, or teaching his son to be a man.

Over the past twelve months, Hari had wanted *so much* to tell Leela of his plans. He had practised how he might explain Ram's arrival; rehearsed meetings in his head; planned dinners, impromptu walks, bedtime conversations. He would take her hand, in these visions, and reveal in quiet, reasonable tones how their family could be. She, in turn, would nod, smile, signal by the touch of her hand on his that her desires concurred with his own. But somehow the correct moment kept slipping away. They seemed to waste so much time at parties, fundraising events and functions. Did they really spend so little time alone? Whatever the reason, Hari failed to find the courage to speak. He waited until he had cancelled their holiday in Paris, had moved paintings and furniture out of storage to their house in New Delhi, had booked their tickets to India – and still he hadn't told her. It wasn't until the morning of Professor Chaturvedi's lecture in New York – after Ram rang to inform him it was taking place – that Hari knew he could delay no longer.

Standing at the window, looking out over the garden, listening to the sad song reach its climax, Hari thought with another pang about his wife. She had never wanted to return to India; staying away from this country was the one thing she had asked of him in twenty years of marriage. And yet, here they were.

But the doorbell rang at just this moment, and Hari, who knew that his nephew had arrived, turned away from the window with his usual resolve. Tonight, Ram Sharma would return here as Hari's son. Tonight, Leela and he would become parents. Tonight, Hariprasad's family would begin to function in the way he had always intended. Everything rested on the filial alliance.

chapter 4

It is with great pleasure and evident facility that I begin my portion of these pages. Not a moment too soon. (Even a mite too late? I should see about getting the order changed.) For words come naturally to me.

Allow me to introduce myself. I am Ganesh, elephant-headed god, misshapen son of Lord Shiva and Parvati; beheaded by my father for protecting my mother's honour; abusively given this flippant elephant replacement; too-long-term resident of Kailash, that icy and unfriendly mountain where my family chose to live; befriended only by my faithful Rat (divine vahana, godly mode of transport). I freely admit that my sworn enemy is Vyasa, pedestrian composer of India's too-long epic, a poem called the Mahabharata, every word of which I wrote.

Even as a very young elephant, I could feel words building up inside me, pressing against the end of my trunk, fighting to get out – and all at once I would lose control, as a great trumpeting, ear-popping tirade came shooting out into the air to disturb the concentration of that self-obsessed meditation hillock they called Kailash. Before my family could reproach me, I would run off to my side of the mountain, crouch over my peacock-feather pen like a guilty adolescent, and write without stopping.

What did I write about? I hear you ask. Well, the inner lives of others, whose experiences jumped, unbidden, into my mind. It brings me to the point of tears to remember how my father Shiva – the famous ascetic – would thwack me with his trident as I sat chattering during his meditation class, transcribing the thoughts that passed through his mind (*Parvati, come to me, honey-thighed princess*); to recall the ill-tempered curses that met my efforts at indicating to my family the folly of their ways; to recollect those long, brave sessions in the solitary company of my dear little Rat – the only member of our household who would prick up his ears and listen, truly listen, as I poured out my woes.

I was certainly brought up very badly. It is indeed nothing short of a miracle – given the unfavourable circumstances of my early elevation – that I was able to maintain my integrity, believe in my bent, and trust in my trueborn knack of telling a good story.

The danger was that, having had it drummed into me that what I did was *wrong*, I would come to believe that what my family said was true: I would start to interpret my creative faculties as the sign of a voyeuristic bore. And I did listen and did feel dismayed when my mother wailed: 'Oh, Ganesh. You cannot always be telling people their own stories!'

But bards are supposed to tell the truth. Did Ugrasravas, son of Lomaharsana, singer of the ancient Lore, compromise on this count? No. Did Homer skip the bad bits? I assure you he did not. Back then, stuck in an eternity of timelessness, a vacuum of art and words, I had no way of convincing my parents of this. I was nothing better than a lonely penman lost to his ignorant family.

But while the repression I suffered would have cowed a less resilient will than mine, I am made of determined matter, and neither my father's scowl nor my brother's prickly arrow points could dent my verbal shield for long. Like Valmikiya (author of

that very minor epic, the Ramayana) I turned 'shoka' to 'shloka'
(sorrow to resounding verse) and realised how far too lavishly I
was endowed to be sitting around on that barbaric goddery-colony
and waiting for my kishti to come in. I had almost reached the
stage of final disillusion with the other gods. My mind was filled
up with serial somethings – they would surface, irrepressible, to
taunt me – and thus was I forced to spend more and more time on
the other side of the mountain, writing it all down, lost in a world
of my own invention. And then something happened that helped
it very much. Vyasa turned up.

Yes, up he came, huffing and puffing through the mist, tramping
through the snow, hyperventilating to the crest of Kailash Hill
– where he threw himself at my feet, laid himself open to my
mercy, and begged me to lend him my famed transcriptional faculties. For by then, even the good god Brahma had heard tell of my
wordy affliction. Vyasa had complained to him: 'O Brahma, a Poem
which is greatly respected, has been composed by me. It contains
the mystery of the Vedas, the hymns of the Upanishads and the
history of time Past, Present and Future. It explains the nature of
existence and non-existence, the rules for the four castes, and the
dimensions of the earth, sun and moon. It reveals the art of war,
the key to different races and the languages of all men. Everything
has been put in this Poem. But I cannot find anyone to write my
Mahabharata down.'

Brahma, being an infinite and beneficent god of creation,
thought that, despite the poem's unmarketable length, it might
be worth a try (it could always be sold as Religion). So he put his
finger against his nose, looked up at the sky, down at Vyasa, and
then he said: 'You have revealed divine words in the language of
truth even from their inception. That's all very well. But now ask
Ganesh to write it out for you.'

So off Vyasa went to find me. 'Ganesh,' he said, when he had got his breath back from the trek up the mountain, 'become the scribe of my Mahabharata, which I have composed in my mind and shall now repeat.' He explained how he had heard from Brahma that I couldn't say no to a saga. And he was right. Being an instinctive elephant, I had already seen the potential of Vyasa's tale in ways its author couldn't begin to gauge. So I said: 'Ganesh will be the writer of the work, provided his pen is not made to stop even for a moment.' Vyasa said: 'Stop writing only when you do not understand a passage.' I said: 'Om.' And so we set to work – going back to the beginning, for like all good stories we had started in the middle and were ending near the start.

Now, in the Mahabharata, Vyasa portrays himself as a holy sage, with matted hair and an otherworldly air, an expert teacher, the counsellor of kings, the wise old grandfather of his characters. He builds up a fabulous portrait: comforting yet aloof, clever yet alluring. I have only one problem with this benign vision: it is totally untrue. In these pages of mine, I will correct the misapprehension under which mortals have languished for so long. I will show how Vyasa disrespected ladies, failed to dissuade his descendants from mutual carnage, gave students of literature headaches with his prose.

Alas, it took an aeon to get the story out. Vyasa was a meanderer, and the sluggish river of his poetry had many tributaries, ox-bow lakes and stagnant pools (not to mention too many narrators). With its gigantic cast, mindbending time span, and extensive locations, his Mahabharata was far too large, even for India. Elephantine. But I tugged and I pulled and I urged Vyasa onwards – until at last the bawling progeny of his experiences and dreams came slithering out through his labour pains, into my waiting pen.

The thing that set these literary efforts of ours apart from any ordinary act of authorship was that while we were up on Kailash (he talking, me scribbling), down below on earth everything Vyasa spoke of was *actually coming to pass*. That much everybody knows: Vyasa's characters peopled India. But the thing that nobody else has yet been apprised of – the glorious twist that I have waited until now to reveal – is that Vyasa's Great Poem was also the fertile seedbed for my own imaginings: for my own invented cast.

Vyasa, like all dictators, was paradoxical. He guarded his story jealously, refusing to let it be published during the lifetime of his grandsons, for they, of course, were in it, and reading it, would have known what was going to happen next. And yet, despite keeping a very strict eye on the whereabouts of the manuscript – regulating exactly who could learn which sections when – he never once stopped to check what I had written. Perhaps, having thought through those one hundred thousand shlokas twice already, he hadn't the energy to read them again. Maybe, illiterate bard that he was, he had no way of checking. Or possibly he credited me with more godly honour than is my divine due. In short, I would still be feeling guilty today, were it not for the fact that, without my specific actions, certain important people – the top quality fabric of the story I am about to unfold – would never have seen the limey light of day.

So there we were. Vyasa – with his version of events. And me – all outward concurrence and inward dissension – with mine. And Vyasa never noticed my interpolations until it was far too late.

In truth, at the beginning, my people were shadowy types, marginal jottings, easily overlooked. They slipped between the pages of Vyasa's text, namelessly traversed the hallowed Vedic scene of ancient Bharat, touched the hem of the holy Pandavas, proffered handfuls of water, vaginas of sex, prostrate bodies for the killing or selling to the waiting, warring clans. Local and imported slave-girls, elephant-riding mlecchas: the barbarian underclass of Aryan dominance, this was my clay. But I was determined to cast them right. My text was their dramatic debut; they were my directorial cue. And I had my eye on posterity. What I needed was a winning formula, a human team of characters who would grow to person-hood within the pages of Vyasa's book, and then reincarnate across the centuries, each successive life giving each individual character the time and space to practise traits and eliminate tics, to perfect qualities and hone actions, until they had mastered my mode and message. (And yet, all too quickly, they slipped from my grasp and started dictating plot twists of their own.)

But I am getting ahead of myself. Let us go back to the begin-ning. Back to those infantile Kailash days. Allow me to unveil my leading lady.

Leela, lovely Leela, came to me one morning in a haze of undis-covered alphabets as I lay sweating on the hillside after a thankless fit of wordsmithery. She emerged fully formed from the froth and foam of my subconscious with the vagueness of a summer dusk: naked, soft, pulsing with promise, her breasts as delectable as monsoon mangoes, her stomach a gentle curve, her cow-lash eyes impossibly elongated. I had birthed a beauty.

Without mentioning a word of it to anyone, I simply dropped her into Vyasa's tale, at one of the few places in the epic where a character didn't have a name – Vyasa's own bed, as it happened – as the amorous slave-girl he impregnated by mistake (after his late brother's widows had had enough of him).

Avatar 1: Fish

Of course you remember the story: Vyasa's fish-born mother conceived him out of wedlock, and then went on to marry a magnifi-cent king, by whom she had two useless sons, one of whom died young in battle and the other of sickness even before fathering heirs upon two wives, the sisters Ambika and Ambalika. Vyasa's mother, who, like every woman, longed to hold her offspring's offspring in her arms (and in this way secure their kingdom), summoned her surviving son and demanded that he foist his sperm upon the sisters. *Go on*, she said, *It's up to you now*. And so it was: Vyasa went to bed with his dead brother's wives.

Unlike most authors, Vyasa was not vain about his own appearance. He described it in disarming, disgusting detail: his appalling ascetic's odour, his hideous hair, that gleam in the eyes that seems to afflict the country's holiest of men. Ambika, whose turn it was first, cowered when she saw him approaching. She shut her eyes tight and refused to open them again until Vyasa had withdrawn himself from her presence and left her to incubate their baby alone. But the sage was not amused by her obvious displeasure. He cursed her as he left – and, true to his word, their child was born blind. Ambalika, who went second, did not like the great epic-touter either. She turned pale with repulsion when he showed his naked body to her, and this time the sage bestowed on their offspring a deathly pale complexion. But these two ill-begotten children were not enough for Vyasa's mother. She wanted a third, and since neither Ambika nor Ambalika wished to sleep with Vyasa again, they sent a substitute, a servant-girl dressed up in royal robes.

This was where I came in. This was where I inserted my precious Leela. It seemed like a brilliant ploy at the time, a subtle and subversive way to inviegle my character into his Mahabharata. Only later did I realise the scale of my error.

Vyasa, you see, was quite taken by Leela: he wouldn't leave her alone, he harried her with kisses, he pestered her with inappropriate advances. She ran from him, threw herself onto the hard stone floor of the temple where the idol of Ganesh was standing, and screamed at the statue with its dull eyes and absurd fat belly. *Save me from this monster*, she implored. What have I done to my creation? I said to myself as I watched her. *You've pimped me to your enemy*, she seemed to scream as she lay there. And if there had been blood in my veins it would have run cold.

I did what I could to wrest back control. I stowed the servant-girl away on a skiff carrying Kashmiri saffron downstream to where the Yamuna joined the Ganga, and sent Vyasa off into the wilderness to indulge in some enforced meditation.

Life expectancy for servant-girls was not very long back then. She lived out the span of her mortal life unharried by Vyasa, and though I bitterly mourned her departure – my first creation, so short-lived, so thwarted – to my delight she was soon reincarnated: this time into the bosom of an inconspicuous and low-caste fishing family who lived in long wooden boats on the banks of the River Yamuna in an out-of-the-way place called Indraprastha. She was born not long before the war that ended Vyasa's story.

Avatar 2: The Wife-Life

Unfortunately, Vyasa had already had the idea to steal Indraprastha as a location for his epic. At first, I didn't notice. It was such a nondescript little village (I thought), a mere collection of huts on the banks of the Yamuna (a lovely stream with its snowmelt, mountain breeze and cold, deeply flowing water). But as it happened, Vyasa's grandsons had lived there in their made-up palace; and later it would become the Mughal headquarters; and subsequently the capital of British India, by then renamed Delhi. Had I foreseen this, I would certainly have moved my Leela on elsewhere. But back then I was innocent of history's grubby paws, and could not conceive of anywhere more discreet than this scraggle of champak trees and small collection of fish-odourated people.

With joy I observed Leela turning from a girl into a woman; smiled as I saw what a headstrong young person my imagination had spawned; laughed to myself as I witnessed how my creation had inherited my love of storytelling. For as she ferried passengers across the river, Leela sang songs of the republics ruled by women in the land beyond the Great Himalaya; of the hill tribes to the west where women danced without censure; of the matriarchal rulers of the south, where mothers gave their children money, moral guidance and even the names they carried (. . . and the fathers, it was whispered, cleaned the house and prepared the dinner). So famed did these rebellious ditties become, so frequently did they turn the heads of the women who heard them – child-brides in fertile red being carried off to their weddings, mothers pregnant with their seventh offspring, grandmothers bent under decades of labour – that they came to the hearing of Vyasa himself, who travelled downstream to take a look at my Leela and gauge the challenge she posed to his avowed mission of peopling the land with the fruit of his loins, with a breed of warriors of particular ferocity.

Leela was not afraid of the wily old Brahmin. She had a low opinion of his cheap narrative machinations, and she voiced it thus to anyone who would listen. She said she had heard the implausible story he had put about of his mother's conception (of how his grandfather, the king, entrusted his sperm to a bird, who dropped it into a river where it fell into the mouth of a piscine goddess) and as far as she was concerned, it stank: a fishy tale, invented by Vyasa to make his mother sound high-caste, and his own subsequent conception purer. Leela herself recounted a more prosaic version: that the queen, Vyasa's step-grandmother, was barren; that the king risked his heirs upon the river ladies who lived in such freedom on the banks of his kingdom; that only an unscrupulous liar like Vyasa could have foisted such an outrageous story on humankind through his deceitful epic.

By now Vyasa was a sage great in austerities and since it was irksome to have one's reputation assaulted by an insignificant ferry-woman, he arrived at the riverbank prepared to silence her. But as he watched Leela rowing passengers across the river, returning with her boat, waiting with one foot on the bank and the other on the prow, her toes stained with henna, her hair uncovered, the five-metre cloth of her sari not even attempting to conceal the curve of her bosom; as soon he glimpsed her – this lithe-limbed lass dressed in very little attire, the cold dark water swirling her unstitched cloth like monsoon clouds around her thighs – he had a better idea. At dusk, he approached the bank and called across to where Leela was sitting with her feet up on an island in the middle of the river. Turning her head, catching sight of his improper looks of longing, she cursed him for his attempts to learn her songs and steal her stories, and for his designs to elevate himself away from the amphibious riverstock of his mother.

Unfortunately, when it came to illustrious matches and the monetary rewards offered by powerful Brahmin sages, Leela's opinion of the matter made no difference to her father. Vyasa went to speak with him; and by the time I came to know of the matter, Leela was wedded to my foe.

At first, I took this sharp maneouvre on Vyasa's part as an attack on my story. Thankfully, Leela wasn't so easily cowed. She refused – so it was rumoured – to behave with propriety towards her new lord and master. She never once (so Vyasa was said to curse) touched his feet or called herself his servant; she neglected to address him as her god; she failed to wait for him to come home in the evening before licking her supper plate shiny clean. Worst crime of all, she refused to bear him a child. 'I need to conserve my energies,' she would repeat, 'for other activities.' When she did give herself to him, it was the wrong time of month, and the time-release ovarian engine was out of sync. She was a scientific lady who knew the rhythms of her body. Her science paid off. She remained childless.

Back then, Vyasa had old-fashioned ideas. He was appalled by her absence of maternal instinct and independence of mind; he believed she was tampering with Nature, contravening the Laws of Life; refusing his genes their eternal due. She spat back with sarcastically culled quotes from a handy precursor to the Laws of Manu: *You have six choices for begetting a son: Foist him on your wife, take him as a present, buy him, rear him, adopt him or find yourself a better broodmare elsewhere.*

In the end, Vyasa did as Manu advised and got himself a bride who came into the house with bowed head and hymen intact at the age of twelve. Vyasa hoped to teach this recalcitrant elder wife a lesson in Vedic ethics; to spur Leela on to jealousy-induced conception; and to receive, in the meantime, the attention he deserved from a younger spouse.

But Leela was delighted with the arrival of her special saheli, her girlfriend. She whispered to Meera: *I am fed up with men.* She explained, over the sound of tinkling bathwater as they lathered each other's backs and winkled grime from behind respective ears, her theory of female emancipation; she elaborated, as they crouched together in the courtyard sifting rice, upon the methods they would deploy to convert their husband to the light; she was very clear, as they picked up kindling from the forest outside, about the means available to them if he refused.

Meera, as pristine as she was voluptuous, had been born into the usual, traditional kind of family. When she returned home, twelve months after the nuptials, not yet pregnant, her head full of extremist ideas, her father quit his boasting and sat down to write a complaining letter to his son-in-law.

But Vyasa was helpless. It was easy for his first wife to strike up an intimacy with wife number two; the river was the channel of their friendship; and Leela, who swam like a nagi, took Meera down to the water the morning after her arrival, determined that she, too, would learn that freedom resided in the waves and the shallows.

They paddled there, below the old abandoned Pandava palace. At dusk, they wandered through the burnt-out rooms, picking their way over fallen rafters, wondering where it was that Draupadi had lived – 'with her five husbands, Meera!' said Leela. At night, Vyasa would return to the hut he had built them just to the south of the palace, and as they prepared the food for dinner, he would begin to recount another of those tales for which he was famous. 'And how,' Meera would ask innocently, 'was it that you fathered the Pandavas' father and uncle?' And Vyasa would begin to explain how his mother's two younger sons were killed by battle and disease, and that she, needing a mate for her daughters-in-law, came to see Vyasa and begged him to procreate with his half-brother's widows. 'On the first night,' Leela interrupted, 'the first sister shut her eyes in horror at the sight of you, and on the second night the second sister turned pale with fright, and on the third night these two women – who couldn't bear your advances any longer – sent a servant-girl in their place.' And Meera would put back her head and laugh, as the tears sprang into her eyes.

In short, under Leela's tuition, Meera grew rebellious, and the unfortunate joint husband – unable to impregnate them – was forced, like his grandfather, to foist his heirs upon the local washerwomen.

As for Meera, towards the end of her life, she became so haunted by a foreknowledge of the child-bearing, shit-cleaning, bangle-jingling existence of wifehood that she knew awaited her in future incarnations, so terrified did she grow of relinquishing the bliss of the present for the monotonous future, that on her deathbed she wailed, beat her breast and begged the gods to let Leela remain with her always.

Avatar 3: The Buddha's Pen

And so it was to be: Leela and Meera reincarnating together for ever after. Nevertheless, I feared the damage this era of Vyasa-scripted epic might do them. And so, at first, as the centuries passed without them putting in an appearance, I felt relieved. But on the ages stretched, and soon I began to get nervous at their absence. Where were they? Wallowing bare-breasted in the warm salt water of the southern seas? Re-born without my knowledge into the forest peoples of central India? Had they dispensed altogether with the hassle of reincarnation by passing Go, collecting two hundred heavenly rupees, and clocking up their time in nebulous nirvana?

No. Only after all memory of the Pandavas' city – of Vyasa and his story – had faded from the Indian imagination did my prudent characters return to the Yamuna. By now a new philosophy was in the ascendance, and Indraprastha was being transformed, under the Buddhist dispensation, into a brick-built city called Indapatta. Leela and Meera graced this brand-new era of handwritten scriptures, of breathless tales from places outside India, of the breaking of corrupt and obsolete idols, working as scribes, turning the utterances of this latest holy man into something long-lasting. Their existence was by and large peaceful. Much later came the rumour that they had left for Tibet, trading exotic carnelian for nuggets of pure river gold, and later still I heard a report that a monk called Vyasa had been knifed through the back as he penetrated a trainee nun in a cemetery on the Black and White Faced Mountain.

Avatar 4: Wanderers

Their coming and going remained mysterious. Life number four, for example, I heard tell of early one morning, just as I was settling down to a tepid dinner of bread (roti) and dripping (gaomedha) in a cobwebby sarai down by the river. A woman was recounting the scandalous tale of a local princess, Leela, and her handsome handmaiden, Meera. She told how Princess Leela had everything that a woman could possibly desire – saris, servants, fruits brought for her delectation from the furthest side of India – but that she had renounced it all in the name of poetic creation. Fleeing the court accompanied by her maid, she was even now wandering as a kind of minstrel, singing hymns in praise of the elephant-headed god (yes, that is what the woman said, I promise). Of course, with hindsight – in retrospect, during the journey from one rumour to the other – some details of this story were changed in other gods' favour. Later, I heard that the Rajput princess was called *Meera*; that the palace was in *Rajasthan*, not Dilli; that the object of her devotions was blue-faced *Krishna*. But it doesn't matter: I breathed a sigh of relief, and rejoiced in my characters' independence.

Avatar 5: Scriptures

Soon the wind began to blow in from the west, bringing with it a new type of people: from Samarkand – from Kabul – from all those arid places west of Taxila. They came to the Yamuna, erected forts for their wives, tent cities for their soldiers, and penned bittersweet poems tinged with sadness at the loss of the snow, the mulberries, the mountains of the lands they had left behind them. One of their sons was named Humayun, and he, like all the others before him, took over the site of the Pandavas' castle and fitted out a palace there with a splendid library.

Meera was the young daughter of one of Emperor Humayun's

courtiers. Her beauty came to his attention, and he requested her specially for his harem. Once ensconced in the fort, however, she developed a debilitating addiction. She could not stop reading tales of intrigue and battle, of spice merchants and river crossings, of avenging lovers − all provided in volumes smuggled across the Yamuna from one of the less reputable sarais, and written by a woman named Leela on paper the ink of which smudged as you turned the pages.

One such story was a yarn of two lovers, both women, deceiving the husband who held them captive. It had been translated into Persian from an unspecified local dialect, and illustrated with portraits of the women dressed as marauders from Herat, entering the city in a caravan of Kabuli melons, and leaving in a cartload of indigo-dyed dhotis.

Humayun began to grow suspicious. Meera, who as a fourteen-year-old maiden had charmed the emperor with her wileless ways, was no longer to be found in the palace apartments at the usual times, and he had grown weary of asking after her whereabouts. At last, an old eunuch told him the truth: *Sire*, he said, or something very like it, *she is reading*. *Reading?* said Humayun, spitting out a melon pip. He got to his feet, and demanded to be shown the offending girl at once.

So the eunuch led the king through the fort, along the ramparts to a small room where, behind a stone turret, there was a secret door built into a room over the river. Humayun looked down through a narrow tunnel to where light and freedom glinted and he could hear the gentle lapping of the river's waters. There, at the bottom of the tunnel, just above the water, sat Meera with her nose in a book.

The monarch confiscated the volume and took it with him to the library. Meera was imprisoned in the masons' tower. When Humayun reached the top of the library steps − reached the page where Leela had written, *Wishing to rid herself forever of the imprisoning grip of subservience to her master, the serving girl pushed a knife deep into his breast* – he gave a cry of pain, stepped forward, entangled in his own garments, and tumbled back down the smooth stone steps.

He died a few days later, calling out as he went, *Tell her she is free.* But Meera had not cared to wait for his approval. She had already escaped from the palace in a bundle of washing – thrown down into a boat where a cocky-eyed woman named Leela was waiting – and nobody except that snitching eunuch (whose name, by the way, was Vyasa) knew what the emperor was talking about.

Avatar 6: The Ghost

In their next life, Leela (on this occasion, 'Leila') came back as the daughter of a functionary at the court of the declining Mughal administration. Meera was her favourite Hindu servant. This time, too, Leela never married but lived on the outskirts of the city in splendid poetic isolation. From the roof of her house you could just see the glint of the river in the distance and the walls of the newest of the Mughal cities, refigured in red, half a day's walk away to the north. Their house was in an unpopular locality, a place where crows gathered to pick through the refuse thrown there by scavengers who had been through it once already. From the balcony, Leela would watch Hindus tipping the ashes of their relatives into the water, and later, at dusk, see the boys who dived from the bridge, searching through the river with its cargo of flesh and orange peel, for the gold coins that were sometime thrown in too, as good-luck charms. From sights such as these Leela composed the singularly bleak ditties for which the pens of other men became famous, and Meera would watch her, puzzled by the ease with which she drew forth similes of such beauty from sights so morbid.

The day Meera was killed by a British sniper, as she ventured out at dawn to look for food, Leela sat keening by the window, watching her friend's inert body lying by the side of the road as the vehicles of the British victors moved past and into the city. The siege of 1857 had been lost, the Emperor Zafar had fled south to the tomb of his ancestor Humayun. Leela knew that the killing and looting would begin, and that even an old lady like she would not be safe from the swords and pricks of angry foreigners.

When darkness fell, she pulled back her hair and dressed herself up like a man in a plain dark shirt and trousers, and went out into the street to where Meera lay; and later that night, as her heart filled up and broke with longing, she paid one of the scavengers to carry Meera's body to the riverside, and performed the rites herself, scattering ghee and water and lighting the pyre of wood with money purchased from the bania in exchange for the three silver rings that Meera had on her toes and her own gold filigree bangle. Then she walked to Humayun's tomb, where the old king, Zafar, was hiding, carrying the last of her verses: compositions of such unalloyed sadness that the emperor wept all the way to Rangoon.

Avatar 7: Epic Dancers

That life ended sadly. Leela and Meera's most joyous incarnation, by contrast, occurred in the early 1920s, when they worked the bars and clubs of old and new Delhi as itinerant dancers. By now the scrubland of the city had filled up with pink-faced invaders, with their spacious, airy bungalows, with their crisp sense of order, with their cramped sense of humour. Each night for nearly a decade, Leela and Meera danced out the story of the Mahabharata. Meera twirled as Urvashi before Leela's ascetic archer, until after one rowdy reception in Arab-ki-Sarai near the tomb of Humayun, a local policeman broke into their makeshift tent. The women he battered to death were discovered the next morning with smiles on their faces, clutching to their bosom Arjuna's deadly bow. The policeman's name, I later discovered, was Deputy Inspector Vyasa.

Avatar 8: Migration

Which means there is just one more tale to recount before I embark on the complications of the present. It is 1947. Meera and Leela are each exactly seven years old in the year that India is divided. They were born in Delhi, in the same week, in the same neighbourhood, to mothers who hated each other. Meera's mother, a Muslim, was tall and thin, always dressed in a plain black cloak, with red-stained teeth and kohl-rimmed eyes staring out defiantly from the moon of her burqa. Leela's mother, a Hindu, wrapped herself in a sari, parted her hair with scarlet powder, and slotted gold bangles over her plump, oil-smoothed hands.

Both women shared a guru: an undefinable Sufi-cum-Bhakti, a mountain man with a taste for southern belles. He often passed through the neighbourhood, bound for Hampi, thence Haridwar, and back again to the Himalayas; and nine months after one such visitation, the offspring these women had always longed for – could easily have relinquished their marital virtue for the sake of, had visited many different shrines and springs and temples and gurus in the name of – were born, in adjacent houses.

The little girls loved each other, and whatever the admonitions of their mothers, took no notice as wrath spluttered and bubbled in their lane just south of that long and crowded street where the whole city came for shopping, Chandni Chowk. The girls were oblivious of their mothers' ire; and for seven years, the city's streets between the Turkman and Kashmiri Gates were all theirs.

In September of their seventh year, a few weeks after they had seen their first carcasses – not of chickens or sheep but of people

– the tall thin beanpole mother called her daughter: 'Come, Mirah' (she hated the way her daughter's worthy Arabic name was phonetically indistinguishable from the common Hindu 'Meera'), 'pack your toys, we are leaving.' And she pulled her daughter inside the house from the street, where the girl had been listening to Leela describing how she had seen from the window a man brought back to his home by his uncles, red stains on his white pyjamas. That night, the tall thin beanpole family left the seventh street, taking a tonga through the shuttered streets to the Purana Qila, Emperor Humayun's old fort built there four centuries before on the site of the Pandavas' prehistoric palace of Indraprastha. 'We are going west, to the Land of the Pure,' the beanpole mother told her daughter, and the child cried and would only go to sleep when her father slipped a nugget of opium between her lips and begged her to be quiet.

The old fort, where Emperor Humayun had tumbled down the steps of his library, stood on a hill in the centre of the city encircled by a wall. Inside, where kings had looked at the stars, and Vyasa's grandsons had managed their kingdom, there were now rows and rows of tents: refugees bound for Pakistan.

To this place, the next morning, came Leela. With her was a political activist from the Congress Party, a Miss Urvashi, who knew very little about the lies children tell, and thus had listened, and felt deeply concerned, when this girl told her that her Muslim family were leaving for Pakistan, that she had been separated from them and must be taken to the camp *at once*. Miss Urvashi walked her charge through the old Mughal fort, the child's hand in hers, her own eyes wide with horror at the sight of row upon row of frightened Muslims, huddled in the pathways, their possessions – everything they had to start new lives in that country to the west – rolled into bedding at their feet.

Leela whistled the notes that Meera and she used to identify each other's movements along the narrow streets near Chandni Chowk, and hearing them, Meera crept out from the tent where she was dozing. Wandering through the crowd, she came to the well that had been dug so many feet deep into the earth, so many years ago, with so many steps leading downwards. Since Meera was too small to see above the crowds of hungry and frightened people, and since the fear of losing Leela choked the reply in her throat, she climbed up onto the walls of the well to look for her and just before she fell – jostled so that she lost her footing and sprawled into the air and down down down onto the sandstone steps below – Leela saw her.

Pulling her hand out of Miss Urvashi's grasp, Leela ran, pushing through the crowd, tripping over bed rolls, jumping over the legs of grandmothers who had already lived through too much to be leaving the place where they had composed families and quilts and letters and lives, to be leaving it for an unknown edge of the vanished British empire, knocking down carefully saved tins of daal, and pots of steaming rice – and heard the thump as Meera's body hit the stone forty feet below. If Meera fell too quietly for the other passers-by to notice, everybody heard the scream that Leela made, and everybody claimed to have seen her jump, trying to save her Meera.

Avatar 9: The Present

This tragic end might have brought my tale to a close. But I was determined not to be downcast – I knew that my story had almost reached its dramatic conclusion – that I had to be patient. And so, barely a decade after India achieved its Independence, Leela was born in a small village in Bengal, and Meera Bose in an elegant brick Calcutta townhouse. The Bose family owned the fields that Leela's parents farmed.

At first I was troubled by this link between them, which seemed too attenuated to be trusted, especially given the talk of land reform, of the old guard being swept away in a fervour of socialist redistribution. This time I decided to intervene directly. I couldn't allow my beloved Leela to suffer, as she certainly would if she lost her companion, her confidante, her refuge, her succour. I considered my options: a famine? A flood? A plague? All these things were regular occurrences in India. But they were too heavyhanded; I didn't want to take out the entire village.

So in the end, I simply gave her parents cholera – and in this way Leela, aged three, was orphaned.

She was a sweet child, with curly hair, inquisitive eyes and a steady smile. It would have been a shame to send her to the missionaries, or to put her out as a servant in one of the bigger village houses. At least, this was the opinion of her late mother's friend, who was married to Mr Bose's munshi. The munshi was a thin, sober man, with a good head for mathematics, employed by Meera's father to manage the estates, to make sure the rent came in on time, to weigh each villager's yield of rice, to divide the crop and to calculate the profit. But he had seven children already; he couldn't possibly take in another. 'She's a pretty thing,' mused his wife one evening. She spooned some more rice onto his plate. 'Take her to Calcutta to see Bose-Sahib.'

Meera's family lived in north Calcutta. There was a courtyard in the middle of their house, and a long, cool flagstone hallway that ran down one side of the house to a library at the end where Mr Dipankar Bose read the papers, dabbled in writing and received his guests. On the afternoon the munshi arrived with Leela, Mr Bose and his three-year-old daughter were sitting in this room, he at his desk with his papers, she at a table under the window with hers. While he studied a bill of transfer, she drew an abstract impression of her family on a piece of headed paper. A jagged purple mass of lines, like a ball of unravelling string, was her mother. Her father was a dynamic streak of yellow. The ayah, the cook and the mali were stubby jabs of red. Even aged three she had a sense of hierarchy and order. But all that was about to be overturned by the arrival of Leela.

Meera looked up from her artwork to see, for a change, a person of exactly her height looking right at her. She held out a crayon, moved along the bench to make room, and as the munshi looked over in approval, the two children bent their heads together, laughing to themselves as they caricatured the grown-ups.

The munshi pursed his lips thoughtfully. Out loud, he said to Meera's father, 'I am on the way to the orphanage at Entally. The nuns will baptise her, but what to do? At least she will come to no harm there. At least she will be fed.' He spread his hands helplessly before him. 'I would take her in. But you know, I have been burdened by too many children.' He bent his head. 'The nuns will look after her.'

Mr Bose had a young, pretty wife who loved him, plenty of money and few real cares. He lived a happy existence, fattened on milk-sweets tinged with nutmeg, kept healthy by pond fish, given meaning by the revolutionary language and equitable aspirations of India's glorious independence. There were two things that vexed him in 1958: the first was the benighted state of India's peasant population, with its truly frightening array of noxious gods – whether indigenous, imported or on loan from elsewhere, they were all as bad as each other. The second was a dim sense that while he himself had talked a lot about revolution, about change, about tearing down the old and building up the new – despite drinking numerous cups of coffee with his comrades and drafting a multiplicity of manifestos – he had not actually done anything to foment the rebellion. He stared distractedly at his daughter sitting with her new village playfellow, at the dust falling through the shaft of light coming in through his window (reminding him that the maid hadn't been in to clean his library today – that the day had passed without him having finished his letter to the *Statesman* on the subject of peasant education – and moreover that it was teatime).

There was a long pause; he turned these thoughts over in his head; the only noise a contented murmur from the children under the window. Then he got to his feet. 'Wait a moment,' he said to the munshi, and gestured to one of the chairs on the other side of his desk. 'Sit here while I speak with my wife. I'm sure we can do something for her.'

Later, neither girl would be able to remember a time before. It was as if they had always known each other. From this day onwards they were bathed by the same ayah, they slept in the same dark room with its high bed and heavy wooden furniture, they went to the same school with their hair tightly plaited.

Of the two, Meera was the child with the most determined sense of rebellion. She enjoyed shocking her parents, who dutifully pretended to be outraged when, aged twelve, she announced that she wished to eat Chinese noodles and British pudding only; when, aged fifteen, she said wicked things about Rabindranath Tagore, the great poet of Bengal; when, aged sixteen, she kissed a boy outside the school gates and the headmistress sent home a letter suspending her. Wisely, the Boses understood that quiet, solemn Leela kept Meera in check, and that as long as the two girls remained at each other's side, no harm could come to either.

But harm can come from unexpected places. On the day Leela and Meera turned seventeen – nobody knew Leela's date of birth, so the sisters synchronised anniversaries, menstruation, decisions

– their mother called them into her bedroom, unlocked her boxes of jewellery from her trunk, and picked out three pieces for them each. She gave Leela her heavy gold pendant with a bright lacquer-work of butterflies and peacocks; some hoop earrings speckled with semi-precious stones; and a gold filigree-work bangle with one large amethyst in the middle, which was Leela's favourite. Meera was given a similar bangle and earrings – the stones in hers were rubies – but when she saw the heavy gold necklace, wide and thick, like a silty river spreading out as it reaches the plain, she wrinkled her nose in distaste. It was a traditional piece: so ornate that she refused to wear it in public, and it was put aside for her wedding day.

But both girls were pleased with the abstract notion of these gifts, which they interpreted as signs of their transition out of girlhood. They didn't realise that for their mother, this dividing of the spoils had little to do with their age, and everything to do with her illness.

Soon afterwards, the sisters began at Calcutta's Presidency College as students of literature, and the house was filled with their cheerful disputes about whether Eliot was a better poet than Tagore, or Bankim a finer novelist than Dickens, though they both agreed that Shakespeare had the edge over Kalidasa. They began frequenting poetry readings and writing workshops, which prolifer-ated throughout the city, and though they read in both Bengali and English with equal facility, when they began writing poetry them-selves, it was English that they chose as their language. So thrilling was this time of their lives, so full of meetings and encounters and conversations and discoveries, that if their mother was paler than usual, or their father quieter, the sisters, immersed in the happy sound of their own precociousness, had little time to notice.

'Come home quickly today,' their mother said one morning as they left for college.

'Yes, yes,' Meera replied as the door slammed behind them. But that afternoon, as they wandered slowly back home, they couldn't resist stopping to buy saris for each other. There was a party at the end of term and they needed something elegant but vivacious, sophisticated and pristine. They searched for hours, Leela eventually picking out a fine tant weave in neem-tree green, and Meera, ever ostentatious, choosing for her sister the brightest sari in the shop: saffron-coloured cotton with a thin golden border. It was late when they arrived back home. They pushed open the front door expecting to find their parents waiting up for them – mother with her proud smile, father with his frown of concern – to listen with feigned displeasure to the girls' triumphant narration of their afternoon adventures.

But the house was quiet, and as they walked down the hallway to the library, they heard nothing but the dripping of the tap in the courtyard and the cawing of a crow in the road outside. The servants were huddled together in the kitchen. *Where are my parents?* Meera demanded. And it was then that their mother's secret was revealed – how quickly the disease had spread through her blood, through her bones, how there was nothing any doctor could do. She died that night in hospital, and Meera, it was said later, never recovered.

Leela had lost her parents once already – but that was in the village. It was silently understood that since the peasantry in the countryside bore all sorts of troubles (bereavement, penury, chronic ill health) without once complaining, such an event, at such a young age, had been easily overcome. If Leela ever dreamt about her real mother, or pined for her unknown face, nobody ever thought to enquire.

But for an educated young girl from the city – well, that was different – such a death, for such a daughter, was a trauma.

Meera mourned her mother flamboyantly and persistently, wearing the marriage necklace at inappropriate times: over her sari when they walked to the fish market, or to lectures at college. She who had always hated cooking learnt to prepare her mother's favourite dishes. As their father wept and did his best to carry on, and Leela retreated into silence, Meera explored the extravagant hinterland of grief.

It was in this mood, one night at dinner the following spring, that Meera announced she had taken a decision. Instead of going to Delhi University for an MA as they had already agreed, she would spend the following two years at Santiniketan, studying Sanskrit at Rabindranath Tagore's university in the Bengal countryside, just as her mother had done before her.

Privately, their father was appalled. Tagore was revered by Bengalis as a kind of saint, and because of this, the university he founded had a reputation for an almost otherworldly devotion to authentic Indianness (whatever that meant). Meera's mother had studied there in the 1950s, and he remembered how, on their first meeting – in Flurys cake shop on Park Street – she had talked with a boldness that belied her mild demeanour of how Santiniketan alone of India's educational institutions was capable of forging in its students a proper understanding of, and respect for, indigenous culture. Sitting there in Flurys, gazing at her lowered eyes, listening to her speaking, he had found the adulation preposterous. Twenty years later, he considered that his witty, cosmopolitan daughter was making a big mistake. The university was no longer what it had been; even for a Bengali, it had become provincial. Gently, he tried to persuade her of the merits of the capital, of the fine teachers in the English literature department at Delhi University. But Meera was not to be dissuaded; and whatever Meera had set her mind on, Leela had to do too. So it was in some perplexity and with many misgivings that early one stifling morning in July, Mr Bose saw his two daughters off at Howrah station, never suspecting, poor man, that the villainous Vyasa, recently appointed as Santiniketan's youngest professor of Sanskrit, was readying himself to enter their lives; unable to predict, as I was, that chaos would ensue.

chapter 5

On the eve of his daughter's wedding, Shiva Prasad Sharma, guardian of the national identity, saviour of pure Hindu India, was sitting at home in his small South Delhi flat, full of thoughts of his Autobiography. This morning he had completed the dictation of his early childhood up to the age of ten. It was at that point in his life – the year being 1945, the month November, fifty-six years ago almost to the day – that he had delivered his first public act of prodigiosity. His assistant, Manoj, a young man from Varanasi whose sole task it was currently to type up the Autobiography, had been greatly moved by the event. 'But, sir,' he exclaimed in Hindi, 'was it possible that as a child you had no fear of speechifying?'

'Ah, Manoj,' Shiva Prasad had replied softly, 'you see, there was no choice. The village elders said to me: *Your turn boy.* And I was pushed out in front of the crowd, where I gave my speech – a very simple, direct speech – declaring that I, too, would become a freedom-fighter: that I, too, would expel the Britishers, their English language, and their non-Hindu ways from our sovereign land.'

Yes, the crowd had cheered, the newspapermen had come to take his photograph, his grandmother had fainted, and his mother had sent him to bed at the same time as baby brother Hari, for being an impertinence, and only ten years old. She feared that her elder son would end his days in a dank British jail along with all the other young revolutionaries. But Shiva Prasad knew that his father was proud of what he had done, and so, early next morning, he took a bath – washing carefully, for he did not know how long it would be until he could wash again – packed a small bag, and bade goodbye to his family, saying: 'I must go to join the protest against the unlawful trial of Indian National Army officers in Delhi. I may come back. I may not.'

As his mother stood weeping in the doorway (baby Hari in her arms; Father, as always, was giving extra tuition at the other end of the village), Shiva Prasad took a staff and left the house in Amarkantak. His home town, situated in the forest at the source of the Narmada river, was not a big place, but it was significant; the omens were auspicious; and as he set out on his journey, Shiva Prasad felt like a rishi in the days of yore. He walked all the way to the railway station in Pendra, climbed aboard, and off he went, to show solidarity in the fight against the Britishers.

A militant young Krishna, Shiva Prasad won over crowd after crowd at Pendra, Gwalior, New Delhi, with his pure, Sanskritic Hindi rhetoric. Even Gandhi-ji, it was rumoured, was impressed. *Who is this infant Churchill?* he was said to have asked, *His words are too stirring.* It was a glorious beginning.

Due to a happy exposure, in the country's capital, to the policies of the Hindu Mahasabha, Shiva Prasad returned to Amarkantak determined to rally the people there with a brave new cry. '*Now is the time for action!*' the eleven-year-old would proclaim. 'We must have pride in our ancient and glorious Hindu culture! We must push back the alienating immigrations of Islam and Christianity and embrace our indigenous Vedic values. Our ancient Arya forefathers gave the world language and science and geometry! Now the time has come for us to conquer once more!'

The crowds continued to cheer, but to his surprise, Shiva Prasad's father took to locking his son in the buffalo shed every time a rally was planned. 'Finish school with good grades,' he said. 'Only once you have left my house may you practise this new-fangled form of fanaticism.'

Shiva Prasad took this minor setback in his stride. He lost no time in displaying his formidable intelligence, turning out to be the cleverest pupil in the district, consistently topping his class in every subject by at least three marks. Before long, he was bidding his mother goodbye once more, and returning to the capital to protect the culture of which he was so proud.

Once in New Delhi, Shiva Prasad finished his BA in record time, completed his MA with special distinction, and was personally headhunted by the Guruji Research Foundation, a new think tank dedicated to promoting native values and rooting out all imported ones. By the time he was twenty-four, Shiva Prasad's melodious tones, beaming forth astute political commentary and cultural critique, were in demand at all his Party's meetings. After he began writing a column for the Party magazine, the publication was inundated with fan mail; he himself received countless proposals from the parents of college-educated girls with wheaten complexions; in certain circles, one could say, 'Shiva Prasad Sharma' became a household name.

Yet each time he returned home to Amarkantak – basking in the glow of recognition and success – it was to encounter an increasingly sterile reception from the one man in the world whom he felt should have been most excited by his eldest son's progress. Why was it that his father had transferred his affections so facilely to that much younger and more insignificant son, tiny Hari, born in the embarrassing tumescence of old age? Their father was the headmaster of an obscure village school – in New Delhi such a position would have been thought inconsequential. And yet, it was undeniable: whenever Shiva Prasad stood back to survey the progress of his own famous life, his dazzling career, it was with a marked lack of satisfaction, a sense of non-completion. He had not yet experienced his father's quiet pride.

In the years that followed, Shiva Prasad strove for this elusive achievement. After he became a fixture on the Party's intellectual scene, he expected political accolades to follow – and on his visits home to Amarkantak, he hinted as much to his incredulous parent. He explained how the Party was coming more and more to rely on his public pronouncements and private convictions. But he sensed that his father didn't believe him, and when the old man proved this, by dying of old age before the son could effect his crucial transition into politics, it was a moment of brutal reckoning. Shiva Prasad was forced to appreciate, as he took the train back to Amarkantak for the funeral, that he had not been able to prove himself to his parent in the way he had once hoped, after all.

In the ensuing decade, this realisation deepened. Shiva Prasad now came to see that although from its very inception his life had promised wonderful things – indeed, it had delivered marvels – it had not continued to dispense them with the speed to which he had once become accustomed. A climactic event was missing, and due to a lamentable lapse on the part of fate he had not been asked to contest a seat in the Lower House. He was not, after the Party got into power, offered a place in the Rajya Sabha either. And by the time his Non-Resident brother Hari went into English-language media, Shiva Prasad was forced to confess to himself that although fundamentally fascinating and deeply important, his life lacked a rounded shape.

The marriages of his daughters were significant landmarks.

After Unmentionable Urvashi ran away with a Muslim, he was at least able to blame his failure to rise on his daughter: that his pet, his favourite, his darling, had defied him to take to the bed of a Muslim – the shame of it for himself as a father, as a man, as a Hindu! He had spoilt her from the beginning, he thought; he had even misnamed her: that lascivious name he had insisted on for his firstborn . . . why had he done it? Against his wife's better judgement, he had invited disgrace to come and lodge in his family. Things only changed for the better when Sunita announced her surprise engagement.

Shiva Prasad debated – only briefly – the positive and negative ramifications of the match. On the negative side was the association with a man who had humiliated him some nine years before in a moment of ignominy. It had occurred when Shiva Prasad agreed to appear as a guest on a political debate show run by one of the new television channels. The other guest was Professor Ved Vyasa Chaturvedi; their scheduled conversation topic, the building of the new Ram temple at Ayodhya; and the conversation was supposed to take place in Hindi. However, so deracinated was Professor Chaturvedi that every now and then he would throw in a word or phrase in English: *historical perspective, apotheosis, divide and rule*. This kind of slip provided Shiva Prasad with the excuse he needed to unveil his fellow guest (with his hollow, treacherous politics) as a fraud, and as soon as he could, he took him up on it with some relish. 'You find the language of your forebears inadequate for self-expression?' Shiva Prasad asked. But the Professor merely leant back, smiled across the table at his interrogator, and when he opened his mouth to reply, what came out was a stream of Sanskrit, uttered in a singsong expression so evocative of ancient forest ashrams that it gave Shiva Prasad a little shiver as he heard it. The awful thing was, his own Sanskrit wasn't good enough to understand what the man was saying. It was only afterwards, as he played the videotape back, that he realised what Chaturvedi had been quoting: a passage from the *Satapatha Brahmana*. 'Hence let no Brahmin speak barbarous language,' Vyasa had said, 'since such is the speech of the demons. Thus he deprives his spiteful enemies of speech; and his enemies, being deprived of speech, are undone.' Vyasa stopped speaking – and there then ensued the worst thing of all, *a terrible silence*. Later, Shiva Prasad thought of all the wonderful put-downs he could have uttered; the equally fabulous quotations from even more ancient texts; the withering tone of voice he could have used to utter these rebuffs. But at the time he said *nothing*, and at last the television presenter turned back to Professor Chaturvedi and the conversation between them drew to a close without Shiva Prasad having uttered a single further statement.

The incident had rankled for some years in Shiva Prasad's mind. He never mentioned it at home, and when his meek little Sunita came to him with the news that she was to be married to Vyasa's son, he didn't mention it then either. He weighed the fact of having been humiliated by Vyasa against the social advantages of the match, and saw that something more significant was required. Something clever had to come of this union, something brilliant, some extraordinary benefit for Shiva Prasad himself in the eyes of the Party. In the end, it was the nascent Arya Gene Project that was the deciding factor in Sunita's favour.

On the day when Ash first visited Shiva Prasad's office, touched his feet, and said, in pure, Sanskrit-inflected Hindi, 'Sir, my name is Ashwin Chaturvedi, I met Sunita while she was undertaking some work for my father, a writer and professor of—' Shiva Prasad had interrupted, in English.

'I know of your father,' he said. Then he paused, seemed lost in thought, pressed his fingers together, shut his eyes; and when he opened them again, it was to announce: 'You may marry her. On my terms.'

Shiva Prasad had already been told by Sunita that Ash was a student at the Centre for Biochemical Technology in Delhi. He had learnt from her that the boy had a specialism in genetics; he understood that Ash was amenable to a project of a scale that would outshine the paltry philosophising of Ash's misguided father. That afternoon, father and son-in-law came to a tacit understanding. Shiva Prasad became convinced that as a science Ph.D. student, Ash Chaturvedi could identify a gene in high-caste Hindus that allowed them to trace their lineage back to the 'race of Aryas', who had composed the Vedas thousands of years ago. More than that, he would prove that these noble bearers of Arya civilisation were indigenous to India. And finally, that Shiva Prasad and his family were themselves Aryas par excellence.

In the months that followed, Shiva Prasad's confidence in his Autobiography grew once more. He told Manoj to put aside the duties he had hitherto prescribed him, of transcribing each and every one of his magazine columns with the long-term aim of compiling a book called *Shiva Prasad Sharma's Cultural Insights*. Instead, they spent the mornings lost in the bliss of dictation. It was the Arya Gene Project that would provide his Autobiography with the fillip it needed; it was this that would bring crescendo, climax, conclusion – the firework or two it required, that extra bit of noise.

It was this, too, that allowed Shiva Prasad to overlook the awkwardness of meeting Ash Chaturvedi's father during the various wedding formalities – the engagement, by way of example – for in the scheme of things, what was the exchange of polite greetings, weighed against the glory that was soon to accrue to Shiva Prasad Sharma's name? Now, whenever he felt irked by Vyasa, or concerned at being humiliated a second time by this unscrupulous anti-national leftist with his preposterous Ganesh theories, one thought went through his head like a soothing forest breeze: the career of his prospective son-in-law, and the use this would be put to by a party eager to advance its ideologies in the areas of education, science and history. All he had to do, as father of the bride, was smile, say something asinine to his great nemesis, and behave, as every Indian knew how, with due decorum.

As it happened, there had not yet been an opportunity for anything more than the most superficial exchange of pleasantries – all other arrangements had been negotiated via their children, or through Manoj. The really important meeting – the union of the two families – would come tomorrow night at the wedding. In Shiva Prasad's dream scenario, three things occurred at this juncture. First, Shiva Prasad upbraided the quisling Vyasa, making him repent of his faulty conclusions about the sacred Mahabharata and its reverend and holy scribe. Then, Shiva Prasad forgave him, saying, 'My dear Brother, do let me introduce you to one or two of India's most treasured businessmen/prime ministers/charitable benefactors'; and as the women in his family caught their breath, as the garden full of wedding guests quivered in expectation, as the stars in the sky held back their blinks in awe, Vyasa-I-am-so-special-Chaturvedi would put his hands together and humbly intone: 'How utterly delightful to meet you again, Shiva Prasad Sharma. How much I have benefited from your incisive commentary over the years, dear sir!' Thirdly, Shiva Prasad would tell Vyasa exactly what his own son Ash thought on the burning issue of the—

But Shiva Prasad's reverie was interrupted at this point by his wife and daughter, calling to him from the kitchen.

'Yes?' he answered.

'Didn't you hear the bell?' one shouted.

'It will be Ram,' called the other. 'Open the door.'

Stirring reluctantly, Shiva Prasad removed his (portly but stately) figure from his carved-wood armchair, and progressed to the front door. He pulled it open.

Three figures stood in the doorway. He saw his son Ram, wearing an idiotic grin. He saw his brother Hari, very bald these days, clad in a badly cut silk kurta. He noticed his brother's dark-skinned, childless Bengali wife standing in the shadows behind them both and holding a box of expensive-looking sweets. Instead of shutting the door in their faces, as they so clearly expected, Shiva Prasad smiled, bowed his head in a grandiose namaskar and said, almost jovially: 'Come in, do come in!'

Then he stood back from the doorway (exactly in the manner of the Prime Minister inaugurating a function, or the President opening a new military training centre) as they took off their shoes and filed obediently past him. 'Sit down, sit down,' he urged his timid guests, still smiling graciously upon them as they settled themselves cautiously on his Maharashtrian sofa. And finally he called through to his wife in the kitchen: 'Our brother is here!' And turning to the party of three, he said: 'Dinner is ready. Shall we eat?'

During dinner, after Hari made his little announcement – he was asking to waive the small matter of the loan for Sunita's wedding – Shiva Prasad's thoughts actually began to crystallise into triumph. Hari had come to plead for his forgiveness. Not only that, he was offering to take unwieldy, sulky, materialistic Ram off his father's hands. Repentant Hari was perfect Autobiographical timing. For the second time that day, Shiva Prasad danced all over his Autobiographical misgivings.

'What does Ash Chaturvedi do?' Hari asked politely as Sunita brought out the dessert (a splendid rice pudding topped with almond slivers).

'He's a scientist,' Shiva Prasad's wife began explaining, as she dolloped spoonfuls into small glass bowls. But Shiva Prasad could contain himself no longer. He interrupted his wife: 'Ash Chaturvedi is analysing the DNA of our family, you know, every one of us!'

'Whatever for?' his brother's wife suddenly asked, shocking everybody (they were almost the first words she had spoken); and Shiva Prasad, realising that he had gone too far with this disclosure, looked to his daughter for guidance.

'Retinitis Pigmentosa,' said Sunita, and her father had nodded: 'An eye condition. He will test you, too!'

'I hope not,' the woman answered back before anyone could stop her.

But Shiva Prasad didn't reply. He was thinking how Sunita's marriage was going to put right everything that Urvashi had disfigured through her union to a Muslim; how this new son-in-law, Ash, was going to prove the genetic purity of the Arya with his DNA project; how Urvashi's treacherous rejection of her upbringing was going to—

'Where does the Chaturvedi family live?' somebody else asked. Shiva Prasad looked up. It was his brother who had spoken.

'Nizamuddin West,' Shiva Prasad said.

'Oh, like your daughter Urvashi,' put in the childless Bengali wife. 'Isn't that what you told me earlier, Ram?'

There was a terrible silence. For a moment, everybody froze. Then they all began speaking at once. Hari mentioned the vital importance of honeymoons for marital harmony. Ram spoke of the virtues of the new cars available in the market and the dangers of driving those old Ambassadors with their terrible suspension. Shiva Prasad's wife began to explain how the recipe for gulab jamuns was cited in the Vedas, and how they were serving this most ancient of dishes tomorrow night at the wedding.

Shiva Prasad himself said nothing. He allowed the conversation to ebb and flow awkwardly around him, for he had nothing to say. It was true: the location of his daughter Sunita's marital home, just a few streets away from Urvashi's, was a great disadvantage. The thought of that place made Shiva Prasad shudder. For while Nizamuddin West was a smart-enough residential colony, well planned, with large houses and tree-lined roads; while it had sprung up after Partition, settled by Hindu traders who had fled their ancestral places and come to Delhi when Pakistan was forced into being; it was also an inescapable fact that it took its very name from the Sufi shrine it stood beside, and therefore from the eponymous Muslim saint, Nizamuddin, who had made this place the centre of his cult. And it was no coincidence that the so-called saint had come here during medieval times, along with all those other grasping, bloodthirsty, jihad-minded foreigners, at the point in history that had changed everything for the worse for India's Hindus.

If that wasn't bad enough, the fact that there was a Sufi shrine on the edge of Nizamuddin West meant, naturally, that there were Muslims. Poor Muslims, but Muslims nonetheless. They lived around the shrine, Shiva Prasad knew, in a chaotic jumble of brick houses built any old how, slums that had gradually congealed into numbered houses and properly paved streets with all the craftiness of a colony of underwater polyps extruding their tender tendrils into coral. The poor Muslims worked for the rich Hindus; the Hindus lived in the planned residential area, keeping themselves to themselves and minding their own business. In this way the two classes and religions of Nizamuddin West remained distinct, and everybody understood the status quo. But recently, so the newspapers Shiva Prasad read informed him, the boundaries had blurred. Muslims from the old city, having become unaccountably rich selling halal meat as their co-religionists' numbers bloated with uncontrolled breeding, and wishing to move away from the squalor of their upbringing, had taken to buying up properties in the Hindu part of Nizamuddin West – and pushing out their Hindu neighbours with their new mosques, their Arabic writing on the gateposts, their ladies hidden away in burqas. And it was here that Sunita was to be brought as a bride. Shiva Prasad pursed his lips and shook his head. There was no avoiding it. The Chaturvedi family did not live in a good location. But there were consolations. The family was well-known throughout India, their house was sumptuous – and the Arya Gene Project would put all other considerations in the shade.

Hari and his wife left the house soon after her awkward blunder, bestrewing their exit with lavish compliments to their sister-in-law's vegetarian cooking. Ram went with them, to try out his new abode; Sunita burst into tears; her mother joined in; and Shiva Prasad, having exacted a promise from his brother before he left that a journalist and photographer would be dispatched from his English-language tabloid to cover the great wedding in full-colour splendour, left his women to clear away dinner as he shut himself into his study (the Unmentionable Urvashi's former bedroom) to consider his new life agenda.

An hour later, when he walked upstairs to bed, to lie on the yogically thin mattress he shared with his long-suffering wife, his reflections on the wedding, on his future, on his coming glory, made his entire body tingle with excitement. Tonight was a watershed, a turning point. The triumphant scene of his future conquest of Vyasa, of Hari, of the Party, of India, ran before him like a Republic Day commentary on television. 'What are you so cheerful about?' asked his wife through the darkness. 'Isn't it enough that you've lost me all my children?'

But Shiva Prasad wasn't listening. He knew now that a whole new life was just beginning. Tomorrow, the cream of Delhi society

– politicians, journalists, shakers and movers – would assemble for Sunita's wedding to the son of India's favourite academic. The reception was to take place in a respectable but not-too-extravagant Delhi location, the Flying Club, next to the old airport. Shiva Prasad had been forced to pay for several immoral alcoholic drinks with an old Air Force acquaintance before he could secure the booking, but it was worth the effort. He had then hired the very best Pure Vegetarian caterers in the city. There were to be three different kinds of chaat and some tasty dry snacks to begin with, multi-juice refreshment throughout, the waiters would be smartly dressed in maroon suits with starched white topis, and the dinner that followed – paneer tikka, tandoori vegetable kebabs, two different kinds of raita, three types of daal, a choice of six subji, missi roti, romali roti, kulcha paratha, butter naan, the standard South Indian fare of idli and vada, three types of ice cream (pistachio, his favourite; mango, the desi choice; and something with dried fruits in it ordered according to Sunita's particular instructions), an array of extremely fresh fruits, Nescafé and/or masala chai – was sure to be talked about for weeks.

As a result of this prestigious event, the following things were slated to occur:

1. He, Father of the Bride, would have a friendly, man-to-man chat with the Father of the Groom in which he urged him in the name of kinship to tone down his unacceptable views on the Ganesh Scriptation Issue. In the name of kinship, Vyasa would hasten to comply.

2. Vyasa would *beg* Shiva Prasad to sit on the board of his new Living Sanskrit Akademi. Shiva Prasad would come to influence the entire motivation and focus of this prominent academic body.

3. Repentant Hari would enlist Shiva Prasad to write a regular column (translated from Hindi) for his English-language tabloid. Shiva Prasad Sharma would graciously acquiesce. The English-reading public, stunned by Shiva Prasad's erudition and political resourcefulness, would clamour for more.

4. Following the wildfire success of the Shiva Prasad Sharma column in the *Delhi Star*, television groups across the land would implore Mr Sharma on bended knee to host his own Hindi-language chat show.

5. Ash Chaturvedi would identify the Arya Gene in his father-in-law, thus solving the hitherto intractable mystery (the 'singular scientific annoyance of our times', according to high-ups in the Party) of exactly who in the motherland was genetically a noble, made-in-India Arya.

6. Bathed in glory in the eyes of the Party, Shiva Prasad's stars would fuse into a galactic political future. He would become Mayor of Delhi. All the major awards for national service would be his, in record time. And finally he would receive that call: to the Presidency of holy Bharat, the most ancient country in the world (and currently and inaccurately called India).

And as his Big-Ben alarm clock put its hands together in a reverent midnight namaste, Shiva Prasad added one extra, clinching clause:

7. Ram would keep his mother in silk saris for the rest of her days.

chapter 6

While her father snored in south Delhi, Urvashi the Unmentionable, 'Pinki' to her sister, Uzma for the purposes of her Muslim marriage, formerly-Sharma-now-Ahmed, woke up in her conjugal bed on the first floor of a twelve-month-old house in Nizamuddin West, weeping.

Sometimes, at the weekends, Urvashi met her younger siblings for tea. Their father had forbidden them the luxury of eating meals together (too much camaraderie) but as a special dispensation he allowed his children the privilege of drinking tea in Connaught Place, in the old-style grandeur of the United Coffee House. They sat under its air-conditioned hum, attended to by cheerful-shabby waiters, soothed by the glitter and glint of the decor, by the tea dripping unhurried through silver strainers, among the scent of old beer, lost crisps and meandering conversation, for an hour or two of strained and unsatisfying chitchat – before Sunita was ordered home again to south Delhi.

The one advantage to this arrangement was that afterwards, having sent Sunita off in a taxi, Ram, who always had taken pleasure in silently disobeying Father's dictates, took Urvashi out to the bars that fringe Connaught Place. Then, while Urvashi drank one daring cocktail all evening and he knocked back an unlikely combination of concoctions, Ram told her stories of his friendships with other onyx-eyed young men: stories that were likely to shock a conservatively educated girl like Urvashi – except that she was now married to a Muslim, and was therefore beyond the boundaries of the wholesome and civilised. She found that her reputation had begun to precede her, anticipating and fashioning her responses to these tales, and so she shrieked with laughter as Ram described his online encounters with other men who wanted to web-chat without women listening. There was one, in particular, who made her giggle. He called himself 'Manhattan Mania', chosen for the cherry-specked, nut-spotted Nirula's ice cream which he liked licking – with Ram? off Ram? (Her brother hadn't made it clear.) Afterwards, at home, Urvashi tried to unravel the outlandish details of the stories of male camaraderie that Ram told her, but her imagination failed her, and she was content instead to dwell on the warm intimacy she had built up with her brother since her elopement; and was glad, in a sisterly way, that he had made so many friends through the modern medium of the world wide web. Somehow she knew never to discuss these matters with her husband. She treasured the fact that somebody, anybody, was confiding in her.

For the past six months, however, ever since Sunita announced her engagement, Urvashi's conversations with her siblings had been dominated by discussion of the wedding. Until now, regarding this event, Urvashi had been in a state of anticipation. She had actually seen the wedding invitations – made from thick, pink, silky handmade paper, tied with gold thread, bilingually embossed with fluid Devanagari script on the front, and squat English writing on the reverse, *cordially inviting* so-and-so to the wedding of *Sunita Sharma and Ashwin Chaturvedi* – which Sunita had shown her one afternoon in the United Coffee House. She had heard all about the groom's family; could list the contents of Sunita's dowry; knew the exact timing of the wedding reception, its location and menu.

Sometimes, because her family was not from the elite of Delhi society like the Chaturvedis, Urvashi even dared to wonder if the groom was disfigured – so unequal was the match. But she had been shown the Engagement Photos, where the groom was displayed in his perfect healthy glory, limbs and all intact. And although Sunita never mentioned it in so many words, the truth was that Urvashi herself had played a critical role in securing this dream man as her sister's husband. It was she, after all, who had mentioned to Sunita that Professor Chaturvedi – who lived a block away from the Ahmeds in the same housing colony – was looking to hire somebody to come in three days a week and organise his library. She had received this piece of news from her maid, Aisha, who also worked in the Chaturvedis' house. 'You know the Professor's home?' Aisha had said one afternoon. 'In G-block?' And Urvashi nodded, for her young maid often spoke of this large shadowy house with its big piles of books and black-and-white photographs that made her think of ghosts. The Professor, it seemed, needed somebody who could read and write in English and Hindi, to catalogue his library. And so Urvashi sent her sister Sunita along with her curriculum vitae printed out on gleaming white paper, and later that day Sunita rang Urvashi to say that she had been given the job as Professor Chaturvedi's librarian! At a tea session some weeks later, a newly confident Sunita told Ram and Urvashi that the Professor had a son, Ash, a scientist – the Professor himself had introduced them. And barely a few months passed before the little sister announced to her siblings that Ash and she were engaged. A love match! Soon Sunita would be married – and then the sisters would be neighbours.

Sitting at home in Nizamuddin during the months leading up to the auspicious day, Urvashi could think of little else. But the event threw up one short-term problem: what to wear? After weeks of deliberation, after looking sceptically back and forth through her wardrobe and consulting a range of fashion magazines, Urvashi summoned her driver, Humayun, and made him take her to Nalli Saris in Connaught Place. There, she spent at least two hours appraising wave upon wave of multicoloured silk, struggled to choose between nude georgette with a dark blue lace border (three thousand three hundred rupees) or printed leaf-green/shell-pink crêpe (five thousand exactly); draped the georgette across her bosom (over the tiny bump of a three-month-old foetus in her womb), stared at her reflection in the long store mirror, and tried to picture herself walking through the crowd at Sunita's wedding. Maybe georgette was too modern, really, for the Sharmas. She picked up a heavy purple tanchoi brocade. There were ornate gold flowers along its six-metre length. There was kalga work on the border. Urvashi held it to her face. So pretty, so refined. She lifted the paper price tag: twenty thousand rupees. Far too expensive. But for her little sister's wedding? She took out her new golden credit card, and placed it on the sari. *An investment for the future.*

The week before the wedding, Urvashi met her siblings in the United Coffee House at half past four. 'I'm going to wear my second-best wedding set,' she said as they waited for their order. 'It's amethysts; they'll match my sari. Tanchoi brocade,' she whispered to Sunita.

'But . . .' Sunita began.

'I'm so excited!' said Urvashi.

Ram looked between his sisters. 'Sunita! Tell her.'

'What?' said Urvashi. 'Tell me what?'

Sunita was sitting with her eyes cast down, a smile playing on her lips. She put a manicured hand over her mouth, and when she spoke, her words were muffled. 'You just don't understand. Father will never let you . . . You married a . . . Don't you see?'

Tears sprang into Urvashi's eyes. 'Did you think I was going to bring my husband?' she said quickly. 'Of course I know that Father wouldn't want him to be there.'

Sunita, who was now smiling intently at her pink glossy nails, made no reply to this, and so in the end it was Ram who spoke. 'What Sunita is trying to say, Pinki, is that father doesn't want you to be there either. We're sorry we didn't tell you before.'

The night before Sunita's wedding, at home in her custom-built mansion, lying next to her hardworking, loving, handsome (Muslim) husband, tears rolled down Urvashi Ahmed's cheeks.

Because Urvashi, formerly-Sharma-now-Ahmed, had married a Muslim, she was unfit to attend her younger sister's wedding. Because Urvashi had married a Muslim, she could not be introduced to her younger sister's fiancé. Because Urvashi had married a Muslim, she sometimes experienced a longing for that past life where there was never a choice to be made between cooking chole bhature or serving mutton rice, where acquaintance was divided into those we know and the rest we have no need to understand, for her former status as the definitely not unclever, undeniably pretty, sister-cousin-daughter to the people she had grown up knowing, and whom now she never saw. Because Urvashi had married a Muslim, a sweet, kind and loving Muslim, she was sometimes very lonely.

Feroze was lying on his side with his back to her, breathing deeply, fast asleep. He was a man of punctual habits, faithful to a set of rules that served him well at home and in the office. Regular meal times was one, uninterrupted sleep was another, and the six or seven hours he spent absorbed in this latter activity were sacrosanct. She knew she could not disturb him with her trivial worries. But as she lay there, a memory came to her from child-hood, of how, when she was a very little girl, and couldn't sleep, it was always her father who took her downstairs to heat a glass of milk, her father who murmured soothing phrases; she had always received so much attention from her father. And even though she was a grown-up woman now, the vision of herself lying here in her marital bed, alone with her sorrow, made the tears fall anew, and she hugged herself in pity.

Urvashi lay awake for a long time that night, staring into the darkness of her bedroom, until she could make out the bedside table, and a chair with a white kurta of her husband's on it, discarded there for washing, and the long blue and gold patterned curtains that she herself had chosen after much deliberation. After a while, her eyes fell on the present she had been given by a young girl-cousin of Feroze, the last time they visited his parents' house in the old city. Not thinking much of it at the time – the sticker on the bottom said *Made in China* – she had placed it, a little irreverently, on the table by her bed. But she reached out now and picked it up, tipping it so that the coloured balls inside the clear perspex fell through the liquid in the darkness of the night, just as snowflakes had fallen through the sky when she shook the glass snowstorm her grandmother had owned and which she had played with as a child, taking it down from the showcase in the front room and turning it round and round so that the snowman inside was lost in a sudden, furious storm. This was no snowstorm, however. It was a holy ornament, an auspicious gift (the cousin said), for it contained two tiny replicas of Islam's holiest places: the black cube of the Ka'aba at Mecca, and the green-domed mosque of the Prophet, also in Saudi Arabia. Instead of snowflakes, glittering balls of silver and green and gold floated down when you shook it.

Urvashi turned the object in her hand, watching the balls as they slid off the roof of the mosque and bounced off the top of the Ka'aba, then fell slowly through the liquid again until gravity put them right. She shivered suddenly, for a thought had struck her: *Allah the Merciful, the Compassionate, would he shelter her?*

And as she stared at the model of the Ka'aba, a warm feeling spread through her – she put the object back on the table in fright and pulled the sheets tighter round her shoulders. For she knew that it was her soul, filling up with yearning for her husband's religion.

chapter 7

Ram Sharma couldn't stop smiling. He smiled at his own good fortune, at the surprise that he, Ram, had sprung on his family with this sudden promotion from provincial Delhi boy to international man of business. He laughed to himself at his father's inadequate reaction to the momentous news that Uncle Hari had broken over dinner: for Shiva Prasad had barely seemed to notice that his own son was being taken from him. He had responded with maddening nonchalance to the fact that his till-now estranged brother was standing in his house, offering to bestow on Ram unheard of riches (that he, Shiva Prasad, was incapable of providing) and explaining what an impressively charming and talented boy Ram was. Ram grimaced at the thought of his father. The old man was very annoying.

But his annoyance hadn't lasted long. In fact, it was already waning by the time Ram bid goodbye to his weeping mother and walked outside to where his uncle's 4x4 was waiting. He got into the front seat, leant back, admired the gleaming windows and sparkling appliances, the state-of-the-art AC and clean comfortable upholstery, and then, as many times before, imagined his life as Uncle Hari's heir stretching luxuriously away before him into the future.

Neither Hari nor Leela spoke during the long drive home to Connaught Place and Ram, who was used to constant bustle in the small, humdrum home he had grown up in, with his father shouting at everybody and his sisters creating their own type of commotion and his mother standing in the middle of it all, calmly dispensing tea and paratha and advice about which gods to propitiate according to which requirement, found the silence distinguished by comparison. It pleased him. They were driving north, and after half an hour they passed the turning to Nizamuddin West, where Urvashi lived. Ram thought of his elder sister with fondness. She, at least, had manifested genuine surprise and enjoyment when he told her about becoming Uncle Hari's heir, and he was half-tempted to ask the driver to let him out so that he could walk to Urvashi's house and regale her with a rendition of the evening's successes: of how it had gone off so very much to the visiting party's satisfaction; of how generous Hari's offer was; of how a reconciliation between the brothers was immediately effected; of how the heir arrangement was received without so much as a murmur; of how Hari, Ram and Leela fled back to their tank-like vehicle at half past nine, full of Ram's mother's food, glad of the gin they drank earlier.

But Ram had an appointment to keep, and so he said nothing, and the car sped silently onwards through the city.

Suddenly Auntie Leela spoke from the back seat. 'Can you stop the car?' she said. 'I want to get a cigarette.'

Ram leapt into action. They had just reached India Gate. 'When we get to the house I'll walk up to N-block,' he said, craning round to speak to his uncle and aunt. 'I'll be back in ten minutes.'

In fact, Ram had a packet of cigarettes in his pocket; but he didn't want Uncle Hari to know that he smoked. He wasn't sure which Uncle Hari approved of less: wives who smoked or nephews who did. How odd Auntie Leela was, Ram reflected, as he watched the car turn into the driveway. He took a cigarette out of his pocket and lit it. This afternoon he had arrived at the house to find his uncle's taciturn wife waiting outside the front door, clutching a bag of fruit, and dressed in such a plain cotton sari that for a moment he mistook her for the maid.

'Auntie . . . may I help you?' Ram had asked, and leant over to take the bag out of her hands. Then he bent down to touch her feet – an automatic gesture of submission to one's elders drummed into him by his authoritarian father. But she moved her feet away from his outstretched hands, and said, 'No need for that.'

'Did you take a round of Delhi?' Ram persisted. 'Are you liking the new car? Did you try the music system?'

'Actually,' she said, 'I took the bus.' The bus. His uncle's crazy spouse used public transport. He hated to think that the lovely white car that Uncle Hari had caused to be purchased for her exclusive use was not being appreciated as much as it deserved.

Ram shook his head in disapproval as he reached Connaught Place. Being November, the chill of winter had already set in, and a forlorn, deserted air had descended like a damp mist on the wide, colonial-era arcades and shabby shopfronts of this place his uncle loved so much. Tonight there was hardly anybody about at all: the smart people were at home in their south Delhi residences. But Ram was too preoccupied to be affected in any lasting way by this isolation. By now it was half past eleven – only thirty minutes to go. He bought the cigarettes for his aunt and walked quickly back down the long, ill-lit street. When he reached the house, he ran up the path in some excitement, unlocked the front door, and strode into the hallway.

Ever since Ram had been allocated, by Uncle Hari, the task of renovating Auntie Leela's house, he had the feeling of walking straight back into the past. Everything about the property was dusty and old-fashioned, from the location to the architecture to the cracked marble-chip floors that Ram had urged Uncle Hari – fruitlessly, as it happened – to replace with something modern. Despite his best efforts, the place still looked antique. This evening, typically, an old Indian film song, crackly with age, was drifting through the house from the record player Auntie Leela had brought with her all the way from America.

But the place had potential. Walking across the hall, Ram caught a reassuring glimpse of his dashingly curved nose and long, black-lashed eyes in the heavy carved wooden mirror opposite (that new pink and green silk tie suited his complexion) and when he entered the lounge area (referred to by Uncle Hari as the 'drawing room', and which he himself thought of as a space for massive and spectacular parties) he found his uncle standing by the drinks table under the window, pouring whisky into tumblers, his bald head glowing. Leela, who had been sitting on the settee reading a newspaper, got to her feet when she saw Ram, took the cigarettes from him with a quick, grateful smile, and walked out into the garden to smoke one, her face turned up to the darkened sky.

Hari held out a whisky to his nephew, and although Ram preferred something less classical himself – the new vodka mixes were more exciting – he sat down with the glass, and picked up the newspaper that Leela had been reading, flipping over the pages as he took a sip. It was the paper his uncle financed, the one that his father so despised: the *Delhi Star*. The gossip column was on the back page with yet another paragraph about the deceased society beauty, Meera, late mother of Sunita's future husband, who also wrote poems.

'Listen to this naughty poem that Professor Chaturvedi's wife wrote before she died,' Ram said, and lowering his voice to a conspiratorial whisper read out some lines: '*They dispatch a servant*

/ In their place, dressed in royal robes, Who caresses and kisses him / And charms him with her ardent moans.' He looked up: 'These Bengalis!'

His levity had the desired effect. Finally, at last – as needed to happen – the two men laughed.

But then Uncle Hari sat down opposite him, and Ram saw that the elder man's smile had vanished. His uncle turned the drink slowly in his hand and took a sip. 'Did my brother ever hold a position in the Party?' he asked at last.

Ram shook his head. His father's expectation – continually disappointed – at being favoured by the party was one of the themes of his childhood. He distinctly remembered, as a ten-year-old, vowing that he would never grow up to be a man like his father: constantly waiting on the Party for favours and promotions that never materialised, forever leading his family with him up false avenues of hope, telling stories that infected their mother, too, so that she whispered to her children that their father was just about to be asked to stand for election to the Lower House, and had only to decide where to contest from: a constituency in Madhya Pradesh (where he hailed from) or Delhi, where the family was now settled. Ram alone, it seemed, understood the truth: that his father was far too ideological to be a politician; that he had no real sense of how things worked; that his school-going son knew better what made the wheels of the world turn than he did. As a teenager, taken along to Party meetings (and the Party was then in its infancy as a political force in India), Ram saw with a jab of humiliation how the big bosses smiled condescendingly on Shiva Prasad for his passionate pronouncements, and humoured him in his vision of himself as a political actor, but that when it came to actually getting things done, there were other, more pragmatic people that they turned to. Shiva Prasad was disappointed time and again, and nobody else in the family saw it for what it was.

Neither Ram's mother nor his sisters dared to look each other in the eye and speak the truth: that their father had spent his entire life waiting for something to happen that never would.

Ram had not spoken of this to anybody before, but now it all came out, and Uncle Hari listened, not with a gleam of satisfaction, but with a sad look of sympathy, that of a younger brother mourning the mortification of the elder.

'You must not forget him, Ram,' said Hari. 'You must still visit.'

It was nearing midnight by the time Hari and Leela said goodnight to Ram and walked across the hallway to their bedroom. As the hand of his watch moved northwards Ram became impatient; but he didn't move from the couch until the bedroom door had shut behind his aunt and uncle and he was sure that they had turned in for the night. He waited a minute further, and then he ran outside and up the steps to his special suite of rooms along the roofline, pushed open the door to his bedroom and switched on his new laptop, brought over by Uncle Hari from America, which was waiting for him on the bedside table. Uncle and Auntie slept one floor down at the other end of the house. Nevertheless, Ram took the precaution of locking the door.

Ram dialled up the Internet connection, logged onto Delhiwallah's House of Sin, entered the prebooked cyber room, and waited. Fifteen seconds elapsed. Then a message: 'Are you there, Man-God? It's me, Manhattan Mania.'

Ram had had boyfriends ever since he was six years old, and he had been having sex since the sultry afternoon of Gandhi-ji's birthday (it was a school holiday) when he did it with the son of his parents' mali. But this one – this shy Internet lover whom he had never met in person – was special. They had come across each other in the House of Sin six months ago: 'Let me touch you,' *Man-God*

(Ram) had written, and *Manhattan Mania*, who had clearly never done anything like this before, typed back: 'Gently then.'

It had begun like that. They would meet at midnight in their chatroom twice a week to stroll around their virtual Delhi, unzip each other's trousers – and faster than it is possible to type with one hand, reach yet another monumental climax. It worked every time.

'Your name, naam batao!' Ram would gasp into the computer, and Manhattan Mania, who was a lot less proficient than Ram at typing quickly, would reply: 'I CANT DON@T ASK.'

In the first few months, Manhattan Mania was cautious – afraid, Ram surmised, of being found out. 'Where in Delhi do you live?' Ram wrote one evening. 'Can we meet?'

'No,' Manhattan Mania replied, and terminated the connection.

Ram remembered all too well how upset Manhattan Mania's ensuing absence from the House of Sin had made him. His Internet partners were usually more brazen. There was none of Manhattan Mania's reticence, his unfamiliarity with the language men use together. Every night for a week Ram logged on only to be met by nothing. Silence.

Then, ten days later, Manhattan Mania reappeared as usual, as if nothing was wrong: 'We walk down Rajpath, arm in arm . . .' he typed, and Ram added, 'When we get to India Gate I pull you down onto the ground and . . .'

Via the ether of their top-floor chatroom, they fondled each other on a boat on the Yamuna ('But the river is disgusting, yaar,' protested Manhattan Mania realistically), on the lawns of the Purana Qila, on the dance floor of the Zed Bar, and went even further when sprawled across the bonnet of a dusty white car parked outside the Income Tax Office. Ram had a taste for the illicit: the Jama Masjid, the Hanuman Temple. Manhattan Mania revealed his more homely streak: Nirula's ice-cream parlour (of course), the INA Market, the Pelican Pond in the Zoological Park.

Later, in broad daylight, Ram would occasionally revisit these places, haunting the sites of their verbal-virtual trysts, trying to catch the eye of passers-by, and wondering. Who *was* Manhattan Mania, really? People told each other such lies over the Internet. He knew that they assumed new identities, personas, even genders, in their Internet avatars. But he himself was just as much Man-God in his real life as during his midnight dates. Was it the same with Manhattan Mania?

Ram looked up from the computer and stared round him at his bedroom. He would like to bring Manhattan Mania here, to show him the trappings of his new life as Uncle Hari's son. The screen was flashing. A message had appeared: 'Do you remember the place we went to first?'

Manhattan Mania was certainly in a nostalgic mood tonight. He wanted to linger on Rajpath longer than usual. He kept asking Ram if he could remember what they had done where. 'What's wrong?' Ram typed at last, and waited patiently for the reply to appear.

'Man-God, if I don't come back, it doesn't mean I don't love you.'

'Where are you going?'

'I'm not going anywhere.'

'Then why might you not come back?'

No answer came. The fear jabbed at him, a premonition.

'Answer me!' Ram typed.

'I'm getting married.'

'NO!'

'Isn't that what people like us do, in India?'

Ram felt, for almost the first time in his life, the hot, maddening throb of jealousy. 'No!' he replied, 'it's not what we do. Not in this day and age!' His hands were shaking. 'It's a brand-new era. Don't you understand?'

He waited again, trying to resist the impulse to discover the worst. But he couldn't resist, and finally, he wrote: 'WHEN are you getting married?'

There was a moment of flickering emptiness, and Ram held his breath as he waited. Then the single word appeared on his screen, and Ram hit the keyboard and turned his head upwards and screamed. But the word was impervious to his troubles; it remained there, suspended before him: *Tomorrow*.

chapter 8

On the morning of Sunita Sharma's marriage to Ash Chaturvedi, Humayun (son of Mohd Hamid, deceased) said goodbye to his cousin Aisha at the Ahmeds' house in Nizamuddin West where they both worked – he as a driver, she as a maid – and pulled the door softly to behind him. Before he left, she had handed him two pails, one for the milk that he would buy in the market, and the other a tiffin of Mrs Ahmed's chapli kebabs for his mother, and he swung these jauntily now, as he walked down the side alley of the house and opened the gate. The route from Mrs Ahmed's house to his mother's home beyond the shrine ran along the far western edge of the housing colony, parallel with the drain. He loved this daily journey, crossing from the large, tranquil place where he worked, into the hectic, densely packed, and much more antiquated settlement where he had grown up. He liked the peace and order of the planned colony; but the familiar people and the places around the Sufi shrine were part of him too: it was like walking from a peaceful riverbank into a forest noisy with birds, he thought, and he was pleased with himself for thriving so well in both places.

It was in good part due to his upbringing. When he was little, Humayun's mother had looked after the Professor's children – she had been ayah to Ash Chaturvedi, the man who Urvashi Ahmed's sister was marrying this very evening. Humayun had grown up around the Chaturvedi household, watching their elegant ways and listening to his mother Raziya's stories about the twins, Bharati and Ash – who had been raised in luxury but without a mother, poor things. Humayun's mother had strong opinions about the family she once worked for, and she had pronounced that the affable young scientist was 'throwing himself away with this marriage'. Aisha, too, who worked not only in Urvashi Ahmed's house but also cleaned for the Chaturvedis every afternoon, found the future bride to be quite unfriendly and over-fastidious, and sensed that, once married, she might be very bossy. Aisha had confided in Humayun that marriage preparations at the Chaturvedi household were very low-key. There were no special lights or flower arrangements, no visiting tailors from south Delhi or jewellers from Chandni Chowk, no breathless delivery boys with huge boxes of crockery and extra-heavy white goods. The only notable thing that had happened, in fact, was that old Mrs Chaturvedi, the Professor's mother, had sent Aisha upstairs to tidy her grandson's room (it was a mess of scientific papers), and then she herself had unlocked the old tin trunk in her bedroom, removed an ancient red and blue quilt, and given this to Aisha to spread on her grandson's bed. That was it. Aisha, who had been expecting marigolds and candles, jasmine blossom and giggling girl cousins, had pronounced herself, in her turn, 'very disappointed'.

Humayun agreed. But he relayed none of this information to his mother, Raziya, despite her frequent questions on the subject. It was important, above all, that he did not allow it to come to her attention that Aisha was working in the Professor's house. Raziya, too, was fastidious, and her greatest disapproval of all was reserved for Aisha's mother. She liked to point out that the two families were only very distantly related; she certainly had more extravagant hopes for her son than marriage to a girl whose father had disappeared, whose mother had sporadic employment at best (she had recently taken to hawking bananas along the ring road), and who, since the government had cleared the illegal dwellings around the Hindu crematorium, was camping next to the chowkidar's hut in the graveyard.

Ever since her husband had died, fifteen years ago, Raziya, too, was making do without a man around, and yet she managed, procuring not only a driving licence for Humayun but also employment at the Ahmeds' – a rich, young and inexperienced couple who had only recently moved into the neighbourhood. Mrs Ahmed, indeed, had been born a Hindu, which made her the perfect employer, for she knew next to nothing about Islam. 'Three weeks' annual leave for performing Haj,' Humayun's mother had told Mrs Ahmed on the day she kindly volunteered her son as their driver. 'Twice annual bonuses for Eid. He will need that extra room at the back of the garage quarters for praying in' – this was, at present, the place where Mrs Ahmed stored her husband's library of such political- and social-minded books as could not go on display in his study – 'and,' Humayun's mother said, 'hot and cold water for ablutions.'

Mrs Ahmed had a water heater fitted and ordered three-dozen bars of Lifebuoy soap.

'He should eat mutton at least once a day,' continued Humayun's mother. 'This is enjoined upon us in our religion.'

With her forefinger, she pointed towards Mrs Ahmed's belly. 'You, too, will need this holy diet when the time comes. Muslim babies need Muslim meat.'

Mrs Ahmed, who had been brought up a strict vegetarian, shivered. But the shiver was merely a reflex from childhood; for some time now, she had experienced many thrills (and gained some extra weight) from eating lamb and chicken with her husband. She had acquired a taste for spicy meatballs.

'Is there anything else?' she asked Raziya, and the older woman smiled.

'New clothes on Eid.' Then she added, as an afterthought: 'And please do send him to the mosque on Fridays. These youngsters are tending to miss even the obligatory prayers.' Humayun's mother left nothing to chance.

It was perhaps in reaction to his parent's strict measure of the world that Humayun began to take notice of a girl whom he met, quite fortuitously, one evening as he was walking home from work. Just as he reached the poorer settlements that abutted the shrine, where the houses suddenly grew very close together, and the alleys were too narrow for cars to pass along, and there was a sudden increase in the volume of raucous shouting and friendly greetings and none of the amazing *quiet* in which the residents of the planned colony wallowed from morning to evening, he happened to see a girl struggling to carry a plastic container of water. She had turned off from the main street and was dragging the container after her through the gate that led down to the narrow, deep river of sewage that divided Nizamuddin from the housing colonies of Bhogal and Jangpura. She was a thin girl, and her headscarf had slipped from her head and was trailing in the dust behind her. Humayun called out and hurried over.

'You are Humayun,' she said shyly as he took the container and hoisted it up onto his hip; as they walked, she explained how they were related through her mother's family. The names meant nothing to him. 'Yes, yes,' he said, as she listed unknown uncles in faraway villages, and, turning his head, tried to catch glimpses of the girl's face, now partly obscured by the readjusted headscarf. When they reached the drain itself, she made as if to cross the small concrete bridge that led up to the bank on the other side.

'But where are you going?' Humayun asked, suddenly aware of where they were standing: on the edge of the drain that curled through the centre of the city.

This was how he learnt that Aisha and her mother lived in the graveyard. She led him across the putrid stream, up the sandy bank strewn with rubbish, plastic bags, little trails of human shit, past the foraging pigs with lines of mud along their backs from wading through the sewage, to the graveyard on the crest of the hill. 'We have to enter the graveyard through here', Aisha explained to him, indicating the green gate enclosing the space where the Muslims buried their dead, to her left. 'In there,' she whispered, pointing to the right, to a high wall topped with shards of coloured glass, 'is the Hindu crematorium.'

Humayun followed Aisha through the gate and between the trees and sandstone headstones to a slight rise in the middle where a white wall enclosed some graves set apart from the rest. Here the watchman lived with his family. Her mother, she explained, rented a tent space for them in the safety of this enclosure. Humayun stared, unable to voice his words. *You sleep here? Alone?* The old caretaker, Aisha told him soothingly – half anxious at the disgrace, half concerned that he shouldn't worry – kept out miscreants and kept an eye on them.

That night, Humayun returned to his mother's tailor's shop in a rage at the shame of it. She had pulled down the shutters and was putting away the articles of clothing her tailors had finished. As he fumed, she listened in silence, picking stray threads off a newly ironed kurta. Finally, she said, 'I won't have anything to do with that woman, and neither will you.'

The very next morning, early, before he had to be at work, Humayun returned to the graveyard, this time carrying a pail of milk. Large lumbering black buffalo were being led through the gate and down to the drain. Humayun walked after them, towards the water, to examine it in the daylight. Early morning was the time he loved most in Delhi, while the mist still sat low upon the roads and the river, and the highways where the buses ran nonstop at the height of the day were almost empty. He stood on the bridge that Aisha and he had crossed the night before and looked along the drain to the east. A huge water pipe crossed the drain, linking Nizamuddin housing colony with Jangpura, and already there were people washing in the water that spurted out from the leaks. Men, half-naked in their lungis, were standing on the Nizamuddin side, swishing the water over themselves, or soaping their bodies as they waited in line. Women stood on the Jangpura end, tipping their long ropes of hair into the water, swinging them up so that rivers curved miraculously upwards through the sunlight. Humayun, whose nose had wrinkled at first against the thick scent of sewage, wondered now whether it wouldn't be more efficient for the concerned officials to mend the leak and install a shower on the pipe which could then be switched on and off. He felt unusually happy.

That morning Aisha, too, felt happy when she saw her robust and practical cousin crossing the graveyard towards them. 'Come with me and I'll find you work,' Humayun said, in what seemed to her a tone of almost otherworldly confidence; and he waited as she picked out her best suit, a flimsy orange georgette with long bell sleeves, and combed amla oil into her hair.

They walked back across the drain and went to a house where Humayun's mother had once worked. The Hindu man, Professor Chaturvedi, seemed pleased to see Humayun, asking after his mother and her tailoring business in some detail as they spoke together in the hallway. Aisha stood outside in the shade of a large glossy leaved tree, overcome by shyness. But Humayun, who had spent many afternoons waiting in this house after school for his

mother to finish work, found it unchanged. He was not fazed by
its strangeness; rather, the feeling it had always induced in him
was a slight, pleasurable feeling of vertigo, so crammed was it
with strange rural objects and pieces of mud sculpture and wooden
masks hanging from the walls, of men with twirly moustaches and
orange turbans, and Hindu ladies with large wondering eyes and red
bindis on their foreheads. On a table in the hallway where they were
standing, there was even a clay pot such as those his grandmother
used in the village, for keeping water cool. 'She can come in every
day for two hours,' Humayun told the Professor – who opened his
hands out wide in a helpless gesture: 'But we don't need an extra
servant, now that my daughter has gone to London.' 'She can wash
dishes,' said Humayun, 'and mop the house.' There was a pause,
and then he added, knowing that this point was indisputable: 'Just
as my mother looked after your two children, so she will be a good
companion for your mother.'

'Who is this girl?' the Professor asked at last, watching the young
man's determined face, and Humayun said: 'She is my cousin. She
is a good girl, I guarantee.'

At Mrs Ahmed's, he adopted a more triumphant tone. 'I have
found you the ideal maid, Mrs Ahmed,' he told Urvashi – who,
not yet pregnant, was spending a very long time in the kitchen
practising simple meat dishes. 'She can clean the house and do the
laundry. She can make daal and vegetables and other little things
that are too tiresome for your mother-in-law to send over' – at
present one of Humayun's tasks was to drive every afternoon to
Mr Ahmed's parents' house in Old Delhi to collect that evening's
meal, prepared by their aged cook. 'Her parathas are excellent,' he
continued. 'She knows everything about korma.' He even added,
extravagantly, 'She can teach you how to make shami kebabs.'

Aisha stood on the doorstep as Humayun arranged the terms of her employment. She could smell the thick, cloying odour of Mrs Ahmed's perfume. This house was even more resplendent than the last. Mrs Ahmed was wearing flame-coloured silk, and each time she ran her hands through her long, long, silky hair, her bangles jingled. The house gleamed with fresh white paint.

Since then, almost a year had passed. Aisha's innocence had touched Humayun from the first, but during the ensuing twelve months he watched with satisfaction as her confidence grew. He remarked to himself how her body seemed to alter with her new composure. Under his gaze, her breasts, still hidden beneath layers of fabric, seemed subtly to swell. He wanted to run his hands through her hair. But he kept his desires to himself, for Aisha was young; and lest the other servants in this colony should gossip to his mother, he was careful to limit his interaction with his cousin in public, collecting Aisha from the graveyard early in the morning on the way to work, and taking her home after dark.

He hadn't broached the subject of marriage with the three women concerned – neither his mother nor Aisha herself, nor Tabasum Khatoon, Humayun's prospective mother-in-law – and his mother at least, would take a lot of convincing. There had to be some forceful way in which he could do it; but given his mother's temper, he didn't yet know how; and the only other person he had mentioned it to was his cousin Iqbal, and Iqbal's prognosis of his success in this matter had not been good. 'She'll never let you,' he had said. 'Inshallah the thing will turn out for the best.'

Humayun was thinking this over as he walked along the path that ran parallel with the black and winding drain that carried the city's sewage away into the river. The drain was invisible from the housing colony in Nizamuddin – there was a park, a high wall, and a line of trees screening it from view – but you could smell it, despite these attempts to pretend it wasn't there. The houses that stood here were the oldest in Nizamuddin West, and even though they were large – two or three storeys high, each divided from its neighbour by a wall and a garden – in the time since they were built, the amount of sewage in the drain had swollen from a trickle to a flood, and the people who lived here lived with the stink.

All of Delhi was built like this, his mother had once told him: pockets of airy, quiet residences where the rich people lived, and right alongside, pushed into the crevices the rich people didn't want, the busy scrum of everybody else's existence. She was proud of the tiny, independent space she had made for them both, her little house on the edge of Lodhi Road; but as Humayun walked, he looked up at the big wide houses, with their drawing rooms, and dining rooms, and their succession of bedrooms with bathrooms en suite, lived in by doctors and engineers, and he tried to imagine how it would feel to live in such a house with Aisha – with all that white space on the walls, all those steps to run up and down, all those doors to walk through and cupboards to open.

The Professor lived in one of these houses, and this morning, as Humayun passed the gateway, he saw that there was a taxi outside, its engine running.

'Humayun!' shouted a female voice. Looking up towards the house, Humayun saw Bharati, the Professor's daughter, standing in the doorway at the top of the steps. She was dressed in tight jeans and had cut her wavy hair daringly to chin-length. Her dark blue jacket was slung around her waist and the white T-shirt she was wearing showed off her smooth round shoulders. As he walked towards her, he could see that the T-shirt ended above her navel.

She beckoned to him. 'Humayun,' she said, 'my father says he sees you every now and then. You are working in Nizamuddin as a driver?'

Humayun raised his eyes to her face. She was three years older than him, and when he was not even yet at school, had forced him into her father's study to learn English words which she read out from a blue and white grammar. She had tried to teach him things, showing him a map of the world, pointing out 'Italy' and 'Spain' and explaining about the Mughal Emperor whose name Humayun bore (and about whom Humayun had, of course, already been told). Once, she had even arranged for him to be taken to the cinema with them in central Delhi; Humayun had felt ill from embarrassment. Everybody could see he was the family servant. 'He works for you?' the man at the ticket booth had asked, but she denied it. 'He's a friend,' she said, turning away. 'Here's your ticket then, young friend,' said the man as he handed over the small yellow rectangle of card, and Humayun had felt ashamed of who he was.

Later, when Humayun's mother no longer worked full-time for the Professor, he occasionally caught sight of Bharati in the market, buying mangoes from the fruitseller, or arguing with the master tailor about the cut of a shirt. It was she, not the usual filmstars, who filled up his dreams; late at night when he should have been asleep, he imagined unpinning those tiny blouses, caressing that smooth skin, filling up the warm dark cavities of her body which beckoned to him like the sea sucking at pebbles.

As he stood listening to Bharati speak, these pubescent fantasies came back to him in shameful jabs. She was speaking fast, explaining that she had just this morning arrived back. 'From America?' Humayun ventured in English. 'From London,' she corrected in Hindi, and added: 'I haven't been in Delhi for over a year.'

He put down the pails. 'Shall I bring in your cases?'

As Humayun climbed the steps with a case in each hand, the Professor came to the door. 'So you've met my daughter already,' he said. She smiled at them both, and Humayun's eyes strayed haplessly over the skin of her midriff.

Looking up, he saw that the Professor had been watching him, and feeling both ashamed and defensive, he said, without thinking about it beforehand, 'I might be getting married.'

'You might be?' said the Professor, with a smile.

'I am hoping, inshallah.'

'To whom?'

'To your maid, Aisha.'

'Why, that's wonderful, Humayun,' said Bharati, and she added, 'You know that your Ash-bhaiya is getting married today?

'In fact,' she went on before he could answer, 'that's why I am here.' She turned impetuously to her father. 'Wouldn't it be good to have a driver to take us to the wedding, and to bring us back?'

The Professor ran a hand over his bearded chin. 'It might.'

'So,' she said, tapping one finger against her lips.

Soon, Humayun had promised to be back after work, to pick up the family and drive them in the Professor's car over to the wedding grounds beyond the old airport. Bharati waved at him from the top step as he walked back towards the road. 'See you at five this evening,' he heard her call.

After dropping off the kebabs at his mother's, and telling her about his work for the Chaturvedis (anything to sidestep her questions about the Ahmeds' domestic arrangements – he had so far only mentioned something vague about a shy little maid coming in from somewhere across the river), and collecting the milk from Mother Dairy, Humayun returned to Mrs Ahmed's house and told her about his work that evening. She stood in the hallway, her eyes filling with tears as she listened to his story – Aisha had told Humayun the rumour she had heard from the Chaturvedis' cook, that Mrs Ahmed had been banned from attending her sister's wedding because her husband was a Muslim – but in the end, after Aisha brought her a cup of tea, she agreed that Humayun could leave work early, and that after Aisha had done her evening work at the Chaturvedis', Mrs Ahmed herself would go to collect her, and she would wait here for Humayun's return. 'She mustn't walk home in the dark,' Humayun said: 'Delhi is no place for young girls.'

'Don't worry. I will go and get her myself,' Mrs Ahmed assured him. She then proceeded to outline her complicated plans for the day. They involved a great deal of driving. First, Humayun had to take her to her mother-in-law's to pick up some household items that the old woman would need when she came to stay during Ramzan; then he was told to drive to Khan Market where a grocery shop stocked a particular brand of haleem spice that Mr Ahmed liked; and when they got back to Nizamuddin West, she made him wait outside the Islamic bookshop in the market. She spent a long time inside, speaking to the staff and browsing the bookshelves, and when she came outside again she was carrying a large paper packet which she held defensively in her arms and wouldn't let him take from her, even though Mr Ahmed had specifically commanded Humayun not to let his wife carry bulky packages in her condition.

It was three in the afternoon by the time Humayun and Mrs Ahmed returned home. Mrs Ahmed was wiping the perspiration off her brow with her headscarf, and proclaiming herself 'very very tired'. Humayun carried the groceries inside, covered the car with a dustsheet (she wasn't going out again that day), and waited until he heard his employer walk upstairs for her afternoon nap.

When he came round to the back of the house, to the kitchen door, he saw Aisha through the grill, sitting on a stool next to the stove, peeling potatoes for the evening meal. She was wearing her favourite yellow chiffon suit and she looked so young and delicate that he suddenly longed to take her in his arms. He pushed open the door and said: 'Today I decided that we should get married.'

She looked up. A bowl of daal was soaking in water by the stove, and the pan in which she had boiled Mrs Ahmed's tea stood with the strainer still in it, on the marble floor.

'Married?' In the moment before she pulled the scarf over her head and hid her face, her eyes moved to his, and he was startled by their expression. Terror or happiness? Perhaps both. He wasn't sure.

The house was silent. In the distance were noises of the quiet afternoon, somebody pushing a handcart, the creak of a gate, men calling to each across the rooftops. Mrs Ahmed was upstairs, asleep; Mr Ahmed was away at the printing works and wouldn't be home until evening. Humayun took the bowl of potatoes out of Aisha's hands and placed it on the floor next to the pan. Then he came close to her. His hands made contact with her shoulders – the fingers of his right hand moving down her back, tracing the ridge of her spine, as the fingers of his other hand moved upwards to clasp her neck. He put his face to hers, smelt cooking oil and soap, and kissed her lips. At first her body went rigid, attentive; then it relaxed slightly in his grip. He thought he felt a tremor move through them both, and he took her by the hand and pulled her after him through the mesh door that led to the alleyway at the back of the house.

This room where he was supposed to come and pray was dark and stuffy. There was a mattress, placed there by the Ahmeds in case he ever needed to work late – but his mother's house was so close he always went home anyway. He locked the door behind them, pushed aside the prayer-mat which Mrs Ahmed had ordered for him, unrolled the mattress and spread out the sheet. Then he pulled Aisha with him down onto the bed, and suddenly, everything happened in a rush. His hands that had never touched her before, felt inside her shirt, felt her breasts, felt down to the springy hair between her legs. He couldn't see her face, and for a moment it was Bharati Chaturvedi's semi-naked body standing in the sunshine on the steps that he saw as his fingers moved over her skin. But when he felt Aisha's own fingers, clasping his back, tenderness overcame everything, and soon he was pulling at the elasticated waistband of her salwar, pinning her down with his weight, parting her legs with his knees. He tried to push himself into her; again and again he tried, and at first there was resistance – he made a wordless grunt of exasperation; and then, just as suddenly, he was in; and the spasms of love and protection followed each other so quickly, so overwhelmingly, that it was all over in an instant.

Afterwards, as he lay there in the dark with Aisha, Humayun could hear the azan in the distance. He felt her shiver, and then there was the warm wetness of her tears on his neck. 'I'll tell Mrs Ahmed today,' he said, putting his arm around her and feeling her body, so thin and tiny beside his own. 'I'll tell my mother that we're getting married when I get home tonight.'

He got up, feeling shy suddenly, and resolute. 'You must hurry,' he said, 'Mrs Ahmed will be asking for you. You will be late for work at the Professor's. I must go there straight away and take the Professor and—' He stopped. 'The Professor and his children to the wedding. Mrs Ahmed will pick you up from there in the evening.'

He knelt down and reached for the box of supplies that Mrs Ahmed had given him, and pulled out a new Lifebuoy soap, still unopened in its white and red packet. He pointed to the door, beyond which was the toilet, tap and bucket. 'You can wash yourself in there,' he said. 'I will be back after the wedding.' He put his face close to hers, kissed her hair, and got up from the bed.

'Shall we have three children?' he asked almost shyly, his face half-hidden in the shadow, as he unbolted the door. 'Two boys and one girl would be best? Two smart boys and one little girl just like her mother.' And when she didn't answer, he pushed the door open, and said as he was going out, 'Don't leave the Professor's house till Mrs Ahmed comes to get you. I'll see you when I'm back from the wedding.'

chapter 9

Bharati, who had touched down at Indira Gandhi International Airport early that morning, watched Humayun walk away down the street, and followed her father back into the house. She was glad to have been the means of securing Humayun this extra employment, superfluous though she knew her father thought it, for he was one of the few Delhi dwellers who actually enjoyed driving in the city. But it would be good to have a chauffeur for the evening – it looked smarter – and Humayun, moreover, was special. He was the only child of Raziya, Bharati's former ayah, a Muslim widow from the settlement that abutted the nearby Sufi shrine, who chewed paan and wore brashly coloured cotton saris, and had been fond of Bharati and her twin brother Ash, in a brusque, preoccupied kind of way. She stopped working for them full-time soon after they turned ten – it was said that she had saved enough money to open a tailor's shop near the shrine – and anyway, by now it was their grandmother, their father's mother, who became responsible for their upbringing, and she was a much more demonstrative person who was fond of telling them stories from the epics and reminiscing about their father's childhood.

Bharati was not looking forward to meeting her grandmother, whose disapproval of Bharati's casual attitude to her own twin's wedding had been freely expressed in the course of several expensive international phonecalls. She was right, Bharati knew; one could easily judge the attitude of the sister by the contents of the suitcase that Humayun had just carried lightly up the steps: containing as wedding offerings no Swavorski crystal, no auspicious statue of Ganesh, but only a stripy blue cook's apron for her brother and a copy of *The Female Eunuch* for his wife.

Bharati had taken a taxi from the airport, and driving silently past the beginnings of new flyovers, in between taxis and autorickshaws newly painted green for the compressed natural gas they now ran on, into the sweet hectic hub of the city she had not visited for over a year – she found that, little by little, with the warm odour of sweat in the taxi, and the sight of mist rising from the road, she was already shedding her epidermal London armour. As she breathed in the scent of the chameli bush by the pathway, the smell of turmeric in the hall, and exchanged glances with the photograph of her mother on the stairs, she felt herself losing what defences she had constructed during her recent, triumphant odyssey through the bizarre tics and peculiar trials of that diminutive island they called *Great Britain*.

Bharati walked upstairs and sat on her bed, the narrow hard little childhood bed with its printed cotton ochre quilt and flat, dense pillow. She had left this room an innocent, sheltered, upper-class girl and come back – she felt – a woman. Downstairs, her father was calling her name.

Hitherto, the family – grandmother, brother, and, by extension, Sunita's father, mother, grandparents, siblings, cousins – had been furious. Bharati had ignored their emails, phonecalls, letters, faxes. They thought she might come home for the summer but instead she had stayed in London, working on her dissertation, even though it wasn't due until the following year. They had inundated her college with messages, sent letters to the library where she was known to spend long hours in a favourite cubicle at the top of the building (there was a *Dickensian* view over London, over the scurrying lawyers of Chancery Lane). But Bharati, who was preoccupied with Indian poetry – and in particular with writing about, analysing and understanding her dead mother's verse – had continued to ignore them. Her tutor had called this first chapter of her MA dissertation 'an exquisite exposition of a particular time and milieu in Indian poetics', and Bharati had emailed these comments to her father, who, she felt, had not been altogether encouraging about the topic of her thesis. She wondered if he wasn't jealous of his late wife's small but perfectly formed poetic *oeuvre*, and she planned to show him how the poems her mother had written were 'the quintessence of the darkening mood in late 1970s India: passionate, radical, disillusioned, playing on the juxtaposition between the golden age of Indian independence, that had seemed to stretch from 1947 into the future, and the State of Emergency imposed in 1975 by Nehru's daughter'.

In London, Bharati proved her difference from her upbringing, by setting herself apart – not from her British contemporaries – but from the life she had left behind in Delhi. In London she:

Slurped bitter with actors in Hoxton;
Sipped absinthe for tea;
Sucked the penises of men from Jamaica;
Snorted cocaine from the stomachs of obliging boyfriends;
Smoked aniseed cigarettes with pink paper tips;
And lived like the bohemian she was born to be.

Until she left Delhi, Bharati was cocooned in the rewarding existence of being the desirable, clever daughter of one of the city's most preeminent thinkers. But in London she was seen as a sex-siren intellectual who had stepped straight from the pages of the *Kamasutra*. She always got good marks, and the tall, pale Englishmen on her course – who read Spivak and Said, who lived in rickety flats strewn with Euripides and Beckett – queued up to kiss her, to lick her, to most enthusiastically bed her, and then – always, always – to take her home to meet their parents over plates of pretty sugared biscuits and tepid, sugarless tea. In London, Bharati discovered, to her pleasure, she was infinitely presentable. (That was when she started broadening the field a bit, checking out the men who moved, silent and unseen, through this sea of pale faces: the Colombians who worked in the kitchens; the Nigerians with their forthright attitudes; best of all, the Pakistanis.)

Her twin brother Ash, by contrast, had always been a good boy. While it came naturally to Bharati to rebel, Ash seemed to go the other way. Even as a four-year-old, he objected to the liberality with which they were raised: on Janmashtami, their grandmother loved to tell her, he actually asked to go to the temple. When she had her first boyfriend in school, he took her aside to lecture her on woman's virtue. He found it upsetting when she went to parties in tight, ripped jeans and see-through tops. He protested against the cavalier manner in which she had disappeared to London without establishing where she would stay, on what kind of scholarship, and why she would be gone for so long.

In London, Bharati often spoke of her twin to her boyfriends. The English ones answered solemnly: 'Filial guilt. He feels the death of your parent. He is mothering you.' Bharati wasn't so sure. And the French boyfriends tended to disagree: '*La mort, qu'est-ce que c'est? C'est rien,*' said the one called Jean-Claude. 'What about poverty, or disgrace, or despair? What is an absent parent to all that?' But Bharati held her ground when it came to her brother: 'He's never recovered,' she said quietly. She saw her brother's lack of interest in parties and dancing and girlfriends as a long-drawn-out mourning. Later, she mused to a different lover (it may have been the one from Peshawar): 'I study my mother's poetry and exorcise this grief. With science, my brother retreats ever inward.' It came out pretty well in Urdu. And the boyfriend, beneath her, fervently agreed.

Bharati had made only one female friend in London – she and women didn't get on in general – an English girl called Linda: skinny, tomboyish, freckled, barely five-foot-one, and yet, unprepossessing as she was, somebody who was continually saying things that made Bharati laugh. The first time they met was in the student bar, almost a year earlier. Bharati was there with her then-boyfriend, an Englishman called Nigel, celebrating her birthday. He was serenading her – singing her Happy Birthday – when five female voices on the next table joined in. Nigel and Bharati turned to look. It seemed she wasn't the only birthday girl in the room. There was another one – Linda.

Despite buying each other drinks that night, Linda and Bharati might not have made friends had they not bumped into each other the following week. It was a bright winter afternoon and Bharati was standing in the street stridently dumping Nigel – he was so tiresomely enamoured – when she noticed Linda leaning against the wall that divided the Union building from SOAS, clutching a stack of books to her chest, and smiling.

'What?' Bharati said, breaking off in mid-tirade.

'I was just thinking,' Linda said, 'that there are more efficient ways of doing this. You could push him into the road. Somebody might run him over if you're lucky.'

Bharati nodded, trying not to giggle. 'You're right.' She contemplated Linda's hair – golden-brown, unruly, never brushed; like something you might see on the head of a vagrant child at an

Indian railway station – and her sunburnt complexion. She wore nondescript blue jeans and a very plain coat indeed. But her face was full of laughter.

'How about a cup of tea?' asked Linda.

'Yes, all right,' Bharati said, and, leaving a battered yet grateful Nigel sitting on the pavement, she followed Linda into the Union bar.

Apart from their height, they didn't have much in common. They had both been raised by single parents – though even Bharati could see that an attentive father, good-natured brother, hands-on grandmother, throughout-infancy ayah, full-time cook, part-time maid and mornings-only mali was not in quite the same category of singleness, exactly, as a lone, Bible-thumping mother in Brighton.

Linda was doing a one-year MA in South Asian Languages and Culture. Where this interest came from she didn't say, but when Bharati pushed her, she admitted that her mother had wandered off to India in her youth and, since she was now too Christian to tell her daughter about her experiences, Linda was having to find out for herself.

That afternoon they exchanged email addresses. 'Chaturvedi?' said Linda, staring at the name Bharati had written in her notebook. 'There's an author on my reading list with that name. Ved Vyasa Chaturvedi. I haven't read his book yet but—'

'He's my father!' Bharati said.

'Your father?' Linda repeated.

'The very same.' Bharati laughed at the wide-eyed look of wonder on Linda's face. 'It's no big deal, you know, having a father who's an academic.'

To Bharati's initial consternation, during that first year of their friendship, Linda began to read Bharati's father's books. She ended up writing her MA dissertation on the development of script in India, and her supervisor encouraged her to expand it into a Ph.D. To Bharati's even greater surprise, whereas when her father spoke about his work, her mind turned, of its own accord, to other more palatable and exotic subjects, with Linda it was different. Somehow, the way Linda described her interests – the transition from oral to scripted culture, the rise of Buddhism, what it meant to write something down rather than to memorise it – made it sound much closer to her own concerns with poetry and the transmission of ideas than Bharati had ever imagined Sanskrit and archaeology and ancient texts could be. Sanskrit, a field that Bharati had hitherto assumed was populated by legions of earnest, bespectacled men – transnational replicas of her father's earnest, bespectacled colleagues in Delhi – seemed, in London, to be something rather different. These days, as her friend talked excitedly of Western scholarship's misreading of Indian epic, Bharati wondered whether she had misunderstood her father, all these years. The thought even crossed her mind that the department in which Linda was doing her Ph.D. might house a nice, handsome scholar whom she, Bharati, could go to bed with.

Sitting in her bedroom in Delhi, Bharati thought about her awkward English friend. She should have persuaded her to come out to Delhi for the wedding; it would greatly improve things to have some faux-pas-prone guest to wreak havoc with the bridal party. 'How can you work on Indian literature without ever having been there?' she had asked her recently. 'Through books,' Linda had said. 'We're not all dripping in money, like you.' The gauche pleasure of Linda's company had helped Bharati survive her first London autumn and the onset of another. Indeed, she thought – forgetting about Linda – if there was one thing she was pleased about in coming home to Delhi, it was the weather. Autumn in Delhi was perfect: not too hot, not too cold.

But her father was calling her from the hallway, and strolling downstairs, Bharati found that he had set the table with his favourite coffee cups and treasured Italian espresso pot. In the place where Bharati always sat was the pull-out section from one of the newspapers, and on the front page was a photograph. It was of Bharati's mother.

Bharati was not unused to seeing her mother's picture gracing the cover of artistic journals. There was one shot in particular they always used, taken by a photographer friend from Calcutta, who had died of drink very young. It showed her leaning forward, one hand under her chin, an almost stern expression on her face, her lips slightly parted. Her dark straight hair was so long it framed her face and neck. Bharati had this picture up on her wall in London. It was, people often said, 1970s India at its most glamorous.

But she had never seen an article about her mother in a daily newspaper. So she sat down, picked up the paper, and read the piece through. When she finished she turned back to the beginning, looked at the name of the journalist – Pablo Fernandes; there was something about it that was familiar – and then she read the article again, lingering over, and returning to, certain words: 'a voice from beyond the grave', 'a mystery co-author or a malicious modern fraud?' Finally, she pushed the paper away. 'What's this, Baba?'

Her father, whose hair was now completely grey (he wore it long, tied behind his head in a way she had only recently grown to like), leant back and stretched his hands above his head. 'Somebody is imitating your mother's poetry, that is all,' he said. 'But I thought you ought to see it.'

'Why?' she said. 'Why would somebody do that?'

A hand reached down to stroke his beard; it was something he did when he was upset. 'I don't know,' he said. 'But many people were in love with your mother, and jealous of her, too.'

Bharati pointed to the space missing from the left-hand side of the page, where he had cut out the poem. 'The poem's not here,' she said. 'Where is it? Can I see it?'

He took the paper from her and there was a moment of silence. 'I forgot,' he said. 'I archived it. It must be in my office at the university.'

'But I'm writing a dissertation on the poetry. I need to see it now!'

Calmly, Bharati's father poured out the coffee. 'I'll get it for you tomorrow,' he said, and handed her the cup. Then he went on, in a musing kind of way, 'There you are, studying your mother's poetry; there Ash is, marrying the child of a man whose politics his father detests. In a sense your brother is the family rebel. Being Ash, he does it with the minimum of fuss, without upsetting anybody.'

Bharati felt her face flush with anger; she had been feeling so glad to be back in her father's company; why was he undermining her work in this flippant way?

She heard Ash's bedroom door banging shut upstairs as he went into the bathroom.

'Baba.' She spoke suddenly, in the rapid way she had inherited from him. 'Ash's marriage. What a strange thing; you didn't try to stop it?' She had always been frustrated by her twin's apparently non-existent sex-life; his baffling lack of interest in all the delectable ladies she had pushed his way during college; her dawning suspicion that there was something *unemancipated* about him sexually. But they had never talked about it – while she was daringly open about everything with her friends, somehow with her twin it was different. In this one most important area of her life and his, she had skirted gingerly around the topic, as if raising the subject of *sex* might bring down some evil blight upon them. And thus, Bharati concluded dramatically to herself, if Ash had an unhappy marriage, it would all be her fault.

'Stop it?' Her father shook his head. 'She is a good person. She comes from a different kind of family, that is all.'

'I don't understand.' She spoke firmly. 'Her father is a Hindu fascist.'

'Ash and she chose each other. It was nothing to do with me or you or Mr Sharma. She will become open-minded. She will make him happy.'

Bharati shook her head. 'It doesn't make sense.'

Bharati had met Sunita once, just before she left for London, before Sunita had become Ash's girlfriend. Sunita had been dressed predominantly in pink. She wore thick make-up, a shade lighter than the skin on her hands, tidily applied lipstick and had carefully painted nails. She had presented Bharati, bafflingly, with a small statue of the god Ganesh, made from a plastic that had been liberally sprinkled with sparkly dust during some point in its creation. Bharati had looked at it and fought with the desire to laugh. 'To wish you luck in London,' Sunita said. Then Sunita asked about the city, what it was like. It seemed she had read a crime fiction book that was based in north London; she explained at great length to Bharati the precise method the man used to kill the female rape victims – a bread knife: '*Incisions*,' she said, and shivered. During the conversation, Bharati had glanced over at Ash, and raised one eyebrow. But Ash seemed distracted that day, and at one point, apropos nothing, had spoken hurriedly and in great detail about one of his scientific experiments. Afterwards, Bharati asked him: 'So you have met Sunita's parents?' 'Yes,' Ash said. 'Her father has been very helpful to me, very welcoming.' And the next thing Bharati knew, her brother and this woman were to be married.

There was the sound of feet running downstairs and Ash stood before her at last, sleepy in his bedclothes, hair sticking up, blinking at her through his glasses, head tilted to one side, smiling.

'Oh, Ash,' she said – and knew that she should have come home sooner, and not allowed herself to become so absorbed in her London life. She thought of her roll call of lovers, of the parade of things she had said and thought and done. She found herself hugging her brother, trying to hold back the tears. She was suddenly overwhelmed by emotion: seeing her mother's photo in the paper; her father's scolding; above all, her twin brother's wedding, an occasion of such significance, which she had treated with disdain – flying in on the day it was actually taking place.

Ash patted her hair. 'What can be ailing our brave explorer?'

Bharati laughed. 'I'll miss you when you are married.'

'Miss me? Where am I going? You're the one who goes away.' He let her go and sat down at the table.

After her father had drunk his coffee and gone upstairs to his library, Bharati sat for a moment, watching her brother. Soon he would be married, and this intimacy would be lost. She vowed to behave this evening. She would be pleasant to Sunita always. She would do her best.

In the afternoon, following her grandmother's instructions, Bharati dressed herself up. In order to do this she drank three more cups of her father's coffee – he always brewed it too strong – and by five o'clock, the time of their departure, she felt manic with the caffeine unloosed in her bloodstream. When she came out of the house with her grandmother, Mrs Nalini Chaturvedi, on her arm, Humayun was already waiting in the garden. She knew that, since the brief moment when they had met this morning, her appearance had changed to radical and pleasing effect. In a green silk sari, with her wavy short haircut showing off her neck, her mother's bangle and thick gold necklace that had belonged to her mother before her, she looked, she believed, something like a starlet from Bombay. She had transformed herself, under her own volition, with the help of shampoo and creams, kohl and gold, thanks to the istriwallah who ironed the sari and to Ash himself, who chose the jewellery from their mother's collection. In the end they had settled on just one of the gold filigree bangles, and the necklace that looked to Bharati like something a warrior would have worn going into battle. The gold looked good against the green silk of the sari. But her father's coffee had destroyed her equilibrium. She felt the need to fuck, to get this excess energy out of her system.

Bharati looked down from the step at Humayun, who was waiting there with all the patience of a feudal servant; and yet, no: she checked herself. There was something solid and well-made about him, which was unusual in the emaciated servant class. She smiled, feeling the effect of her greatly enhanced, glossified beauty in the look of astonishment he gave her back. Next to her, Bharati's plump grandmother – who ate too many sweets, who was wearing a pale silk sari, whose long silver hair was bound up behind her head in a tight coil – tightened her grip on Bharati's arm.

Her father and brother came out of the house, and Bharati, clasping her bespangled purse in her bangled hands, hoping silently for a quick wedding, helped her grandmother down the steps. Her father's mother had made it clear that grandmother and grand-daughter would stand beside each other at the wedding, greeting guests and behaving with decorum. Still, Bharati prayed that she wouldn't have to watch her brother sitting uncomfortably among his obnoxious in-laws for too long, and that she wouldn't have to endure too many gossipy comments about her mother's posthumous poem.

'We won't know so many people this evening,' Bharati heard her grandmother say, 'but tomorrow for the wedding lunch all your cousins from Bombay will be there. Including Indrani's daughter who is your age and already has a son.'

'What's in your shopper?' Bharati asked, as Humayun opened the car door, for her grandmother was carrying a plastic bag tied tightly at the top. It bulged with packages.

'My pills,' her grandmother said, and retorted, a little sharply, 'What's on your arm?'

Bharati, who had climbed into the car from the other side to sit in the middle, looked down in surprise. 'It's Ma's bangle,' she said, trying not to sound hurt.

'Ah,' said her grandmother, and shut her lips tight.

If there was one thing Bharati hated about her sweet, darling grandmother, it was the tone in which she talked about her mother. Generally, the old woman avoided the topic altogether, but occasionally, very occasionally, she let a comment drop, and it was as if a veil had been whisked away, so that the laughing, happy young woman from the black-and-white photos was banished, and in her place Bharati was forced to see the naked outline of her lovely, defenceless mother standing there, unable to answer back, as hurtful accusations were hurled at her: *frivolous* was one; *thoughtless* was another; and the word that touched Bharati most deeply, which made her hesitate sometimes about her own actions, even when she was far away in London: *flirt*. Had her mother been a flirt, even after marrying their father? She had never dared ask; and she had refrained from discussing it with Ash for fear of upsetting him. She turned these words over and over in her head, and all she was left with was a desperate, hopeless desire to question that headstrong young woman who had given birth to her twenty-two years ago, and then – barely had Ash and she opened their eyes and looked around them at the world – disappeared from their lives for ever.

Bharati turned the bangle slowly on her arm as Humayun drove them carefully through the streets of Delhi. Ash sat in the front seat, staring fixedly ahead of him out of the window. Bharati had always thought they looked alike, her twin and she; except that while she had their mother's grace and bearing, he had inherited her round face, dimples and fair complexion; and what was striking in her was endearingly gawky in him. Somehow you could tell just by looking at him that he was a scientist. That was what their grandmother said, anyway; she liked to mention how he was the exact copy of her famous ancestor who had solved a mathematical conundrum and stunned the whole of British India. As for Bharati's long eyes, dark skin and wavy hair – here her grandmother spoke rather gratifyingly of an aunt whose beauty had bewitched every eligible man in Benares. 'That's where your eyes and hair come from, anyway, my dear,' her grandmother would say; and Bharati herself had often reflected – as she liked to tell white-skinned lovers in London – that had she been born into a less liberal family, her dusky skin would have been a problem. '*Really?*' they always answered – sounding suitably shocked, and perhaps a little gratified, by this subcontinental barbarity.

As they approached the end of Lodhi Road, Bharati opened her purse and slipped her hand inside to feel the foil of the condom she had brought with her from London. 'Isn't it amazing to think that Humayun was just a little boy a few years ago?' she said out loud in English at one point (since she knew he couldn't understand). But nobody answered, and it was the only comment passed between Nizamuddin and the Flying Club.

Because the family had hired no band, no white horse, and had called no entourage, Ash, who was wearing a new, dark, single-breasted suit, his hair still sticking up in that unruly way, looked just like any of the numerous guests who were milling around the entrance to the wedding grounds. But Sunita's family had been waiting for him, and a shehnai began playing as soon as he reached the flower-strewn archway. He was taken by the arm, a jangle of relatives Bharati didn't recognise closed around him, and she watched as he was ushered into the garden and over to the stage where his future wife was to be brought out to him, no doubt as resplendent as an apsara in a haze of gold and silk.

Bharati had always hated weddings – the social tediousness, the extravagance annoyed her – and on this occasion the gleam of gold, the excessive amounts of food, the silken, heavily powdered wives of the bride's family, was particularly distressing. Incredible, it seemed to her, Ash's capacity for tradition.

It was not yet six o'clock and it was already getting dark. Bharati and her grandmother followed Ash slowly across the lawn, everything lit up by strings of lights – but above all by the constantly swivelling flashlight of the photographer's assistant – to the stage where the bride's family was waiting. Her grandmother gave Bharati a sharp nudge: *smile*. Both families were to be photographed together, in a crowd of jostling saris and jingling jewellery.

From the dais, Bharati stared out over the crowd of silk-clad guests. Tables, spread with white cloths, lined the edges of the garden. Benches and chairs were dotted here and there. Her eyes moved methodically over the crowd, but she saw very few people whom she recognised: as her grandmother had said, the cousins, the aunts, the schoolfriends and the teachers would all be coming, instead, to the wedding lunch tomorrow. Around her, the bride's family were shouting to each other to keep still for the photographer, and Bharati glanced contemptuously at the assembled group, in their shimmering saris and stiff sherwanis. They all looked atrocious and she leant over and whispered as much in her grandmother's ear. Standing three places away to the right was a thin woman of around her father's age, dressed in saffron-yellow silk. Bharati noticed her because of her haircut: it was cut short in that defiantly sharp way that Bharati herself now preferred. No other women at the wedding had hair as short as that. For a moment they gazed curiously at each other – something about the woman was familiar. The next instant, to Bharati's astonishment, the saffron-sari lady had collapsed on to the person in front of her.

Bharati couldn't help laughing. There immediately ensued what her grandmother would term a *hullabaloo*. Several women shrieked. The posed family shot disintegrated. The father of the bride, his wedding turban sitting astride his head like a stately ship, shouted instructions about how to carry the fainting woman away: 'Out of the wedding garden, *out*, at once!'

'I'll get us some drinks, shall I?' Bharati said to her grandmother and father, and climbed down from the stage without waiting for their answer. She moved through the crowd, feeling regal and absurd in her stiff, slippery silk. At the drinks table, it turned out that the wedding was dry – the bride's father was too pious to serve alcohol – but she queued up anyway for a nimbu pani, between a woman wearing such tight bracelets that the flesh bulged around them, and a thin old man with a shawl slung around his bony shoulders.

'Hello,' said a voice behind her, and looking round, Bharati found herself staring up at a very tall young man with curly hair. She felt a sudden stirring within her, and frowned, trying to remember where she had seen him before.

'I think I know you,' she said. 'Do I?'

chapter 10

In the first few moments after it happened, Hari didn't actually realise that it was *Leela* who had fainted. Since they had arrived at the wedding, he had been so preoccupied by everything that was happening around him that he had barely given a thought to her. In the short walk across the lawns to the nuptial dais, he had spotted a politician from his home town, a Joint Secretary from the Ministry of Commerce, and that man from Kanpur who had made a mint selling software services to Americans (it was all about the time difference). Of course, none of these apparitions mattered in a material way to Hari Sharma, whose days of hassling for contracts, of passing money across desks with the nonchalance of hand-shakes, of throwing booze and girls at the underlings of ministers, were behind him. But although it was no longer his duty to butter up bureaucrats and cultivate politicians, despite the fact that he nowadays had other men to do this sweaty-palmed work for him, nonetheless, as he looked across the crowd of people assembled here for his niece's wedding, he felt a kind of grudging admiration for his brother. It was a significant social success to have collected this array of powerful allies together – not just bureaucrats and politicians, but journalists also, businessmen and hotshot lawyers.

Hari thought of what his nephew had told him last night about

Shiva Prasad's political ambitions, and the sadness he had felt then for his brother's failures gave way to a sense of exclusion: to an equally sad sense of being cut off from his sibling's thoughts and feelings and ambitions. During the years of their dispute, Hari had missed his brother, and it was only his own sense of stubbornness that had stopped him giving in and throwing over the newspaper project. And so, at their reunion the previous night, Hari had expected embraces, would not have been surprised to find himself weeping, beating his breast, asking for forgiveness (regardless of the fact that it was he who should have been doing the forgiving). It was strange and upsetting then that there was no opportunity for any such drama. Shiva Prasad, in truth, had not really risen to the occasion. It was as if the very thing that linked them – the fraternal tug that had once been as sturdy and immovable as a peepal tree, as instinctive as pain – seemed to have dissipated altogether, and now, as Hari looked over at his brother, he no longer saw the distant and awe-inspiring figure of authority from his childhood: just a banal old man, striding about the garden, bestowing obsequious greetings, and generally behaving like the centre of attention.

As they stood on the stage for the photographs, Hari was pleased to see that the usual vast contingent of cousins and home town connections had not been sidelined at this wedding. Their aged aunt, Pita-ji's youngest sister, was here, a woman who, like their father, had worked as a schoolteacher all her life, never practising graft, never vying for promotion, year after year producing at least a dozen students who went on to study for degrees at college. The young man in the mauve Western-style suit: he was the son of Hari's prettiest cousin, who had done unexpectedly well for herself by marrying a graduate from Bombay whom everybody else considered faltu – useless – until he suddenly went into stocks and shares and a year later bought a house in Bandra. And the little old man dressed entirely in white, Hari remembered with a shudder (after some moments of staring and not being able to place him), was the owner of a cloth shop in Amarkantak, who also ran the town's RSS training camp (which Shiva Prasad had tried, and failed, to make his younger brother attend with him in the hour before school).

It must give such a wonderful feeling, Hari thought as he gazed out at the wedding party, to be able to stand here in Delhi, giving away your daughter like this, to such a respectable family, in such grand style. He felt a little throb of emotion deep inside him at the thought that he himself would never be able to do such a thing, would never have a lotus-eyed daughter of his own to bestow on some lucky bull-like hero. He thought of his brother's two perfect daughters, Urvashi and Sunita, and once again he asked himself – as he had asked himself so many times before – how could Shiva Prasad have done it? To disown one's younger brother for a business deal you disapproved of – that was bullying of a stubborn though comprehensible kind. But to renounce the child you had sired because she chose her own husband: what kind of hotheaded foolishness was that? And for no better reason than that the man your daughter loved was a Muslim.

He looked around. Where was Urvashi? He leant across his wife and addressed his aunt. 'Where is my niece Urvashi?'

Hari's aunt wrinkled up her face in a grimace. 'She wasn't invited.'

'What? Because of . . . ?'

'Because of that, yes.' And the old lady shut her lips tight.

For the first time since returning to Delhi, Hari actually felt sickened by his brother's ideology. He himself had always had a soft-spot for his niece Urvashi. In the early years of her life he had made a point of visiting the family home whenever he was in Delhi, and he found her to be an open, affectionate child who lisped the word uncle – *Chacha* – in a way that made his heart melt. She was much less aloof than Ram had been at first; with none of the formal distance acquired in time by her younger sister, Sunita; prettier and more becoming than her mother. Hari's brother knew this: he had palpably doted on his firstborn. 'There is no comparable joy in this life,' he had disclosed to Hari late one night, in the days before they stopped speaking to each other. And Hari had nodded, never suspecting that such a joy, in his own life, was to be denied him.

How stupid his brother was, to have cut off this most wonderful part of himself, and all in the name of religion. Hari thought of the wedding *he* could have thrown for just such a daughter, of the crores of money he would have lavished on the occasion, of the forts in Rajasthan he would have rented without a moment's hesitation, the elephants he would have hired to march the guests around on, the filmstars he would have flown in from Bombay to dance at the party, the chefs he would have booked for the reception, the designers he would have requisitioned to dress up his daughter like a nymph from the epics, the jewels he would have chosen.

He glanced across at Ram, a little shyly. There was a man who would soon have to choose his life partner from among the many candidates available to him. Wouldn't he, Hari, as his new father, have a role in choosing the bride? And this time, when Hari's eyes roamed across the garden, they ignored the middle-aged men in suits, and searched instead, among the many nubile beauties, for Ram's ideal companion.

Weddings were the perfect place to find a bride. If Ram could begin looking tonight, Hari himself would make further enquiries, Leela would cast the deciding vote with her unerring sense of moral character – and before a year was out, Mr and Mrs Sharma would be throwing their adoptive son a stupendous wedding party in New York – something truly sumptuous, in one of the museums, perhaps, Leela would know what was currently most stylish. Hari sighed to himself as he visualised a room full of distinguished New Yorkers, with waiters circling round them carrying flutes of champagne, prawns speared through with little sticks, pastries filled with blobs of caviar. They could hire the roof garden of the Met, let off fireworks at midnight, fly a rock star in from Karachi to show the Americans the meaning of *open-minded*.

'Namaskar Leela, how are you?' somebody was saying to Hari's left. Turning his head and looking down the row of guests lined up for the photo, Hari saw to his surprise that the woman greeting his wife with such familiarity was none other than Professor Chaturvedi's mother. He couldn't believe it. Did Leela know the Chaturvedi family? She had never mentioned it. So how was it possible that—

Before Hari had time to finish that thought, the Professor himself, standing next to his mother, also turned graciously to Leela and spoke to her in an intimate tone, as if he knew her: 'Welcome back to Delhi, Leela.'

Astounded by this interaction, Hari glanced at his wife. She had said nothing in reply to the Chaturvedis' greeting but nodded politely back at them as if nothing was wrong, as if this familiarity between them was utterly natural and to be expected. Hari felt wholly confused. What was going on? How was it possible that she knew the Chaturvedis?

'Did you meet at the lecture in New York?' he whispered in her ear but she shook her head. 'How then?' he insisted.

She refused to answer – she was staring straight ahead – and he felt not just puzzled but mystified by this secretive, implacable woman he had married. Why was it that she kept him at such a distance?

Just at that moment, two things happened. An excited murmur ran through the crowd assembled on the dais – the bride was at last being brought across the wedding garden to meet her groom; and a young woman in a green sari, standing just beyond the Professor and his mother, said something to them in a low, ironic undertone, which made Leela glance over with an abrupt turn of her head. Hari, too, turned his head and sized the girl up. He saw at once that she was not at all the right type for Ram, what with her cynical expression and very skimpy choli. Ram needed somebody simple and loving and unaffected. But he was distracted by his aunt, on his other side, tugging on his sleeve. Hari bowed his head to her – noting wryly that she was the only woman at the wedding wearing cotton – and asked courteously after her health, and the welfare of her sons, before explaining in reply to her questions exactly how it felt to have lived away from India for all these years, and why they hadn't come back before, and where it was that they had moved to in Delhi.

'Arre,' cried his aunt suddenly, and Hari stopped speaking.

The party was in commotion. Men were exclaiming, women were tutting; it seemed that somebody had fainted. And Hari, turning back to Leela, saw to his horror that she had disappeared from view. It was *she* who had fainted – as silently as a cloud passing across the sky – right onto the woman in front of her, narrowly missing the bride.

Unfortunately, as Ram explained later, she had fainted just at the moment that the photographer clicked the shutter, moments after the bride had finally been seated on the dais, when all eyes in the garden were trained upon them. She had thus fainted in front of Hari's entire family – not to mention the assembled grandees of Delhi society – and, of course, the Chaturvedis.

Hari went swiftly to her side, kneeling over her anxiously, shouting for somebody to bring some water. His first panicked thought was self-accusing: had his coldness towards her just now wounded her so much? Had he made a huge mistake, in bringing her back here, to India?

But matters were quickly taken out of his hands. The air was filled with voices: his brother, calling for assistance; a grunt as three men lifted Leela off the dais; the cry he made as he ran after them across the garden; a yell in his ear as somebody told him to ring his driver. And before he had time to protest that he was sure she would recover, that he would rather spend the rest of the evening here at the wedding, that there was no need to worry, the large white car that he had bought for her was drawing up at the entrance, they were bundled inside, the doors slammed shut behind them, and the driver was carrying them away down the lane towards the city.

Hari, sitting in the front, looking pointedly away from Leela who was stretched out along the back seat, felt an unfamiliar strain of suspicion mingling with his usual, insurmountable affection.

chapter 11

When Linda was fourteen, she worked as a paper-delivery girl in Brighton. Aged fifteen, she spent all of August in a chip shop. At sixteen, she waited tables in a summer-season cream-teas-only beach hut. Seventeen brought a spell in Topshop. Throughout her eighteenth year she ran an organic burger van in Hove (a local gang slashed the tyres and graffitied the windows), and at uni she was manager of the comparatively tranquil college stationery shop. Thus, by the age of twenty-two, she was more than familiar with work that was poorly remunerated, intellectually unchallenging and socially taxing. But when Linda tried explaining this recently to Bharati, her Indian friend shook her head.

'You're doing a fully funded Ph.D.,' she said. 'What do you need the extra money for?'

'I need to save,' Linda said. 'The funding's not enough if I want to . . .'

'You could spend your Saturdays going to art galleries or the theatre.'

Linda took a sip of beer. It was a cold evening and they were sitting in the student union bar; soon the barman would call Time and Bharati would wander off in her sparkling T-shirt and super-tight jeans to some club or other – and Linda would return to the scruffy hall-of-residence room she called home. She knew there was no point in trying to explain how unreal it seemed, to be given money by the government just to do something she loved so much; that she needed a rubbish job in order to keep things in perspective; that if she didn't, somewhere deep inside she would start to panic. 'I like the café,' she said at last, 'it has—'

'What?' Bharati interrupted. 'What exactly has it got going for it?'

'Well . . .' Linda began. Set at the end of a mews to the west of Euston station, the Nine Muses was not just blessed with an address – 9 Drummond Mews – that lent itself to the kind of punning jokes so beloved of London locals, it was also run by a woman called Liz who was large, practical, red-haired and straight-talking. Her clientele was numerous, regular and demanding, the meals were simple, the ambience pleasing. Linda had grown to admire the nonchalant culinary élan of the Bap, the Sarnie, the Toastie. Eight hours on a weekend buttering scones, chopping up cabbage for coleslaw, slicing cakes and making coffee, made a blissful break from a week crammed full of Sanskrit philology. She amused herself thinking up new ways of cutting tomatoes (little slivers with a sharp kitchen knife; wild and violent chops with a cleaver) and novel means of assembling cheese and pickle sandwiches. She listened to the radio, chattered blithely to Liz, kept an eye on the customers, noting that the place seemed to attract men of melancholy dispositions.

'Why don't you come by during my shift tomorrow?' Linda suggested. 'I'll make you one of our super-strength coffees.'

But Bharati, who was snobbish about the institutions she patronised in London – she drank her coffee at an Italian place in Soho – wrinkled her nose in distaste. 'Thank you but I have to pack tomorrow,' she said. 'I'm going back to Delhi for my brother's wedding.'

'Are you?' Bharati hadn't mentioned it before.

'Just for a week.' Bharati sighed. 'Let me tell you, if there's one thing that's intellectually unchallenging, it's a bloody Indian wedding.' She drained her glass.

Linda sighed. 'I wish I was coming too.'

'Come!' said Bharati.

'I couldn't possibly afford it,' Linda said. 'The college has a travel scholarship for postgraduate researchers and I've applied for that, but I haven't heard anything.'

'Why don't you apply to give a paper at my father's Living Sanskrit conference? It's in Delhi on November the fifteenth. They want to support uptake of the classics among the youth. You'd be perfect.'

'Really?'

'Yes!' Bharati said, 'Put in a proposal. What harm can it do?'

Linda suddenly felt defensive. 'Of course I wish I could visit India,' she said. 'I long to do that. But I'm reading texts in Sanskrit. I'm thinking about words that were composed thousands of years ago. I don't know how much help modern India would be to my area of—'

'Of *course* it would help,' Bharati interrupted. 'You can't just talk to these non-resident types. You've got to go there and see for yourself. Modern India thrives on its ancient culture. The old temples and the forts aren't just sitting there as tourist attractions. They're living parts of our political and cultural landscape. On top of that,' she added, 'you should taste the kulfi and the chaat—'

'Kulfi?'

'Oh Linda, really.' Bharati looked quite fed up, and Linda – thinking of the country she knew through the words of ancient men (Kalidasa, Panini, Krsna Dvaipayana Vyasa) and the modern land she had sensed in hints and snatches (the hefty Indian hero of the film she saw once by mistake in a musical epic at the Mile

End Genesis cinema; a spicy balti she had shared with a girl from her Sanskrit grammar class at the Taj Palace restaurant in Brixton just last weekend; an Indian scarf of her mother's she had worn as a teenager) – nodded. Her friend was right.

The morning after her beer with Bharati, Linda was woken earlier than usual by a knock on her door. A voice, which seemed familiar, was speaking her name. Opening an eye, she realised she had fallen asleep with volume one of the Chicago translation of the Mahabharata splayed across her pillow. Her glasses were perched on the end of her nose, her bosom, wrought by the fervour of something she had dreamt in the night about India, was heaving.

'Hello, dear?' said the voice again, a little more anxiously now, and Linda knew at once who it was.

'Mother!' she said, sitting bolt upright in bed and gazing around her in horror. Her anxiously beloved, just-turned-forty, very-single parent prioritised cleanliness in all areas of her life, but especially the domestic. The flat where Linda grew up smelt of Pine toilet-cleaner and the lemon spray with which her mother doused the air every morning; it was thoroughly dusted every Saturday so that, on Sunday, her mother could sit back and appreciate the godly effects of these efforts. Linda knew that her hall-of-residence room, which smelt of beer-scented breath, which coughed-up used underwear with every exhalation, which could not disguise the mouldering curry-dinner under the bed, was not a safe place for a woman of Mother's sensibilities.

So she jumped out of bed, pulled on her café clothes and shouted as she tugged a comb through her hair, 'Mother! What are you doing here? I'll be out in a tick. I was just going to work.'

Half an hour later, having sat her mother in front of the Nine Muses' full-strength brew and slid a plate of cupcakes across the counter, she at last learnt the reason for this pilgrimage to London. Last night, in the queue for the supermarket checkout, her innocent parent had flicked through a parenting magazine and discovered there that it was the duty of single mothers with only daughters to *nurture* the maternal bond. Nurture, she read, meant close physical proximity, impossible sex-talks, long restaurant dinners, exhausting high-street shopping trips, and, wherever possible, bonding through mutual hysteria: 'a cleansing cry together'. It was for this that she'd caught the 6.03 to London and forced herself to wait an extra hour on a bench in King's Cross, before riding the 253 down the Euston Road to see her daughter. 'Mother!' remonstrated Linda, and sloshed more boiling water into the round brown teapot.

But her mother was undeterred. 'I've decided to take my annual leave over Christmas,' she announced as Linda set out the croissants and wiped down the counter. 'I shall come up to London to be near you. We can go to the theatre. Do you need some new thermal undies? Have you got a boyfriend? Are you happy? Are you taking adequate precautions?' And looking up bravely from her cuppa, she fixed her only child with a wavering smile.

Linda tried not to blush as she made herself a triple espresso.

Linda couldn't remember her father, who had keeled over quite cleanly and died, in 1982, one day when Linda was at playgroup. All her memories were of her mother, and the tiny flat where they lived throughout her childhood, within shouting distance of the seaside. But despite her fondness for her widowed parent, despite the fact that they never argued, despite Linda's desire never to offend her fragile sensibilities, the woman who had brought her into the world remained inscrutable. She worked as a nurse, yet they had never discussed the mechanics of reproduction. She was an unwavering Christian and yet, at twenty she had spent five anomalous months in India, travelling there on the strength of a job she had got with a Methodist charity. She had loved her husband, and yet they never ever saw his family. Throughout Linda's childhood, she had pestered her mother for more information about these two topics – her father, the Indian adventure – to no avail. The mental image of her father was obscure. He existed in her imagination as a hazy version of the man from the photograph: clean-shaven, dressed in a brown corduroy suit, standing in the distance on the steps of a church, with a slip of a girl in a simple white dress on his arm, whose barely perceptible bump (Linda) was only just covered by the long lacy veil. But the travels to India took on a life of their own in Linda's mind. As a ten-year-old, Linda pictured her mother riding through a desert on a purple-painted elephant. As a teenager, she had imagined clouds of opium smoke, naked holy men, and jingly prayer beads. During the stint in Topshop, the vision had been sartorial: red cotton saris, swishing skirts, extravagant beaded throws. Only when she reached the age of twenty herself did she stop thinking about it. It was all too implausible. But she couldn't help it if the question occurred to her now and then: how did her mother – this woman now timidly drinking her tea, a cornflower blue bobble hat on her head (she had bought it at the Harvest Festival church fair), who found London daunting, who lived for cleaning the house and going to church – have the know-how to travel alone through Asia and get a job there? Not for the first time, Linda was tempted to ask her mother to explain this daring, once and for all. But she was distracted by the arrival of one of her regulars.

He was a harassed-looking man of forty odd, always dressed in faded jackets and chinos that looked like they had been slept in. Linda disliked him because he was immensely fussy about the way they made their coffee; he liked to send back cups that weren't strong enough, or ask for extra jugs of hot milk, or insist on a sprinkle made from *pure* cocoa rather than the drinking chocolate that 'ruined everything with its added sugar crystals'. This morning he carried a briefcase bulging with papers. Pushing his way into the café, he nodded absently at the women, plonked himself down at the table under the window and began leafing through his papers with an air of desperation. Mother, Liz and Linda regarded him dubiously from the elevation of the bar.

'He doesn't usually come in till the afternoon, does he?' Liz said.

'What's he brought all that paperwork out for, on a weekend?' Mother added, more loudly.

'*Shush*, Mother,' Linda said, refilling her mother's teacup and turning away to make the chinos-man his macchiato.

Because she had her back to the door, she thus missed the visually arresting arrival of her favourite customer: a middle-aged Indian man who dressed on the outside in a grey duffel coat and sandals with socks, and on the inside in long colourful shirts (startling orange, blue or yellow – he made her think of an African parrot), who liked to sit at the table under the window, who only ever ordered a large glass of water, a cappuccino, and an egg and bacon bap to follow, and who, as she brought his order over, seemed to emanate the whiff of something spicy – the aroma of camels, palm-trees, glinting surf. She had nicknamed him 'the Dictator' because he would spend the morning sipping his coffee, nibbling his bap and whispering into a dictaphone that he always carried with him, and then leave in a hurry to avoid the lunchtime crush.

'Who is he?' Linda's mother asked in an anxious whisper.

But Linda didn't reply. She was watching the Dictator march up to the table where the harassed-looking gent with thinning hair was already sitting, and place himself in the spare chair under the window. As the women looked on, he arranged his possessions on the table top, called over to Linda to bring 'the usual', and turned on his dictaphone.

The harassed-looking man began to protest: 'Actually, do you mind, it's just that—'

But the Dictator took no notice. He held the dictaphone up to his mouth, leant back in his seat, clicked Record and started talking.

'I say, hold on a sec,' began the man, and Linda held her breath. She feared very much that there might be an altercation.

But chinos-man no longer sounded angry. He stubbed out his cigarette in the ashtray and, leaning over, addressed the Indian man directly.

'Where are you from?' he said.

The Dictator glanced up. He pressed Pause. 'From?'

'Where are you *from*?' the other man persisted, 'Are you . . . ?'

'India,' the Indian said. 'I'm from India.'

'And what are you doing?' asked the other.

'I'm composing,' the Dictator said, in a tone of great irritation. 'I am composing a work of literature.'

'Ah,' said chinos-man, and sat back. 'In the writing trade?'

The Indian man put down the dictaphone and fixed his interrogator with a disapproving glare. 'You could say that,' he said.

'Really.' The other man leant forward again. 'A writer. I need one of those. An Indian. Do you sell your work here?'

Linda couldn't quite hear the Dictator's reply, because she was back behind the counter now, toasting the bap and frothing milk for the coffee. She scrambled the egg extra fast, assembled the coffee in its cup plus sugar crystals, and carried the whole lot over on a tray, eager to hear their discussion.

'So,' chinos-man was saying as she put the tray down on the

table, 'I'll give you twelve weeks to get me a book. I handle all rights. You rake in the royalties.'

The Dictator looked dubious. Chinos-man held out his hand. 'I'm Bill,' he said, as if that explained everything. 'Bill Bond, but my friends call me William.' He placed a business card on the table. *Literary Agent*, it read, *Specialist in Foreign Literature*.

He tapped a second cigarette against the tabletop. 'Now it's your turn,' he said, and added encouragingly, 'Who are your characters?'

Linda had no time to listen to the answer, however, because by now the café was filling up with customers. For the next two hours, as she cleared away coffee cups and totted up bills, and Mother sat at the counter reading a series of yesterday's tabloids, Linda heard only snatches of Bill's conversation with the Indian.

'This might come in handy,' she heard Bill say at one point, pulling some stapled sheets of A4 out of his briefcase. '*Notes for New Writers*: a little publication of my own. I give it to all my new recruits.'

'Dear sir,' the Dictator replied loftily, 'I've been in this game far longer than you. I'm not sure you should categorise me as a "new writer".'

Linda could see that Liz, who was usually tolerant of the establishment eccentrics, did not share her fascination with the two gentlemen in this instance. The fact that they had not even ordered so much as a second coffee was trying her patience.

Things came to a head at one o'clock, by which time the café was crammed with customers seeking a table.

'Now, gentlemen,' Liz said, 'what's taking you so long?'

Bill and the Dictator both began speaking at once.

'We were just doing a deal on a book,' Bill said.

'I was telling him about Leela,' put in the Dictator.

'He is in the grip of his artistic inspiration,' Bill added.

'Well, if you don't mind,' Liz said, 'I think it's time to wrap things up.'

The Indian pointed to the dictaphone. 'I have to get this onto paper,' he protested.

'He needs a typist,' Bill objected.

'I suppose I could do it,' Linda said suddenly.

Everybody turned to look at her.

'Linda, what are you saying?' her mother exclaimed. 'How can you do it? And who knows what these tapes contain?' She had gone quite pink.

'They contain a wonderful story,' said the Indian confidently. He looked to Liz for guidance. Liz looked at Bill. Bill looked at Linda. Linda found herself nodding. 'She's a *postgraduate*,' Liz said. 'A student of literature.' And that settled it.

'So you listen to what I've recorded here,' the Indian man said, holding up the dictaphone for her to see, 'type it up, read through it correcting any mistakes, and have it ready for when I return from Delhi—'

'Delhi?' said Linda.

'I'm going to India for an important wedding,' he said. 'I'll be back at the end of the month.'

And then he got to his feet, wedged his *Notes for New Writers* under his arm, and, waving at them all, was gone as suddenly as he had come.

'Linda dear,' Mother said, her cheeks now quite florid. 'Do you think this is entirely proper?'

chapter 12

The sight of his brother's wife fainting had both sickened and annoyed Shiva Prasad. It was not just the woman herself – whom he instinctively disliked – but also something more visceral about what she represented, that empty, yearning womb, that childless-ness. Looking up at Sunita, sitting on the wedding dais in all her golden finery, a memory came back to him of his youngest daughter as a baby, gurgling with pleasure as her grandmother tickled her belly. She had been content and docile as an infant, and she was content and docile now – as content and docile and compliant as any father could wish for. And so it infuriated him to remember how, for at least a year after she was born, a debate had raged about her in the family. It was Shiva Prasad's own mother who had insisted that he should give Sunita away to childless Hari: *That is the tradition,* she kept pointing out; *that's how brothers have always helped each other. You have three, he has zero. With two healthy children already, what do you need one more for?*

Shiva Prasad might have felt differently if Hari himself had been obedient to tradition – if he had stayed here in India, lived under one roof with his family, been kind and attentive and behaved like a loyal little brother. But Hari hadn't done that. He had married some aloof, unknown woman, and immediately emigrated to

America, where, to make matters worse, instead of struggling with the cultural and religious void which was the USA, instead of working all hours of the night and getting only visa hassles and debt issues for his troubles, instead of coming home sheepishly to the family scarred and subdued by the whole experience, Hari had seemed to *flourish*. It was unbelievable: each time he returned home he seemed more confident, more cultured, more moneyed. It was one thing to hand over a surplus third child within the joint family to a grovellingly grateful junior bhabhi – but it was another prospect altogether to give away a child to rich American émigrés, as if the baby herself was a needy third-world victim, as if back home in India her parents should be grateful.

Shiva Prasad couldn't do that. So when his mother raised the question, he simply refused on point of principle: no child of his, he raged, would ever be import-exported to that temple of mammon over the Atlantic just because of a failing of Hari's dark-skinned whatever-her-name-was.

And here she was again, ruining things. Summoning a peon, Shiva Prasad ordered him to help Hari and his spouse as quickly as possible from the wedding grounds and into their car. In the meantime, he continued to greet guests, to receive their congratulations and to direct them up to the dais to be photographed with the bride and groom. When he sensed somebody coming up behind him, he turned towards them automatically with his hands folded in a pious namaste, words of welcome already forming on his lips. But it wasn't any ordinary guest. Shiva Prasad found himself coming face to face with his tapasya – his ascetic trial in the manner of the Vedic seers of yore – *Professor Ved Vyasa Chaturvedi.*

At last, they were about to have an encounter. Not just across a row of flashing cameras, or namaskaring guests, or on either side of a Harmonious Wedding Pose, but a close encounter, such that Shiva Prasad Sharma could see each wiry hair on the (slightly) younger man's chin, reassess the quality of that telegenic nose and examine the scraped-back coiffure that the Professor clearly didn't bother dyeing. Shiva Prasad looked about him. No ex-prime ministers were on hand to solemnise the greeting. The only important-looking person in the vicinity was a large woman wrapped any old how in yards of blue silk, with not a gold necklace in evidence on her physically intimidating person. Shiva Prasad couldn't remember who she was, though he vaguely recalled that she was something to do with the university. But he greeted Vyasa boldly, beckoned the lady with a cupping motion of his hand, and said: 'Ahhh. Namaskar ... Deb ... Geet ... Urv ...' (What on earth was her name?) 'My dear madam: it is so wonderful to see you here at my daughter's wedding. And now it is my pleasure to introduce you to the groom's father, Professor Vyasa—'

'Oh hello, Vee,' the woman cut in. 'I've been meaning to tell you that I can't come to the wedding lunch tomorrow. I've got my Shakespeare seminar.'

It seemed that the two already knew each other. 'We teach Literature in rival faculties at north campus,' Vyasa explained to Shiva Prasad with a slight smile, 'but we've been friends for years. Ever since Oxford.'

The Lady Professor turned to Shiva Prasad: 'I hope you don't mind that I gatecrashed the wedding ceremonies this evening.' And she laughed, as if she was sure that he didn't.

'Not all, not at all,' said Shiva Prasad. 'Any friend of Professor Chaturvedi is a friend of—'

But the Lady Professor was no longer listening. Instead, raising her eyebrows emphatically as she addressed him, she said to Vyasa: 'What I've been meaning to ask you, Vee, ever since I read about your New York lecture in the papers, is: doesn't this obsession with the ancient texts worry you a little? This preoccupation with Hindu-era epics, surely it obscures subsequent matters? You aren't worried that it will play into the hands of those who hark back to an invented Hindu golden age?'

Shiva Prasad Sharma looked on in bewildered silence as Chaturvedi put back his head and laughed. 'But it's our common heritage,' he said, 'our history. If you like, the storytelling of the epics – it's an alternative to the holy books. It's extremely important to remember that this is the primary legacy of a text like the Mahabharata. One can, I think, distinguish culture from religion.'

'But these texts are appropriated by Hindu nationalists in an attempt to divide the country's religious communities,' said the Lady Professor.

Shiva Prasad could stand by no longer while his culture was vandalised by ignoramuses. 'My dear lady,' he said loudly, fearing as he said it that she might poke him in the eye with a pencil, or step on his feet with her heels, 'it is our *sacred duty* to honour the holy book of our ancestors.'

The Lady Professor gazed at him briefly. 'But it's not a holy book.' Then turning again to Vyasa, she said: 'So what *does* the book represent to you?'

'To me?' Vyasa shrugged. 'War, principally. The carnage of war. Power. Land. Hegemony over people, honour, tradition. The fight between cousins. And also sex. Reproduction and inheritance are central concerns.'

Sex? Shiva Prasad felt his outrage mounting. Clearly, the man was not prepared to keep his foul views about the nation's most sacred texts to himself, not even at his own son's wedding. It was distinctly compromising to be standing here conversing with him. It was people like this who allowed planes to be hijacked, and innocents to be kidnapped, and chaos to be unleashed on a blindly permissive society that was only now reaping the rewards of decades of compromise and negligence. He peered around the garden for political allies. This would be the perfect moment to achieve lasting fame by exposing the hollowness of the 'Ganesh Theory' that had caused such consternation in high-up circles. Shiva Prasad knew that the ruling party was considering sponsoring a wholesale import to Delhi of the Ganesh Chaturthi festival which Mumbaikars enjoyed every year with such devoutness. He felt sure that he himself might well be offered the important job of editing a dedicated Ganesh full-colour booklet, tasked with explaining the true history of the god, how he had lost his head defending the virtue of his mother – for there were many wonderful legends about Ganesh that would need to be put in context. But how could this go ahead if Shiva Prasad allowed Professor Ved Vyasa Chaturvedi to purvey his scandalous views like this, in mixed company, in front of an impressionable woman?

The Lady Professor continued to natter away to Vyasa in her hoity-toity Oxbridge-English tonality. 'The funny thing about Hinduism,' she was saying, 'is that every year millions of people continue to be born as Hindus, by virtue of being Indians, but those with an education don't believe one half of the tenets of their religion. Of course they don't; how can they? A god with a blue face? An elephant-headed scribe? Phantoms of trees and mountains? But it is precisely the inherent ridiculousness of Hinduism which is its own best defence. Who could argue with a religion as silly as that?'

'Sacrilege!' shouted Shiva Prasad Sharma at last. Having achieved a rapt silence, he placed his finger on the large lady's arm in emphasis. The large lady, alerted by his voice, turned towards him, his finger slipped – Horror of horrors! – skidded, skated across the defiled aryavarta expanse of her breast, only narrowly missing the Himalayan cedar tree of her nipple. 'Impossible!' he said again.

'Ganesh was the scribe of our great Mahabharata. He is at the heart of the hallowed literature of Bharat. How can you claim that the son of Lord Shiva and Parvati is silly, as you say?'

'My dear sir,' the large lady said, seemingly unperturbed by the pokage of her bosom, 'you mention Lord Shiva. Ah, well, yes. Who is he? Why, Shiva is an adivasi, he is one of the indigenous forest-dwelling people, a fierce, undomesticated god, remember? That is the point. A god of mountains, of wild places. He is the one whom Arjuna mistakes for a backwoods archer. You don't think that he was one of those prehistoric Aryan invaders, do you, Mr Sharma?'

'Aryan invaders?' Shiva Prasad repeated the phrase: 'Aryan? Invaders?'

'She doesn't mean invaders,' Chaturvedi was saying, wearily. 'Let's try to keep things decent. Migrants might be a more accurate term, historically. You know very well,' he said to the Lady Professor as she laughed flirtatiously, 'that using the word "invader" is deliberately controversial.'

But Shiva Prasad had borne enough. 'It hurts me, it truly hurts me,' he said, 'that you liberal types think we Indians haven't been invaded enough times through history that we must invent yet another such invasion in the realm of the distant and glorious past! It is a figment of some academic speculation! It demeans our precious Indian culture! India as it was thousands of years ago before these Mughals and Britishers came in and ruined it – in Vedic times, the time of our holiest scriptures – that time was a sacrosanct one, an era of the incubation of all our greatest achievements and inventions and philosophies, one that the greatness of this land is founded on. And you have to turn that time of purity into yet another colonisation from afar, by warriors from the West? You people have gone to an extreme with this undermining project. What atrocity will it take for you to realise your foolishness?'

'So, for right-wing Hindus the golden age is a time lost in the fog of prehistory? Lord help us.' The Lady Professor raised her eyebrows.

But Shiva Prasad ignored her. His voice grew resonant as his argument – his disquisition – gathered force. 'Everything,' he said, 'every single thing that we know and honour as good, derives from that time only. And people like you – educated people with suspect loyalties – want to take it away from us. You tell us that our precious indigenous Arya culture was brought to India on horseback by prehistoric Europeans, is it? Just as the modern Europeans brought us trains and bureaucracy, is it? You know that these former British colonial masters of ours, who held India and bled it for over two hundred years, that it was they themselves who invented this theory, about their forefathers coming here and making us into Aryas? My dear lady, your whole mindset has become enslaved to a corrupt colonial paradigm. I pity you.'

With that, Shiva Prasad turned away disgusted, only to witness another outrage from the Chaturvedi family. At the far end of the garden, sitting on a bench, not taking any notice of the sacred wedding celebrations around her, was Professor Chaturvedi's daughter – a young woman who had chosen to leave her native place to study in England, about whom he had heard (from a shocked Sunita) rumours of loose European habits and sexual misbehaviour – looking up into the eyes of a handsome youth with lascivious longing. As he watched her, Shiva Prasad felt a cold fear take hold of him. Chaturvedi himself had just made it quite clear: everything his family stood for was counter to everything that Shiva Prasad's held as best. The worst of it was that, somewhere deep inside him, Shiva Prasad had known this all along. He had allowed himself to turn a blind eye to the faults of this wedding union because of the Chaturvedis' wealth and social standing. And because of the benefits of the Arya Project with Ash, of course. Above all, he had deluded himself into believing that Professor Chaturvedi would come to appreciate the great qualities of Shiva Prasad Sharma himself. That was never going to happen, he knew it clearly now. Ash's father had not sought his opinion once in all the time that they had been conversing together. He had ignored him, rather, and had given his attention instead to this wholly insignificant Lady Professor of literature.

And meanwhile, over in the corner of the garden, Chaturvedi's daughter suddenly stood up, put out a hand, and pulled the tall lanky youth to his feet. Chaturvedi's wicked Sex Daughter, Shiva Prasad saw with mounting indignation, was in the act of profaning the holy nuptials.

chapter 13

'I was at school with your brother Ash,' the young man said to Bharati as they stood in the queue. 'Until Class Nine when we moved back to Bangalore.'

She tilted her head to one side, appraising him. 'So we haven't met since we were . . . ?'

'Fourteen,' he said.

'Fourteen,' she repeated, amused at how that *very* shy and gangly boy had turned so pleasingly into this serious-faced – almost handsome – person.

'Were you one of the ones he played chess with always?' she said with a smile, and the man, whose name was Pablo, nodded.

Bharati added, with teasing grimness: 'And what's more, you were a *birdwatcher*.'

'Ah,' he answered solemnly, 'I still am.'

'And do people still mock you for it?' She remembered how *uncool* she and her teenage schoolfriends had always considered Ash and his posse, with their spectacles and long words and erudite passions.

'It seems they do,' he said, smiling at *her* now.

'And what are you doing these days?'

Pablo had moved back to Delhi four years ago for college, and now he was working as a journalist for the *Delhi Star*. He was a junior reporter, so he covered everything: schooling, health, politics. He liked doing stories on literature and culture. But the environment was his speciality: smog, river pollution, species extinction. He began to talk about wildlife with an enthusiasm she dimly remembered from their schooldays. Delhi, he said, was built over the Khandava forest. 'Do you remember,' he asked, 'the ecological genocide in the Mahabharata? When they burn down the forest and all the snakes and animals perish?' She shook her head. 'Well,' he said – and launched into a long description, which culminated in an even longer list of each and every local bird species that was facing eradication. 'Despite everything we are doing to this city there are still good places to see birds, though,' he went on and Bharati pinched her toes together under the hem of her sari and dared herself to lean up and stroke him on the cheek to make him shut up. She didn't dare, however, not quite yet. 'Did you study environmentalism at university?' she asked, when she could bear no more armageddon.

'No,' he said, looking over at the stage, where Ash sat garlanded with jasmine and marigolds, 'Literature.' He regarded the bride and groom in silence for a moment and then turned back to her again. 'You know that I wrote the story on your—' he began, and then stopped.

'What?' she asked. Her eyes had been roaming over Pablo himself, reappraising his long red cotton kurta and faded jeans, his thin dark face and curls, and as he turned to look at her, she suddenly felt very hopeful.

'Nothing,' he said, and she took him by the arm.

'Hey,' she whispered. 'Let's get away from here.' She pushed him through the crowd, across the garden, until they reached a bench against the far wall where an old couple was sitting in silence, watching the party.

'How strange to be married so near Diwali,' Pablo said, as they sat down.

'The bride's father insisted. He called an astrologer. And although Ash is a scientist, he still didn't object.'

'Your brother,' Pablo said, after a moment, 'was always very kind to me in school.' And as he talked about his life, about the small, modest privations of which she could have no conception, she felt the warmth of his arm, the pressure against her bare skin . . . and her own desire, thickening within her.

It was now quite dark and the scene in the garden was both illuminated and blurred by the thousands of fairylights slung through the trees, along the hedges, over furniture, around tables. It was while he was saying something about the originality of her father's scholarship that she leant over and kissed him on the mouth, her parted lips pressed to his, her tongue touching his. In London she had done this to virtual strangers many times. But now she sat back, breathless, both alarmed and pleased, and waited. Of course he couldn't kiss her back, they were at a wedding, sitting beside some old relatives of the bride's. But when he bent down to whisper in her ear, instead of words, she felt his tongue, his teeth, on her earlobe. She looked round, and wondered if there was anywhere they could go.

There were food tables all along the edge of the garden, draped with long white cloths taped to the bottom of the table legs so that guests didn't trip up on the fabric. The tables had been empty until now, but waiters, young men of around her age, were just beginning to bring out the food. They were lighting the tabletop gas burners, and setting over them steel tureens of curry, trays of rice, and bowls of daal. Most of the tables were laid out end to end near the entrance to the garden, but there was one, set back from the rest, under a champak tree, and this was still empty. The waiters would probably put the desserts or tea there later, after the first course had been eaten. The table was in semi-darkness; whoever had draped fairylights around the garden had forgotten to wind some through the tree's branches.

Bharati stood up. 'Follow me,' she said, and took him by the hand.

Under the champak tree she knelt down behind the table, out of sight, and unpinned one side of the cloth. She crept in first, and he came in behind her, pinning it back. She laughed, pleased with her daring. It was dim under here, and the grass was damp. She closed her eyes, allowing the sounds and smells of the wedding to waft around her.

'Wait,' he said. 'It's your brother's wedding; are you—'

She put her lips on his to shush him, and then, as she had wanted, she felt his hands, moving under the silk of her sari, reaching under her sari petticoat, up her legs, until his fingers brushed across her knickers.

Above them, there was a sudden thump as somebody put something down on the table. 'Mmmm,' he said in his turn, and his voice was muffled as his mouth bit at the silk of her blouse. There was a clang and the sound of lids being lifted from pots. She grabbed at him, pushing up his shirt, pushing at the button on his jeans. The murmur of voices around the table grew. She could smell the blandness of a generic curry, and she heard her own voice, mixed with that of a waiter calling across the lawn, as he pulled up her sari. 'Quick,' she was saying, and she reached for her purse, for the condom brought all the way from England, bought from a supermarket near her college. She ripped off the edge, filling the air under the table with the un-Indian smell of spermicide and latex.

They struggled against each other for a moment, cloth and

foil and skin, until Bharati felt him moving inside her with hot, warm jabs, and after that she could no longer hear what she was saying, although she thought she heard her grandmother's voice, and as she twisted her body away from his, she laughed again at her own audaciousness, and then gave in to the shudders of her pleasure.

Afterwards, she lay back and waited for Pablo to ask, *Was it good?* so that she could thwart any illusions he had about his sexual prowess – men often had them – with one of her sharp-edged speeches about how a woman's sexual pleasure was all of her own making, that the man was merely a cipher, that the whole idea of some men being good lovers was an utter invention. But Pablo merely slipped an arm around her waist and said nothing, and despite her own wish to keep her resistance intact, she lay back against him and ran through her mental catalogue of the lovers she had had: the ones with special finger movements, the others with supposedly acrobatic thrusts, or practised and choreographed scripts; and then that other type, who blithely poked, blandly prodded, without even asking or noticing or thinking that it mattered whether or not she was enjoying it. She often liked to say – to shocked Indian girlfriends – that she could *see* why lovers turned to whips and ropes and drips of hot wax. Either that or anonymity. Only between strangers was frisson not entirely lacking.

He spoke. 'Have you got a boyfriend?'

She answered eagerly, pleased by the opening: 'Yes, two or three.'

'Oh?'

'I'm living in London now,' she explained.

'And?'

'And I'm polyandrous, like Draupadi in the Mahabharata. I always prefer to have more than one man on the go.'

'That wasn't Draupadi's choice exactly.' Pablo sounded amused.

'She was won in a competition, remember? And the man who won her was duty-bound to share everything with his brothers.'

'Still.' Closing her eyes, Bharati smelt the sugary scent of tea and heard the ebb and pulse of the voices above them. 'I like the idea.'

'And you have two or three on the go right now?' Pablo asked.

'Three or four.'

'But you are aiming for five, like Draupadi.'

'Five would be ideal, yes.'

She felt him lean forward and kiss the back of her head.

After the crowd moved away, and the waiters lifted off the tureens, Bharati and Pablo came out from under the table. Bharati stood behind the champak tree and adjusted the pleats of her sari.

'Look,' she heard Pablo say. The garden had emptied, and the bride and groom were no longer sitting up on stage. Over on the bench were two young children, licking ice creams. But he was pointing to a cloth canopy at the other end of the garden where a priest sat chanting Vedic shlokas. There was a small fire, and walking round it, their garments knotted together, were Ash and Sunita.

'We've spent my brother's wedding under a table,' said Bharati, feeling both pleased and appalled.

Pablo didn't answer. He was watching the moment, the act of being wed, the ancient sacred steps around the fire.

'Well, at least this means it's almost over.' She spoke again: 'Let's go back to your place? I can't stay here. Look at me, so crumpled.'

He smiled at her. 'I like how you look. But we can go if you want.'

In the car park, Bharati couldn't see Humayun. She gave a message to one of the other drivers to let him know that she had taken a taxi home. But there were no taxis, and Pablo had come by motorbike. Because she was wearing a sari, she had to sit sideways. 'It'll be cold,' he warned her.

It was. The Flying Club was a long way from the main road, and between here and there were the empty dark grasslands of the airport. They set off down the lane, Pablo driving slowly. It was dark, and the hedges were high, and Pablo found the quiet and the night, the fields and the trees, the unexpected empty space in this city filled with people, an interesting prospect. But it was different for Bharati. Every now and then a car would pass them, carrying wedding guests back into Delhi. 'Somebody's going to recognise me,' she complained, pulling her sari pallu over her head. 'What?' he said, not being able to hear her because of the wind, and slowing down even more as a result. 'It doesn't matter,' she said angrily. 'Just keep going.'

They had just reached the bend in the lane where it veered towards the main road when they were overtaken by a white saloon car with more red roses taped onto it than there was white space. 'That's the wedding car,' Bharati said, turning and waving, so that she almost lost her balance and had to grab hold of Pablo – but the driver didn't see her, or chose to ignore her. 'My twin brother, married.'

She was quiet by the time they reached the main road, and cold right through. Her feet hurt, and the thought of spending the night with this schoolfriend of her brother's – the thought was suddenly ridiculous. She said nothing as they drove up Lodhi Road, the wind pushing her pallu away from her head and slipping like a thousand icy hands under her sari. She didn't speak even when the bike curved around the blue-domed monument – 'Sabz Burz, it used to be green' he yelled back at her didactically – and into the entrance to Nizamuddin basti. They wove awkwardly between beggars and mullahs, men and boys, past the kebab stands, took a right, and eventually came to a stop outside a tall thin house with blotched and blistered paintwork. 'Is this where you live?' she asked, as he wheeled the bike up the path. 'Yes,' he said. 'I'll heat you up some

dinner since we didn't eat anything at the wedding. After that, if you like, I'll walk you home.'

She followed him through the little broken gate and along a path lined with empty red plantpots. 'The bulb has gone,' he said, and went ahead of her up three flights of steps in the dark, lighting a candle that had been left in an alcove next to the door at the top. He lived on the top floor of the building in the cheap barsaati flat.

With a small silver key he turned the lock and pushed the door open. Bharati stepped after him into the flat. As he turned on the lights she saw a small kitchen to the right with a gas bottle, some pans and a shelf of spices in packets. Beyond it was the bathroom; a bucket caught the drips from the tap. She followed him out onto the roof terrace, where, against the wall, was a line of pots with grimy leaved plants. And there, to the right: Nizamuddin, as she had never seen it before, the higgledy-piggledy houses of the basti, and the long, crenellated wall of a mosque, as solid as an elephant's back in the dark. There was an acrid smell – 'The public urinal is directly below the house,' he apologised again – but mingled with it was the familiar sweet-thick jasmine-cardamom scent. 'You have a chameli tree,' she said. The branches, loaded with almost invisible flowers, brushed against the wall of the terrace.

'It's not chameli,' Pablo said, and she felt a prick of annoyance. 'I think the true name is *saptaparni*.' And he opened the double wooden doors leading to his living quarters and flicked on the lightbulb. 'In the Himalayas it can reach twenty or thirty metres. But it's stunted by urban life.'

'Like so many Delhi residents,' she said drily, following him in.

She saw a room, lined with books. There was a mattress spread with a pale flowered sheet and piled high with cushions. He apologised a third time. 'I never normally entertain such honoured guests.'

She took off her shoes, and stepping into the room in her bare feet, felt the chill of the concrete floor. 'I'll get you a drink,' he said, and while he was fetching glasses from the kitchen, she walked slowly round the room, examining the shelves of books, and glancing over the table which served as his desk. She opened a small wall cupboard. Inside were several freshly ironed, carefully folded shirts. She looked at the black-and-white photograph pinned to the wall above, of an old man with the same curly hair, only white; Pablo's father, presumably.

By the time he came back, holding two glasses of rum, she was sitting upright on his bed, her legs folded neatly in front of her. He sat down beside her, leaving a decorous space between them, and she took a glass of rum and sipped. Perhaps I will stay the night with him after all, she thought, and waited for the rum to take effect.

chapter 14

Unbeknown to Bharati, Shiva Prasad had watched her lead the young man across the garden to the table below the champak tree, and continued to watch as she disappeared under it with him. He was so angry and disturbed at this further insult from the Chaturvedi family – he couldn't help thinking of what that girl was up to, of the wickedness she was engaged in; was, in fact, inflamed by these thoughts – that he ordered the pandit to begin the fire ceremony as soon as possible. He wanted to get things over and done with. Then, instead of luxuriating in this moment of national communion with the past, he stared at his daughter as she walked obediently round the fire with her husband and wondered if he had miscalculated on every level. Urvashi had fallen through the net of caste and religion into the abyss; was Sunita to be lost to him in a different way: ensnared within the anti-national orbit of father-in-law and the sexualised zone of her husband's sister? His gaze shifted beyond the nuptial couple to the family members sitting round the fire. His wife was weeping; the aunts and cousins were looking on, their faces profound with the reflected solemnity of the moment. Only Professor Chaturvedi was smiling to himself. Shiva Prasad Sharma shook his head angrily. He must do something. He must confront the man now, and save his daughter from these unholy liberals.

As soon as the ceremony was over, he walked over to where Chaturvedi was standing. 'Now that our two families are . . .' he said, and with his hands he mimicked their convergence. 'Now that our two families have come together,' he finished.

Chaturvedi inclined his head slightly. 'Yes?' he said, a hint of condescension in his voice.

'I would ask you,' Shiva Prasad went on stubbornly, 'not to make any further public pronouncements about our holy Hindu scriptures of the type that might cause harm or grief to your daughter-in-law.' Shiva Prasad felt a bead of sweat trickle down his brow.

'Pronouncements that might cause harm or grief to Sunita?' Chaturvedi repeated, as if he had never heard of such a thing in his life before.

'For example about Lord Ganesh and his role in the epic,' Shiva Prasad said emphatically, for he had realised with a flash of intuition that academics worked with heavy tomes and turgid texts, and did everything by *inference*, and that this, by contrast, was a time for speaking clearly. He waited a moment for Chaturvedi to reply. But the man said nothing, he seemed to be thinking deeply, and this gave Shiva Prasad new courage.

'I wish you,' he went on, 'to recant your Ganesh thesis, which has caused such harm to Hindus up and down the country.'

All at once, Vyasa burst out laughing. 'Oh, Mr Sharma,' he murmured, 'I am so delighted that our two families have . . .' And he mimicked Shiva Prasad's convergence gesture with his hands. 'Such hours of happiness it will give me in the future.' And he stood looking at him with such a look of benign amusement on his face that it took Shiva Prasad a moment to realise that, very possibly, he was being mocked.

He turned away, short of breath, and to dampen the fury that was dancing inside him, immediately launched himself into another, more innocuous discussion that was taking place in Hindi between an aunt of his wife's and the family doctor (who was so helpful last Holi with Shiva Prasad's ingrowing toenails) concerning the treatment of angina. But all the time he was asking himself in disbelief: why had he allowed his daughters to behave in this way – to marry Islamists, to marry secular atheist agents of foreign powers, to marry without his express consent, and choice in the matter, and permission? Even so, never once in his life had he imagined that his own daughter's wedding could go so wrong for him, ideologically speaking. He wondered what the Party bosses would say to his disgrace as a Hindu, as a party-member, as a father.

When it was finally over in double-quick time, when the nuptial couple had been waved off in their rose-dabbled car, and Shiva Prasad saw Professor Ved Vyasa Chaturvedi walking around the garden looking for his mother and daughter, he knew at once that while he couldn't possibly confront Chaturvedi at the wedding, in front of his own life's sum of business acquaintances, colleagues and family from farflung parts, he also could not let the slight of this evening go unchecked. He would have to speak to the man and establish, once and for all, a clear understanding between them. He would drive to Chaturvedi's house tonight, meet him at the door and demand that he show some respect for his daughter-in-law's father: some respect, some proper deference and some humility.

Once Shiva Prasad had decided upon a course of action, nothing could be done to change it. Of course his wife objected to his leaving the wedding early – he should have stayed to wave off every last guest and attend to each distant acquaintance. But Shiva Prasad was adamant. Cutting through his wife's protests, telling her that one of her nephews would drive her home in the Corolla, he walked out into the car park as quickly as his dhoti-clad legs could carry him and summoned the taxi driver from where he was smoking a cigarette with the other servants.

Shiva Prasad had never learnt to drive, but he had hired three cars for the evening – Sunita's white wedding car, a silver-grey Corolla for the rest of the family, and a taxi from the stand below the house to carry around the remaining riff-raff, such as surplus cousins and the pandit. 'Nizamuddin West,' he told the taxi driver, who stubbed out his cigarette and assumed an air of anxiety, presumably at the thought of his venerable employer frequenting Muslim neighbourhoods. 'Urgent business,' said Shiva Prasad, and gave him Vyasa's address.

By the time they reached Nizamuddin West, it was well past eleven o'clock. In the market, Muslim boys, huddled into drab grey shawls, were sitting together on park benches. In the streets, white-capped madrassa men were clustered round telephone booths, probably, thought Shiva Prasad, arranging international terrorist atrocities. The air was thick with the smell of sewage, which drifted across the night from the city's open drain.

Shiva Prasad ordered his driver to park just in front of Vyasa's house, which was in near darkness; there was not a single light proclaiming the imminent arrival of the holy festival of Diwali. He could see one soft bulb on in the hall. There was no car in the driveway.

Shiva Prasad got out of the car feeling hot and clammy, opened the gate, walked up the steps, and pressed his finger against the doorbell. He waited for a moment, but nobody answered. He didn't like standing here uninvited by the door like a common kabariwallah. He wondered what to do.

He had walked back down the steps and was standing in the road, thinking it over, when he heard the soft click of Vyasa's front door opening and a slight female figure dressed in pale yellow appeared in the light from the hallway. There was a pause, and then the young girl spoke.

'Mrs Ahmed?' she said. 'Humayun?'

For a moment, Shiva Prasad didn't reply. 'Mrs Ahmed' was his daughter's married name. Why was this servant girl – a Muslim, clearly – uttering the name of his Unmentionable daughter? Was it a trap? A further humiliation by Vyasa?

'Is Chaturvedi-Sahib in?' he asked at last.

The maid drew back, closing the door so that he could only see a sliver of her: fearful eyes looking down at him, bright yellow Punjabi suit. She shook her head.

'I will come in and wait then,' he said, starting towards her up the steps. She still hadn't moved from the doorway, but he put out a hand and roughly pushed the door open. It gave him a thrill to do that: to treat this maid of Chaturvedi's roughly.

Feeling his hand on her, pushing her backwards, she shrank against the wall, dropping her eyes from his face and pulling her headscarf back over her hair. Without looking at him, she gestured to him to sit and wait in a large room overlooking the front garden where there was a couch and some chairs. She was a very small, slight girl, and she seemed to merge back into the shadows of this large and ill-lit house, and he would perhaps have forgotten about her altogether if she hadn't spoken again, drawing his attention to her presence.

'Would you like some tea?' the girl asked.

'A glass of water,' Shiva Prasad said, sitting down on the couch. He heard the girl walk through to the kitchen, and as he waited for the water to be brought out the thought came to him that this was the maid whom Professor Ved Vyasa Chaturvedi had hired to wash his daughter Sunita's clothes, to lay out her intimate undergarments, to prepare her tea in the morning. This Muslim girl had been paid to pick up sari blouses from the floor of Sunita's bedroom, to chop meat and vegetables for her unholy dinners, to pollute her Hindu body with Muslim exudations. He thought of the smile on Chaturvedi's face as he listened to Shiva Prasad's speech about family harmony, and of how Chaturvedi's whore-like daughter had committed unmentionable acts at the wedding. And then he thought of the unmentionable acts committed by his firstborn daughter Urvashi, and when the girl returned with the glass he looked up at her and all his suppressed anger seemed to surge through him, through his blood, into his hands and throat, concentrating in his loins, scorching, iridescent.

Later, Shiva Prasad would know that it had been a palpable, even divine, force of retribution; that the power of Lord Shiva had in fact entered him and illuminated the route to purity and forgiveness, to the assuaging of Shiva Prasad's own failings as a father, to the avenging of crimes against innocent Hindu populations, to revenge against the barbaric Muslim man who had taken virginal Urvashi as his nautch girl.

But at the time he wasn't thinking about what he was doing, or about where he was. He thought only of the girl, and how he had her in his power, how he could turn her round, strip her of her clothes, bend her in half and break her, if he chose. First he pulled her down on the couch so that the tray she was carrying fell to the ground with a desperate little clatter. Then he pulled apart her legs, observing to himself to what delicate advantage the synthetic fabric of her dupatta draped itself over the contours of her young and perfect body, and as she began to whimper pathetically he spoke for the first time. 'Don't complain,' he said, and he held his hand against her throat as he unwound his dhoti and yanked down her salwar and pressed his penis inside her. Shiva Prasad, who hadn't performed the sexual act for years, who had assumed that this chapter of life was closed to him, was amazed. He was overcome by an emotion stronger than any feeling he had ever felt when conjoined with his wife, a feeling which rushed through him, suffusing him with a warmth that spread quicker than any poison. His climatic moment came quickly, too quickly, and all the humiliations he had suffered at his own daughter's wedding seemed to have been transported somewhere very far away. As he came, he cupped the girl's face in his hands and cried the name of his Unmentionable daughter. Afterwards, as the girl lay there on the couch, he stood, rearranging his garments, feeling like Arjuna, the ascetic Pandava brother who, after years of austerities, finally embraced a woman – the Pandavas' shared wife, Draupadi. This act, too, had been a mystical experience.

The girl whimpered again, and on hearing that noise – like something emitted from a small hurt animal – Shiva Prasad remembered where he was, and what had happened, and he hurried out into the hallway of the house without looking back at her. The last thing he did before pulling the front door shut behind him was to reach out a hand and knock over a large turquoise water pot that stood on a table in the hall. It fell to the marble floor with a satisfying smash and Shiva Prasad felt sure that it had broken into at least a thousand pieces.

The car was still there in the road but his driver, oddly, was nowhere to be seen. Shiva Prasad paced up and down, growing worried that Vyasa might return at any minute and find him. At last there was a clang of the gate and the driver emerged from the garden of Vyasa's house, smoking a cigarette. 'Sorry, sir,' he said. But Shiva Prasad wasn't to be appeased.

'You,' Shiva Prasad said, 'go back to the wedding grounds and see if there is anyone else who needs collecting. The pandit, for example. Give me a lift to the market. I'll take a taxi from there.'

'Yes, sir.' The man opened the door, and Shiva Prasad settled back into the seat with some relief. His dhoti was only slightly soiled.

By the time Shiva Prasad arrived home, his wife was asleep. He took off his clothes in the bathroom, sloshed water over his naked body, and lathered himself all over. His hands moved carefully over his skin, investigating each crevice and crack, hunting out sweat and juices and the salty traces of sex.

chapter 15

Sunita sat in the wedding car, half-happy, half-afraid – a married woman – as Ash and Ram walked across the tarmac and into the lobby of the Taj Man Singh Hotel. So far everything had gone perfectly. Ram had driven them here from the wedding as planned, making only a few jokes about the joys that lay in wait for Sunita on her wedding night. Ash had held her hand tightly and given her shy smiles. She was now waiting for her husband to come round to her side of the car, to pick her up and carry her over the threshold as if he was the hero of a film and she, his fair-hued heroine. She had seen this scene many times, in many different films, with many different casts and costumes. But Ash did not come to collect her. She could see him through the glass doors, looking at Ram and laughing at something as they walked over to the desk to collect the room key. And so, in the end, Sunita got out of the car, walked across the tarmac, and entered their wedding-night hotel alone.

By now she was very tired. It had been a long and sweaty evening, and the initial yearning she had experienced at the wedding – to climb out of her heavy wedding clothes and extra-heavy wedding jewellery bought for her by her extravagant father, to wash herself in clean running water, to step into a cool, breezy kurta-pyjama – had returned. Sunita was studded, wrapped, enveloped in gold. There was gold around her neck and on both wrists. The American-style engagement ring with its triple diamond spray, which Ash had slipped onto her finger three months ago, glittered on one hand. A thick traditional Indian gold wedding ring was connected by a fine chain to a thick gold bangle. There was a gold tikka in the parting of her hair, and long gold drop earrings in her ears. The gold diamond-studded nose-pin which she wore was linked by a fine gold chain to the earring, which in turn was joined to the tikka. Round her neck was a Rajasthani-style choker. Her clothes – the tight bodice blouse, the full lehenga with its beads and layers of silken tissue, the heavy embroidered dupatta – had been hand-sewn with golden thread. On her feet was a pair of golden high-heeled slippers and she no longer noticed the blisters they gave her. Her hair had been curled and styled, and the jasmine flowers with which it was clipped and plaited had been falling against her skin, lodging under the neck of her blouse, all evening. Her face, painted with several layers of fairness cream, kohl, eyeshadow, powder and lipstick by an irritable woman with bad breath from the Ashoka Hotel, had become sore from smiling.

At the wedding, after sitting still for an hour (and for four hours in total), Sunita had tried to imagine cool buckets and showers of clean water trickling over her. She imagined scooping and pouring, lathering and scrubbing, rubbing and rinsing. She looked over at Ash and imagined him as a part of her bathing ritual. For he, too, was finding the flower garlands irritating; he kept scratching at the skin of his neck with his finger, where the white flowers were rubbing.

Then Uncle Hari's wife fainted, and during the ensuing commotion, Sunita was suddenly made aware of the fact that she didn't know where she was any more. It was dark now, and the wedding garden – so full of lanterns and fairylights, of tasteful white loops and bunches of silk-effect awning draped along the hedges, of sprays of flowers, of tables of food, of red-velveteen chairs, of guests, above all, so many guests in shiny and sparkling saris, expensive jewels, colourful wedding turbans – no longer resembled the place it had been before. 'Mother,' Sunita whispered, after Uncle Hari's wife had been carried away, her face strained with the pressure of being a bride, 'can I have one of those painkillers you mentioned?'

After she swallowed the pill her mother gave her Sunita stopped caring about these inconveniences – the weight of her garments, the sweat trickling slowly down her legs and her breasts, the video cameraman and the light boy, who hovered and buzzed, darted out behind the wedding guests, swooped back again to leave her dazzled and perspiring, swarmed around another configuration of wedding guests, and then returned to the stage where Ash and she sat, to dazzle her once more. Whatever it was that Mother gave her brought the tender and innocent smile back to her face, and as she greeted wave upon wave of shining and congratulating, long-life-and-many-children-bestowing relatives and wedding guests, she drifted away, flying up through the wedding garden, out above the club, and across the city, skimming the top of India Gate, flying on through Old Delhi. And as she flew, she became the goddess Sita: spotless, mythical, cleansed and pure as snow.

Piano music was playing quietly in the hotel lobby as Sunita and Ash – husband and wife – said goodnight to Ram and walked towards the lift. They were staying in a Deluxe Room on the second floor. When the lift doors closed behind them, Sunita stared across into the mirrored wall at her husband. He smiled at her, and when they reached their floor, stepped out of the lift before her, crossing the landing and opening the door of their bedroom with a flourish. Entering the room after him, Sunita saw the big double bed, and the bouquet of flowers and a box of chocolates on the table by the window. She sat down on the bed. 'Will you help me take off my jewellery?' she said.

She thrilled to the touch of his fingers as he unclasped the choker, tenderly pulled out the tikka, unhooked her bracelets, undid the watch, slipped off her rings, and even removed the golden slippers. Sunita was respiring with excitement by this stage. She felt as if they had never before sat so close together.

'Your feet are all swollen!' Ash said as he placed the slippers carefully on the floor.

'All swollen!' she echoed.

'Why don't you have a bath,' he suggested.

'A bath!' she said.

'And I'll go and order us a drink?'

'A drink?'

He kissed her on the forehead and left the room.

Sunita sat motionless for a moment, alone in their marital bedroom. Then she removed her clothes, folding them in a bulky pile on a chair. She left on only her knickers and her bra. Opening the bathroom door, she saw herself in the mirror, smudged make-up on her face, curled hair coming down in tendrils, and below that the breasts, encased in a lacy bra, the stomach which her husband would soon kiss, the parts below, which . . .

Sunita stood under the shower, letting the warm water stream over her body. In her imagination, she placed Ash next to her, under the same jet of water. As she soaped her body, she imagined soaping his feet with this floral-smelling soap, and his shins and calves, and his knees and thighs, and . . . But her mind could go no higher.

Sunita took a long time in the shower. She dried herself slowly. When she walked back into their bedroom, wrapped in nothing but a towel, she expected to see Ash, ready and waiting for her clean, pure, washed body. But the bedroom was empty, and so she searched in the bag that had been left out for her, chose one of the shorter nightgowns with revealing lace along the corsage (bought for her by her sister) and got into bed.

After a while, she heard a noise in the passage. The door opened and Ash entered, carrying a tray with two cups of steaming milk. He placed the tray on the table by the bed, and sat, smiling at his wife. Then he kissed her, very lightly, on the lips. Sunita remained still, her eyes closed in bliss.

When she opened them again, Ash was stirring the cups with a teaspoon. He handed her one, telling her to drink it all down. She found that it tasted a little sweet, a little sour, a little strange. 'What is in it?' she asked.

'Whisky.'

'Whisky!' Her first taste of alcohol. She drank it all, and after it was finished, she handed Ash the cup, put her hand to her face, smiled lovingly at her husband, and leant back sleepily on the pillow.

Ash turned off the lights, lay down on the bed beside his wife, held her gently, and waited. He waited for a long time, even after she had fallen asleep (lulled by his inaction) and was snoring lightly. He lay and thought about her, and his marriage, and about her brother. He had no idea what was happening to him. Nothing like this had ever happened before. All he knew was that there were two Ash Chaturvedis: the normal, everyday one, lying here next to Sunita, and the other, midnight Ash who for over a year now had been having passionate conversations on the computer with somebody who called himself Man-God. And this evening, Everyday Ash and Midnight Ash had been forced to come together, and Everyday Ash knew for the first time that Midnight Ash was stronger.

Ash gave a violent shudder. Hitherto things had always been so simple. Midnight Ash was hidden from the world, from Everyday Ash, from Father, from Bharati, from all his friends, from everybody at the lab, from Sunita. Everyday Ash was the one who had decided to behave like everybody else and get himself married.

And he *had* married Sunita, and had done so to quash his hidden, midnight self, and his feelings for Man-God. And yet in some hideous, monstrous, marvellous way, this marriage, which was to have made everything straightforward and right, had only brought the midnight temptations closer.

Ash lay like this for nearly an hour, switching from Everyday Ash to Midnight Ash, trying to reconcile the one against the other. When he eventually got up from the bed, he half-hoped that Sunita would wake and stop him. But her snores went on uninterrupted, even when he tiptoed across to the door and opened it quietly.

As he stepped into the lift, he had another moment of hesitation – she had looked so innocent and sweet with her head on the pillow – but Ram was waiting, and Ram had been waiting long enough already. The lift stopped at the sixth floor, the door pinged opened, Ash walked along the corridor and knocked on the door of the room that Ram had booked in the name of Mr Manhattan, and there he was: Man-God, standing before him, not as some shadowy computer avatar but real and in the flesh. *Beautiful Ram, his wife's brother.*

'Eat this,' Ram commanded; and the pill dissolved onto Ash's tongue even before he got through the door of the bedroom.

'Did you know beforehand, then?' Ash asked. 'Had you guessed?'

'That stupid ice cream,' Ram murmured, as he nibbled Ash's nipple.

'Oh,' moaned Ash – Ram's aquiline nose nudging his being with tremendous jolts of pleasure.

It was Ash's grandmother who had triggered their coming

together. Following the pleasant distraction of Sunita's New York auntie fainting, the bride and groom had resumed the endless, thankless process of being snapped; their every movement, their slightest smile, their inadvertent grimaces recorded. Flash! The photographer's light boy shone the lamp in Ash's face. Flash! Behind him, Sunita's father coughed, and adjusted the angle of his turban. Flash! Sunita's brother Ram, a handsome young man with a curved nose and mischievous eyes and ruddy red lips whom he had met only once before, at the engagement party, changed his weight from one leg to another and shifted his hand to the arm of Ash's chair. Flash! Both their grandmothers were sitting together, directly below the stage, eating ice cream. The old women were arguing about something. Ash's grandmother was raising her voice and saying to Sunita's: 'It's Nirula's ice cream! I tell you it's Nirula's!'

'No,' said the other, 'Sunita ordered it. Kishmish, badam, American-type name—'

'Manhattan Mania!' the first lady shouted. 'Manhattan Mania, that's his favourite.' She pointed her spoon at Ash: 'Isn't that so, beta?'

'Yes, Granny,' he replied obediently, 'Manhattan Mania.'

Suddenly, an unfamiliar hand moved to rest lightly on his shoulder. Flash! The hand tightened around his collarbone. Flash! Ash turned his head to see. Flash! Ram was staring down at him, smiling. 'Ram?' he said, and then, before he could stop himself: 'Man-God?' Flash! The look they gave each other was captured forever on a roll of Fuji Superior Colour Film.

'So that was when you knew?' Ash asked helplessly as Ram licked his way up Manhattan Mania's legs towards his groin.

'I wasn't one hundred per cent sure . . .' said Ram. 'But the way you said those words, *Manhattan Mania*, it gave me such a shock, I couldn't help myself. *Sorry.*'

'You should never have told me,' Ash said as he felt his limbs quiver and melt under the pressure of Ram's tongue. 'You should never—' He broke off. 'And what will I tell her? What will I tell Sunita?'

'Come on, yaar. What does it matter?' Ram drew back, looked up, and said: 'Brothers-in-law. So convenient, na? Happens all the time. How do you think these marriages keep going? Because of this only.'

Then Ash felt Ram's tongue on his naked skin again, and any further speech was muffled.

chapter 16

Her eyes ran over the lines of the text, the neatly enumerated lines, not understanding but striving to understand, taking comfort where best she could – in the familiar-to-India nouns: the garlic and lentils, the yellow cow, the gardens in which rivers flow – and trying not to let fear prevail at the rest: the lightning and thunder, Satan and the angels, the Book, always the Book, invoked like a warning; and, above all, there at the back and the beginning, beneath and above, poised and powerful, flexed like a cobra ready to strike, Almighty Allah, the unknowable entity to which she was seeking to entrust her battered heart.

Urvashi had opened the Qur'an in the evening after dark. Aisha had left for the Chaturvedis' in the afternoon, and Humayun had gone before that to drive the Professor's family to the wedding. Feroze was away at the printing press at least until nine. At first she had sat alone in the large hallway, in front of the window, watching the shadows slowly and painfully gather, willing the night to descend and clothe the house in darkness on this evening of her sister's brightly lit wedding, indulging her misery with a roll call of the loneliness that had been visited on her since her marriage. Her mind shied away from thoughts of her family. Instead, she recalled a visit by her two best friends from school. She had not dared invite them when she was living in the old city, in the privacy-free haveli where Feroze grew up, with its legions of pale, languid cousins dropping in and out all day long, and the old aunts shelling peas on the roof terrace, and the teasing, familiar, young boy cousins who came by after work still dressed in their pant-shirt, to drink tea with Feroze's Hindu Bibi and to spy on how she kept the house. She had not wanted to subject her schoolfriends to that – getting them to the house itself would have been difficult enough, for it was in the heart of Old Delhi, a ten-minute cycle rickshaw ride from the cinema on Daryaganj, through a warren of tiny streets, with only the occasional Hindu neighbourhood in evidence. But once Feroze and she had moved into their own house, in a respectable colony away from his family, and once she had looked around and approved of the paintwork and chosen the furniture, and generally ascertained that domestically speaking it was all just as she remembered it from the houses of her childhood, she rang up her two best friends, whom she had known since she was at least nine years old, and they both agreed to come over one Thursday lunchtime.

Afterwards she knew that she hadn't been mistaken: on the telephone she remembered inviting them for lunch, and she remembered them agreeing, and hence that Thursday she spent all morning in the kitchen with Aisha, preparing this thing and that thing and sending Humayun out twice before twelve o'clock to pick up curd and some sweets her friend Shobha liked from a shop in Defence Colony, and by the time the two of them rang on the doorbell it was all laid out on the long dining-room table – the yoghurt curry and pulped aubergine and stuffed bitter gourd and daal topped with coriander – and the rice was done, and Aisha was standing in the kitchen rolling out chapatis.

At first, everything had seemed almost as normal. The three of them sat in Urvashi's big front room, on the chairs she had arranged under the window, sipping milky tea with just the right amount of ginger, as prepared by Aisha. The friends looked around them and admired the house, its scale, its brand-newness. She took them upstairs, through their bedroom, to the roof terrace, and downstairs again to appreciate the garden that Aisha watered every afternoon. By now forty minutes had passed; it was time for lunch. And so Urvashi led her friends towards the dining room.

'But we've eaten already!' her friends said in unison as they stood on the threshold, looking at the table with its line of covered dishes. 'We ate before coming!'

'How can you have eaten?' Urvashi asked in wonder. They lived in Saket, so the drive to Nizamuddin must have taken them at least half an hour. She had never heard of anyone eating lunch at eleven o'clock.

The schoolfriends glanced at each other. 'My bhabhi made me eat some of her uttapam just before I left,' said Shobha. 'She loves this south-Indian khana.'

'I am on a diet,' said Shoma with a giggle.

'Come, try just a little,' Urvashi urged them, still not understanding. She pointed to the dishes she had spent all morning making. She tried to force them, taking an empty plate, and spooning a little bit of curry onto it, tearing a chapati in two and placing half on each plate, anything for the sake of decorum. But her friends wouldn't lift even a morsel of the food she had made to their lips. They wouldn't so much as sit down at the dining-room table. They don't want to eat in a Muslim household, Urvashi realised suddenly. But it isn't a Muslim household, she felt like saying. It's just me, and my husband who happens to be Muslim. It wasn't until this day that Urvashi realised how far she had been cast out.

When Feroze came home that evening he found his wife in tears, and the fridge crammed with more food than they could eat in a week. He packed the aubergine and curry and karela himself into tiffin boxes, and rang his mother and told her to send the driver to collect it. But Urvashi was inconsolable at the rejection.

Yellow cow, lightning strike, Allah the Beneficent, the Merciful. No longer able to bear thinking about her friends, Urvashi went to sit in her husband's study, the Book on his desk, illuminated by one strong desk lamp. The text was in English and Arabic, its pages whispered as you turned them, strangely devoid of images, unlike her Hindu books, which had been illustrated with pictures of Arjuna and Krishna and other ancient heroes.

At nine o'clock Feroze rang to say that he wouldn't be home for another two hours. 'What are you doing?' he asked. She answered truthfully: 'Reading the Qur'an.'

'Oh, Urvashi.' His voice was full of concern. 'Look,' he began again, purposeful this time: and told her that he had rung his mother, that they were expecting her for dinner, that some cousin was visiting from Aligarh, that she must promise to call a cab from the market and go to the old city at once and not to spend any more time sitting at home reading the Holy—

Urvashi promised. But sitting in the taxi, watching the city pass, she thought of her in-laws' questions and their eager, concerned faces, and the whispers that would have gone round all the relatives' houses about her having been excluded from her sister's wedding, and the rich oily biryani they would force her to eat, and the pink sugary sharbat which she hated that they would make her drink. She couldn't face it. By now the car had reached Daryaganj. Soon she would have to get out and take a cycle rickshaw. She thought suddenly of the great mosque where she had been taken by Feroze one Saturday afternoon to admire the beauty of the architecture (he was never interested in explaining his religion). 'Take me on to the Jama Masjid,' she said to the driver.

But when the car turned left towards the great mosque and she saw it looming above her, lifted up from the squalor and the crowds by its flights of red sandstone steps, again her courage failed her. She couldn't approach that place alone at night, a Hindu woman.

She was aware that her mind was behaving erratically but there was no point making a pretence. 'Take me back to Nizamuddin West,' she said to the driver, the panic fluttering inside her, not caring if she appeared contradictory and wilful. It was ten o'clock already. Feroze would be home by eleven.

The taxi headlights scrolled across the front of Urvashi's house in Nizamuddin and her first thought was that Feroze wasn't home yet: his car wasn't here. The taxi lights came to rest on a figure slouched against the pots and ferns just inside the gate. The taxi driver braked. 'What's happened?' asked Urvashi. The driver left the engine running as he went to look.

'A young girl,' he said when he came back. 'Something's wrong.'

Urvashi got out of the car. The body, lying just inside her front gate, was still. But she knew who it was immediately – from the yellow chiffon suit she wore. Her first reaction on seeing the limp body of her maid under her tobacco plants and Himalayan ferns was one of fear: *What have I done?* And then she remembered that she was supposed to have stopped by to collect Aisha from the Professor's house at the end of her afternoon shift.

'Help me,' she said to the taxi driver. 'We must take her inside.'

The house had three floors. On the ground floor, opposite the dining room, was a suite that Urvashi's husband had designated for his mother, who was coming to stay with them in a week's time, for this, Urvashi's first Ramzan in her own home. On the first floor was a balcony room overlooking the garden – Urvashi and Feroze's bedroom – and a nursery for their unborn child. The entire second floor, a barsaati of sorts on the roof terrace, was completely empty. It was waiting, like Urvashi's life, to be filled by the future.

'We'll put her in the ground-floor room,' said Urvashi.

Between them, they carried the maid across the marble entrance hall, and laid her on the double bed.

'Rape,' the doctor said later. 'How old is she? Older than she looks, I imagine. Endemic undernourishment. Bathe her, feed her, and then let her sleep.'

'Shouldn't we report it?' Urvashi asked.

'You can,' he said, 'but where is she from? Nizamuddin basti? It was probably someone in her own family. Try to get her to eat something.'

'But it's a crime,' Urvashi said.

The doctor, a middle-aged man with a spreading waist and a kind face, said, 'She won't want to make a fuss. These victims never do. And the police won't be interested in pursuing justice for a girl from Nizamuddin basti.'

'Isn't there anything you can do?'

He sighed. 'If you insist, I can take samples, in my private capacity.'

'Samples?' said Urvashi. She had no idea what they were for, but she answered firmly, 'Yes, please do.'

Half an hour later, as the doctor left, he wrote a prescription: 'You'll be able to buy it first thing in the morning. It's the best precaution, after the event.'

Urvashi nodded; but she still recoiled at the injustice of burying the crime, and as soon as the doctor left, she phoned the Nizamuddin police station and told them what had happened.

'We had better examine the victim,' the policeman said.

'The doctor's seen her. She's asleep now.'

'Who else lives or works in the house?' the policeman asked, and Urvashi gave the name of her husband, Feroze, and her driver, Humayun.

The policeman called over to a colleague. They conferred, and then he said to Urvashi: 'You should bring her in at the earliest. The duty officer arrives at nine.'

'I'll bring her in the morning,' she replied, and before he could argue further, she put down the phone.

Feroze came home from the press an hour later. 'What's wrong?' he said when he saw the agitated expression on his young wife's face. Urvashi had tied back her hair. Her dupatta was knotted behind her and her kurta was wet. But she had managed to clean the girl up.

'Aisha is here,' she whispered. 'She's been raped. I found her outside the house. I gave her something to help her sleep.'

'So what is she doing in our house?' he said. 'Send her home. She'll need her mother. It isn't our business. She's our servant; you don't know their ways. Her people will deal with her. Not you.'

Urvashi shook her head. Ever since she and her husband moved away from his family in the old city, and into their own house, she had been beset by anxiety and relief – relief at her independence, anxiety at how she would manage to run a household alone. Servants were her main source of worry and hope, and she was as eager to make friends with her young maid and driver as she was not to be misled by their mysterious and unfathomable servant-class ways. But Feroze, instead of bolstering her confidence, challenged her at every step: reminding her again and again of her Hindu ignorance about the way these people – these Muslim servants – lived. He who had lectured her while they were living in the old city on the essential similarity of human beings – telling her that what seemed familiar in her parents' home and alien in his was nothing, just an illusion – now found her empathy embarrassing. Now he emphasised only the distance between them.

Urvashi looked at him; remembered how she had held Aisha, had washed her skin and soothed her: *You're a man*, she said to herself, *what do you know?* And as she opened her mouth to disagree with him for perhaps the first time since they were married, Urvashi felt a flattering sense of righteousness.

'Aisha won't go home,' she said. 'She's scared. I'm keeping her here. And she's stayed before. Last month when you were away in Bombay. As soon as Humayun gets in I'll send him to her mother's house to tell them she'll be back in the morning.'

That night, Urvashi sat with Aisha until the girl fell asleep. Humayun hadn't returned after driving the Chaturvedis to the wedding, but Urvashi barely noticed. From her chair by the window she kept watch over Aisha. The girl's forehead was hot, and her hair, which she wore oiled and stretched into a tight plait during the day, spread across the pillow, like tentacles, or the leaves of the spider palm, or the outstretched arms of the angered goddess Kali. Aisha fell asleep at last, and Urvashi looked down at the gently parted lips, watched a smile that moved across Aisha's face as she dreamed, and tentatively, furtively, she tasted the sweetness of charity. She was doing something good, at last. She listened to the hall clock, to the approaching, receding tapping of the night watchman. Could Aisha take me to the mosque? she wondered drowsily. Could we go to the Jama Masjid together? And the thought occurred to her: Our baby will be like this. A Muslim. A girl like Aisha.

'They don't wear bindis,' her husband had said to her when Urvashi gave Aisha a packet of gold-embossed oval stickers on the morning she started work, and showed her how to press them onto her forehead.

'They don't put up photographs,' he said again, when Urvashi tried to please her new servants by taking out her camera. 'They aren't like you.'

But you take photographs, she thought to herself. *Your cousins wear bindis. And you're a Muslim. Why is that?*

'Why are you marrying a Muslim?' Urvashi's sister Sunita had asked her, wide-eyed, in the days before they stopped discussing such things. And Urvashi answered her sister's question with the impervious, age-old reply: 'Because I love him, of course.'

But sometimes she felt it wasn't true. Did she love him enough? Not enough to understand his mother. Not enough to be happy in the house he grew up in. Not enough to read about the prophets. Not enough to ask about the cousins in Karachi, or to learn his aunt's recipe for biryani. *I will try harder,* she thought now, stroking Aisha's forehead and flushed cheeks.

Feroze was asleep by the time Urvashi walked upstairs to bed. She slipped in beside him, willing the sleep to come, but her heart was beating too fast. She was remembering how, the week after her schoolfriends refused to eat the food she had prepared, she had walked to the market in Nizamuddin to visit the tailor and noticed the new Islamic bookshop on the corner by the sweetshop. After glancing through the shelves of religious books and guidance pamphlets, she picked out two books and took them to the counter.

'Are you a Muslim?' they asked her curiously, when she handed them the fifteen-rupees *Glossary of Muslim Names* and Mufti Allie Haroun Sheik's twenty-five-rupees *Islamic Principles on Family Planning.* Urvashi had not known what to reply. But back home, she showed the first book to her husband, and he was pleased. 'Look,' he turned to the page where his name was written: 'Feroz: Emerald. Your jewel of a husband.' But then he picked up the second book and shook his head. 'No, Uzma, please. Not this. Don't read it.'

Urvashi had read it, however. It dealt with contraception (azl, she learnt with embarrassment, was the Arabic term for withdrawal); with abortion and polygamy; with homicide, Jihad, apostasy, adultery and highway robbery (under Section 3.5: Accepted Reasons for the Termination of Life). It also dealt with rape. 'The essence of rape,' the writer explained, 'is that it is without the consent of the woman, and herein lies the difficulty. Modern psychiatrists have amply studied the behaviour of errant young girls and women coming before the courts in all sorts of cases. Their psychic complexes are various, distorted partly by inherent defects, diseased derangements or abnormal instincts, bad social environment, and partly by temporary physiological or emotional conditions. One form taken by these complexes is that of contriving false charges of sexual offences by men. The unchaste mentality finds incidental but direct expression in the narration of imaginary sex incidents of which the narrator is the heroine or victim. However, too often the real victim in such cases is the innocent man.'

'Did he rape you?' Urvashi's mother had asked in a whisper when Urvashi went to her, before she eloped, with the news of her baby. 'Should I tell your father he raped you?'

'Don't be stupid, Ma,' Ram had said. 'They wanted it, they're in love, they're getting married, can't you see? They're going to have a child.'

But Urvashi was never sure what she would have said if Ram hadn't been there. And that night, when she left home for ever, taking with her only a suitcase of clothes (all that remained of her childhood), her mother stood in the doorway quoting the Gita: 'The intermixture of castes drags down to hell both those who destroy the family and the family itself. The spirits of the ancestors fall, deprived of their offerings of rice and water. Such are the evils caused.'

One week later, barely a week before their wedding, when Urvashi miscarried, she remembered those words and went to Feroze to tell him that he was free (that she was free, that no intermixture of castes and faiths and classes need occur). To her surprise, he declined her offer. 'I want to marry you anyway,' he said. 'Don't you know that?' But she had not known. And it was then she discovered, to her surprise, how honourable his intentions were – and how honourable that made her feel.

And in Nizamuddin Urvashi fell asleep at last: her baby inside her, her good cause shielded from any further harm, her mind uplifted by its new resolve.

chapter 17

On the night that Aisha was raped, a rumour spread through the huts on the edge of Nizamuddin's sewer: *the Elephant-headed Demon has returned*. This creature – with its whirling eyes and whip-like trunk, which murmured curses at a pitch that only babies and old crones could hear – was seen by a woman as she walked down to the pipe to fetch some water. Everybody who grew up in certain neighbourhoods of Delhi knew about these demons, which came periodically to terrify the city. Only six months earlier, during the hot summer, slum dwellers from the illegal settlements down by the river had fled their houses during the apparition of a Monkey Man: a creature like the Hindu god Hanuman, but wicked, which could leap over houses and kill children with its hands. Newspapers testified that children were crushed in the stampede of residents trying to escape from the slum. Ministers took the opportunity to bring forward their hygienic plans for urban cleansing. One woman, convinced that she was being pursued by the Monkey Man, leapt to her death from a two-storey building.

The Elephant Demon rumour began when a group of women and young girls arrived at the nala pipe with their buckets, to find their neighbour standing and pointing to the sky: 'A demon leapt across the drain from bank to bank,' she said. 'It pulled itself up by its trunk.' Perhaps at any other time of year, the women would have accused this harassed mother of having visions. But on this night, so soon before Diwali, less than a week to go before Ramzan, at a time of hikes in the price of everything from kerosene to sugar, when the flour sold by the ration shops was blackened with mould, when there were reports that the government was planning to clean out unsavoury migrants from the centre of Delhi, the rumour tipped them into panic. One by one, frightened parents grabbed their children, left pots of rice where they were boiling on tiny fires, and ran across the sewer and through the streets of the basti, to hide from the demon's machinations in Nizamuddin's shrine.

By the time of the last prayer, almost two hundred parents and children from Nizamuddin's poorest and dirtiest quarters had gathered around saint Nizamuddin's marble-fretted grave. The keepers of the shrine tried to quell their fear by insisting that *as Muslims they shouldn't heed such stories.* But everyone here had grown up with the knowledge of djinns. The crowd continued to talk in frightened voices; soon respectable parents from adjacent houses began to gather in the shrine; and before long, those with more colourful imaginations were terrifying even nonchalant bystanders with visions of what the demon might do to the poor, to the elderly and, above all, to those of the minority religion.

Perhaps none of this would have mattered had not a house by the drain, belonging to a family of waste collectors, caught fire. Sometime after midnight, three weeks' worth of waste newspapers and plastics, bought from the neighbourhood's maids and housewives, ignited and burnt so quickly and blackly that soon all the nearby houses were filled with smoke. There had recently been attacks on Muslims in other parts of India, and when the panicking residents smelt the smoke, they thought it was arson. Running into the street, they saw the flames reach the buffalo shed. By the time the police arrived, at least six houses had been destroyed. It was even said that a rich Hindu woman had been nabbed in the act of stealing poor Muslim children under cover of the chaos.

Later that night, after sceptical junior reporters had filed stories on the fragile mental health of India's poor – illustrated with maps of the basti, and an artist's impression of the demon – and had jocosely regretted amongst themselves that something more colourful hadn't happened (a shooting, perhaps, a riot, a gangland war), and the two dead bodies had been taken to the Muslim graveyard, the speculation began. The talk circulating in the rich colony was pontificatory: the fire had been started by the Hindu land-mafia to clear the space along the drain of unwanted Muslim poor – for a huge new residential complex was planned, with shopping malls and parking; a motorway, someone else said; a cricket pitch, countered others. The temple priests, in their turn, cast aspersions on the Muslims: they were forever attracting attention to themselves! Shankar Raj, a grocer from Jangpura, told customers in a lowered voice that in his opinion these dirty places could do with being cleared; the Muslims were heavy breeders; soon they would try to take over India again, as in the time of the Mughals. And in the graveyard on the slope above the drain, Aisha's mother, Tabasum, waiting for her daughter to come home, wondered with a shudder whether the rumours were true: that the Elephant Demon had come back to get them.

Earlier that evening, at around the time that news of the Elephant Demon first emerged, a car was speeding north along one of the wide avenues radiating out from India Gate. Anybody glancing in through the window would have assumed the same thing of the elegant woman inside that people always did. Seen across dinner tables in Manhattan, Leela had appeared perfect: beautiful, well-kept, in good condition for a woman of her age, her education worn lightly, her opinions delivered calmly. Only two things generally gave beholders pause: her husband – that businessman with his sweet face, bald head and singular lack of conversation – where did she pick him up? And then: a certain stillness in her; a kind of sadness; at the very least, a marked reserve. Was it because they had no children? But of course. Poor thing: this was the cruel thread that bound her to him. Here was the sadness offsetting the beauty.

Only, it wasn't quite true. The world was wrong in its assumptions about Leela Bose.

Hari and Leela drove back to Connaught Place in silence. She felt the thickness of the silence, its awful weight, but somehow she didn't care. All she could think about was why she had stayed away so long, why she hadn't returned before. There was her sister's son, Ash, and that exquisite, precious girl, Bharati, already all grown up before her eyes. She saw how obtusely she had nurtured an image of the plump little babies she once held in her arms; standing before them at the wedding, she felt the full scorn of her years of absence. The children were barely two years old when Meera abandoned them, walking out into the road in despair. And yet Leela hadn't done what Meera asked her. *Come home,* her father had written, *The children are alone with him now.* But she had not gone home. The same despair that had settled on her sister like a mist now floated across the seas and lodged with her, too: as a lethargy, a blindness, a capacity to shut out what she couldn't see and to forget what she couldn't bear.

In the car she refused to talk, and Hari would say nothing in front of the driver. But as soon as they reached home, and the front door closed behind them, he walked across the drawing room to the window, and poured himself a glass of whisky. 'So, what's the big secret?' he said, his back turned.

Leela hadn't moved from the hallway. There was an edge to his

voice that was new, and she saw that he had reached the limits of
his forbearance. He would try to force her to talk about her past.
'You and I made an agreement,' she reminded him. 'We moved
to New York; I forgot my life in India. That was what we agreed.'

'But why didn't you tell me?' As he turned towards her, she could
see his eyes glistening in the light from the street outside. She had
never seen him this angry before.

'Tell you what?'

'That you knew Ved Vyasa Chaturvedi.'

'What does it matter?' she said.

'It matters,' Hari began, his voice rising, 'because our family
is joined with his now. Our families are joined in marriage. Such
things matter. I repeat: how do you know him?'

She looked at him, this man she had married, through calm,
appraising eyes. She hadn't married him only to escape the world
she came from, she reminded herself of that; not just because he
promised to take her away. She had also admired this Hari of hers;
took pleasure in his practical way of seeing the world; experienced
the logic of his mind like a solace, his brain which effortlessly
calculated numbers, judged situations and people with accuracy,
and yet shied away from expressing itself in words. She had weighed
up her chances and found that the peaceful solidity she felt in his
presence was better than the pragmatism of arranged marriage,
more steadfast than changeable love.

'He was married to my sister,' she said. 'Meera, his wife, was
my sister.'

Hari hadn't expected this. He stared at her. 'You don't have a
sister.'

'I did.' She contradicted him matter-of-factly. 'My parents, who
adopted me, had a child already.' She repeated the name again for
emphasis. 'Meera.'

'So why?' he began.

'Because by the time I met you,' she said, 'my sister and I couldn't see each other any more. That was why I didn't tell you.'

'But all this time . . .' He sat down in the chair by the window. She watched as he drank his whisky, thinking through what she had said, and then immediately got to his feet again to pour himself another.

'All this time,' he repeated slowly, 'you've kept this from me. Why would you do such a thing?'

'I didn't want to talk about it,' she said; and though the memory began to yawn and scream inside her, she spoke calmly, as if it was of little matter. 'My sister left me at Santiniketan and married Vyasa. She died not long after we moved to New York.'

They looked at each other for a moment. Again, she considered telling him her lonely secret. There was something she had done, twenty-two years ago, of which she hadn't spoken since. Something shameful, which demeaned her, something she had barely been able to explain in all the time that passed. This was the tragedy of Leela Sharma, sister of Meera Chaturvedi, adopted daughter of Dipankar Bose. It was no good telling him now. She began to walk away towards the bedroom.

'Come back,' Hari shouted after her. 'Come back here and tell me why you kept these secrets from me all this time.'

She had reached the veranda at the back of the house when he threw the glass. She heard it smashing against the floor and flinched, turning in time to see him flinging the whisky bottle after it. Then he tipped the glass drinks table over with an effort, heaving it up in his arms, and she watched as the bottles slid slowly along the shelf and fell to the ground in a series of merciless tinkles.

'Hari,' she said softly. 'Hari, it's not as—'

'You embarrassed me this evening,' he interrupted, standing

amidst the violence of the shattered glass. 'You refused to talk to Professor Chaturvedi, whose son is marrying my niece, and yet' – his voice rose again – 'we are living here in Delhi. Our families are joined together. How are we supposed to interact with them now we are back, will you please tell me?'

'It was you who asked me to come back,' Leela said. 'I didn't ask for any of this.' She gestured around her at the house. 'You made me return here. You put me through this. You went against our deal.'

'I love you, Leela,' he said. 'I have given you everything I can. It is you who have kept things from me. It is you—' He pointed a finger. 'It is you who wouldn't give me the one thing I wanted as a husband.'

And he began to cry, now that he had said the one unsayable thing that stood between them.

She looked at him as he wept, his upper lip trembling with self-pity, and her instinct was to go to him and hold him, to tell him that she loved him too. But she couldn't. She still had to keep some piece of herself intact, before it all fell apart. So she watched him standing before her, beseeching her with his anger, and then she turned away, into the bedroom.

She closed the door behind her and sat on the bed, listening to the breathing and whispering of the house around her. As soon as Hari's back was turned, her father's house shrugged off its triumphant new incarnation, slipped its arms out of those freshly painted walls, untied from around its waist the modern paintings, peeled off the carefully chosen furniture, and became the house of Leela's errors again. Underneath the warm polished teak, she could smell the scent of Delhi then: the brown fog in the early morning, the perfumed trees at night, that aroma of betrayal which wafted towards her with every breeze that came in from the garden.

She lifted her head and listened. There was still no sound from outside, and she realised that she had expected him to come meekly to the door of the bedroom, in a spirit of penance, seeking her forgiveness. Just as she was about to start to her feet, she heard the crunch of glass. His feet made no sound as he walked towards the front door but the house reverberated slightly as he pulled the door to behind him.

She jumped up from the bed and ran out onto the veranda. 'Where are you going?' she called after him, but there was no one there. 'Hari?' she cried. All her calm authority was gone now. 'Hari?' She ran down the hallway to the front door and pulled it open. She was just in time to see his huge car pulling out into the road.

Back inside the house she looked at the pile of glass shards he had assembled there in his anger, and which the maid would have to clear up in the morning, and the thought came to her suddenly of the two young people they had been: he so fresh and hopeful, she with the scar running invisibly through her. He had wanted everything, her Hari, expected all the happinesses of the world to arrive in his arms with the easeful delight of a child running to greet its father. They had stood outside this house as he expressed his wonder that she had agreed to be his. Standing on the path, the key of the house in her hand, she had smiled back. She had felt his hopefulness and allowed it to infect her. She told herself that she could turn away from the sadness of the past, from Vyasa and Meera, from the sorrow and mourning that her father lived in: that she could step away to the new world with this unknown and optimistic man, leaving everything that was wrong and tainted behind her.

She walked quickly across the hallway, into their bedroom, throwing open the closet and pulling out a shawl. Catching sight of herself in the mirror, her thick black hair shot through with silver, the saffron sari that she had picked out of Hari's collection – solely for the way it spoke to her of Meera – she laughed out loud. What a role she had made for herself.

Nobody ever told her she had to be the sensible one, the responsible one; such a thing was never even mentioned. Her parents never asked her to act as Meera's keeper. But she knew she had been taken in from outside the family, and hadn't fully understood the bonds between them; had always sensed that the tenderness they felt for this waif could not but be conditional on her good behaviour. Even as a very young child she told herself that it was Meera who deserved the greater portion of their love. So she became adept at being well-behaved. She watched over Meera. She was careful.

Foolish woman, she told herself now. Meera may have exploited this vulnerability – but your father loved you.

And picking up her bag, she went out into the street to hail a taxi.

She only remembered the children's ayah when they reached Nizamuddin basti. Leaning forward, she asked the driver to stop. 'Next to the police post,' she said, looking out at the entrance to the basti, crowded with light and stalls and people.

She felt scared suddenly. She didn't know Nizamuddin well. In the few months she had lived in Delhi, between Santiniketan and New York, she had only visited it twice. She had gone there the first time to see Meera – and instead met Vyasa's mother. The house Vyasa lived in with his sister was tall and stately, on a street lined by trees. There was a maid and a gardener, and the children had an ayah called Raziya. This woman, a Muslim, was also newly married, and she lived with her husband's family in a small set of rooms near the shrine. Back then the basti had the feel of a village, with buffalo outside the huts and chickens in the yards and lines of washing linking the tatty but cheerful shacks where the poor Muslims lived. But in the years Leela had been away, a mesh of concrete buildings and partially paved roads had grown up like vegetation, obscuring the shrine. There was a line of cheap hotels facing the road, with shops below selling services and things to those who were only passing through: a bed for the night, a person to sleep with, a shawl to lay over the holy man's grave.

She didn't know where the ayah lived, but she remembered her saying it was on the other side of the shrine, between the drain and the road. The place had changed so much, though, that as she walked up towards the shrine through the market – past travel agencies, dogs, telephone offices, madrassahs, beggars with sticks and men pushing trolleys laid out with kohl for the ladies and elastic for everybody's trousers – she found that her memories meant nothing. She didn't want to hesitate and stop in this place late at night, and so she walked on, following the path as it led up past the Urdu poetry academy set up almost over the grave of the poet Ghalib, towards the shrine of Nizamuddin the saint, through a square of shuttered food stalls, and into the tapering passageways lined with flower sellers and shoe tenders. She slipped off her shoes, carrying them in her hand, her bare feet tickled by the pitted marble path. The nearer she got to the entrance to the shrine, the damper the path became, and she trod with distaste over the faint muddy outlines of countless other feet.

Everything had been so quiet in the streets outside that she was expecting to come down the steps into the shrine's courtyard and find it almost empty of other human beings. But as she rounded the last corner in the passageway, she saw that the shrine was full of people.

There were hundreds of them – poor people – in their worn-out clothes, carrying only a few belongings, murmuring and crying, lying and sitting together, or standing and talking with uneasy, fearful faces. They weren't here to pray for any private purpose –

for children, for gold, for good luck in a business venture – nor
had they come for the music, to lose themselves in the sacred,
imploring singing. These people, she sensed immediately, were
here because of some collective drama. Mothers sat holding tight
to their children; the men conferred in anxious groups. Old women
rocked themselves backwards and forwards, emitting a thin sound
of fear. Leela saw people glancing up and catching each other's eye:
the crowd had a strange, shared awareness of danger.

She addressed an old man in an astrakhan cap who was sitting
on the steps. 'What's going on?'

He looked up. 'Haven't you heard?' He put a finger to his lips
and whispered, 'The elephant-headed demon has returned.'

'And because of a demon these people are here?' she said, not
caring to keep the disdain out of her voice.

He considered her briefly for a moment before looking away.
'Careful, lady.'

'And what does the elephant-headed demon do?'

'Some remember him coming before. Then five people died.'

Leela looked out across the crowds of people. 'Do you know
Raziya?' she asked at last. 'She was ayah to Professor Chaturvedi's
children in Nizamuddin West.'

But it was the old man's turn to sound contemptuous. 'Which
Raziya?' He shrugged. 'You only know one? But there are so many.'

Pushing her way impatiently around the huddled families and
subdued children, over legs and bare feet, Leela crossed the courtyard, ignoring the saint's marble grave, and entered the narrow
passageway on the further side that led round the deep, open well
with its scum of green murky water. When she reached the northern
gate, she slipped on her shoes again, lit a cigarette and looked
around her. The street was dark but there was a light coming
from a small office a short distance away near the main road. She

smoked quickly as she walked, not caring if anybody saw her, and when she reached the streetlight where the insects danced, she stubbed the cigarette out and called to the three men she could see through the dirty window. According to the board outside, it was the Nizamuddin office of local Congress activists; they were playing cards and drinking rum, but a small man with hennaed hair came to the door, and she described the ayah to him, reiterating the point about Raziya's employment at the professor's. The man consulted with his colleagues. 'Try the tailor's shop on the right-hand side,' he said when he came outside again; 'just opposite the butcher's shop.' He slapped a mosquito away from his neck. 'But be careful. The people are saying there is a demon about.'

She laughed, and the man gave her a look of affront.

'It was your accent,' she apologised in Bengali. 'I haven't heard it for so long.' Her explanation was only half untrue; in America, Hari and she had almost always spoken in English, but here in Delhi she felt her mother tongue, Bengali, and the Hindi she had once known, unfurling inside her, reaching up through her lungs from some dark hidden place, freeing up more and more of her early life like the tendrils of a plant reaching out towards the light.

She said goodbye to the man and made her way along the darkened street where the butcher's shop was supposed to stand. All the shops were shuttered, and many of the signboards were written in Urdu script, which she had never learnt to read. But on the way back down the street she saw a shop sign with a hand-painted picture of a woman in a billowing salwar kameez, and from the scattering of coloured threads and little oddments of cloth on the ground outside, she guessed that it must be the tailor's. The shutter was down but the light was on inside, and when she drew close she could hear the clattering of a sewing machine. She walked up the steps and tapped on the metal. 'Raziya,' she called, 'Raziya.'

She rapped again, and the sewing machine paused. Leela spoke louder now: 'I need to speak to Raziya.'

'Who is it?' The woman's voice was cautious.

'A friend.'

There was the noise of a shutter being unbolted and pushed upwards a few feet, and when Leela crouched down, she found herself looking into the eyes of a woman of about her age, who was wearing an austere blue cotton sari, the end of which was pulled up to almost cover her hair. The woman's eyes widened when she saw it was Leela.

'You looked after the babies. The Professor's children,' Leela said in Urdu.

The woman shook her head. 'I don't remember you,' she said, drawing herself back, sitting on her heels.

'We went to Humayun's tomb. I gave you some jewellery, that gold. You must remember. You looked after the twins. Twenty years ago.' Leela leant in, so close that she could see the wrinkles around the other woman's eyes, and the proud line of kohl. 'Do you have the jewellery still?' she whispered. 'I would like it back. I can give you money for it.'

The jewellery was ornate and finely worked – but more than that, it was Leela's link to her childhood, to her dead mother, to that part of herself that she had all but excised. When she had given it to Raziya it was all she had. Now she could buy it back with just the cash she carried on her. She wanted it badly: as a gift for Bharati, a way of establishing the link between them. But when the ayah spoke, her words were barely audible. 'I sold the gold. I stopped looking after children. I cannot help you any further.' She looked beyond Leela, out into the street. 'Now you must go.' Then she moved back, pulling the shutter down so that it clicked into place on the ground, and Leela could hear the noise of a heavy padlock securing it in place. But they both remained there on either side of the shutter, two women, crouching and listening, disappointment in one heart, fear in the other; and before she got to her feet again, Leela said softly: 'Was Vyasa's wife happy? Was she happy as a mother? Can you tell me?'

But Raziya made no reply, and Leela was suddenly ashamed at herself for having come here like this. It was not the woman's fault that she had done what she did; Leela had used the gold to tempt her. But again she wished she had that jewellery. She had a yearning for it – her inheritance – and to hear more about the children Meera had left behind. She stepped down from the tailor's shop and continued along the street, her mood slipping in that familiar way, from defiance to sadness. She reprimanded herself for her self-indulgence; and the thought of those intimidated people, cowering from superstition in the shrine, came back to her like a taunt.

The road she was on skirted the outside edge of the basti, through an area even poorer and more neglected than the rest. Leela felt an apprehension about crossing through this place dressed as she was in her glowing wedding silk. Nor did she yet have a clear idea of what she was going to do or say when she reached Vyasa's house. She walked on as far as the crossroads where the buffalo stables jutted out into the kabariwallah settlement. Then she saw the burning.

The flames were spreading quickly, licking at timber and plastic as the air filled with heavy black smoke. Buffalo, scorched in the heat, had begun to bellow. People were stumbling out of their homes, carrying children and hastily gathered belongings. The wind drew a plume of filthy smoke towards her so that she had to stop and cough and wipe her eyes. When she straightened up again she saw men sloshing small buckets of water over the blaze, swiping angrily at the flames with blankets, their faces slick with sweat from the heat and exertion. But the fire was spreading easily through the houses, embracing small television sets and crackling with joy as it set upon dowries and precious clothing collections. There was a small group of women, standing with the children and babies pulled out of their beds in the middle of the night – all so thin and small, with tiny limbs and alert eyes – and Leela wondered suddenly if she had appeared to Meera's father like this, fragile and helpless, on the day the munshi brought her from the village. Both parents had liked her eyes: large black ponds of gaiety that belied her brush with death.

A small child, a girl, stood alone on the edge of the crowd, her mouth puckered up with tears, and Leela, seeing that she had been forgotten, stepped forward and picked her up. She was very light and wore a long yellow dirty shirt. 'We'll find your mother,' Leela said, kissing her dry, tangled hair. 'What's your name?' she asked, but the child only began to cry. 'Sssh,' Leela said. 'Don't be afraid.' But there was a shout from behind them. 'Let go of her!' It was a woman's voice, and then a second joined in: 'That lady is stealing our children!' And suddenly a crowd of angry women had surrounded her, tugging the girl out of her arms, shouting that she was abducting their children to take them to an orphanage, or to sell to rich Saudis, or to send to the brothels of Bombay. 'I was trying to help her,' Leela heard herself saying, but the women only shouted louder, jostling her with their hands as Leela tried to back away, her arms raised in self-defence.

'Hey!' It was a man's voice now, reprimanding and commanding. 'Leave the lady alone.' The women turned, and saw a tall young man waving a notebook in the air at them as he approached. He was too young to be an official, or anybody of importance, but he spoke with such a show of authority that the women retreated to a distance.

'Quickly, come this way. The whole basti is in hysteria,' the man said in English to Leela, and she followed him along the small lane that led up out of the basti towards the colony where Vyasa lived. A little further on she sat down on the wide doorstep of a shuttered shop, still trembling from the women's anger. 'I'm going to stop here for a moment,' she told the man, wiping her face with the end of the sari. She looked up at him. 'Thank you.'

'Are you all right?' he asked.

She nodded.

'Let me get you a cup of tea,' he said, and she watched him return to the fire with his notebook.

She sat there alone, thinking of the people she had seen in the shrine tonight: how exactly they resembled the poor people from the dreams and memories of her childhood, how despite everything Hari said, some things hadn't changed in India. She remembered how her father always gave coins to the beggars who came to the door of their house in Calcutta. She closed her eyes and remembered the terrace of her parents' house, and the light that flooded in through the windows in the morning, and the scent of tulsi between her fingers, and the smell of the rough block of soap that stood in a dish on the bathroom floor and always made her think of her mother. She thought of Father after their mother's death, and how hard he had tried to dissuade Meera from studying at Santiniketan. He was determined that she and Leela should go to Delhi University. He said he was going to open up his house in Delhi for them, and put them in touch with friends who had formed part of the literary circles of his youth. He grew excited by his memories of studying there himself. He told them about the streets around Chandni Chowk, and a haleem maker he had known with a long white beard whose entire family had gone away to Pakistan, and a thick, treacly sweet you could buy there on winter nights.

He spoke of the awe-inspiring mosque, the poetry recitals he had attended in Civil Lines, the qawwalis he had heard at Nizamuddin's shrine on Thursday evenings. He wanted his daughters to see the country they had inherited, he said, and they should begin with the capital. Afterwards they could go to Bombay, and the Western Ghats, and Tamil Nadu. But first they must go to Delhi, as he had. It was his conviction and he spoke of it often.

Leela opened her eyes and saw the young man returning. She and Meera *had* eventually come to Delhi – but not in the way that their father had wished.

The young man was carrying two small glass bottles of lemonade with thin straws poking out the top. 'No tea shops were open,' he said as he handed one to her, and she smiled.

They sipped the sweet cold liquid, and after a while he said, 'You were at the wedding this evening, weren't you? Ash Chaturvedi's wedding.'

She looked at him and raised an eyebrow and smiled again, this time at his earnestness. 'I was the one who fainted.'

'You did,' he said, 'I saw.' He smiled back at her. 'You're Meera's sister, aren't you? Leela Bose?'

She put down the lemonade bottle. 'How do you know?'

'I wrote the piece about the *Lalita* poem. I did some research.'

'What kind of research?'

'I was the one it was sent to, "The Last Dictation".'

'Why you?'

'I don't know. It wasn't you who sent it?'

'Why would I do that?'

'But you wrote them together?'

She got to her feet, suddenly very tired. The poems didn't matter. Why was he asking about the poems?

She looked away, watching in silence as a fire engine arrived at last from the Lodhi Road end of the basti and was manoeuvred into place. The heavy blasts of water were poured onto the flames and there was a loud, slow hiss as the fire was extinguished.

'Why are you out in the basti so late?' the young man asked next. 'Did you come to see the fire?'

She hesitated. 'I came to find something I lost.'

'And did you find it?'

'I've only just begun looking.' She stared at the outline of the charred and broken houses. 'Why are you out so late?' she asked.

'I heard the noise and came downstairs. I live on the edge of the basti.'

'So you are going to write about the fire?'

'The fire and the demon.'

'And about a Hindu woman caught stealing Muslim children?'

He laughed. 'No.' After a moment he added, 'I would like to write more about the poems, though. Would you tell me about them? I'd invite you to my house for a coffee, but there's somebody sleeping there and I don't want to wake her. The coffee shop at the Oberoi Hotel might be twenty-four hours, though. And there's an all-night tea stall at Nizamuddin East railway station—'

'I don't want to talk about the poems,' she interrupted, and then, seeing the disappointment on his face added, more gently, 'But thank you for your interest. I have to get on now.'

'Good to have met you.'

She pulled the shawl around her shoulders. 'Thank you for rescuing me.'

'It was my pleasure,' he said gallantly. Then he took a business card from his wallet and handed it to her. 'In case you change your mind,' he said.

Leela took it from him without looking at the name, which she remembered from the article – Pablo Fernandes – and put it in her bag. She stood for a moment longer before leaving, gazing at the people surveying their ruined houses, and then she gave the journalist a final wary nod and walked on down the lane to the edge of the basti. Here the slum suddenly gave way to wide, leafy streets, generously set with large, airy homes, each with a garden and a gate and at least three floors. She found Vyasa's house easily, despite her tiredness: it was on the road facing the drain and his name was written on the gatepost. She stood in the street, looking up at the house, thinking how, in comparison with those in the basti, it was a miracle of solidity. The garden was full of trees: bamboo and frangipani, an ashoka, and somewhere nearby was a raat-ki-rani, filling the night with its flowers' perfume. She leant against the wall of the public garden opposite, which bordered the drain, took another cigarette from her handbag and lit it, listening to the lowing of the night trains passing through Nizamuddin railway station, and to the tap of the chowkidar's stick in the distance, and to the occasional competitive yelping of the neighbourhood's dogs. She knew that she ought to ring Hari – but the more tired she felt, the more her mind turned to the things she tried to forget. She pulled the shawl tighter round her shoulders, and just at that moment, a light came on in Vyasa's house.

chapter 18

The Professor and his mother were among the last guests to leave the wedding grounds, and Humayun one of the last drivers. They weren't staying out of choice, but because they were waiting anxiously for Bharati. The Professor and his mother hadn't seen Bharati all evening; but still they insisted on waiting. 'Where is she?' the Professor asked Humayun in some annoyance, as if he was supposed to know her whereabouts. 'Haven't you seen her?' Humayun shook his head, and the Professor said brusquely, 'Wait outside then, till we call you,' and Humayun returned to the fire where he had sat with the other drivers earlier in the evening and waited there on his own, thinking about Aisha.

At first the other drivers, all Hindus, had welcomed Humayun into their circle – despite the fact that he was so different from them in his mood and preoccupations. Their festival of Diwali was in a few days' time, and they were eager that evening for what they called some 'seasonal' gambling. As soon as it was dark, one of the men took out a pack of cards. Somebody else produced the dice. A third man even pulled out a bottle of hooch, and it was passed, somewhat surreptitiously, around the circle. Humayun, the only Muslim, refused all of these things. He had never gambled and he didn't want to drink. But the other men remained friendly. They asked about his employment, where he lived, and how he came to be at the wedding. He told them about his temporary work for the Professor this evening, driving his family to and from the wedding. 'My betrothed works in his house, looking after the Professor's mother,' Humayun said. It was a quiet boast, and they all murmured in admiration.

After they had been fed what remained of the wedding dinner, several of the drivers drank more hooch and became wilder in their gambling. Then an old man lost a hundred rupees, and he cursed his opponent for taking away his earnings, and the Diwali presents he was going to buy his granddaughters, and got to his feet to move away before anything worse could happen. The mood changed; somebody spoke of how the Muslim taxi drivers were taking their custom this Diwali – they worked right through the holiday for inflated rates, regardless of neighbourly feeling. Things got even more heated when somebody mentioned the Ram temple: 'The government should build it quickly, now that our people have got rid of the mosque Emperor Babur put up over Lord Ram's birthplace!' 'Sister-fucking Muslims, saying that this is their land too. How dare they?' said an older driver. One of the younger men made undulating curves in the air with his hands. 'They're jealous of our women. We have goddess Sita, Ram's wife, so beautiful. Who do they have to compare with her?' 'Their women sleep with any passing man,' cut in a thin man in a blue shirt and trousers. 'That's why they have so many children. Putting them in burqas is just a joke.' He looked up at Humayun as he spoke.

Humayun got to his feet reluctantly. They were trying to provoke him. 'What you say is dishonourable,' he said slowly.

The card playing stopped. The firelight picked out the eagerness on their faces. They wanted a fight. 'Dishonourable?' It was the thin man in the blue shirt who spoke. 'Name me one virtuous Muslim woman.'

'The one I am going to marry.' The instant he said it, Humayun regretted his boast. The circle of men looked at each other and laughed.

Before anything worse could happen, Humayun moved away from the fire. He sat at the top of the lane in the Professor's car, occasionally glancing out at the departing wedding guests, their women in opulent silk saris, blues, greens, purples, leaving the wedding garden and returning to Delhi. He wished for such a sari for his Aisha. He would buy her one when they were married. Sitting there, he closed his eyes and felt another twinge of worry: about what they had done today in his room, about what he had done to her. He must announce their engagement to both their mothers immediately.

After some time, Humayun heard the clamour of the wedding couple departing. He got out of the car and walked a little way down the lane, from where he could see the Professor's son leaving on the start of his nuptial journey, driven away with his wife in a white car covered with red roses. One by one, each party from the bride's large family began to disperse also. Soon, all the gambling drivers had left the fire, and all the dark shapes of the cars that had lined the road leading up to the Flying Club lit up, reversed, and disappeared along the lane like fireflies in the night. Humayun was now the only driver left.

Since it was cold in the car, he returned to the fire, and was sitting there, dozing, when he heard somebody calling his name. It was the Professor. 'We must leave,' the Professor said. He seemed agitated. 'My mother is too old to wait any longer.'

While the Professor went back into the garden to collect his mother, Humayun hurried along the lane to the place where he had left the car beside the Flying Club tennis court. He was opening the door when he heard a taxi in the lane ahead coming towards him from the city. It slowed down when it caught Humayun in its headlights, and stopped when it drew level. A window opened slowly. Humayun heard the voice speaking before he saw the face.

'I just dropped a guest in Nizamuddin,' the voice said, 'and I've come back to collect the pandit. I have to tell you something. I've seen a Muslim girl at the Professor's house where your betrothed works, being taken by another man. Chaturvedi is the name, isn't it? In a tall house just opposite the nala?'

It was the thin man in the blue shirt, the one who earlier this evening had spoken disrespectfully of Muslim women. Humayun tried to reason with himself; surely the man was mocking him? But the tremor in the driver's voice could come from nothing but fear or pity.

The driver spoke again: 'She was wearing a yellow suit of clothes, wasn't she? You'd better hurry back and find her.'

'Who was it who attacked her?' Humayun said.

But the window slid upwards, and the car accelerated away towards the entrance of the Flying Club. Humayun's hands trembled as he tried to fit the key into the ignition. He saw the thin man get out, walk quickly into the wedding grounds, and shout something through the jasmine archway. The Professor and his mother were just coming out. Nobody spoke during the short drive home.

When they reached the Professor's house, the front door was ajar. 'Aisha,' said Humayun. He leapt out of the car, instead of hastening over to help the Professor's mother as he should have done. 'Aisha,' he shouted as he ran up the steps.

The Professor's house was in near darkness; one light was on in the kitchen and another in the hallway. Humayun almost skidded on the clay waterpot, which was in pieces on the floor.

He ran up the stairs, calling Aisha's name, turning on lights, opening the door into bedrooms and bathrooms, and eventually reaching the library on the top floor, where the Professor kept his books. The bookshelves loomed up aggressively like well-trained soldiers. In the centre of the room, Humayun turned on the desk lamp and crouched down to look under the table. He even unbolted the door to the veranda and walked round the terrace, looking over the wall and down into the garden.

When he ran back downstairs, the Professor was standing in the hall.

'What are you doing?' the Professor said. 'Where is Aisha?' His voice was low and angry. 'What the hell are you both up to?'

'She promised she would wait here until Mrs Ahmed came to collect her,' Humayun said.

'She broke my mother's vase!' the Professor said. 'It's lucky that nobody walked in through the open door and took the rest. Aisha is young and clumsy and distracted. Go and look for her at that other place she works and tell her not to come back here.'

Humayun didn't reply. But as he walked away towards the front door, the Professor called after him. 'Take this,' he said. Humayun turned, and saw that he was holding out an envelope. It was his pay for the evening.

Humayun pushed the envelope into his pocket and ran up the drain road towards the basti to look for Aisha at the graveyard, thinking over what the Hindu driver had said as he ran, and asking himself if he had been guilty of lust. It was because of his own dirty thoughts about the Professor's daughter that he had forced himself on Aisha before they were married, made her late for work at the Professor's, failed to make proper arrangements to collect her after the wedding – and even trusted flighty Mrs Ahmed when she promised solemnly to fetch the girl herself as soon as it got dark. If what the driver said was true, then it was his fault. It was just as his mother had said – Humayun clenched his fists together as he ran – men were the cause of all the world's sorrow.

He had almost reached the gateway that led down to the drain, when he heard the shouting in the lane ahead, and smelt the burning. 'What's happened?' he called to a group of people who were standing under the trees near the drain. During the day, the waste collectors' wives sat here weighing beer bottles, Old Monk and Royal Challenge whisky bottles, mango pickle jars, English and Hindi newspapers, and all kinds of slop-stained plastics. A man in a blackened shirt, holding a baby, turned towards Humayun. 'Can't you see? The kabari settlement caught fire. The fire spread into the next gully. The wind was coming from across the drain, and we thought the whole basti might catch, but thanks to God it has only affected twenty or thirty houses. We've managed to contain it.'

'Is anybody dead?'

'One young girl, maybe two, died in the smoke. Also, a baby from the other side of the basti. Many people have taken refuge in the shrine. The bodies have been taken to the police station.'

'Which young girls?'

The man's baby woke up and began crying, and he turned away from Humayun and handed the child to his wife.

'Which young girls?' Humayun repeated, shouting now. 'What were their names?'

The man looked up again. 'Our house is full of smoke,' he said, 'my children are crying from fear and cold. I don't know the girls' names. Go and ask for yourself at the police station.'

Humayun hesitated a moment, and then he ran – pushing through the crowds of men who stood in the street discussing the burning with dismayed but resigned expressions – choking and coughing on the smoke as he skirted the edge of the basti in the direction of the main road.

At the corner of the basti market, scared anew by the thought of approaching the police station alone on a night like this, he called out to the carpenter who was sitting on a bench outside his workshop, dangling a grandchild on his knee and watching sceptically as his son planed the top of a table. 'Did you see the girls who died in the fire? What were they wearing? Was one of them in yellow?'

The carpenter, a big man, looked up and shrugged. 'Yellow?' He looked over at his son. 'Was one of them in yellow? Yes, maybe she was. But you should go and—'

Humayun, however, hadn't stayed to hear any more.

By the time he arrived at the thana he was breathless. The police station was beyond the market, on the outside edge of Nizamuddin, in the armpit of the two main roads which ran along the colony's northern and eastern edge, and was set back from both, in its own garden. After the noise and fear in the basti, the place was oddly quiet.

Humayun walked up the driveway and climbed the steps to the door. As he stood there, getting his breath back, he had another moment of hesitation. Nobody he knew would ever willingly go to the Hindu officers of Nizamuddin police station for help. Then he thought of Aisha – raped or dead or dying – and put out a hand and knocked. The worst they could do was to send him away without an answer.

A tall policeman with a large paunch answered the door. He was speaking to a colleague about a particular chicken dish: 'No onion, no garlic, only coconut. Fried in ghee with a little tiny pinch of poppy seeds. Yes?' he asked, looking down at Humayun.

As politely as he could, Humayun explained that he had lost his cousin; that he was concerned that she had been harmed in the fire; could they confirm that none of the recently deceased was named Aisha?

The policeman opened the door wider, and pointed to a long wooden bench by the entrance where Humayun should sit and wait, opposite a desk where another policeman sat making notes in a large register. He called through to the room beyond: 'It's fried hard till the skin pops. A special Bengali trick. My sister-in-law does it' – and from a nearby room, three other male voices burst out laughing. The chicken-loving policeman turned to face Humayun: 'What did you say her name was?'

'Aisha,' repeated Humayun.

'Aisha.'

There was a sudden silence. The policeman at the desk looked up from his writing. 'And your name?'

'Humayun.'

Again the policemen looked at each other, and the fear entered Humayun and made him grip the bench with both hands for reassurance.

'Do you know what happened to a girl called Aisha this evening?' the man at the desk asked eventually.

Humayun opened his hands to show he knew nothing, not being able or willing or inclined to ask these men about the other thing that might have happened to her. 'Sir,' he said, 'I hope she has not been caught in the fire.' He didn't want to hear these men talk about Aisha; it would make him go mad.

But a third policeman, sitting in an inner room, got to his feet and came to the door. 'Something much worse for a woman's reputation than that.'

The policemen looked between each other again; and the man at the desk nodded.

The chicken-loving policeman stepped forward, leaning over

him so close that Humayun could feel his warm breath. 'Is that mud on your trousers?' the policeman asked, and he took a pinch of the material on Humayun's thigh between thumb and forefinger. Humayun glanced down at the mark. 'It's ash from the fire,' he explained.

The chicken-loving policeman cuffed him round the head. 'Sister-fucker, it's mud,' he said. 'Have you been involved in a struggle?'

'A struggle? No, sir.'

'Are you married?'

'Married?'

'Have you had carnal relations?'

'Sir?'

And Humayun heard the man at the desk say in a tired voice. 'Take him out of my sight. The interrogation room.'

'But, sir,' Humayun said, and as they pushed him towards the room at the back of the thana he heard his own voice rising: 'Don't you understand? My fiancée is Aisha. I am engaged to be married. Tell me what you've done to her!'

A door in the corridor opened and Humayun felt himself being pushed from behind. He sprawled into the dark room, tripping on a chair so that he lost his balance and half fell, half tumbled to the floor. Somebody turned on the light. Humayun lay there for a moment and he remembered how he had pulled down Aisha's salwar that afternoon, how the warmth had flowed between them in their first private moment together; and as the chicken-loving policeman loomed over him, and Humayun scrambled to his feet, he tried to balance this vision with that of Aisha in her yellow suit, being led away by another man and violated.

'Did you fuck her?' the chicken-loving policeman said, making a lewd motion with his hand. And then Humayun did something stupid, something that, even at the time, he knew he would immediately regret. He lunged for the man, grabbing him by the shirt, and then they were on him. One of them hit him round the head. *Sister-fucking terrorist*, he heard them shout. Another punched him in the chest. He felt a pain in his leg and back where a third was kicking him.

They spent a few moments seeing to his incapacitation, and then they dragged him to the cell at the front of the station, and locked him in.

Part Two

chapter 1

The alert reader may have noticed, while I was sitting and talking through my project with the literary agent Bill Bond in London, that circumstances had forced me to effect one key transition. I, Ganesh, had taken human form.

It happens to gods at strategic moments in history. Krishna did it; Jesus tried it; and I, too, took my turn. In the beginning, up on Kailash, I debated with myself only briefly about the type of avatar I should choose. A holy man? A warrior? A merchant? No. I needed to be able to influence events, to get my errant characters back on track, to wrest control from Vyasa. And how to do that? Through my pen. This was the truth I had taught Vyasa. This was the way I would observe my characters across multiple lives, and pursue them through numerous ages, and eventually get them together as one grand cast. I dabbled in it across the centuries, leaping down to earth to be the scribe of courts and sarais and mushairas, to preserve literary traditions, to transmit cultural ideas . . . and always with my elephant's eye on my own cast of characters.

But now that the time of their great meeting had arrived, I realised the stakes had been raised. I couldn't be just any old scribbler. I was determined that everything would happen just as I had planned it. I had readied myself for the crisis (prepared the ground with hakims, astrologers, christenings – all the right and proper proper names) until everyone I needed was walking the streets of my city, masquerading under the identities I had chosen. It was time to make them mine again.

'Of course, when I say I need an Indian writer . . . I mean, you do write in . . . *English*?' said the eager agent when we met at the Nine Muses café, a look of doubt suddenly crossing his schoolboyish features.

I sighed. If he only knew. Yes, I wrote in English, but the *pain* of it, the *sacrifice*.

When I began the narrative exploration of which the following is the fruit – the sugary, gram-flour laddu – I of course had very little idea about what I was letting myself in for. I am now in a position to inform the Reader that my principal task during the tracking of my cast across the yugs was the problem of keeping pace with exactly how to record their exploits and activities. That is, I did not wish to vote, as Vyasa did, for the elite and high vehicle of Sanskrit. No, my aim was more demotic. I wanted my story to be disseminated in every script that was being scribbled in the land now known as India, all of them. And that changed the dynamic completely.

For thousands of years my task was fairly straightforward, merely a matter of migrating across the country from tribe to tribe, town to town, readjusting myself to the ins and outs of a basic set of scripts and tongues. Right to left and left to right. North to south and east to west. I learnt Brahmi and Kharoshti, Maurya and Shunga, Gupta, as the emperors grew in stature and demand. I was ready to master Munda and Kolarian; or Persian to soothe the Sultans; and so from the loins of Sind-Hind-Ind sprang a dynasty of people infused with the love of a good line and the thrill of an intricate plot. I was the first to admit that the collusion of cultures breathed into my story glorious dimensions the likes of which had never been seen before.

The Europeans, meanwhile, had been arriving: the French, Dutch, Portuguese and English, on and off for years. None of us took much notice at first; but slowly, steadily, insidiously, they began marching us down the great long straight Roman Road of no return, and we fell for it without fully understanding how, or pausing to reason why. The Roman letters came and saw and conquered, little by little, drip by drip – a printed sign here, a paper notice there, a transcription, a contract, even a translation or two (of the Ramayana, the Gita – though they have never to this day scaled the heights of the mountainous Mahabharata). All these things were small enough to go unnoticed in the hectic vortex of busy India, until the British forced upon us English education, and then our minds became Miltonic, iambic, full of loony vowels and foggy climes.

But I, at least, retained the desi aroma. I had Leela on my side, didn't I? That's what I told myself, anyhow.

'The people still love me,' I whispered to Bill as he looked on sceptically. 'The ones who don't speak English do; all those who prefer the thick vowels and agile consonants of the mother and father and brother cousin sister tongues still do puja to Ganesh. But how can I answer their prayers? When I can barely sing their songs, feel the rhythms of their rhymes, trill their prose? I had a multiplicity of tongues, and I abandoned them, to write in English only!' And I added (overcome with self-doubt, prone by nature to exaggerate my woes): 'I have become a vernacular illiterate! There! It is true.'

'And a good thing too,' said Bill, taking out a draft contract. 'Now, run me through your characters. Pronto.'

Bill, you see, is an Englishman born and indelibly bred. His instincts are racy, his sense of structure hinges on the cliffhanger (I quote from those now much-thumbed *Notes for New Writers*). He wished for none of this sensitively explored, infinitesimally detailed, psychological study of character. No. He has banned interior monologue, pathetic fallacy, poetic ambiguity. His creed is: 1) character exposition: *Boom!* 2) Plot plan: *Wham!* What he likes best are broad sweeps of local colour, clouds of unusual odours, plenty of exotic women. 'Strictly no disjointed postmodernists, limbless cripples or impoverished persons,' is Bill's mantra.

I began to explain. 'There's Meera and Leela whom we've talked about already, there's Vyasa and his mother, Shiva Prasad and his wife. Then there's Bharati, Sunita, Urvashi, Ash and—'

'Wait up,' Bill said, holding his head in his hands. He had been trying to take notes and his pad of paper was a mess of scrawlings. 'Bharati, Sunita, Urvashi and who?'

'Ash,' I said. 'The genealogist.' I looked over at him and added (a little defiantly), 'I need some help keeping track of my characters' origins. You should try reading the Mahabharata. It is *obsessed* with lists of sons of sons of sons of. Aren't you following?'

He shook his head. 'All these previous lives!' he grumbled. 'It could go on for ever.'

Of course, it wasn't Bill's fault he was slow to catch on. But at least you, dear Reader, will have gathered by now that these precious products of human striving take longer than a lifetime to accumulate. Character, like culture, is cultivated gradually over millennia. It is formed by historical reaction – something like dominoes, or osmosis, or the migration of ospreys along an interlinked series of watercourses, gathering plumage, shedding it, changing in flight. Characters I invented at the beginning of time have lived and relived their lives, winding their way in and out of history, right up to the present, adapting, growing, maturing – but with always a glimmer of their original being. You have seen this already in my first and most important character, that wondrous lady Leela.

O my Leela, my heroine, my muse; the quintessence of my creation, that triumph of rebellion from Vyasa, the best that I gleaned from my under-rewarded, conspicuously sidelined act of literary transcription.

Having resolved that direct divine intervention in the scenes of my creation was the only way I could ensure that the plot would come to fruition in Delhi, I sped across the heavens, dreaming of Leela all the way. I allowed myself to wander indulgently through her eight successive lives: recalling how unequivocally she refused Vyasa's advances just before the Bharata war, how prettily she danced out the epic with her sister, how wilfully she plunged to a watery death in the refugee camp at the Purana Qila. The further we flew through the clouds, the more my mind was intoxicated by our propinquity. When we landed at Indira Gandhi airport I barely noticed the changes to my beloved city – the Yamuna, a once beautiful mountain goddess, now shrunk to a black sewer – so caught up was I in the idea of her existence.

Without any time to lose, I went straight to the wedding, to witness and intervene if necessary in my characters' collisions. I was pleased, of course, that Ash was marrying Sunita with exquisite good grace and according to my express intentions, though this was mere background music, incidental detail to the central drama. I stood amidst the throng, eating a substantial vegetarian meal and patiently awaiting Leela's arrival. And when at last she entered, dressed in wheatfield-crocus-sunspot yellow, my heart went pitter-patter. I would have known that sweet fragrance, that beautiful haste, that defiant glance anywhere on earth. Her voice seemed to reach across to me like a tendril of forgotten language – a rush of remembrance, strains of half-forgotten songs. She was ushered onto the stage, and I trembled. Jealously, I watched the movement of her head as it turned towards her husband, the brooding of her arms as they clasped each other, the sweet promise of her wavy hair. I longed to stand beside her; I watched with envious eyes as others did; as others eyed the woman who by divine right of creative things was mine, all mine.

Now, I have never, in the whole history of mankind's narration, known it to happen before, so there was, on reflection, no reason to expect it to happen then; but somehow it did. A form of recognition passed between the creation and the creator. She happened to gaze out across the crowd – glorious Leela, lovely Leela, fragrant as frangipani, amla, jacaranda – our eyes locked together, and before I could prevent it happening, I had revealed myself to her in all the glory of my godhead – in my numerous representations: elephant-head, arms holding a lotus, an axe, a rope, a trident, a rosary, a plate of sweets, one hand raised up in blessing, Rat at my feet, a mottled ear, a parasol, a saffron-coloured dhoti, four faces . . . Even I began to feel dizzy; and as this vision flashed before her, naturally, she fainted.

I felt consternation. What had I done? In my human form I wished to influence events, but not like this. My aim was to make Leela strong. Filled with dread, I wandered the wedding crowds, eavesdropping on conversations, smiling when I saw my characters fully inhabiting the roles I had carved out for them (Sunita, so shy and retiring, a punching bag for spectators to define themselves against; the passive player they are probably most like, but pretend they would never be), my happy elephant-features wrinkling with worry when I realised that at least one of my cast – Urvashi the Truthteller – hadn't made an appearance at all.

That worry, though, was as nothing to the shudder of anger

that went through me when I overheard the following comment. 'A god with a blue face?' said a voice behind me. 'An elephant-headed scribe? Phantoms of trees and mountains? But it is precisely the inherent ridiculousness of Hinduism which is its own best defence. Who could argue with a religion as silly as that?'

I whipped round in horror. The woman who had just uttered these words chuckled – and then turned for affirmation to a man whom I recognised, in one horrified heartbeat, as Vyasa. My enemy! My nemesis! Of course I had been expecting him; I knew what he had done to Leela and Meera in this life; but still, I felt the strength drain from me – I was in danger of collapsing there and then. No, dear Reader, this return to Delhi was not a mere lissom frolic through the pages of some happy-go-lucky fiction. It was the culmination of an epoch-old battle between two opposing forces. It was the final chapter of our mutually effacing carnage. It was war.

Before we go any further, I would like to remind you that I have not been alone in my attempts to wrestle control of this text from the Great Dictator. Even before Vyasa came to me with his writing project, he had attempted to pass on the Mahabharata to five separate pupils. All of them learnt the text, but only one was allowed to transmit it. Why? Because one pupil's version was too censorious of Vyasa's grandsons; another's didn't stress Vyasa's valour. Vyasa discarded the unfavourable portraits and chose that which presented him as a hero – rather than the villain that he is. The Mahabharata that has come down to us is truly epic: *a vast and sycophantic distortion.*

Like a true strategist, Vyasa stifled dissent, popularising the convenient though ridiculous notion that what is not found here is found nowhere. All lies! There were many variant accounts of Vyasa's own behaviour outside the Mahabharata. Some ancient commentators I spoke to pointed out that the old lecher slept with his dead brothers' wives – was not that against Dharma? Others cried that he had fathered offspring whose actions led directly to the cataclysmic bloodshed of the war. Still more drew attention to his failures as a priest and negotiator. These voices denigrated Vyasa. Why, they asked passionately, was Vyasa honoured? And yet for centuries, for millennia, their questions and accounts have been silenced by the power of the Vyasa Propaganda Machine. But no longer.

For too long now, Vyasa has held this tale in the palm of his hand, tweaking uncomfortable episodes, twisting embarrassing accounts. He has become the judge and the jury – and the criminal! – of India's great epic. How is that fair? And what about the victims? *Where was their story?*

Standing in the wedding garden, watching Vyasa converse with his odious female sidekick, I reminded myself that centuries of antagonism had led to this moment; that the intellectual propaganda I was witnessing in Delhi was thoroughly in line with everything I knew about Vyasa's endeavour to push me into the margins; that ever since I wrote down the first word of the Mahabharata, Vyasa had been on a quest to manipulate Indian history. But now Vyasa's hegemony was teetering on the brink of the abyss. To bring the action to its crisis, I needed to enlist the help of my arrow-carrier, a boy I had always intended as Leela's protector. *Pablo.*

There were, it must be admitted, some problems along the way with this character's incarnations. The first problem lay in his name. When I slipped him on to the battlefield, somewhere towards the middle of Vyasa's Mahabharata, he was barely fifteen years old, and fresh as the flocks he once tended, with pleasing curls and a long strong nose. I gave him a good name, made up of three strong consonants: puh, buh, luh: PABAL, or PUBLI, or PABLO. But this was an era of Sanskrit theology, my grasp of that over-polished language was always very faulty, and I soon found that despite the nice combination I had chosen for him, my character was a linguistic lacuna; there was no such word in the whole of the Sanskrit language.

For centuries, P—o was unable to feature in my drama as anything more than a whisper, a shade, a ghostly figure of fireside stories and riverside rumour. In some places the people called him The Pale One, in others they named him The Dim, and elsewhere The Faint. P—o's greatest gift, at this epoch, was to enrich the imagination of humans as a figure of folklore. In the coastal regions to which he futuristically belonged, P—o gained some renown as the tall curly haired netter of a thousand fish; thereafter P—o was given provincial status as a fishing deity; and local newly-weds would visit the shrine (today the foundations of the Municipal Corporation) to dab the pale stone visage with red paste and offer pennies in exchange for a firstborn son. Who knows how such legends arise.

It wasn't until 1498, when Vasco da Gama touched down in Calicut bringing the name with him – along with the common cold, St Anthony's Fire and other nasty Occidental diseases – that at last my Pablo came to earth as the fruit of a seaside union between a lustrous loud-mouthed fisherwoman and a burly Portuguese sailor (with a nasty habit of sucking garlic in the morning to ward off the Indian evil eye and migratory European vampires). The sailor's name was actually Paulo but they'd called him Pablo in the Spanish way to distinguish him from the other Paul on board, Vasco's brother, and this was the name that the father gave to his India-born son.

Paulo had come from a small village near Lisbon where his wife laboured bottling tomatoes for the winter months and skimping on supper to feed the six children her husband had sired between 1488 and 1495. Having docked for a spell on these coconut-fringed shores, Paulo soon discovered that his brand-new fish-fed baby boy, with his large interested eyes rimmed by his loquacious mother in mustard-seed kohl, was ample compensation for the scrawny old-world offspring he had abandoned to the 1496 tomato blight; that the fresh sea fish she fried far outweighed the horror of thrice-cooked sea biscuit on the arduous return journey; and so he was happy to put off his homecoming by visiting the small salt-sprayed hut to fuck the mother and bounce the boy on his knee; and as for the boy, when he was four years old, his father sent him south to Cochin, and when he was ten, north to Goa, according to the movements of the Portuguese governors. Thus was Pablo trained up to be of his papa's people.

Except that baby Pablo missed the sea. He visited his mother on every feast day, and when he came to man's estate, happily swapped the prickly velvet, lambs'-wool pyjamas, and under-spiced food of the Portuguese for the muslin freedom of the airy-around-the-genitals dhoti and pungent-on-the-tongue fish. In short, this sperm product of a migrant militant became – dah-dah! – a local.

Thereafter, things were more straightforward between Pablo and his creator. In one life he dallied with chronicle-writing for the Mughals; in another he drew cartoons that pilloried the new and even more foreign King Emperor; in another he . . . But here I must stop myself for I gave Bill Bond my word that I would not continually backtrack through these fascinating prior existences. In short, wherever he went, whichever way his peregrinations took him, I was utterly unable to persuade him to fall in love with Leela. Perplexing. He was nice to her, of course; he supplied her with paper for the books she was writing in the age of Humayun; smuggled her food when the British laid siege to her city. But he never fully inhabited all the nuances I had intended with the word 'protector' – not in this life either – as I discovered this evening.

I had done my research beforehand, and had been pleased to learn (from Rat) that Pablo was working as a journalist for a local Delhi paper. Since he always did have a flair for words, a head for puzzles, and since it had come to my attention that in this, her ninth life, Leela did not know that Vyasa had published their poetry in Meera's sole name, nor that he had chosen to suppress the poem that directly alluded to his questionable behaviour, I put two and two together – and generated a noisy local scandal in Vyasa's backyard. Long ago – before Meera's death, during a previous visitation to Delhi – I had heard her recite a poem called 'The Last Dictation'. I copied it down and stashed it away, knowing that the truths it revealed would one day come in handy. How right I was. I bided my time, and then, once I judged that Vyasa's twins were ready for my great denouement, I posted the poem anonymously to Pablo at the newspaper he worked for; and this piece of paper was the catalyst for my drama's unknotting.

To unknot it further, I located Pablo at the wedding, watched his under-the-table antics with little-Bharati, and followed him home to Nizamuddin, where the people of the basti – more attuned to the existence of the supernatural than those at the wedding – fled from my presence, crying of mischievous demons and cantankerous spirits. Once the fire had broken out in the kabariwallahs' settlement, my ploy to contrive a meeting between Leela and her protector was simple. Divining that my beloved needed his help, I shouted 'Fire!' as I stood below Pablo's window, 'Fire! Death! Destruction!' When that provoked no reaction, 'Scoop!' I yelled – and after a moment, his terrace light came on and I could see him standing and staring down through the dark to where the yellow and green flames had turned the streets below his house into a glittering, glimmering spectacle.

chapter 2

On the morning after the wedding, Bharati woke up to find herself staring into the face of a young man she didn't know. She lay very still, a little scared, confused by the deep brown ponds of his eyes. Was he the one from Peshawar?

Then he spoke – 'I'll make some coffee and get the papers from the terrace' – and she frowned, remembering: her brother's reception. Delhi. Last night. Pablo? The memory of what they had done, of how she had behaved, came back to her in swathes of clarity. Did she really do that, at her brother's wedding? Certain images were distinct – the embraces, the writhing, she was sure of that – then they got back to his flat, undressed, got into bed, she remarked how cold it was, and he apologised: no heating, no air conditioning. What happened after that?

'Last night . . .' she said. 'What did we do after we got home?'

'You fell asleep in my arms.'

'I did?'

He got out of bed. She heard him walking outside onto the terrace, and she lay on her side, wrapped in the sheet, thinking. After a while, he returned to the room, dressed in jeans and a shirt, and carrying a tray, with a bundle of newspapers under his arm. She sat up and pulled the sheet prudishly around her breasts as he handed her a glass of coffee. It smelt sweet and very milky and she wrinkled her nose.

'It's south-Indian filter coffee,' he said, 'from Coorg. Try it.'

Bharati took the cup and sipped; and her warm breath made clouds of mist in the morning air.

Pablo was kneeling down in front of his clothes cupboard. She watched as he rifled through it and she felt, to her relief, that she approved of her choice. She hadn't been mistaken. He hadn't been cast in an over-flattering light by the intensity of the evening or her own familiar insatiability. There was something distinctive and particular about him; something to do with the way he moved, or the way he looked at her when he talked.

Pablo looked up and caught her studying him. 'Put this on,' he said, hiding his embarrassment by holding out a much-washed blue kurta. 'It's colder this morning.' He threw her the shirt, and then he opened the bundle of newspapers.

'There was a stampede last night in the basti, and a fire,' he said. 'The people saw a demon and I filed a story. It's been printed.' He held up the paper. 'They cut a bit.'

'A stampede? What kind of stampede?' She pulled on the shirt as she spoke, slithering boldly into it, pleased again to be showing off to him her perfectly naked body.

But Pablo wasn't interested in admiring her legs. He handed her the newspaper and she sat down in bed again, tucking in the covers, turning her eyes to the piece with his byline above it.

Pablo's article described, in quite long sentences, what he called the 'psycho-sociological phenomenon of India's urban poor'. 'This is the second such disturbance to take place in the low-income areas of Delhi this year,' she read. 'The phenomenon is believed to be connected to slum dwellers' mental and economic disen- franchisement from the fast pace of technological progress in the rest of India, and the social inferiority and lifestyle stress that they experience on a daily basis.'

She frowned again, feeling somehow annoyed that these dramatic events had taken place without her knowledge. She stared down at the words he had written, trying to take them in, but soon closed the paper and handed it to him. 'So you went out after we got back?'

He nodded.

'Leaving me here asleep? I can't believe I've come back to this crazy city.'

He nodded again and picked out a guava from the bowl of fruit he had brought in on the tray from the kitchen. He peeled off a thin layer of skin with a knife, cut the guava neatly into eighths, placed four of them on a small plate which he handed across to her, and then he said – in a hurt but curious kind of voice – 'What have you got against Delhi?'

She shrugged as she bit into a piece of guava. 'Take your pick. The stupid politicians, the unfairnesses, the caste system, the traffic' – she waved her hand towards the window – 'the drain. It's endless.'

'And your answer to all that is just to get up and leave?' He smiled at her. 'It's your country, Bharati, and you don't even see the good things.'

'What good things?'

'The people, the history, the energy, the culture.'

'Oh *really*,' said Bharati, sounding scornful.

'After you finish your studies, you should come back here to work, really get to know it.'

'And you know it so very well yourself, do you?'

He nodded. 'Thanks to my job.'

'Ah, yes, your wonderful job. And last night, during the fire and the stampede, did you have time to reflect on the people, the history, the culture?'

'Yes,' he said. 'And guess who I met.'

She rolled her eyes. 'I have no idea. Lord Krishna.'

'Leela. Leela Sharma.'

'Who?'

'She's married to Hariprasad Sharma, your brother's new chacha.'

'What was she doing there?'

'Looking for something, I think she said. She's an interesting woman. Not what you would expect.'

'You mean, not as terrible as the rest of Sunita's family.'

He smiled and didn't answer. Then he said, 'I believe they're childless. They've come back to India because Hari has made Sunita's brother the heir to his entire fortune.'

'Wow,' Bharati said sarcastically.

Pablo got to his feet and came to sit next to her on the bed, his long legs in their blue jeans stretched out before him, so that even through the bed covers she could feel the warmth of his body. She thought for one moment that he was about to kiss her, but instead he began talking again.

'You know,' he said, 'that Sunita's father works for one of the worst right-wing think tanks?'

She sighed. 'Yes.'

'Well, they've come up with some spooky ideas in the past, but the latest thing is genes. They want to identify an Aryan gene in Indians. They think that genetics will allow them both to single out the true Hindu elite of this country, whose origins go back to the priests who first composed the Vedas three thousand years ago, and to reintegrate into the Hindu family those Indians who call themselves Muslim or Christian today but whose ancestors were converted – forcibly, they believe – during the past thirteen hundred years. They want to rescue their long-lost Arya brethren.'

'Don't be silly.'

'It's true. But the point is Shiva Prasad believes Ash is going to do it for them. He thinks Ash is going to lead a private research project into the Aryan—'

'That's ridiculous, how can he think that? I don't believe you.'

'You've spent too long out of India. This kind of thing happens nowadays. The ruling party funds this sort of project. They pay palaeontologists to prove that horses were indigenous to India – when actually everyone else thinks they were probably brought in with migrating tribes from Central Asia – and fake archaeologists to—'

'Yes I know,' she interrupted again. 'But what's this got to do with Ash? He isn't doing that. His project is to do with blindness, and forensics; he's looking at how disease runs in families.'

'Ash told me that Sunita's father was encouraging him to undertake a study to discover the genetic purity of Hindus. That he could secure the funding from Party coffers.'

'And what did Ash say?'

'That's the point, I don't know. The man is his father-in-law, he's married his daughter, how blunt do you think Ash is capable of being?'

Bharati laughed. 'Ash doesn't need to be blunt,' she said, 'he can be *scientific*. Believe me, nobody has any idea what he's on about when he describes his research. I have no idea and I'm his twin. He could say anything to the man to get him off his back.' But she didn't feel as confident as she sounded. She didn't want to show how hurt she was by Pablo's insinuation that Ash would get himself involved in his father-in-law's politics. It was one thing to dispense criticism of one's twin; another thing to hear him criticised. Pablo, however, wouldn't stop talking.

'That's his university work,' he said. 'You ask him about this other idea, see what he says.'

'Have you asked him about it?'

'At first. Then we had a disagreement and stopped discussing it.'

Bharati made a sound of disgust. 'It's nonsense.'

She lay down and pulled the sheet over her head.

'The worse thing is,' he went on, 'that his father-in-law boasts about this gene project to the Party—'

But she had pulled the sheet tight around her head so that only her face was showing and stuck her fingers in her ears. 'I can't listen any more,' she sang out.

His face broke into a smile. 'You look like an Afghan lady in a burqa,' he said, and then he leant down and at last he kissed her, and she was just beginning to feel appeased when he said, 'I've been wondering how he made his money so fast, this Hariprasad, Sunita's uncle.'

She sighed. 'And?'

'There must be something he did to get where he is. His family background is very modest.'

'Some people just work hard,' Bharati observed, growing annoyed now with his sanctimonious observations. 'Rich people aren't by definition corrupt.'

'But there's his brother's RSS links. I just have a feeling: that it may go beyond the usual shoddy employment practice, the fake account holdings, blah blah blah.'

Bharati shrugged and sat up, pulling the sheet off her head. 'Give me some more coffee. I really don't want to think about Sunita's family.'

What she was thinking was how annoying everything was; how stubborn her father was about her work, how silly Ash was for marrying Sunita. The only good thing right now was that after breakfast, Pablo and she would go back to bed, and forget this nonsense about her brother's new family and his scientific research.

But Pablo continued to talk, leaning up on one elbow and looking at her; and she understood finally that this was his big drawback as a boyfriend: he talked too much. She was used to being the loquacious one. She was used to stunning her boyfriends with her eloquence and erudition. It was annoying to be upstaged. It was irritating not to be bathed in constant adulation. 'Remember I said I met his wife Leela in the basti last night?' Pablo was saying. 'Well, she was the one who fainted at the wedding. And it happened just after you climbed up onto the stage. I was watching. She took one look at you and fainted—'

'Maybe she did. I didn't notice. Probably her blouse was too tight.'

'So last night I realised something that I've been wondering about for a while.' He looked embarrassed. 'After I was sent your mother's poem I began to—'

'*What?*' Bharati had sensed that Pablo was holding something back and now she saw why.

'I was sent your mother's poem,' he said in a voice of protest and innocence. 'The envelope was addressed to me, at the newspaper. I did the research and wrote the story.'

'Wait. So you slept with me as a subject of research?'

'No!' he said.

'Isn't there some ethical code preventing journalists from doing that? Shouldn't I report you?'

Pablo got up from the bed, picking up the two coffee cups and placing them on the tray. 'Don't be silly,' he said eventually. 'I didn't sleep with you for that.'

'But you are researching my mother's poetry?'

'Yes.' He regarded her for a moment. Then he said: 'You *did* read the new poem that was printed in the paper?'

'No.' She felt a tiny prick of anxiety in addition to her crossness. 'My father mentioned it but I haven't seen it yet.'

She tried to sound nonchalant, but as she watched him walk over to his desk, open a drawer and take out an envelope, she felt queasy. Supposing it *was* one of her mother's precious poems? And when he handed her the envelope, she felt a sudden resentment against her all-knowing lover, and swivelled round in bed, so that her face was hidden from Pablo as she read. She pulled out the single sheet of creased and folded paper, inscribed in faded ink by a hand she didn't know.

THE LAST DICTATION

Book one, a hundred chapters in,
Vyasa tells how his bastard
Birth, his mother's marriage with a
Brahmin king, and the princes' death,

Leaves the line without an heir. But
His fish-born mother, resourceful,
Has a plan. She summons her dead
Son's pretty young widows and says:

Vyasa is here: your husband's
Hermit brother. Go. Lie with him.
Do exactly as I say. And
The two sisters, fearful, obey.

But seeing the seer, hairy and
Naked, in her bed, the first girl
Shuts her eyes in fright. Vyasa
Is displeased: *Due to your error,*
Lady, your baby will be blind.
His mother sends the second girl.

She, too, turns pallid with disgust.
Again, the seer blames his lover

For the child's flaws: *And your son*
Will be ashen, pale, wan as death.
The third time, then, the sisters take
Revenge. They dispatch a servant

In their place, dressed in royal robes,
Who caresses and kisses him
And charms him with her ardent moans.
Vyasa, soothed by her pleasure,

Bestows a boon: *Your son will be*
The wisest of men. And Meera
Smiled and said: *Look, my own sister,*
Learn from the fate of these women.

As we write, defend our children,
This last poem is our weapon,
A sisterhood of blood and ink:
Proof of our collaboration.

Santiniketan, November 1979

It was strange – a little menacing – the exact culmination of the
process she had noted in *The Lalita Series*, of a gradual ceding of
the nonchalant aura of youth to something more sinister. Why
hadn't her father showed it to her yesterday? She read it again,
and when at last she looked round, she could feel Pablo's eyes on
her. But her mind was too full of the images within it, and of the

peculiarity of its discovery, and on top of that of the tenseness of his expectation, to formulate a ready opinion. Casually, she put the poem aside, and leaning forward, fished out a packet of cigarettes from her bag and lit one as she walked over to the door that led onto the terrace. She sat down on a stool by the open door, her bare legs cold after the warmth of the bed.

Pablo was impatient. 'Well?' he said. 'What do you think?'

She shrugged. 'My mother could have been a great poet.'

'But don't you think it's weird?' he said. 'The subject matter and the tone?'

'For fuck's sake,' Bharati said, 'I'm the one researching the poetry. Leave it to me, OK? It might be a fake.'

'I don't think it is,' he insisted. 'Look at those lines about sister-hood and writing.'

'What about them?'

'It's obvious to me that Meera was writing the poems with someone else. She had a collaborator –'

'Oh, *fuck* off, Pablo,' Bharati said.

'– and that her poetic collaborator was her sister—'

'Don't be ridiculous,' Bharati said, getting up and stubbing out the half-smoked cigarette in a plantpot on the terrace. She felt furious suddenly with Pablo for making her think about things that were upsetting, and for the evident ease with which he had discovered things she should have known.

He spoke in a rush. 'One of the senior editors on the paper was at college with your mother in Calcutta. He told me she had an adopted sister—'

'I know.'

'You knew?'

'Of course I did. You think there's been some conspiracy of silence not to tell us? Don't be stupid.' She had known of the sister in her mother's past ever since she could remember: an orphan brought to Calcutta from the village in a kind of charitable act by her maternal grandfather – that was how her father's mother, their Dadi, had put it. An orphan given everything a child could want – and who nevertheless turned against the family when she grew up. She had married, moved away, and all contact with her had been lost. Nobody ever spoke of this unfortunate episode in the family's history. The twins had always understood that silence and respected it. There was no way of tracing her, and no point. Their mother wouldn't have wanted it.

'So you'll also know,' Pablo said, 'that there was some falling-out after your mother was married. The sister married and emigrated to America.'

'And?'

'And guess what her husband was called?'

He stared at her defiantly but she had no answer.

'Hari Sharma.'

'Hari Sharma?' She couldn't help the look of surprise and horror on her face.

'Leela Sharma is your aunt,' he went on, a look of triumph on his.

'Right, well, I've had enough of this crap,' Bharati said, shaking her sari out from the heap where she had left it at the bottom of the bed. 'I haven't got time to listen to your paranoid rantings.' She pulled on the blouse and did up the hooks. 'It's Ash's wedding lunch today—'

He interrupted: 'I'm going to Calcutta, I can't come to the lunch, there's a story they want me to—' but she spoke over him.

'And I have to go there and be a good sister.' She stepped into the petticoat, pulled it tight around her waist, and began winding herself into the sari. 'You know nothing about my family, or my mother, or her poems.'

'This woman Leela Sharma is your mother's sister. I asked her about it last night when we met and she didn't deny it. Think about it, Bharati.'

'Leave me alone,' she shouted, and grabbing her bag from the table, marched out of the flat, slamming the door behind her as hard as she could, hoping with this action to instil fear and repentance into the flippant heart of this over-talkative young man who presumed to dictate to her about her mother's poetic creation and her brother's scientific activity.

chapter 3

In her house at the other end of Nizamuddin West, Urvashi Ahmed stood in the kitchen feeling giddy with resolutions. She would be a good person, she thought as she took the packet of tea out of the cupboard. She would use this opportunity offered by the dreadful fate of young Aisha, she told herself as she turned on the gas, to do something meaningful with her life – to do something for someone else. She would get to know her husband's family, she murmured as she took the tea and parathas through to the dining room, where Feroze was sitting and reading his morning paper as usual. She couldn't say any of this to him, of course. She watched him as he sipped his tea and silently turned the pages. After he left, she prepared a new pan of tea, and fried some more parathas, and took them through to Aisha in the guest room.

When Urvashi pushed open the door, she saw that Aisha was awake, but lying absolutely still in bed. Only the young maid's eyes moved, following Urvashi as she put the tray down on the table by the window and drew the curtains. *Poor little thing*, Urvashi thought; and then she remembered how she, like Aisha, was alone in this world – abandoned by her parents, her sister, her schoolfriends, with only this frail little maid servant for company.

'Where is Humayun?' Aisha asked suddenly, interrupting the dramatic reverie.

'Humayun?' Urvashi answered in surprise. 'But it's Diwali soon, he must be on leave?' She looked at her maid's distraught face. Her responsibility now was to take Aisha's mind off what had happened to her last night. And so, after Aisha had eaten a little breakfast, Urvashi led her straight upstairs to her bedroom where she threw open the walk-in wardrobe and began pulling out clothes. 'Take this!' she exclaimed girlishly, draping Aisha in a pale blue georgette salwar kameez. '*Mashallah*,' she said, enjoying the taste of the Islamic word on her tongue, 'you look so fancy!' The suit had been stitched by the Muslim tailor in the market, who, in the weeks just after they moved into the colony, when Feroze was working especially hard, and before the servants were hired, was Urvashi's only real contact with the outside world. It made her feel lonely just to look at it. 'Or what about this?' she said, holding up a burnt-orange raw silk suit with blood-red velvet appliqué work at the cuffs. 'It comes from that boutique called Nirvana, the one in Greater Kailash N-Block market . . .' She looked round. The girl was standing with the blue suit draped lifelessly over one shoulder, her eyes filled with tears.

Urvashi responded with bustling practicality. She led Aisha downstairs again to the guest room, demonstrated how the shower worked, ran a bucket of hot water for her just in case, and then she waited impatiently in the hall, where she checked that the doctor's prescription was in her handbag, and wondered which chemist to go to, and also how to get there. Apart from the two of them, the house was empty – Feroze, as usual, was at the printing press. Urvashi could have called a taxi. But instead, when Aisha appeared, wearing the new sky-blue clothes, her hair all wet, Urvashi took the car keys out of the bowl on the hall table.

She had been taught to drive four years ago by Feroze, when they were classfellows, and courting. Feroze would borrow his father's car – a long white Cortina – and they would drive south together, out of Delhi, past the towering, curving sharpness of the Qutb Minar, past the familiar squat outlines of the Chhattarpur Mandir, and over the border, into Haryana. It was like eloping. Only after they were married, and Feroze took over the family business and no longer had any time to devote to obtaining his wife's licence, did his father insist on her hiring a driver; his Hindu daughter-in-law was far too scatterbrained to drive a car. But she had been good at driving once and had always enjoyed it. Urvashi felt a rush of excitement as she led Aisha outside to where the car was parked next to the house, pulled off the cover as if she was a magician performing a really clever trick, and clicked the electronic button that pushed up all the locks.

Holding her breath, Urvashi sat in the driving seat and switched on the ignition. Carefully, slowly, she reversed the car out from under the tree, straightened it up, changed gear, and moved away down the lane that skirted the edge of F-Block. It was as easy now, she found to her relief, as it always had been – it was such a pleasure, after such a long time. What freedom. It felt like flying.

She hadn't yet decided which chemist was best; the one in Nizamuddin was out of the question, obviously. She considered going to Sunder Nagar but as the car took them up over the flyover, she realised that they were on the wrong road, and at the last minute before the turning, decided on Khan Market. She veered left through the traffic and when they reached the market, turned right without indicating, so that the guard waved his stick and shouted at her. But she was unperturbed, and parked on the edge of the road in the middle of the taxi rank; and although the drivers honked at her angrily she remained serene, getting out of the car without trapping her gauzy headscarf in the door, and taking her handbag and Aisha with her.

At the chemist's shop the girl refused to go in, waiting for Urvashi on the pavement with lowered eyes. There was a crowd of women inside but the pharmacist handed over a paper cup of water, along with the pill, and Urvashi bustled importantly out again and made Aisha swallow it then and there without delay.

'Would you like an ice cream? Or some cake?' she asked, feeling quite overcome with the scale of the expedition and her heroic role in it, and it was only then that she glanced down and saw the tears on Aisha's face.

'I am so sorry,' she whispered, and repeated, in a tone she had heard in many Bollywood films, 'I am *so* sorry, Aisha.'

She hurried her back through the market, past all the smart ladies with their fragrant hair and lipstick smiles, clutching the hand of the sobbing girl. A policeman was standing by their car but Urvashi pulled out her purse and shoved some money at him and bundled Aisha into the car without anybody stopping her. She drove all the way down the Lodhi Road, and only as she reached the roundabout near the basti, did she remember that she was supposed to have taken Aisha into the police station to give a statement.

Urvashi parked lopsidedly in front of the police station, gave the keys to a parking attendant, and led Aisha inside. They waited for a long time. Eventually, they were shown into a small room where a constable took down Aisha's version of events. 'Do you know who raped you?' they asked several times. 'Did you recognise him?' And when Aisha repeatedly shook her head, they at last got angry and said, 'What about this man Humayun?' Aisha began crying, and Urvashi spoke up: 'He is her cousin, our driver, why are you asking all these questions?'

The inspector wrote out a note for Urvashi, telling her to return with Aisha tomorrow for a meeting with the clinical psychologist. Then he took Urvashi aside, so that Aisha wouldn't hear, and said to her: 'Madam, she is underage. We need her family's permission to make a full physical examination and to lodge an FIR.'

'FIR?' asked Urvashi.

'First Information Report,' said the inspector in English. 'After that,' he resumed in Hindi, 'we take the victim to a government hospital for a medical check-up.' His voice became more hushed. 'Usually hymen based.' He wiggled his finger. 'Doctor judges whether hymen is intact or ruptured. Presence of semen, abrasions, state of genital area, mental distress, condition of apparel – often difficult to judge so long after the event. If there is semen, maybe a DNA test is possible.'

'You'll find out his genes?'

He nodded approvingly. 'Ninety days elapse. Case goes to Lower Court. Rape is a state case, victim will be granted government lawyer. After first hearing, with deposition of witness list, et cetera, process can take three years. Accused if under trial and not on bail, goes to Tihar Jail. Victim is a minor: any type of intercourse is an offence. If girl's family decides to file a case they will have to do it quickly. But bear in mind trauma for the girl. Such things are a dishonour. I don't need to tell you about comments being cast on girl's character by unfortunate mishaps such as these. Very rare for victims to receive compensation.'

Urvashi, standing in the doorway, held her stomach protectively with one hand.

The inspector went over the basic facts again. 'First lodge FIR. To do that, speak to the family. She is minor. Parental assent to effect that case can go to court – essential. Provide doctor's medical examination, and check-up and all from gynaecologist. Then get statement from the girl. That is most important.'

Urvashi put a hand to her forehead.

'And hurry,' he went on, 'we have a suspect.'

'You do?'

He ushered both women out: 'Strictly confidential police information.'

chapter 4

At first, Ash Chaturvedi didn't notice that his wife's parents hadn't come to the wedding lunch. He stood in the Rose Garden at the India International Centre, dressed in the embroidered white kurta pyjama that Sunita had selected for him, holding a glass of beer – and trying to keep it together.

In the midday sunshine, the Rose Garden was crammed with people: all the professors and activists and teachers and writers and visual artists and documentary filmmakers of his father's acquaintance whom Ash had grown up with. Dressed in colourful cotton khadhi, drinking beer, eating ruddy chunks of chicken tikka, they chattered nonstop, ruefully praising their one-maximum-two children, ruefully complaining of their two-maximum-three servants, eagerly exchanging notes on the small coterie of private schools to which they sent their offspring, passionately denouncing the Hindu-right government, generally expounding on minority religious culture, and specifically disavowing adherence to any faith bar the socialist-feminist-atheism of their own milieu. Not one of them, in short, was crassly middle class; nobody's English diction was lacking; there was not a soul here who believed all the flim-flam about Lord Ram's temple at Ayodhya needing to be rebuilt over the demolished mosque, a view that the Hindu-led government was endorsing. Ash had already talked to three of his father's colleagues from the university and exchanged pleasantries with a range of cousins and aunties, and was now being lectured to by an acquaintance of his father's – an old man with a thick grey beard who ran a charity monitoring educational facilities in the slums of Delhi – on the dangers of the current government's attitude to Muslims and other minorities, and the monstrous things that they might try to do, legislatively or otherwise, under cover of the hysteria emanating from America. And thus, had he stopped to think about it, Ash would have understood entirely why Sunita's parents had not put in an appearance at such a godless gathering.

But he had no time to think of it. He had just witnessed the arrival of the one other person – aside from Sunita – who didn't belong here: her brother Ram. He saw Ram making his way slowly across the lawns towards him and tried to correct the stricken, fearful expression on his face. But it was no good. The look had taken possession of his features since the early hours of the morning.

It would be fair to say that all Ash Chaturvedi's hyperactivity, the exuberance of his wedding night, had disappeared at dawn: the moment he awoke and found himself sharing a bed with his wife's elder brother. He had hidden his face in his arms for a moment and then – praying that Ram wouldn't wake – stumbled out of the door, pulling on his crumpled groom's attire as he ran, not forgetting to grab his glasses, and arrived at the bridal suite where he found, to his great relief, that Sunita was still asleep.

Standing by the bed, Ash had looked down at his wife and wondered if he had made a huge mistake, marrying this innocent young woman whose opinions he had helped to form – but whose kisses he barely knew. He hoped that the strange ethereal gasps he had heard himself uttering in the arms of her brother were some kind of trick played by the body on the mind, that his marriage was the truth. He hoped that the fearsome, exhilarating feeling he had felt last night with Ram – of something fluttering inside him trying to get out (a bird, he had thought, a bird flying higher and higher through a dark space, soaring optimistically upwards to where the air was thinner but the light hovered) – he hoped that those thoughts and feelings were a sham. But he wasn't sure.

Despairing at himself, he had walked over to the hotel window and pulled back the curtain. From this angle, at this height, Delhi was a mass of green trees and gardens, with only some tower blocks in the very far distance. He breathed deeply, soothed by the sight. It was as if he and his wife were sleeping in the middle of a forest.

His wife. Now that he thought about it, everything to do with this marriage had been to avoid one thing – to cleanse himself of this Internet romance, and the illegal, concomitant desires that had troubled him so much. Sunita had provided the solution. She had mentioned marriage in her innocence: and suddenly he saw the way. This was how he would exorcise his inappropriate obsession with the sweet chatroom friend who called himself Man-God.

Ash closed the curtain and returned to the bed, watching Sunita as she slept, the breaths she took dilating her nostrils slightly, her eyelashes fluttering. After a moment, he undressed, pulled back the sheet and got into bed beside her. She made a slight, protesting noise in her sleep, but he inched forward nevertheless until his body was cradling hers. She was soft, and smelt faintly of something foreign and flowery. He put an arm over her, feeling her naked skin touching his, and wondered how he had been foolish enough to get himself into this situation.

Ash had been embarking on his Ph.D. in Genetics when his father first introduced him to Sunita. 'What do you think of her?' his father had asked that evening; and Ash had to admit that the librarian was very nice. 'She seems to enjoy your company,' his father commented the following week at dinner, 'more than mine, at least'; and Ash looked up in surprise: he wasn't used to girls enjoying his company. But the concept pleased him; and in the weeks that followed, he began to notice that this neat, quiet girl did seem to listen when he spoke; she looked up when he came home from the lab; she brought him tea on the terrace, preparing it herself (she said the maid didn't do it right); and he, in his turn, began to appreciate Sunita. With her quietness and sincerity, she was quite unlike the other young women he had known in his life – the sharp-tongued girls from school, his witty cousins, his dazzlingly confident sister. And he began to notice a certain feeling in the air when they were in the room together; he felt with no lessening of surprise how sensitively she continued to respond to his most mundane statements. He began to sense that here was a mind that he could shape, even. Obliquely, he sounded out her politics; asked questions designed to reveal her cerebral acuity; gently examined her on culture (Indian and foreign), on religion (Hinduism and the rest), on her role as a wife and mother. After some months passed, he was gratified to notice that the opinions Sunita espoused were becoming more sophisticated; that the books she now read were of a higher grade than those she had talked of when they first met. He came to think of her as the original innocent; a mythical Sita to his imperfect Ram.

On the day when Ash went to ask for Sunita's hand in marriage, Mr Sharma brought up the question of locating an 'Aryan gene in India's upper-caste population'. The way he phrased it, Ash reflected afterwards, sounded very much like a requirement.

'There has been very little work done on it as yet,' Ash said, trying not to look ignorant. He racked his brain for whatever it was they were taught in the first year about early genetic studies of population; 'In the nineteen thirties, of course, Haldane was looking at the prehistoric migration out of India. He proved it by looking at blood groups.'

Mr Sharma had thumped the desk. 'Fantastic!' he exclaimed.

'But since that work was done so long ago,' Ash went on, feeling rather surprised at how delighted this prospective father-in-law seemed with his credentials – didn't they generally want you to be a doctor or an engineer rather than an ill-paid researcher? – 'obviously it would need updating—'

'Wonderful!' said Mr Sharma; and he began talking about the historical references to the Aryans in India's ancient Sanskrit texts. 'If you just prove this Arya gene with science,' he said, pacing around the room, 'I can secure you funding for further—'

'Oh, no,' Ash had interrupted, 'I can conduct all the necessary research as an adjunct to my Ph.D.'

But Mr Sharma was no longer listening. He was shaking Ash's hand, patting him on the back, and sitting down again in something of a flurry. Then he exclaimed, in clear English, 'Absolutely marvellous! Bravo!'

Ash had already chosen two of his Ph.D. topics. There was to be a chapter on gene defects as a cause of disease: he was looking at the degenerative eye condition, Retinitis Pigmentosa; another chapter using Short Tandem Repeats for rapid forensic applications – the identification of individuals – which he was doing in association with a lab in west Delhi; and meanwhile everyone at CBT was talking about a new national 'mapping project' in which institutions across the country were collaborating on a countrywide database of genotypes. If he pursued a line of enquiry related to this in a third chapter, Ash thought, it would give him plenty of material for publications. And so he began to consider exploring whether there was a marker on the genome that could be traced back to an ancient Aryan people.

Mr Sharma was very happy with the tentative steps Ash was taking in this direction. Whenever the two men met, the elder would talk enthusiatically to the younger about Vedic references to fair skin-colour and intelligence – in Sanskrit, 'arya' meant 'noble'. He argued that Ash only had to identify a *nobility* gene in him, Shiva Prasad, to hit on the elusive question of who in India was Arya and who wasn't. He said that the Sharma family's fair skin colour (the women always made good marriages because of it) proved that they were Aryas as distinct from the dark-skinned Dravidian population (mercifully confined mostly to the south of India) but Shiva Prasad was well-read enough to know that skin-colour alone wasn't enough: he needed the genes to prove it.

Much as Ash wanted to please Shiva Prasad, his research didn't provide such easy answers. To gain some elucidation on the matter he tried to broach the subject with his father. His father, however, answered in professorial mode – saying something complicated and incomprehensible about the Indo-European language group and the names of rivers common to Iran and India. So Ash brought up the subject with his schoolfriend, Pablo, who had returned to Delhi from Bangalore four years ago, absolutely brimming over with history and sociology and innumerable abstruse theories about India and its place in the world.

Unfortunately, Pablo wasn't at all impressed by the parameters of Ash's gene proposal. 'I don't understand. Are you looking at an Aryan migration into India or out? Where do you think the Aryans came from?'

'You tell me,' said Ash, feeling confused, and pushing his glasses back onto his nose with his finger.

'Some people say Iran, others the Caspian sea, or the Middle

East,' said Pablo. 'But as far as I can gather from my reading, the evidence is highly contested either way, which is why it is so easy for people of one particular persuasion to hijack the debate. The problem with your contribution is that in order to prove which way this so-called Aryan people went, you'll have to look at the DNA of population groups from Europe to India at least as far east as Bengal – wherever the Indo-European language group stretches, in fact. Whereas you are telling me that your study will focus on a maximum of ten Indian individuals. What this will prove I have no idea.'

'I am trying to identify an historic people,' Ash said in a tiny voice.

'Why?' asked Pablo.

'For intellectual interest,' Ash said, his face growing hot with displeasure and unhappiness.

'All that will happen,' Pablo replied, 'is your research will play into the hands of the nutcases currently running the country.'

'But isn't it worth finding out for sure? Sunita's father thinks he is a pure Indian Aryan.'

Pablo laughed. 'What has he got to do with it?'

'He's really interested in my research.'

'Ash,' Pablo tapped his head with his hand. 'Sunita is very nice – but believe me, her father is a crackpot. You know the kind of unscientific rubbish those people speak, surely. They condemn as anti-Indian anyone who thinks the Aryans might not have been indigenous to this country.'

'You just told me the evidence goes either way,' Ash said.

'I also said that there are groups in this country who use that extreme complexity to befuddle people and tell them that the debate is cut and dried when it's not. Shiva Prasad is linked to—'

But Ash, feeling defensive about his betrothed and her family, was no longer listening. To his own relief, after months of confusion and internal debate, things were made very simple one warm afternoon when he broached the issue with his supervisor at the lab. Instead of throwing up his hands in horror, as Pablo had done, the man sat back, unwrapped a boiled sweet and sucked on it for a while. 'Interesting, very interesting,' he murmured at last. 'I suppose you could try to prove the Aryan migration by examining data from, say, east India, Pakistan, Russia, Germany . . . Though if you find nothing conclusive – and given your expansive canvas, such a thing is not unlikely – the right-wingers will use it to prove that this Aryan gene is indigenous, of course—'

The statements petered out, and Ash realised that the man was thinking. They sat together in silence, and finally his supervisor said: 'I like it. Go ahead with this Aryan idea. If you find something juicy, we'll send it to one of the journals.'

Ash was pleased – relieved – and he threw himself into the work. To his father-in-law's delight, Ash took blood samples from each member of the Sharma family, subjecting the samples to routine forensic analysis, and adding them to his population database for the Aryan chapter. From then on, whenever Mr Sharma asked him what he was up to, and how the research was going, Ash murmured something equivocal about history and something specific about genetics – imitating to perfection the manner of his own supervisor – and this kept Sunita's father happy. No spanners were thrown into the works of the wedding preparations.

'Ash!' said two voices at once, and Ash saw two people converging on him at the same time from the other side of the Rose Garden – Bharati, dressed in a heavily embroidered pink and red salwar kameez, her eyes made up with kohl, and Ram, looking sexy and nonchalant, clad all in white but for a long indigo cotton scarf draped over one shoulder.

'Hello,' Ash said to both of them at once and neither in particular, hoping that his consternation didn't show, presuming – praying – that Ram, who had caressed him so lovingly that night, would know how to behave with him in public. He thought to himself, as he had thought during the night, *This is Man-God in the flesh*, and the idea that the mystery man he had Internet-chatted with almost every evening for a year was here in front of him gave him a whoozy, disorientated feeling. He wished he could get away from this party, he longed for it to be over, he felt incapable of making chitchat. He had no idea how he was going to get through the next four days until he and Sunita left for their honeymoon in Goa – a departure that had been delayed until after his birthday, so that they could attend the opening of the Living Sanskrit Akademi, which was a major event for his father. He didn't want to talk to anyone. But Bharati was saying something to him with all her usual intensity.

'Ash!' she repeated. 'I've got to speak to you. Privately.' And she smiled sweetly at the old man with the beard, and glared at Ram, clearly expecting them both to get the message and disappear.

The old man obediently melted away. Ram, however, was not to be put off by the rudeness of his lover's sister.

'Namaskar,' he said to her, placing his hands together respect-fully – and also pursing his lips, so that Ash couldn't help but remember the pleasures and traumas those very lips had so recently unleashed in his being. 'It's so good to meet you finally. Sunita has told me you are living in London, that you have fled our despic-able city. I imagine you living in a large house in . . . Chelsea.' He smiled at her, knowing full well that such a vision was impossible. 'Or Mayfair, or Hampstead—'

'Please give us a moment,' Bharati said, no longer smiling. 'I need to speak to my brother in private, it's important.'

'Oh,' Ram said, 'of course.' But he wasn't taking her seriously.

'I mean it,' Bharati said, uncompromising in her rudeness.

'Yes, madam,' Ram said, sounding put out for a moment, but he immediately recovered his poise. 'Shall I fetch us all some drinks?' And he pointed to the bar at the other end of the garden, where three waiters in turbans were presiding over a display of wine bottles, beer and whisky, and gave Ash a wink as he departed.

'Oh my god,' Bharati said, taking Ash by the arm and steering him over to the far end of the garden, 'that boy is dreadful, poor you. But whatever are you thinking? What are these rumours?'

Ash's face went hot, and inside he felt sick and cold, as if icy hands were gripping his entrails. So she had found out. Did everybody know?

'It's not like that,' he began miserably, staring at the drink in his hand. 'It's nothing. We were just fooling around. It's no harm. Have you told Sunita?'

'I don't give a fuck about Sunita,' Bharati said. 'These people are dangerous, Ash, and this is history – or the perception of history. How can you compromise your work by having any dealings with them? Isn't science supposed to be above politics?'

Ash looked at his twin, puzzled.

'Surely Father has taught you that,' she went on. 'You can't meddle with this pseudo-stuff. Indigenous Aryan genes – that's what Pablo says. What are you researching this nonsense for? Did Sunita make you?'

'Oh,' Ash said, relieved, and smiled.

'What are you smiling at?' she demanded. 'What's so funny?'

'Pablo's got the wrong idea. Actually, my research is looking at it from the other direction – I just haven't got round to explaining that to Sunita's father yet.'

She looked up at him through narrowed eyes. 'I hope to God you are telling the truth.'

'Of course I am.' He felt such relief that her anger was directed at the silly project about Aryan genes, and not at his friendship with his bride's brother, that he smiled again and pinched her arm.

'You great big deceiver,' she said. 'How badly you've misled Sunita's father! It's really quite funny. Anyway, where is he? Didn't he show? I can't see him.' And then, before Ash had time to answer, she said, 'And where's our father anyhow?'

'Baba? I don't know.'

'Ash?' she said, suddenly all serious.

'Yes?'

'Did you know that Ma's sister was in Delhi?'

Ash could feel a headache coming on. The twists and turns of his sister's conversation were making him feel vertiginous – and all the while, out of the corner of his eye, he could see Ram chatting up one of the waiters. He was trying to think who on earth Bharati might be talking about when she exclaimed again. 'There he is, the bastard,' she said. 'I'm going to fetch him.' And she pointed over to the far side of the garden where their father was talking to a young woman – one of his students, probably – who was looking up at him adoringly. Bharati shook her head in disgust. 'These women get younger and younger. He's such a bloody flirt.' And without waiting for a response from Ash, she made her way purposefully, scornfully, across the garden towards their parent.

Ash, left alone at last, felt miserable again. Though he was pleased to have his twin back in Delhi, he wondered why she always had to exaggerate minor things. It was *his* wedding and here she was making dramatic pronouncements about their mother's sister. Presumably she meant the adopted village sister that their mother was supposed to have fallen out with before they were born. Ash thought of his long-dead mother, whom he knew of exclusively from photographs: smiling out at him from the black-and-white print that hung on the stairs at home. He wished that she was here, by his side, so that he had somebody in his family to discuss his problems with. He couldn't tell Bharati, who would laugh at him for loving a man like Ram, the type she considered 'dreadful'. He couldn't tell his father about the deception he was practising on Sunita. But he had to decide this thing with Ram, one way or the other. It couldn't go on as it was. And how was he to decide on his own? His mother, he thought sadly to himself, would have been the one to confide in.

Ash looked round the garden for his wife and caught sight of her, standing talking to a man whom Ash knew painted enormous male nudes for a living. She had dressed herself up so carefully this morning: in a bridal-red silk sari, with red colour on her lips and special thick red bangles all up her hennaed forearms, and the sight of her marital attire touched him. A sudden rush of tenderness flowed through him. He pushed his glasses back on his nose. The very sight of her made him feel calm and relaxed, whereas the sight of her brother made him shiver with excitement. Which feeling was right? Which one was better?

He walked over to join her. 'Where's your father?' he asked, after greeting the painter (who had been telling her his theory about the predominance of the lingam in Hindu iconography; 'Lord Shiva's phallus has prevailed,' he said, 'over the rest of the body'). Sunita looked like she was about to cry. 'I don't know,' she whispered, and again he felt the same tenderness, and taking her hand in his own, said, in his kindest voice, 'Shall we go and ring them? Most probably they are stuck at home. Some emergency may have happened.'

chapter 5

Vyasa returned, exhausted, from his son's wedding lunch. He settled his mother in her favourite chair by the garden window, dismissed the former ayah who had come round to ask him to attend, today of all days, to some insignificant business of hers, and then, to soothe his nerves (and because the coffee they served at IIC was undrinkable), he took the packet of expensive, imported coffee beans out of the fridge, ground some in the machine, and when the silver pot was coughing its delicious aroma into the air, carried it upstairs, so that the whole house was strewn with fragrance. He pushed open the library door to the terrace, sat down at his low stone table and sighed. It wasn't meant to be like this – surely he didn't deserve this fate – being cross-questioned by his own daughter on the subject of Leela Bose.

But Bharati had been ruthless. She took no heed of social decorum. She had pushed her way through the party to where he was standing (discussing something important with one of the prettier MA students from the faculty), and said, straight off, without even introducing herself, 'Guess what I learnt this morning?'

'What?' he said, and smiled apologetically at the student for this rude interruption.

'That one of Ash's new aunties, Sunita's uncle's wife, is our mother's sister!' And she looked up at him with disingenuous frankness. 'Did you know that?'

So, the moment had come – and Vyasa wasn't prepared for it. For several seconds he was lost for words.

After Meera died, both he and his mother knew – without ever discussing it – that they shouldn't hide from the children the fact that Meera had a sister, but that it would be better not to tell them anything about her, either. Concealing her existence completely would have created its own drama: Ash and Bharati were bound to find out from a schoolfriend of their mother's, or a cousin in Calcutta. The much wiser policy was to let them know of her in a vague way, but to give them to understand that the estrangement was permanent, as unfortunately occurred sometimes (not uncommonly) in families, even in ones as loving as theirs. Of course, Vyasa had steeled himself for questions and curiosity. But somehow they had never come. The twins had bought the story – which, after all, wasn't in itself a lie – and that was that. They had more than enough to ask, and dream about, concerning their dead mother. They had no interest in her long-lost sister.

How ridiculous then that, even though the inevitable meeting between the twins and their aunt was of his own making, Vyasa was still caught without a ready retort when his daughter looked up at him and said – something in her face betraying that she knew more than she was letting on – 'And, what's more, Ma wasn't the only author of her poems; she wrote them with her sister. Did you know that, too?'

Vyasa pulled himself together. 'No,' he said firmly, 'I didn't. But, Bharati, is this really the time—'

She took no notice, however. Instead of listening to her father, she scanned the garden full of guests. 'It's that woman who fainted last night at the wedding,' she said. 'I can't see her here now but she's married to Hari Sharma. You must have known that, Baba?'

He cleared his throat. 'Yes, I recognised her,' he said.

'And you must have taught her at Santiniketan?' she said, frowning up at him. 'Did you?'

'I must have. Very likely.' Their father took a long gulp of beer. 'It's hot here,' he said. 'Shall we move into the shade?'

The pretty MA student, who had been standing there all this time, listening to this awkward exchange, smiled sympathetically at Vyasa, and said, 'Shall I get you another drink?'

'No, no,' Vyasa answered. 'I'll just have a word with my daughter.' And he drew Bharati aside. 'Listen,' he whispered, 'this isn't the right moment to have this particular conversation. It's very difficult for all of us that Leela Sharma is now related to us through marriage. Your mother fell out with her before we were married.'

'Why did they fall out?'

'I'll tell you another time. I can't tell you now.'

'When will you tell me?' she asked childishly, pouting.

'Later.'

But Bharati refused to give up. She had carried on so relentlessly in this injurious vein that in the end Vyasa used a deliberately derogatory word to describe Meera's sister, a word that had angered him when he heard his mother use it: he called her a *foundling*. On top of that, since he did not want Bharati to realise that the poem published in the *Delhi Star* linked him and the two sisters, nor that he himself considered that he had married the *wrong* sister, he steered the conversation in a different direction entirely by criticising his daughter for her own sexual behaviour, something he had always sworn he would never do. He had only meant to criticise her for the undue worry she had caused them by leaving the wedding yesterday without telling anyone. But instead he enquired coldly, 'Who was it you disappeared with last night?'; and Bharati looked up at him as if he had slapped her. She left soon afterwards and he went home with his mother.

But why was she stirring things up like this? he wondered as he sat on his terrace, sipping his coffee. Didn't she realise, didn't she feel grateful, that the family that could have come apart with Meera's death had been kept intact by him and his mother? The children had been given the best, the most loving upbringing possible; nothing was lacking, nothing was amiss. And yet here she was, misbehaving because of Leela Bose. And guiltily Vyasa blamed his daughter for seizing on the one thing in his life that most distracted and dismayed him.

Seeing Meera's sister at the wedding, Vyasa had at first felt only a youthful, amorous delight: *Leela, home in India.* The beauty and candour of the time he had spent at Santiniketan swept over him with the freshness not of memory, but of reality itself – as if he was still that bold young man, and she that alluring aloof young woman. He could easily have dropped then and there at her feet and pledged her his love, swooning with the intensity of it. Instead, it was she who fainted, and the ecstatic moment of their meeting was cut rudely short by her departure.

Since then, Vyasa had barely been able to think of anything else; and even though this was what he had planned and schemed for, he felt utterly thrown by Leela's precipitous re-entry into his life. During the wedding lunch, for example, he had felt thankful that Leela and her husband had stayed away, but he had worried that she might turn up late, and then when she didn't, he worried about what her absence meant. Vyasa hadn't felt this lovesick for years – for his career, yes; for his children and their ambitions; but not for a woman. Women seemed to come and go in Vyasa's life with superb tact. Young or middle aged, sexy or outwardly chaste; it didn't matter. Somehow they seemed to intuit the delicateness of his position as a widower father, and however hastily he brushed them off, they acquiesced without complaint. Yes, until Leela's return to Delhi, Vyasa had been managing things – his life, his legacy, his lovers, his children's lives – superbly.

Even when the poem suddenly appeared in the *Delhi Star*, he had not surrendered. He had kept his cool. He saw straightaway that it was the only poem he had withheld from the published collection, *The Lalita Series*. It was clear that Leela had sent it to the paper, and as he winced at the angry feminism of the verses, he knew there was a strong possibility that the whole history of the poems, and the events surrounding their composition, would be exposed to the public. Delhi was a city that loved a mystery about one of its own. There would be an inevitable juggernaut of gossip trampling over Meera's reputation – and his.

Vyasa was determined to stop this destructive force in its tracks. When the journalist responsible for the article called him for a comment, Vyasa pointed out that Meera was never a nationally acclaimed poet; that her output was small. 'She only became known for her poems after her death,' he said, 'and if somebody is imitating her now, what can I do?' The journalist had been a little incredulous. 'Everybody has heard of Meera,' he countered. But Vyasa was unfazed. The poet Lalita – so he told the inquisitive young man – had written Bengali-besprinkled verses in English. The early poems had whole lines in Bengali script; subsequently she threw in the occasional Bengali word; and the latter poems were entirely in English. But what this meant was that 'Lalita' was really read by only a *very* small coterie of English-speaking Indians, and Bengali-conversant ones at that. That such people had a political and cultural standing in the capital far surpassing their numerical presence in the country, and that a sentimental Bengali professor at Delhi University had put her poems on his reading list, created a false sense of her importance. But the President hadn't heard of her. The book pirates didn't bother to distribute her work at traffic crossings. And Vyasa didn't say this out loud, but he thought it to himself: his wife's poetry was only really loved by those who had known her personally, or had wished they were her lover, or had felt socially honoured to be invited to her raucous parties, notorious, above all, for the voluptuous beauty of the hostess.

Vyasa had been pleased, until now, with how he had handled things. But sitting upstairs with his coffee, he realised that he hadn't given sufficient thought to how to manage any crisis that might be precipitated in his daughter, who was actually studying the Lalita poems. He got to his feet, went back into his library, and retrieved the offending copy of the Delhi Star from where he had left it on his desk. Meera's face stared out at him mockingly. She would have laughed to see how badly he was coping. And what about Leela? What would she think? From the pile of daily papers that he had flicked through this morning, Vyasa found and re-examined the spread of wedding photos in the society pages of the Delhi Star, illustrating last night's festivities. There was only one of Leela. It was a group shot – he was there too – and it must have been taken moments before she fainted. He studied it carefully. There was a sadness in her eyes, a kind of wisdom, perhaps; and he remembered the calm, self-contained expression that had attracted him so in Santiniketan. And he, had he acquired wisdom? He thought of his youthful arrogance and winced.

Vyasa had grown up hearing tales of his namesake, Vyasa of the Mahabharata, and there was one story in particular he had always admired. It was a tale of male potency; an ancient example of his namesake's virility; a legend, moreover, which was the key to the epic. The story told of Vyasa's triple insemination of two sisters and a servant. By sleeping with these women, the Mahabharata's author had brought forth children and grandchildren – the cousins who waged war on each other – and in this way engendered the cast of his epic. Professor Ved Vyasa Chaturvedi had never revealed to anybody else the extent to which, at one youthful, egomaniacal epoch of his life, he had allowed himself to be guided by this legend. He generally tried not to over-analyse the meaning of that long-ago carnal autumn and self-indulgent spring. And yet what he had done at that time was, in its own way, life-changing.

Vyasa's infatuation with the legend took its final shape at Santiniketan, his first teaching post. He loved transmitting knowledge to young minds; and when two beautiful sisters appeared in his class, every aspect of his personality – and physique – leapt outwards in response.

Meera, the more vocal of the two, was easily won over. She responded in all the usual ways to his looks, to his words, and, eventually, to his caresses. But it was the other sister, Leela, whom Vyasa yearned for. Leela was tougher. She appeared not to notice Vyasa. This made him reckless, and he dallied ever more frequently with her sister, not leaving the room until Leela returned, filling the space with his smell of sweat and maleness. Leela took no notice.

In the midst of this frustrated courtship, Vyasa developed an embarrassing genital itch, and one afternoon when classes were over, he walked three kilometres out of Santiniketan, on the Ilam Bazaar road, to the new mission hospital in the neighbouring village, run by Methodists. Like all these places, it was designed as a way of making conversions among the local Santhal tribals. But it also served those local people who were too poor to pay the university hospital fees – or who didn't trust the sub-district hospital in Bolpur. For Vyasa's purposes the mission hospital was anonymous and clean – and he even found the earnest evangelism charming (given how doomed it was).

Sitting there in the waiting room, along with fifteen poor

villagers, Vyasa took out a paper from the pocket of his waistcoat and unfolded it. Meera had given it to him that morning, following a class assignment to write some verse with a mythological theme. Perhaps inspired by Meera's name, Vyasa had taught a class earlier that term on her namesake, Meerabai, the medieval Rajasthani princess who had renounced her husband and the royal court, to travel the desert singing hymns in praise of the blue-faced boy-god, Krishna. Meerabai took with her a handmaiden, Lalita, and it was she, so the story went, who edited Meerabai's verses, collecting together these exquisite productions of divine ecstasy and ordering them into a coherent body of work. Every Indian poet needed a pen-name and it was this one – Lalita – that Meera had chosen as hers. It was a clever touch, for the lines wove a story of love and obsession. The last stanza even mentioned him by name:

> O saffron-hued woman,
> In your previous birth you were a cowherding girl.
> Once, you sang of your love for Krishna.
> Renounce now those childish things,
> Hold out your hand to me, Meera.
> Just as Ganesh wrote the epic for Vyasa,
> So proclaim in these verses your love for Lalita.

Vyasa laughed out loud in pleasure. The rewriting of Meerabai's love-songs – the winding in of a theme from the Mahabharata – was exquisite.

Just at that moment, the nurse opened the door and called out to him. The voice was English, unmistakably, and young. Vyasa looked up. She was slight, slim and blonde, barely out of her teens, with her hair tied behind her head in a bunch and tucked away in front under the white nurse's cap she wore. As he followed her into the

room, sat on a wooden chair and explained his problem, desire made him lightheaded. She was pulling on her gloves. 'Please, show it to me,' she said, avoiding his eyes as a slight blush came up on her cheekbones.

He took it out, she took it between her gloved fingers, and then it seemed to come alive, moving upwards in a slow and stately procession that Vyasa was unable to control. They both stared at it for a moment as it swayed there, as if with some kind of crass confidence in its own beauty. Her hands fluttered backwards; her face was now flushed red. But she turned away, pulled off her gloves – and by the time she was ready to face him again, Vyasa had pushed it down into his trousers where it strained, painfully, against the fabric.

'There's nothing seriously wrong with you that I can see,' she said. 'It looks like a bit of dermatitis. Use a moisturising cream, and if it hasn't cleared up, come back after a week.'

When he returned as ordered, a week later, the nurse was still blushing. By now, though, he felt sure. And inside her room again, when he slipped one arm around her waist, and bent his head and kissed her, she turned her face up to his and he tasted the peppermint of her clean, nurse's mouth. Her skin was so smooth, so white, every emotion was reflected on its surface; and when Vyasa laid her down on the bed where she examined her patients, and ran a hand up her thigh, even ran a finger inside her, she sighed and didn't stop him. Her blush remained as he jabbed at her carefully, moving this way and that, so that she turned away her head, not quite moaning.

The third time he went back to the hospital, however, he found that the young English nurse had gone, and her replacement, a much older and sturdier woman, wouldn't say where, or tell Vyasa her name. He mourned her privately for some days, remembering the look in her eyes as he pushed his way in; but the sharpness of the loss was quick to fade. By now Meera had spoken to Leela – and thanks to her efforts, the second of the sisters, the silent, dismissive, alluring one, was his, at last.

Women didn't usually say no to Ved Vyasa Chaturvedi; he had learnt very early on that persistence was generally all that was required – that and an absolute confidence in one's own desirability. The unique and maddening thing about Leela Bose was that she said no, the first time, the second, throughout his wooing of Meera, said no even at the point when, to please her increasingly unhinged sibling, she finally gave herself to him. She said no even when Vyasa begged her to set aside her fight with Meera, and come to Calcutta for their wedding.

Yes – Vyasa married Meera. Life was unkind in its comparisons: it hadn't been like that for Vyasa of the Mahabharata. After performing his duty as the impregnator of his brother's two wives, Krsna Dvaipayana Vyasa stepped away into the shadows – to observe his progeny and cast, and to write his story. But in the Santiniketan of 1979, stepping away wasn't an option for Ved Vyasa Chaturvedi. In May, towards the end of the academic year, Meera told him she was three months' pregnant.

They married in haste – a simple Arya Samaj ceremony in Calcutta, to please her father – and as the heat of the summer stretched on and on, smothering the country, they moved away to Delhi, where Vyasa had managed to find a teaching job at Hindu College. Since the new academic year began in late July, Meera and he spent the time that remained setting up house in Nizamuddin West.

They were blissful months, in retrospect, and not just for their contrast to the horrors that came later. During her pregnancy, Meera seemed to glow with pleasure. Everything about their new life pleased her; and in his eyes, too, this marriage that he had made took on a special sheen of its own: one that compensated, in part at least, for the intellectual disadvantages of marrying oneself off in the first place. Once in Delhi, Meera declared that she had felt as he did about Santiniketan: both of them were city people, both thrived in the urban thrill. And at first, Meera lived it to perfection. As her cheeks filled out, as her belly began to swell, she seemed to embody the perfect wife: witty, desirable, elegant, daring. This was before the days of her poetry recitals, before the tedious coterie of young admirers. She organised dinners in their home, bringing together literature professors with social activists, journalists with the cleverest students from the faculty: setting up encounters and rencontres that ebbed and flowed with ease and passion, as if she was conducting not conversation but a concerto.

There was only one dark spot. During these months neither Meera nor Vyasa mentioned Leela. Since becoming a wife, Meera refused even to speak of her sister. Vyasa's silence was driven by necessity. He was terrified he might reveal to his wife how, when she occasionally pulled him down onto the marital bed and forced him to make love, it was Leela's phantom he touched and caressed, Leela's tongue he dallied with, Leela's face he saw as he uttered long anguished cries. Serious though Vyasa's distress at losing Leela was, he concealed it. Or so he hoped.

In the autumn, just a few weeks before she was due to give birth, Meera took the train back to Calcutta. She said she wanted to be in her father's house for the birth; Vyasa, now in the middle of a busy term of teaching, stayed in Delhi.

A month later, his wife returned. To everyone's delight she had given birth to twins, a healthy boy and a healthy girl. They named the boy Ashwin – after the mythical twins who were both men and women – and the girl Bharati – in a nod to his work.

But during that month away, Meera had changed. At first she said nothing, and he took her silence for the preoccupations of motherhood: the constant demands of not one but two small mouths, not one but two helpless bodies. It was when she started asking him about his previous couplings that he knew something had gone wrong inside her. She asked tentatively at first; later demanding that he retell these stories, these cruel vignettes, over and over in ever more ghastly, lurid detail. Who he had slept with first, what the other women were like, who cried out most, who gave him most pleasure; but all this was a mere prelude: she wanted him to tell her every detail of that brief and unsatisfactory moment of coitus with Leela. Vyasa was outraged. She was turning his unconventional sexual daring on its head; bringing the horror of bourgeois values into their marriage, to wreck it from within.

As the hard Delhi winter turned to spring – as the twins filled the house with their cries of hunger and frustration – Meera stopped taking care of the children. In the evenings, he would come home to find her slouched on their bed, a glass of gin in her hand. The twins had an ayah, a woman from the basti, and Meera, who spent her days at home, like many other Indian housewives, did no cleaning or cooking. She did not even feed the children. 'What do you do when I am out? Are you writing?' he asked one day, more from curiosity than suspicion. She looked up at him slowly, as if she didn't understand him, as if his words were being transmitted from a very far-off place. His words were a taunt.

It was early spring the following year before they heard the news from her father: Leela had moved away. She had married an unknown man, informing no one and choosing America, of all places, as her home. The depression into which Meera had already dipped – and into which she now plunged like a swimmer – was blamed on her post-natal condition. But Vyasa knew better. It was the shock of being separated from the one woman on whom she had always depended. But he only understood part of what was happening. Later, he realised that the thing that grew inside her during that first year of the twins' life on earth was much more subtle, much quieter – more frightening – than anything that could be seen from outside.

During this era of his wife's undoing, Vyasa had a revelation of his own. He was teaching the Mahabharata to class after class of young, desirable students. But now the formative stories of his namesake began to seem a curse. As he stood up in front of a class full of eager pretty faces, he thought for the first time of the women in the epic – cowering as they were shoved into the bed of the dirty, hirsute sage; crying out as they were made to copulate against their will; protesting at being receptacles of substitute sperm – and he felt angry that modernity, diminishing the epic dimension, had bequeathed him this belittling perspective.

In the autumn, soon after the twins turned one, when the air in Delhi was filled with the perfume of raat-ki-rani blossom, and the unbearable heat of summer was behind them, Meera's mind suddenly warped once more, and this time into an upswing. It was a change for the better, and Vyasa felt such a relief as he had never known before or since. She was coming out of the darkness that had enveloped her at last. She was getting up early in the morning, and dressing once again in that flamboyant way she always had, and best of all, she was playing with the children. He didn't mind that she began to throw parties that became the talk of the town; that she became famous for the shiver that ran through the audience during her poetry recitations. He could see that she enjoyed the attentions of her many young male admirers. He guessed, and remained unmoved by the thought, that she bestowed more than literary pleasures on the luckiest of these men, as he had already done on other women.

If anything, this new hard paradoxical fragility of hers made him love her in a way that he hadn't bothered to before. Now, when he took her, he thought of their mutual betrayals – and he mistook the bitterness and loss that they were visiting on each other for a new profundity of feeling.

So misled was Vyasa by this era of their marriage – reading its silence as respect, its despair and duplicities as solitary freedoms – that the tragedy, when it came, was unexpected. It was soon after the twins' second birthday; Vyasa was away in Bombay on a work trip, and it was his mother who rang him with the news. He took a train back to Delhi and a friend in the police sent a car to meet him at the station. To his surprise he was driven out, past India Gate, and up over the spine of the Ridge. What had she been doing here? This was the newest of New Delhi, with neither the grace of nearby Shahjahanabad nor the space one usually associated with Civil Lines; a dusty, marginal place of slum workers and railway lines. When the car finally glided to a stop, Vyasa looked out of the window and saw the red and blue of a Delhi police station. No, not a police station. A police morgue.

The yard of the morgue smelt sweet, an undefinable smell then, but one that, later, Vyasa would know meant death, inert flesh, the violence of life's end. He was led towards a room at the back of the yard, and told to wait. Two policemen were lounging with their backs to him in the doorway of the Cold Room. Moving forward, Vyasa saw that they were laughing at a woman who was lying in the entrance. She had enormous breasts, and only her face was covered, by a dirty cloth. She was so white and waxy, she looked unreal, not dead, and Vyasa had to remind himself that she was a human being. Around her, in a heap, were other naked bodies, prostrate on a pile of rags. 'Train crash,' the policeman said, and pointed to a man lying at the back of the room, his head turned towards the wall. 'Vagrant.' His finger picked out another lump of body, the head tumbled on the vagrant's legs. 'Murder, from Karol Bagh.' The finger moved on.

'Hooch death in a construction camp. Rickshaw driver, crushed by lorry. Hungry girl, ate dead pigeon off the road.' The dead were all pale, their skin seemed to have achieved an identical tone in death, they looked related, as if they came from the same family once.

Somebody was calling. Vyasa turned away, and found that the inspector had returned. He was shown into another room. In here it was cleaner. There were only two dead bodies, both on light blue stretchers. One was an old man, also naked but for a piece of white bandage on his toe. His hair was white and wiry, his nose a handsome hook. A man in blue overalls was leaning over him, sewing up the skin on his neck. The string yanked the head up off the stretcher, the man let it fall, yanked it up. The stitches were huge. The head fell with a thud.

The other body was a woman. Her skin, too, was pale. Her face was bruised, she was naked, she had bled. You could see the ruptures on the skin of her arms and legs. 'We found her on the road near the hospital,' the policeman was saying. 'It was difficult to tell where she was from. No identification. An old green sari . . .' He pointed to a pile of clothes on the workbench. 'She came in yesterday morning. We didn't know what kind of woman she was. No jewellery. No gold. Not even a watch—'

'And yet not a servant,' somebody interrupted. 'Skin too smooth on the hands.'

'That's why we put out the Hue and Cry.'

The fender of the truck, Vyasa learnt later, had struck her head, the wheel caught her body, crushing her legs. She would have died instantly. The policeman was still talking. 'No knowing who the driver of the lorry was. No knowing why it happened.' He glanced surreptitiously at Vyasa. 'No further questions. All over and done with.'

The funeral took place the next day at the burning ghats up near the university on the banks of the river. Vyasa had already rung her father in Calcutta but there wasn't time for any of the other relatives to take the train and come to Delhi, and the white-clothed mourners who stood with him at the funeral pyre were mostly his own colleagues and relatives, as well as a few of Meera's youthful admirers: the long-haired young men who had come to sit on Vyasa's terrace to drink his rum and swoon as his wife recited her poems. It was they who wept as Meera's ashes were scattered into the Yamuna.

Meera's father betrayed no emotion in front of his son-in-law. The only signficant thing he said was: 'I will inform Leela.' And Vyasa nodded.

It took months for him to begin going through his late wife's possessions. When he did, he found the stack of poems almost immediately. Meera had filed them away, each one dated and numbered, each one signed with the name, *Lalita*. Vyasa sat down and read them through. They were good: youthful, witty, assured, with an occasional turn of phrase that even made him gasp.

Vyasa showed Meera's poems to a friend (all except one, which he withheld because of its embarrassing content), and the man, who ran a small publishing house, grew excited and voluble and declared that he would print five hundred copies in a special commemora-tive volume, with a sketch of Meera's face on the cover, and special footnotes translating the occasional Bangla word into English. The slim cloth-bound book was called *The Lalita Series*. Journalists wrote articles in esteemed literary journals. With the second print-run of eight hundred copies, there was a generally expressed sense of regret at the loss of this promising poet. Comparisons were made to Rajasthani Meera, and to English Keats.

Vyasa longed for some praise from Meera's father for this act of kindness to the dead, but the old man never brought it up on the occasions when he came from Calcutta to visit. Dipankar Bose doted on the twins; but he had always held himself slightly aloof from the marriage Meera had made – Vyasa felt – and now that his daughter was dead, he did not invite intimacies with the grieving husband. And so, even though Vyasa longed to discuss Meera's work with Dipankar – the creative breadth her ebullience had masked, the agonies and depths that her depression had exposed – he did not dare. Perhaps he felt ashamed of revealing all that he, the husband, had never quite understood.

Meera's father passed away some three years later.

'I suppose you'll have to tell Leela,' his mother observed after he returned from yet another funeral, on the banks of another river, in a different city. Vyasa nodded. He commissioned his lawyer to find out from Delhi's civil marriage registration records who Leela had married.

When the truth came to light, Vyasa was surprised at how jealous he felt. She had made a bad marriage, taking as her spouse a man in import–export called Hariprasad Sharma. Vyasa did a little research of his own and discovered that Hariprasad was the younger brother of a voluble Hindu nationalist called Shiva Prasad who was currently making himself felt as an irksome presence on the fringe of right-wing Hindu politics. Shiva Prasad's non-resident Indian brother Hari, however, had acquired a range of business interests and a lot of money. Vyasa composed a formal letter to Leela about her father's sad demise, and addressed it care of her husband's office in Delhi. He hoped that it might spark some correspondence between them. But her reply, when it came, was curt; and although he could see that the letter had been sent from America, she left no forwarding address.

He was hurt by her words – the lack of them. And although he did debate with himself whether he should send her a copy of Meera's poetry collection and tell her how well it had been received, he surmised in the end what her letter made clear: she had no wish to be reminded of that past life, with its over-generous share of sorrow.

Time passed, the years became decades, the children grew up, and many other women came in the place of Meera and Leela. But while, as a young man, Vyasa had rationalised his actions at Santiniketan with the hindsight of history – men had always done what he did; women had always responded in the way the sisters responded – he found, with fatherhood, his views changing of their own accord. Of course he had always spoken out on women's rights, on the sexual revolution, on feminism; he believed in these things with a fervour that was almost physical in its intensity. But it wasn't until he had a daughter of his own – a child whom he brought up to be independent and headstrong, uncowed by tradition and convention – that his personal behaviour began to disturb him. Suddenly, in middle age, he was left with a distinct sense of having acted wrongly in the past, and of having got off very lightly, given what he did. And he felt bad for his children. The twins had needed a mother. But there was nothing to be done except make the best of what they had and be grateful that the lives they were living were as rich and full as could be expected.

The month before Bharati left for England, Vyasa advertised the post of librarian for his extensive private book collection. The library on the roof needed pruning and ordering and setting to rights, and, moreover, as head of the faculty, it behoved him to give in to this indulgence. Countless college girls applied, and one afternoon, Vyasa's assistant at the university sent him home with a huge pile of CVs; all he had to do now was select a shortlist for interview. But as he walked up the front steps to his house, and the young maid came to the door with a glass of water, Vyasa found that there was somebody waiting for him, sitting bolt upright on a chair in the drawing room, a blue folder perched on her knee.

She explained that she was applying for the post of librarian, and as she handed over the folder with her CV inside it, and rattled off her personal details and modest accomplishments, one detail caught his attention. Her father was Shiva Prasad, member of a right-wing think tank; Hari Sharma was her uncle; she was Leela Bose's niece. And so, instead of choosing the St Stephen's alumna with a string of As, Vyasa hired the B.Sc. (Hons.) Home Science graduate called Sunita Sharma.

His librarian was a pleasant, competent girl, and when she deliberately befriended Ash, a shy boy, Vyasa didn't exactly encourage the union – but nor did he discourage it. He observed, from a position of comfortable proximity, their coming together, despite their very different social milieux, and he smiled to himself – when Ash came and told him – that they wished to be married. For what this meant, in a secretive, roundabout way, was that Leela was coming back into the family.

The wedding date was set, and Hariprasad Sharma, Vyasa heard, was flying over from New York to attend the nuptials. Then the Lalita poem appeared in the papers, and as soon as Vyasa read it, he knew the journalist was right. How could he have been so blind? It was obvious: the verses that Meera had recited so often at Delhi parties, and which, after her death, Vyasa had conveniently attributed to her alone, had been written with Leela. She had recited them as a lament for the sister she had lost. And twenty years later, Leela had decided to publish this missing poem – the very one he had been careful to keep out of The Lalita Series because it cast him in an unflattering light. But why? As a warning. But a warning of what?

Vyasa cast the newspapers aside and got to his feet. It was not in Leela's interest to generate any scandalous talk about their past – she was a married woman. So maybe she had published the verse as a plea for recognition. And if so, then surely she would be open to a constructive dialogue on the issues that concerned them both. He could consult her on the extent of her authorship – he might even suggest a collaborative project – they could bring out a new volume of poems with a short biography of both poets and an introduction by Vyasa, their most formative teacher.

As he strode back and forth across his terrace, the idea – as good ideas do – blossomed in Vyasa's head. By the end of half an hour he was firmly convinced that it was a good idea – an excellent idea – and one, moreover, that he would take some pleasure in executing. It would require a little work, to expand on some of the more briefly explored ideas; but it would not take much time. Vyasa was used to this kind of project by now, and the writing would come with great felicity. He did not want the work to be too long. A little gem of a book: nothing pompous or verbose. Something pithy and to the point. A comment on modern India. An exploration of its diverse poetic traditions.

Sitting down in the sunshine, Vyasa felt pleased with himself all over again. His essays about writing in the Vedic tradition had proved controversial; there had been protests and speeches and letters to the papers. But it was like a flock of noisy starlings or myna birds, this reaction: it acted as a chorus to his more powerful solo voice. Nothing was frothier than these temporary expressions of emotive modern politics, and their recurring obsession with religion. Vyasa felt sure that his work would last longer than the current government, which had almost exhausted its store of goodwill due to its near constant harping on mythological Hindu figures, none of which – the populace of India would gradually come to realise – had any control at all over grain prices at harvest, or the rate that moneylenders charged in the market, or the distance that their children had to walk to the nearest functioning school.

And with the Delhi opening of the Living Sanskrit Akademi,

Vyasa was about to enter a new epoch in his career. He had wielded all his academic force, all his powerful connections, to persuade the Archaeological Survey of India to let him use the old fort – Indraprastha itself – as the location for his lecture. He would open the proceedings with a brief speech, and following this introduction – a shortened version of the lecture he had given in New York – some of India's finest intellects would speak to the audience. Vyasa, who was pleased by how assiduously he nurtured new scholars, had encouraged his committee to fund both a young researcher from Calcutta and another from London to come to Delhi and give papers too. The Akademi's key remit was to promote a vibrant and engaged study of this ancient language and its literature. Nobody could accuse Ved Vyasa Chaturvedi of not making a significant contribution to the national and global commons, to the cultural and intellectual life of India.

But all these achievements would seem hollow until Leela Sharma added her voice to the general chorus. Why couldn't she get over her petty pride and become part of his life again? What was stopping her now? All the other women he had loved remained close to him; they were the most privileged, happy, lucky women in Delhi – in India – in the world, and they knew it. Only here were they granted unrestricted access to his marvellous brain. Only here were they given amazing intellectual insights, coupled with radical exposure to popular culture. He was liked, and praised, not just in Delhi and Bombay but in London and New York. Paris hadn't passed him by, Berlin radiated on his consciousness, Sydney and Melbourne had felt his mark. All this could be Leela's.

And as he picked up the tray of coffee to take it downstairs, Vyasa couldn't help indulging the vision of her in his arms as he made love to her that one time – so gently and sensitively – nor avoid recalling the unforgettable look of disdain on her face when it was over.

chapter 6

Raziya Begum, Humayun's mother, screamed and shook the
messenger – one of her dead husband's brothers' sons – by the
shoulders. 'Who? Who is he said to have raped?'

'The girl Aisha, daughter of Tabasum.'

She raised her arm, and the nephew cowered. After she let him
go, he ran home through the streets of the basti and told his father
and uncles that Auntie Raziya was mad with grief.

Raziya had her wits about her, however. Her first action was the
practical one of going to visit the Professor, who knew the family
well, in addition to having employed Humayun the night before to
drive them to his son's wedding. He would provide a good reference with the police, as well as an alibi.

The Professor wasn't at home when she arrived – the whole
family had left for the wedding lunch off Lodhi Road – and Raziya
was forced to talk to the family cook, a chubby, opinionated Hindu
man, originally from Sindh, whom she disliked. 'The Professor's
son was married yesterday,' the cook said provokingly, as if Raziya
didn't know the family business. 'We haven't seen your son since
he drove them home from the wedding and then went out to look
for the maid, this young girl Aisha.'

'Aisha works here?' Raziya clenched her fists behind her back.

'You didn't know? Your own son Humayun came and asked on her behalf.'

Raziya's knuckles turned white. The cook opened the door wider. 'You can step in and wait. Make yourself some tea, you know where everything is kept.'

Raziya followed the cook into the hallway of the house where she had spent so many years of her life, raising these two children, and raising her own son, and looked around her. Everything was exactly the same as before. The house, so carefully arranged by the Professor, with its paintings and photographs, its thick, richly coloured carpets and elegant objects, even smelt the same.

There was a photograph on the stairs that she recognised, of the Professor's wife. Raziya was standing at the bottom of the stairs looking at it when the Professor arrived home. He seemed preoccupied. 'Whatever you have to say must wait until tomorrow,' he said. 'I'm too busy now.'

'But, sir,' she protested.

'Enough,' he said, raising his hand to stop her. 'Please come back tomorrow.' And before she could say anything further, he walked away upstairs.

Standing outside in the street, her head bowed again with the horror of her son's predicament, Raziya felt helpless. She looked up at the house. She would have to come back again tomorrow and wait to see him at the house. She would wait every day if necessary. And eventually he would help her – he had to – in return for the care she had lavished on his motherless children. That was only fair.

Raziya's arrival in the Chaturvedi household twenty-two years ago had coincided with a difficult period in the Professor's life. His young wife had just given birth to the twins, but she found the feeding painful, and Raziya, who herself was trying to conceive, felt scornful of this woman, this half-mother, this creature who couldn't even cook her family dinner, who barely spoke to the ayah or cast an eye over her son and daughter. It was her husband, Ved Vyasa Chaturvedi, who represented the only link between the parents and their offspring.

Raziya and the twins spent long hours alone together. Once, during a spring afternoon, when Raziya was out walking them in their pram, a woman approached. Raziya stopped still and felt the chill of the winter sun making the hair on her arms stand up in fear. She recognised the woman from a photograph the Professor used to have hanging on the wall of his top-floor library. In the picture, a pair of young students were staring boldly at the camera. Every time Raziya dusted the picture she would stare back in wonderment at the brash smiling confidence of Meera, and the extraordinary beauty of the young woman who sat just behind her. One day, after the Professor had been arguing with his wife, Meera threw the photograph to the ground and the glass smashed and scattered its brilliance all the way down the stairs. Raziya had been sent to sweep up the tiny shards. But though she collected the glass together, the print, the black-and-white photograph, this she had hidden under a pile of papers on the Professor's table. It was her first act of defiance against her mistress.

When she saw the beautiful woman from the photograph in the flesh, then, she sat down on the bench and looked at her curiously. The woman came quite close and held her breath. Bharati and Ash were asleep, their dark eyelashes fluttering slightly. 'Which one is the daughter?' the woman said, and Raziya pointed her out. 'That one.'

'May I hold her?' the woman said.

'She's asleep,' Raziya said.

'Is she a peaceful baby?'

'Very peaceful.'

'What is she called?'

And after a pause, Raziya told her: 'Bharati.'

'Bharati.' The woman turned the word on her tongue. Then she sat down on the bench and slipped something into Raziya's hand. It was a bangle. A thick, gold bangle. 'I will sit here with you until she wakes up.'

They sat together in silence, watching Bharati. The sun sank lower in the sky, and the park filled up with young boys and girls. Raziya said eventually, 'I'll have to take them back to the house. They might catch a chill.' She leant over the pram, lifted up the sleeping Bharati, and placed her gently in the woman's arms. The baby stirred slightly but didn't wake. When Raziya took her back again, barely a minute later, the woman gave a little sob. Bharati, still sleeping peacefully, had curled her fingers around the woman's finger.

They walked together with the pram over to the entrance of the park. 'I would like to see them once more,' the woman said. 'Will you be here tomorrow?'

And Raziya answered without any hesitation: 'We'll be here tomorrow morning at ten.'

'Ten o'clock tomorrow morning,' the woman said.

As a reward for this second meeting, Raziya received some gold earrings and a necklace. The woman lay on the grass with the babies on the rug beside her, and although they had only just begun to smile, and neither of them had laughed yet, the woman seemed tirelessly to examine Bharati's face, to watch her waking eyes register the leaves and shadow; and it was she, the woman, who laughed out loud when the baby's little face smiled.

As for Raziya, she told nobody about the gold, not her timid husband, nor his brothers' wives, nor even her sisters on the times they came to visit from the village. She hid the jewellery at the bottom of her trunk and said nothing – but the knowledge was like a warmth within her. It gave her a sensation she had known neither in her childhood nor in her marriage. It was not just the hard fact of the gold itself. It was as if the strange pretty woman had handed her a chance for independence.

For months, the way in which she was to take this chance remained opaque. Then, one evening, when her mistress was dressing for a party, Raziya entered the room to find her angrily pulling off an embroidered shirt. 'The cut is wrong,' Meera said, standing before her, naked but for a skirt and bra. She held out the shirt and dropped it to the ground. 'Can you fix it?'

Raziya nodded. Her father had been a tailor; she had grown up hearing the whirr of his sewing machine. He made his money from the dull, straightforward clothes that men liked to wear, the simple long shirts and baggy cotton trousers with their endearingly limited range of variation. But he also made clothes for his daughters, and although Raziya had never been encouraged to think that she might practise this profession – of course not – she had learnt it de facto. She had learnt how to sew and cut and hem. She had been taught about the fall of certain fabrics. She knew, above all, how to achieve with her needle and scissors the things that made women happy.

And so, as she sat on the veranda in the afternoons, the twins asleep in the room behind her, one of her mistress's silk blouses in her hands, she began to imagine a small shop in the basti, designs from catalogues pinned to the walls, an array of coloured threads, the satisfying snip of her tailoring scissors. As a first, tentative step, she sold the thick gold earrings dotted with jewels that the woman had given her, and bought a sewing machine. After that, she began to take in the odd bit of sewing for neighbours. Over the next few years, she continued to dream of this shop and the life it might entail.

Then, by the time the twins turned three, Raziya got pregnant at last. Remembering the morning at the tomb, she named her boy Humayun. Her husband, cautious at the best of times, agreed that it was a nice name, though unusual; her mother-in-law openly disapproved, complaining that people would think her grandson was a Shiah; but Raziya was adamant. She wanted her son to remind her of how she had acquired ambition, and how, one day, she would secure him a life different from her own.

Perhaps nothing further would have happened if her husband, sickly as he was, had not contracted dengue fever and died. Raziya was now a widow, with a weaker position in her in-laws' home than before. She knew that if her business was to thrive, she had to move out. She could never achieve financial independence if she stayed: her brothers-in-law would circumscribe the hours she worked; her sisters-in-law would interfere and say disparaging things to her clients; all of them would want to take a cut.

There was a building she had seen on the Lodhi Road side of the basti. The cheap top-floor rooms were for sale; the commercial property at the bottom was being put out on rent. The living space that went with the shop was crucial. So Raziya went to see the Professor and told him what she needed. Humayun was only four years old – she was a widow, with a tiny son, he couldn't very easily refuse her. She showed him the work she was doing; she explained about the commercial opportunity she, as a female Muslim tailor, offered in this neighbourhood. She would continue to come in part time, for a year or so, to take care of his children. But soon they wouldn't need an ayah. They were already busy with school – their grandmother was living with them; and by the time her shop was established, Raziya calculated, she would have looked after the twins for long enough.

What the Professor suggested pleased her: he would buy the shop and the residence outright from the owner, she would buy it back from him in monthly instalments. By the time the property was entirely hers, she would have paid him three per cent more than the original selling price, in line with inflation.

And that was what happened. He had papers drawn up, which she signed; she took her son and moved to their new home; and throughout the years that followed, there would come moments when she would look up – at her workers, at the rail of ladies' suits, at the measurement book where the statistics of every woman she sewed for were recorded – take a deep breath and go slowly upstairs to her bedroom, to unlock the trunk and unfold the cloth bundle with its thick gold bangle and long Hindu necklace, and remind herself of how it had happened.

Even though many years had passed, Raziya had remembered the woman immediately when she passed by the shop after closing time – still the same wavy black hair, the same erect bearing, above all the same impossibly elongated eyes. But things were different now – Raziya was a businesswoman, not a servant – and she refused to speak to the woman about the gold, even though she hadn't sold it. She had kept the thick bangle and the chain with its pendant. The bangle would be good for a daughter-in-law; the pendant, with its lacquerwork butterflies and peacocks, would probably have to be sold. But the woman's peremptory tone annoyed Raziya; she wanted nothing further to do with her.

As Raziya walked away towards the basti, she knew that Humayun and she were alone in the world, and that nothing but her quick mind could save him from being falsely accused of rape, and that the next visit she had to make was far more humiliating even than the fruitless one she had just paid to the Professor. She had to beg for help from her late husband's brothers.

They lived altogether in a joint family house behind the shrine, a portion of which technically belonged to Humayun. They had done well for themselves – one brother owned a small shop, another was an autorickshaw mechanic, and the house, though small, with whole families sharing tiny rooms, had a large, electricity-guzzling fridge, and a toilet for their exclusive use. They hadn't, however, done as well for themselves as Raziya had, with her tiled kitchen and bathroom with a tap. She had done the best of all, and her brothers-in-law knew it and found the insult difficult to take.

The brothers – who in their pious old age had abandoned the spit-slick hairstyles and Western-collared shirts that had helped them get on in their chosen professions, and were wearing instead the spotless, pressed, white salwar kameez that identified them as respected and senior members of the community; who played with prayer beads and dropped Arabic phrases into their speech like a sprinkling of almonds on a fine white kheer – had to contend with her anger. They could see it in the way her eyes flickered between them, in the colour of her cheeks, in the movements of her head and hands, and most of all in the words she spoke about Aisha and her mother. 'But, Raziya,' they began, once she had explained that Aisha's accusations of rape marked her out as a whore like her mother, 'these women are from our own family.'

'My son has been slandered. I demand retribution.'

Raziya paused, restraining herself from speaking too much. During the silence that followed her speech, she could hear the clink of beads, the clearing of a throat, the steady swish of the overhead fan, the whine of the neighbour's television. She felt irritated with their ponderousness; it was as if, somehow by virtue of being men, they had accumulated wisdom and worthiness. It irritated her, too, that although she had managed her own affairs ever since she became a widow – had taken nothing from her husband's useless brothers – now that the police were involved, being a woman and a mother was no longer enough, and so she had to come to these people and beg.

From the mosque came the first notes of the call to prayer, and looking around her at the men assembled in this crowded basti room, with its glossily painted walls and line of trunks on the shelf, where every breath of air carried with it the sweet fetid scent of too many humans living together, Raziya thought again of her tailor's shop, with its living quarters that overlooked Lodhi Road, its three sewing machines and newly painted sign, its terracotta plant pots with tulsi and mint and coriander, its roof terrace, its simple but clean living space: one bathroom, one bedroom, one kitchen. It was luxury, and nobody could comprehend how a woman, a widow, could have done it alone. When she heard these doubting words, Raziya would mention Khadija, the businesswoman and widow who had married the young Prophet of Islam and supported his mission. That shut people up. How could they know, how could they guess, all the hard work that had got her this far? She would do anything for Humayun.

Suddenly, somebody spoke. Without turning her head, Raziya knew who it was: Iqbal, Humayun's best friend, the weakling youngest son of one of Raziya's husband's younger brothers – a boy who had not yet learnt the value of parroting his elders.

'Chacchi,' he began, 'Cousin Humayun wants to marry Aisha. So it is impossible that Aisha accused him of this crime. That is not the reason why Humayun has been arrested. Police prejudice must be to blame for that. The truth is that both these young people are in trouble and we should be doing our best to help them.'

Since learning of the arrest, Raziya had been told several things that she didn't want to hear about the relationship between Humayun and Aisha. When she walked back through the basti, the fruitseller on the shrine road murmured something to her concerning it; at her shop even one of her own tailors referred to it. None of these people had ever spoken to her on personal matters before; and yet now that she was in crisis, everybody wished to impart their knowledge concerning her affairs. She understood that she was partly to blame, for of course she would have known these rumours about her son as a matter of course had she not moved away to the outer edge of the basti; she would have been able to stifle this gossip had she not set herself apart from the family she married into. This was why families stuck together with suffocating closeness – it was for crises such as this. And so, listening to Iqbal, she felt the old anger rise into her throat. Aisha's mother – that witch – with her claims of blood kinship to Raziya's husband's family, whose own husband had abandoned her and gone to some other part of the country. She hated to remember how her husband had mentioned Aisha's mother just before he died – he had known her since childhood, had grown up in the same village in Bihar, and he had always nurtured an affection, who knew how deep, for that stick-thin woman with her hungry-looking face and squinting eyes. Even more, she hated how this woman had got her hands on Humayun by using her daughter to tempt him. Raziya knew also that she should have arranged for his marriage before now. She thought of all the mothers who had come to her door with proposals for her son, offering him their pure, fair-skinned daughters, pious beauties, Qur'an hafiz, undefiled. Every one of them she had proudly turned away, for her son was to aim still higher.

'She has created this story to trap Humayun,' Raziya said at last. 'How will he prosper if he has bound himself in marriage to the child of that whore?'

But Iqbal answered back before any of the elders had time to stop him. 'The police arrested Humayun last night when he went to report Aisha missing from the Professor's house.' He raised his eyes to Raziya's. 'It is the laziness of the police that has put your son inside that cell. Humayun feels strongly and with great respect towards this girl, Aisha, whom you so distrust.'

Raziya stared at him. Who was he to talk about her child? She could hear the plaintive voice of animals outside, being brought to the butcher; the calling of hawkers selling dinner tickets to pilgrims. She had seen the blackened mess left by the fire last night and all this unimproved disorder made her throat tighten as a kind of involuntary animosity coursed through her. How right she was to have taken her son away from this chaos, to their own house on the edge of the basti; she would do it again – she would go through that hard, lonely work three times over for Humayun. She did not want her precious son to end up in the clutches of skinny Tabasum's daughter. She wasn't even able to say why she hated that woman so much – it didn't matter why; it was a woman's instinct. She straightened her back and folded her hands tightly in her lap. 'You must send Aisha and her mother away from Delhi,' she said.

'No,' said one of the younger brothers – it was Iqbal's father. 'We won't do that. The marriage should take place at once. Then the police will have to drop the charges.'

Raziya shook her head. It was a ploy; she saw it clearly now. They wanted to bring her son, with his driving job and excellent prospects, down a notch, to below their level.

'You are condemning my son,' she said. 'I turned away many better daughters and you know it. I wanted something more for Humayun. Because that girl has got herself in trouble she wants to drag Humayun in after her, and you are all going to abet her.'

There was another uncomfortable shifting in the air, and finally, the eldest brother cleared his throat with a great phlegmy rattle, and said, 'We won't let any harm come to Humayun, Raziya. He is part of our family, our dear brother's only child. We will speak to the elders in the shrine after prayers, and they will advise us. They know how best to manage police procedure. This work, at least, is best left to men.'

'No!' Raziya interrupted shrilly. 'Don't do this to my son, don't—'

But the man raised his voice over hers. 'You will do nothing,' he continued. 'We are all agreed on that. Please leave it to us. We will sort the matter out. Now it is prayer time.'

And Raziya's brothers-in-law got to their feet and ushered her out of the room.

Aisha saw her mother waiting by the gate when Mrs Ahmed brought her home from the police station. 'How thin your mother is!' Mrs Ahmed said, waggling a finger backwards and forwards in disapproval. They looked through the car window at her frail parent, hunched over with her permanent cough, dressed in a faded sari. Then Aisha got out of the car and put her arms around her mother. She breathed in her warm familiar odour. The two of them wept.

Mrs Ahmed, meanwhile, had unlocked the front door. She led Aisha and her mother inside, and briskly disregarding Aisha's tears, took her into the kitchen to help heat some food for her starved-looking mother. 'I need to talk with your mother alone,' Mrs Ahmed said to Aisha sternly, as she took out the leftover daal and subzi from the fridge. 'You understand?' Aisha nodded. She watched Mrs Ahmed put the food in the microwave, and then, when it was ready, carry it through to Aisha's mother, beckoning her into the study, and sending Aisha off to sit in the guest room and wait.

Aisha sat on the bed looking out of the window into the garden. Until now, she had done exactly what she had been told. She had stayed in the Ahmeds' house, picking at the food set before her, wearing the clothes Urvashi handed to her, and all the time going over the events of the past twenty-four hours, remembering good moments from the last six months. She worried that Humayun had heard what had happened and wanted nothing more to do with her; she would wipe her eyes and tell herself that this wasn't true. Then an image would come to her of the old Hindu man's face as he lay on top of her – frozen, as if in agony – and after that she would sit for a very long time, hunched up, immobile, staring out of the window, until Mrs Ahmed came to find her.

Last night, after the Hindu man had left her in the Professor's house, Aisha waited until she was sure he had gone, and only then did she get to her feet, feeling giddy and ill, pulling the dupatta so far down that it completely covered her face, and made her way slowly down the Professor's garden path and along the quiet road that ran between the Chaturvedis' and the Ahmeds'. Humayun had warned her not to leave the Chaturvedi house until Mrs Ahmed came to collect her, but now that the Hindu man knew where she worked, she couldn't wait there. She approached the Ahmeds' house slowly, reassured by the familiar sight of its long glassy windows and large wrought-iron gate. The house was in darkness and she opened the front gate and curled up there under the plants, in her familiar place where she waited for Humayun in the time between swabbing the floors at Mrs Ahmed's and beginning at Professor Chaturvedi's. Late in the afternoon, on the days he hadn't picked up the milk in the morning, Humayun would hurry to Mother Dairy with the pails she had cleaned, to queue for milk, and Aisha would water the plants in the front garden, looking out through the leaves at passers-by, at their shoes, their saris, their necklaces and blouses, watching the goings-on of the neighbourhood – waiting especially for the girls of her age in their blue school dresses who came home across the bridge, punctually every day at half past two – and eventually she would see Humayun coming down the road, swinging his milk pail as he walked, and smiling, because he knew that she could see him. She had closed her eyes as she lay there and the next thing she knew, Mrs Ahmed had arrived and was carrying her across the threshold of her house and into the guest room.

Aisha got to her feet and opened the bedroom door. She wanted to know, now, what it was that Mrs Ahmed and her mother were talking about in the study. She moved silently across the front room in her bare feet and put her head against the study door. Her mother was speaking in a low voice, and Aisha could only make out a few words: Bihar, she heard, and Mamu, uncle, and then that word, Shaadi, marriage. She wondered why her mother wanted to take her to Bihar for a wedding; they never went there any more. The last time had been when Aisha was very small. She remembered her Mamu, a fat, kind-faced old man, whose wife had died long ago and whose children had grown up and made families of their own. But the village – she didn't like the village – it had very bad electricity connections and no running water.

Her mother raised her voice slightly, interrupting something that Mrs Ahmed was saying: 'But it is the only way to save her honour.' She sounded both sad and indignant, and Aisha stepped back from the door as if she had been hit. So it wasn't a cousin's wedding they were going to. Her mother meant for her to be married – to her Mamu. She stared around her wildly, trying to find something familiar in Mrs Ahmed's front room to focus on, but her eyes roamed over the polished furniture and ornamental objects that she had dusted so often, without finding any solace. She knew that this was what women always warned of, in sharp but hushed voices: the advantage men would take of young girls. She thought of Humayun's promise to marry her – and how he had immediately taken her into his quarters and laid her on his bed. She was stupid to have gone with him; everybody would say she had only herself to blame. But he had promised to marry her, and maybe the promise would have been honoured if she had not opened the door of the Professor's house to the old Hindu man. Nobody would forgive her for that. And now this third man – this aged village uncle. She hit her forehead with the palm of her hand. There was nobody to trust, nobody. Even Humayun was to blame. He should have married her first, in front of their whole community, and then taken her into his room and forced his children upon her. That was the proper way in which things were done.

Her mother was speaking again, louder now, sounding frustrated and tired. 'I have been told that his family is against us,' she was saying. 'They think the reason the police have locked Humayun up is because Aisha accused him of the crime.'

'But why would they think that?' Mrs Ahmed asked, sounding shocked, and when Aisha's mother uttered a wordless sound of exasperation, Aisha knew that nothing she could say would make her employer understand. She walked silently back into the guest room and sat down on the bed. So Humayun was in the police station, that was the reason he hadn't come to see her.

Aisha's mother had always told her that life was difficult, that life was unfair. She knew that Humayun's opinion was different: with hard work, he thought, you made your own luck. Now it was Aisha's turn to see her choices laid out before her. She could do as her mother said, and go to the village, and never see Humayun again. Or she could tell the police they had taken the wrong man. Then Humayun would owe her something. If she freed him from the police, he would have to save her from shame and marriage to her uncle.

But if she went to the police station now, who knew what the police might do to them both. Today at the police station, the tall, angry constable had mentioned doctor's tests, and Aisha did not want to be tested again. The doctor whom Mrs Ahmed had called to the house last night had made her lie on her back on the bed as he pulled up various parts of her clothing and removed items from her skin – and even from deep inside her. He had touched her here and there, asking about scratches and bruising. 'What are you doing?' Aisha pleaded at last, chilled and scared by being semi-naked in front of yet another strange man. The doctor had sighed and apologised: 'I am sorry, my little one, I have to collect these samples, just in case.'

Aisha couldn't confide in Mrs Ahmed, who was a Hindu and didn't understand some things that everybody else seemed to know. She couldn't tell her mother about the promises Humayun had made. It was too late for that. If he had announced his plan to marry her just one day earlier, everything would have been different – his mother may have objected and made difficulties, but Humayun could have persuaded her. Now it was impossible.

There was only one other person Aisha could speak to, and that was Iqbal, Humayun's cousin. He lived in the basti in a small brick-built house, not far from the shrine. Humayun had shown her the house once, when he went to collect his cousin on Eid. But she bit her lip in worry: how would she get out of the house without Mrs Ahmed hearing, and how to get to the basti without being recognised by Humayun's family?

Then she remembered. Yesterday, Mrs Ahmed had come home from the market with a paper-covered package from the Islamic bookshop. 'Look at this,' she had told Aisha, and opened it up. The silky black material had spilled out into the air as if Mrs Ahmed was a djinn controlling a stormcloud. 'Do you know what it is?'

she asked, and Aisha had nodded. It was an Arab-style burqa, such as some women in the basti now wore. Mrs Ahmed pulled the layers of georgette over her face and tied the string around her chin. Then she laughed. 'I'm not going to tell my husband just yet,' she said. 'He may disapprove. I'll have to hide it.' She pulled it off, and pushed the burqa back into the paper bag. 'I'll put it in the rice store.'

That evening, after she had said goodbye to her mother, Aisha ate dinner sitting alone in her bedroom, a plate of food on the low table near the window. She dragged the roti round the plate until it was clean. Then she waited for Mrs Ahmed and her husband to go upstairs, and once the lights had gone off and everything was quiet, she crept out of the guest room, across the marble entrance hall, and into the kitchen. First, she took a stool and reached up to the crockery cupboard. There, right at the back, hidden under the piece of paper lining the shelf was a slim envelope with this month's salary from Mrs Ahmed in large denomination notes. She pulled it out and put it in her pocket.

The rice store was in the cupboard next to the gas cylinder below the window. Aisha felt inside for the bulky paper packet. Standing by the stool where she had been sitting when Humayun kissed her, she unwrapped the burqa and tied it around her body as Mrs Ahmed had done. It was too big for her, and the folds flowed down from the crown of her head.

Outside in the street, she lifted the gate back on to its latch. Tonight there was no moon and the trees lining the road created a canopy that frightened her, made denser and more impenetrable by the layers of material in front of her eyes. But she walked slowly down the street, passed the Professor's house and then, reaching the entrance to the basti, slowed down because the houses were built so very close together, and the street, with its small shuttered shops and stalls, was quiet, and she didn't want to miss the turning to Iqbal's house. She walked slowly, trying to see the outline of the houses through the burqa; they were blackened by fire, their roofs caved in, and she remembered what Mrs Ahmed had told her that morning, about the stampede and the burning.

Iqbal's house was near the shrine, beyond the kabariwallah settlement, right up the hill just before the girls' madrassah. It was a distinctive house, brick-built, only two storeys high. There was a dog lying in the road, and Aisha heard the drone of cars on the main road in the distance. When she approached the door, she could hear voices inside and wondered what she should say. At last, she raised her hand and knocked on the wood and somebody came to the door almost immediately. 'Yes?'

In a low voice Aisha gave Iqbal's name, and said, 'A message from Aunt Raziya.'

It took some minutes to bring Iqbal to the door. 'Excuse me, Auntie,' he said when he arrived, 'I was eating.'

Iqbal had recently become very religious, and he wore a white cap and shaved his upper lip; but his beard was still so exceedingly thin and wispy that Humayun liked to tease him for it. Aisha motioned him away from the house, around the dog, to the other side of the street. The wind was blowing the colour supplement of a newspaper across the road; a film actress with long billowing hair and a modern slinky sari smiled up from the banner of the paper.

'I am Aisha,' she said.

'Aisha,' he replied, his voice full of wonder, and she felt the hope that had left her when the Hindu man pushed her into the house return like a flock of brightly coloured birds alighting nosily in a tree.

'Humayun is in trouble,' she said. He bowed his head in acknowledgement. 'Brother,' Aisha went on, 'I am in trouble too.'

In a hushed voice she explained about her mother's plans, about the wedding, about the uncle, and the village. 'If I stay in that house,' she said, 'they will come and take me.'

'Yes,' he said, nodding. Then he added, 'Humayun's mother will never let him marry you.'

They stood together in the road as the wind blew the newspapers and fire ash around them in a dirty, colourful squall. Aisha knew that they would have to hurry; if they stood here any longer, Humayun's uncles would grow suspicious and come out to question them both.

At last, Iqbal spoke. 'You should wait in the shrine,' he said. 'It is the safest place. Can you do that? You may get cold. Wait by the grave of Princess Jahanara, it is the most secluded part. Tomorrow, either Humayun or I will come and find you. You will have to wait for many hours, all night. You will have to be careful.'

He took some money from his pocket and handed it to her. 'Buy something to eat from the stalls outside the shrine. If anybody questions you, say you are praying for a son, and that after some time your husband is coming to collect you.'

He turned to go, and then stopped. Aisha saw him stoop down to the ground and pick up a piece of blue string that had been used to tie up a bundle of newspapers.

'Fix this on to the hem of your burqa,' he said, 'so that I can tell Humayun to look out for this mark.'

She thanked him.

'Alhamdu lillahi allaa kulli haal,' Iqbal said, and turned away towards the house. Praise to Allah in all circumstances.

Aisha watched him go, and stood there, alone in the street, thinking about what he had said. At last she set off, walking very slowly, towards the shrine, but as she walked, she thought about the police, and the crime Humayun had been accused of, and the marriage her mother wanted to make for her in Bihar, and the act that Humayun had performed, which bound him to her, and the more she thought about it the more clearly she saw that Iqbal's advice was wrong.

She walked on, past the turning to the shrine and out to the main road. When she arrived at the police station she didn't hesitate. With her envelope of money clutched tightly in her hand beneath her burqa, she walked up the steps and announced to the policeman on the desk what she was there for and that they had taken the wrong man. Then she held out the money.

Humayun was sitting on the ground with his back against the wall when he heard the sound of the door being unlocked from the outside. 'You,' he heard the policeman say, 'there's a woman here to take you. Get up. Quickly. Go.'

He shook his head, unbelieving. He had been in the police station for less than twenty-four hours, but already it felt as if days had passed. 'Get out of here,' the policeman was saying as he got to his feet, 'and don't come back. If you show your face again in Delhi we'll do to that girlfriend of yours what we've done to you.'

Why weren't they asking for money? Humayun wondered as they unlocked the cell and let him out. Then he felt in his pocket: they had taken the envelope with his pay from the Professor.

His mother was the last person he wanted to meet. But when he stepped outside, he saw two things: that it was night, and that the person waiting for him near the entrance was not his mother. It was a woman in a burqa. She was waiting for him at the end of the path by the gate.

'Who are you?' Humayun said as he approached.

She answered in a whisper: 'I am Aisha.'

He stood speechless for a moment, staring at her. She was wearing a heavy black burqa with some gauzy thin material over the eyes, and he peered at her, disturbed by the distance this tiny piece of fabric put between them: it was as if they were seeing each other through a crowd of people.

'What have they done to you?' she said, looking at him in the light from the thana. 'Is it just your face or anywhere else too?'

'Nowhere else,' he lied; but his body was hot with pain. 'Just my face. What did you do to get me out?'

'I went to see your cousin Iqbal. He told me to wait for you in the shrine. But I thought of you with the police—' She broke off, unable to describe the terrible things that had occurred to her. 'So I came here instead.'

He lifted away the cloth from over her face and looked at her. 'You saved me,' he said. Every hour that he had lain in that cell the worst imaginings had preyed on him: that she had accepted another man's advances, that she had allowed herself to be taken. Now he wanted to press her closely to him to shut out all the things that had happened.

'We have to leave the city tonight,' she said. 'My mother wants to send me to Bihar to be married.'

He nodded. 'Do you have your salary?'

'I gave it to the officer. Do you have yours?'

'They took it from me.'

There was silence between them for a moment, and then he said, 'I'll have to go to my mother's and get some money.' The police station itself was quiet, but to get to his mother's shop they would have to pass through the market. 'Pull the veil across again and walk behind me.'

They set off towards the market. Where the main street intersected with the road leading up to the shrine, Humayun feared coming across one or other of his uncles, who often went there to pray or to meet their friends. But it was night-time and nobody stopped them. When they reached the street before the tailor's shop, he found a place for Aisha to sit on a wall next to the large domed tomb by the road, which had recently been cleared of the families living in it by the city authorities. 'Don't move from here,' he said. 'Don't speak to anyone. I'll be back as soon as I can.'

His mother's shop was closed when he reached it, the shutter down, but the light was on, and he knew that she was inside, working. She would be sitting at the front of the shop, checking a garment that one of her workers had finished, examining seams and stitches – and proudly glancing every now and then at the little pile of coloured business cards that she had just had printed. He stood there sullenly, like a child, wondering what to do; trying to keep the memory of Aisha intact inside him before his mother trampled it again with her anger, her passionate denunciations, her histrionic yet accurate version of the world as a place of whoring daughters, traitor sons, emasculated fathers and lascivious Hindu police constables.

At last he came to a decision. He walked down the alleyway that ran round the back of the shop and climbed the outside staircase. At the top he unlocked the padlock to the kitchen door, crept in, fumbling as he reached the bedroom, and slipped his hand under her mattress where she kept the key to her trunk. He lifted down the trunk from the shelf. She stored the gold at the very bottom, below her few good saris and her best kitchen utensils. She never wore the jewellery, and once, when she showed it to him, she told him she was saving it for her daughter-in-law. That was long before Humayun fell in love with Aisha.

The gold was still there, wrapped in a purple-flowered cloth. There was a bundle of notes in there, too, and he put it all into the jute bag he had used for schoolbooks when he was a child. Finally, he reached his hand down the side of the trunk and felt for the plastic-wrapped packet of papers where she kept the ration card and school leaving certificate and, most importantly, his driving licence. He left the ration card for her in the trunk. The rest of the papers he put in his pocket. Then he locked the trunk again, heaved it back onto the shelf and before leaving the house, he wrote his mother a note.

> Mother, Aisha came to free me from the police. The police have beaten me and told me to leave Delhi. I know that you don't support our marriage but it is too late to do anything different. I have taken the jewellery you set aside for my wife and the money. Please forgive me.
> Your son, Humayun

He left the note on the bed, looked around him one last time at the house where he had spent most of his life, and before his sense of panic had time to take hold, he locked the door and slipped away down the street. They would escape from Delhi with the money. He would sell the gold, and they would marry, become husband and wife, and start a family. He would buy them train tickets tonight to a place high up in the hills, or next to the sea. Aisha had never seen the sea.

chapter 7

Normally Shiva Prasad thought of his morning visit to the bathroom as a time for fertile meditation, for flashes of inspiration even, but the day after the wedding he was unable to think about his family, or his parliamentary ambitions, or his Autobiography without the memory of the girl – her soft skin and petrified eyes – tripping up his thoughts. He crouched there, naked, and all he could see was her small, dark, terrified face. Eventually, he tried to rouse himself by splashing cool water from the bucket over his person. He stood up, soaped and rinsed, soaped and rinsed, three times, but still that strange aura of the girl wouldn't leave him; it was as if her dirty-sweet odour had become lodged for ever in his nostrils.

Try as he might, he couldn't forget her; he turned again and again to that moment of the great gushing forth, that amazing spiritual tingling, the erupting of a spring of soma, the unforeseen bestowing of the sacred effluence of his body. His mind filled with parallels from India's distant past. There was Lord Arjuna who was a great practiser of austerities, but even during his years of celibacy he abducted the girl Subhadra (at Lord Krishna's sugges-tion) and seduced two princesses. Arjuna also spurned the nymph Urvashi, and was cursed by her to become a eunuch for a year; didn't every Hindu man know that to refuse an amorous lady was to risk emasculation? Such were the lessons of history. And Shiva Prasad sat and remembered the moment of embrace, when he had uttered a cry that sounded unearthly and remote, as if a message was being transmitted from some distant, snowy place.

There was a rapping on the bathroom door. 'What are you doing in there?' his wife called.

Shiva Prasad lifted his towel down off its hook and carefully dried his body, pulling on the clean kurta his wife had left out for him and removing the wax from both ears with a finger. As he did so, he gave himself over to rational thought. There were several significant things:

1. She never said no. She never actually said no. He was overcome by amorousness and she responded to his advances of her own volition. (Why didn't he pay her? Should he say that he paid her?)

2. A jury would believe anything they were told about those dirty, fundo Nizamuddin-dargah Muslims – especially a carefully selected Hindu jury. He would tell them that she beckoned to him, that she led him inside, that she behaved like one of the dancing girls from Emperor Babur's harem.

3. Of course it would never actually get to court. Shiva Prasad knew those families – they had no desire to publicise such dishonour, unless they saw money in it. Shiva Prasad, on the other hand, was a pillar of the Delhi establishment. They couldn't possibly win.

4. Where was the proof?

Feeling better, he exited the bathroom, called his wife into their bedroom to cut his toenails and powder the soles of his feet until they exceeded even their customary silky softness, and then, as she began opening cupboards and jewellery boxes – preparing, in the usual fussy way of women, for Sunita's wedding lunch – he dressed himself in his finest cotton dhoti and locked himself into his study to make a new life plan.

For an hour, Shiva Prasad sat absolutely still, staring out of the window and listening to the cooing of the pigeons who had made their home in the water-cooler, and going through his options. Certain key lifestyle changes presented themselves for his perusal. The first one was the easiest and the best: from henceforth there was to be a total boycott of his son-in-law's family. Since there was no time like the present, Shiva Prasad summoned his wife into his study and communicated this stricture to her in no uncertain terms. From this day forward, he explained, they were to circumscribe all social contact with Professor Chaturvedi on the grounds that the man was an anti-national secularist, who had refused to modify his heretical statements about key Hindu gods, and thus posed a personal danger to Shiva Prasad's standing with the ruling party. 'Social contact' included the wedding lunch today – he had been thinking it for some time and there was nothing she could say to change his mind – and before she could argue, and regardless of her tears, he picked up the telephone and rang the India International Centre, informing the Manager at Reception that he and his wife would not be attending Professor Chaturvedi's function, and asking him to convey a message to the Professor to that effect. Then Shiva Prasad summoned his assistant for some emergency Autobiography dictation.

Strictly speaking it was Manoj's day off, and when he arrived an hour later, looking flustered and hot, he was carrying a small electronic item in a battered cardboard box. 'A dictaphone, sir,' he explained. 'You speak now, I transcribe later.'

Shiva Prasad regarded this innovation doubtfully. He had been enjoying the sight of his words flowing out of his employee's black

Parker pen. But Manoj placed the object on the study table, pressed the red button, said, 'Hello hello, testing testing,' and then played his own voice back to his employer.

Despite himself, Shiva Prasad was remarkably pleased by this clever device. For the rest of the day his wife had to explain to the non-stop wedding visitors who arrived with boxes of sweets and smiles of goodwill, that her husband was working hard on his Autobiography and could not be disturbed. Every now and then, in between visitations, she put her ear to the door of the study and listened to the murmuring of his voice as he rehearsed the great, unparalleled glories of his life so far – and his life as he foresaw it, stretching away into the even more glorious future.

But the next morning, when he woke up, Shiva Prasad remembered his dream – he was being butchered, slowly and with great precision, by the girl's father and her brothers. 'He's in good shape,' they said to each other. 'He'll sell well on the bone.' They stripped him of his clothes and called a washerman, an old man with a long white beard, who wrapped Shiva Prasad in a burqa that smelt of semen, and carried him down to the sewer. The girl was there, washing herself in the stinking water. 'You should use Ayurvedic soap,' Shiva Prasad called out to her. 'Do it halal,' the girl replied.

When his wife came upstairs with his bed tea, she asked him, 'Why did you make so much . . . moaning in the night? You were thrashing about so much, I thought you were having a fit.' And Shiva Prasad remembered how he had twisted and turned, trying to break free from the tight swaddling, trying not to be drowned in the dirty nala water.

He sat up in bed, sipped his tea and regarded his wife warily. His dream had precipitated a decision – one dictated by fear, but he couldn't tell her that – and he wished to implement it without delay. 'I have been a student,' he said eventually, 'I have been a householder, successfully siring children and marrying off my daughter. According to the holy texts, the first two stages of a Hindu life are thus complete. Dharma now requires that I retire to the forest for a period of celibate austerity. My wife may accompany me if she wishes (but that is optional). Then, after some years, I will reach the fourth stage, when, renouncing all worldly possessions – including you yourself – I will wander Bharat till the time of my passing, living on alms only.'

To his regret – but not, he had to admit, his surprise – she burst into tears. He had no clear idea why, however; for they had not been intimate for many years. If it was not the celibacy that she feared, it must be the loss of material things. The tea parties, the silk saris, the visits to her favourite hairdresser and cousins. Yes, she must be crying for those superfluous items. But he couldn't help it. This was Dharma. Nothing could change it.

'We will leave in three days' time,' said Shiva Prasad in a tone of grave finality, picking a number out of the air and not caring how inconvenienced this made her.

Then – having told his wife to prepare for the trip home to Amarkantak; having sent a boy to the railway station to buy the tickets – he washed, dressed and went downstairs to the study to shut himself in with the dictaphone. He pressed Record.

'I shall now, Manoj,' said Shiva Prasad Sharma in Hindi, 'endeavour to explain why, from this day onwards, I have chosen to divert the splendidly glittering course of my life into yogic renunciation. As with astrological science, the following orally given, script-disseminated predictions will reap bountiful harvests in the public forum. Only a certain amount of fate can we leave to karma. (That is off the record.) Is your pen ready? Have you evacuated recently? Then I will begin.

'Thus it was, one could say, that India's most shining and brilliant example of hope and dedication to the motherland (cross out *shining*, Manoj, and replace with *iridescent*; delete *brilliant* and insert *outstanding*) entered his sixth decade. By this epoch or aeon or yug, Shiva Prasad Sharma had achieved many things of distinction and quality in the tradition of the finest Brahmin priests of yore. He had become a renowned oral historian of the human condition, speaking fluently over the airways on the history of these ancient lands. He had campaigned nobly for glorification of the Hindu people. He had endeared himself to the people without shying from criticism of the ruling parties. The ministers, bureaucrats and presidents all loved him for his quick tongue and nimble views. Frequently he saw policies proposed by himself over dinner materialise into parliamentary edicts on the morrow. Many were the times when his friends and colleagues urged him to understand that the only way forward was Governmental. "You will become President in no time!" they told him.

'But one day, Shiva Prasad took to the floor with a dramatic decision. "My dear friends," he announced very softly, trying not to traumatise them, "I am returning to Amarkantak. I am renouncing the world and travelling back to the source itself, to the holy river. My time as a householder is over. I must give all my energies up to the people who need me. I must leave India's capital and turn to a life of sacred seclusion in the forest."'

At this point the batteries ran out, and Shiva Prasad listened to the clunk of the machine and reflected with something of his old, excited tingle, on the disappointment he would inflict on his Party. He knew that sooner or later he would have been offered a glorious ministerial post, and that over the coming months, people all over India would shake their heads and say, *Shiva Prasad is instead becoming a Vanaprastha – what a loss to Indian society! How nobly he is* retiring to the forest before even collecting his worldly accolades! What an inspiring example he sets for us all!

Nothing could harm him now – not the outrages of the Chaturvedi family, nor the marriage Urvashi had made, nor the spurning of his talents by the Party. For thousands of years, twice-born Hindus in India had reached this stage of life, and become noble Arya Vanaprasthas. Now it was his turn to bow his head to Dharma and peacefully follow where they had led before.

chapter 8

They were swimming underwater, the current rippling over their bodies, the pale green light washing through them as they moved through the river – so fast that even though her eyes were open she could sense but not see Meera beside her, her sari streaming out, sinuous as seaweed. The telephone began ringing. 'Answer the phone, Leela,' Meera said, her voice commanding, and when her sister turned towards her, Leela looked into her eyes, large and questioning and angry, and saw the wound on her head where the truck had struck her. She picked up the receiver and put it to her ear.

'Where were you last night?'

But Meera and she had never learnt to swim, it was something she did after she moved to New York.

'Where *were* you?' Her husband's voice.

'Last night?' She couldn't remember what had happened.

'You didn't come home. I rang throughout the night.'

'I came home,' she said logically, looking around her at the bedroom. 'I'm here now.'

'It's four in the afternoon. Where were you during the night? Where did you go?'

The light was coming in through the curtains. She remembered suddenly. 'I went to see Vyasa's children,' she said, momentarily triumphant at the recollection. 'I went to see their ayah.'

She remembered everything now: Raziya, the shrine, the fire, the journalist who knew about the poems, Vyasa's mother. Nothing had happened as she had wanted it to.

'Why?' Hari was asking.

'There's something I needed to discuss with them,' she said reluctantly. 'But I didn't manage it,' she added.

'What is it you have to discuss?'

'I can't tell you till I've spoken to them.'

'Why not?'

'It concerns my sister.'

'Is it something serious?'

'Yes.'

'And what is so serious that you can't tell your husband?'

'So many things, Hari,' she said. 'So many things are so serious that I can't discuss them with you.'

'You don't want to?'

'I want to.'

'Then why don't you?'

'I just can't.'

'Tell me.'

'No, please, not on the telephone.'

There was a silence, and then Hari said, very slowly, for he was issuing an ultimatum: 'I am going to come home now. And if you can't tell me what has been going on—' his voice broke, 'and whatever it is that's so serious, then . . . I don't know how we can go on together.'

He put the phone down and she lay back in bed, closing her eyes, trying to return to that river where she had been swimming with Meera until the phone rang.

But she couldn't. She got out of bed and walked through to the bathroom to stand beneath a cold stream of water. Meera was gone, and after twenty years she had still not atoned for the things they had done to each other.

This was what she had achieved last night: the realisation that the way she had acted all these years was selfish, cowardly and wrong. If she had learnt a single truth from her childhood it was that it didn't matter who brought you up, family or strangers, as long as those people were capable of giving you love. She, who had divined the preciousness of this bond at the earliest age – who could not remember anything of the family she had had before; who felt, as a young woman, that this chance had taught her life's most important lesson – had learnt of Meera's death twenty years ago, and done nothing. Instead of returning to Delhi to offer Vyasa's children her presence and love, she had allowed her fear and resentment to stifle the one thing she believed in. And as the water streamed over her body, filling her eyes and ears, Leela willed herself to think on that one last promise she had made to Meera as they said goodbye in Santiniketan. *If anything happens to me, you will look after them, won't you?* And Leela answered: *Yes, Meera, I will, I promise.*

It had been the darkest hour of the night when Leela opened the gate of Vyasa's house in Nizamuddin West. She had seen the light come on in the downstairs window and hoped that it was one of the children. But when she stepped through the flowerbed and up to the window and saw the plump, contented old lady with her plait of white hair, she thought to herself: *Good.* Better to have the conversation about her sister's last years with the mother than with her son. 'Hello, Mrs Chaturvedi,' she said, and the old woman – her given name was Nalini – looked up at the sound of Leela's voice and peered out into the garden.

Vyasa's mother had come downstairs that night, unable to sleep. On nights such as these, when the sleep wouldn't come, she waited until everybody else in the household was in bed, and then she made her way down to the kitchen, where she prepared for herself one of those special dishes which she loved, and which her over-anxious doctor had tried to abolish from her diet: sliced bread fried in ghee with a fried egg on top. The young Tamil doctor complained it was bad for her weight, and thus for her diabetes, and consequently for her eyesight. But it tasted good; and how many more sights did one need to see at her age? She had seen her son married, her son widowed, and now her grandson take a wife. She had lived through Partition and the Emergency and this 'liberalised' phase when young girls had boyfriends and self-respecting ladies wore skimpy tops. She had heard her relatives gossip about her grand-daughter's behaviour; had seen the blue and turquoise vase – her oldest possession – smashed by the maid. She had seen enough.

She took her plate through to the front room, sat down in her favourite chair next to the open window – the breeze came in but the wire gauze kept the insects out – and allowed the small frugal bites which she took of this delicious concoction to bring back the peaceful feeling that had gone ever since Bharati returned to Delhi. This evening her mind couldn't leave the subject of her grand-daughter alone. She loved Bharati, and yet she was also aware that the girl, pretty and clever though she was, was nevertheless not all she could have been. She lacked a certain gravitas, and that lack was quite improper; it saddened Mrs Nalini Chaturvedi to see that an old-fashioned type of modesty had all but been eradicated from the manners of those women who moved in her son's academic circles. For Bharati, in particular, it was a shame, and Nalini felt quite strongly that it went against the very matter of womanhood itself. The girl was composed of too much emotion. She was all *heart* – she wore it on her sleeve, on her skirt hem, wherever the fancy took her – and not enough *common sense*. It was at this point in her ruminations that Leela spoke.

Because it was dark outside, and the lamp at her elbow cast a warm light across her person, and there was in addition the mosquito gauze that mercifully divided them from each other, the speaker's outline was blurred. But Nalini knew at once who it was, standing in the front garden, wrapped in a shawl, half-hidden by the bamboo bush. She bravely suppressed a yell at this ghostly vision, having never forgotten the girl who had come to see her on that day in January 1980 – thin and dark and mournful, like a sad lady from one of those Kalighat paintings: an unlucky village orphan, snatched from one life and placed, with such disregard for social strictures, in another.

Back then, Nalini knew just by the look on Leela's face that the girl was dangerous.

'I think my sister lives here,' the young girl standing on the doorstep had said; but Nalini was unmoved, and replied in her grandest manner: 'My daughter-in-law doesn't want to be disturbed. She is busy with the twins'; for she had overheard a conversation between her son and his troublesome wife in which Meera had shouted that she no longer wished to see her sister, and it had been difficult for Vyasa to calm her down.

Leela dropped her eyes and left the house without another word; and Nalini heard nothing more of her. And now, here she was, making trouble again. 'It's rather late,' Nalini said, in an unfriendly voice.

Leela smiled and said, 'I'm sorry to disturb you, Mrs Chaturvedi. I came to Nizamuddin to pay a visit, but there was a fire in the basti and that delayed me.'

Nalini raised her eyebrows. 'I'm glad to see you've recovered from your fainting fit,' she observed. 'It must be all the travelling you've been doing.'

Leela gave a nervous laugh. 'I'm so sorry. It was a lovely wedding. I hope it didn't spoil the event. It's never happened to me before, but after twenty years away everything feels so strange, and yet so familiar.'

'Our families have collided again, it seems,' Nalini said.

'It is especially odd being here without Meera. And then, seeing her children, grown up.'

Nalini said nothing.

'It must have been difficult for them, growing up without a mother,' Leela went on.

'My son was there to look after them,' Nalini was moved to correct her. 'I was there too.'

'Yes,' Leela said. 'They certainly seem to be very nice children.'

'I have been blessed,' Nalini said. She studied Leela through the gauze, wondering whether to invite her into the house. She decided against it. 'Do you have any issue of your own?' she asked.

'No,' Leela said; and Vyasa's mother shook her head at the involuntary pity she felt for this thin dark foundling.

'Meera wrote about you in one of the letters she sent me after she was married,' Leela said after a moment, in her low voice.

'She wrote that she didn't like me, I imagine.' Nalini was under no illusions about the extent of her daughter-in-law's betrayal. Meera had been a Calcutta urbanite – exquisitely turned out, educated to excess, as lovely, so everybody said, as a champak flower. But Vyasa's mother never trusted her daughter-in-law. She had wanted her son to marry a good, fair-skinned U. P. Brahmin; not a Kayasth fish-eating Bengali. She suspected that Meera didn't love Vyasa; and Meera certainly didn't love his mother. Worst of all, she appeared not to love her children. Only after the ayah arrived did the babies flourish. And only after Meera died, two years later in that strange accident, did Vyasa's mother grow to love his children.

Leela said, 'I think she sometimes wished she was back in Bengal without the responsibilities of—'

'That was her destiny,' Nalini interrupted. 'It's the destiny of all of us. What's more, she chose it. She had nothing to complain about. Her husband loved her and provided well for her. He gave her this house—' She gestured around her with one hand. 'What did she have to complain about?'

'She was homesick.'

'All young brides are homesick. I was homesick once. It's what happens.'

'She missed home.'

'No, she didn't. She never wanted to visit her father in Calcutta.' Nalini peered out at Leela. 'You never wanted children of your own?'

Leela shook her head, and Nalini felt displeased. Something about the way this foundling carried herself gave the old woman an impression of . . . she wasn't sure what; something she couldn't quite distinguish or define; *poor woman*. Not to have borne a child; not to have suckled an infant; to have been denied every woman's greatest achievement.

'Mrs Chaturvedi, may I wash my face before going home?' Leela said. 'I feel quite shaken by the fire.'

This time, Nalini nodded quite benignly. 'I'll open the door,' she said, and got to her feet. Neither of the children were here – it could do no harm.

She unlocked the front door and pointed up the stairs. 'Use the bathroom through the bedroom straight ahead of you,' she said. 'The only other person here is my son, who sleeps on the floor above.'

Nalini nevertheless waited in some trepidation as Leela walked upstairs, and was glad when she soon returned and took her leave. As she watched Leela Bose walk away down the street, something about their conversation hovered like a wraith in the back of her mind. But she couldn't seem to get any firm purchase on it, beyond a feeling of having been compromised in some way. She locked the front door again and walked slowly upstairs to bed.

Almost the first thing Leela saw as she stepped through the door of Vyasa's house was the framed picture on the stairs of Meera. It was taken on the first day of their BA degree at Presidency College in Calcutta – and you could see that she was happy. Such plans they had, what grandiloquent visions, as teenagers they had dreamt of rich, meaningful lives. They were going to be poets, like Rabindranath Tagore, and they had enrolled on the literature degree to read and learn from the canon – from Milton, Wordsworth, Shakespeare. Many years later, Hari would tell his friends, *My wife has a degree in English!*, as if she had joined some exclusive, international club; but Leela herself never questioned the politics of what they were doing until one night, a few days after their final examinations, when Meera came and announced her decision: to leave Calcutta for Tagore's university in Bengal, to study Sanskrit and Bengali, to write other, better poems in a more authentic environment. 'You want to go and live out there, in the middle of nowhere, away from the city?' Leela said in an unbelieving voice, well aware that the things that engaged her sister most were city pleasures (late-night conversations over coffee, midnight walks, throngs of elegantly dressed women, chance meetings with loquacious men). In the end, however, she agreed with Meera's plan; their grieving father, always trying to be liberal, let them go; and it was there, at Santiniketan, that Vyasa found them.

Leela made no comment on the photograph in front of Vyasa's

mother. All she would let herself think as she walked upstairs was: So this was the house where Meera spent the last two years of her life.

The bedroom door on the landing was jammed open with a pile of books and Leela took a quick, sudden breath when she reached the threshold. Clothes were strewn across the room: silk saris had been discarded on the bed, flung down upon the ochre-coloured quilt like rivers winding down from the mountains. There was a heavy, black and red embroidered skirt hanging from the back of a chair which she immediately recognised as Meera's. This must be Bharati's room.

Leela stepped over the half-emptied suitcases and made her way to the desk under the window. The desk, too, was piled with books, and the volume that was uppermost had a scarlet cover and a black etching of a woman's face. Meera's profile stared haughtily out at the world. Leela picked up the book. She had known about the publication only since reading Pablo Fernandes' article on the plane; this was the first time she had held it in her hands. It was a slim volume, of barely sixty pages. She flicked quickly through it – The Lalita Series, it was called – and turned back to the copyright page. It had been published after Meera died. There was a short introduction from the poet's bereaved husband.

Leela slipped the book into her bag, and when she came downstairs again, she said goodbye to Vyasa's mother and walked away down the road. She found that she was clasping and unclasping her hands as she walked. It was nearly three in the morning, and the night was cold. She thought with pity of the prone bodies she had seen as she arrived in Nizamuddin that evening, lying wrapped in their slices of cardboard against the urine-stained wall of the colony.

At the taxi rank in the market, Leela roused a taxi driver from sleep. Before going home to Hari she wanted to read the poems in solitude. She told the driver to take her to one of the five-star hotels near Connaught Place.

The Park Hotel smelt incongruously of incense, and as Leela walked into the coffee shop, she found to her relief that they had at least turned off the music which during the day came incessantly out of the speakers, permeating all conversation with its dreariness. She sat at a table by the window, ordered a coffee from the young, sleepy waiter, and opened the book. Her collaboration with Meera was among the things she had treasured most in the years that followed. Nobody could say whose lines were whose; the point was that they had done it together. It had been sacrosanct, the pact between them. Leela made the two manuscript sets herself, copying the poems out twice in the months after Meera left Santiniketan to marry Vyasa. She wrote them out in the evenings with the black fountain pen that their father had bought her, and that autumn, when Meera returned, she presented them to her as gifts from one sister to another.

Vyasa's brief foreword explained how he had found the poems among his late wife's papers. He evoked the febrile atmosphere of her parties, one of the main attractions of which was her poetry recitals, her modern-day mushairas. He described how happy he was to have discovered this neat stack of verses, autographed with the poet-name his wife had chosen for herself, *Lalita*. He trusted that the reader would take as much pleasure in the poems' youthful expressiveness as he himself had.

Leela called to the waiter and asked for the bill. A thought had struck her. Why was it that in their poem 'The Last Dictation', Meera and she had written about two of the sisters from the epic – Ambika and Ambalika – but had neglected to mention Amba? Amba was the one who, unlike her compliant siblings, refused to be given away as a bride to a man she didn't love. So incensed was she by her treatment at the hands of Bhishma, Vyasa's half-brother, that she burnt herself to death in order to be reborn as a warrior, and during her next life, when nobody else was able to kill him, it was she who appeared on the battlefield and defeated him. That's who they should have taken as their model, Leela thought. Some angry, rebellious woman full of defiance.

She walked back home to Kasturba Gandhi Marg through the deserted streets, thinking of the three months she had spent in Delhi as a twenty-two-year-old: trying to decide what to do with her life, and how defiant to be. Meera had written her numerous letters from Delhi that December, each one full of unhappiness at being a wife and mother, with bitterness at the turn her life had taken, with resentment for Leela's free and solitary existence. When Leela showed them to her father, he begged her to be careful. 'Don't interfere,' he said. 'She's an adult woman with responsibilities of her own. She needs to make a go of marriage and motherhood.' Though Leela found it difficult to protect herself against these letters – their words seared themselves into her mind – the silence that followed was worse. When the letters stopped coming altogether: that was unbearable. On the day she left Calcutta, telling her father that she had to go to Delhi, in case Meera needed her help, he repeated his advice.

Leela only ignored his warning once during the whole time she spent in Delhi, when, on the morning she arrived from Calcutta, exhausted by the journey, she went straight to Vyasa's house in Nizamuddin to see her sister. But it was Mrs Nalini Chaturvedi who answered the door of the grand house where her sister lived. She turned Leela away.

'Will you tell her I called, though?' Leela said as she left, and Vyasa's mother had nodded.

Yet no word came from Meera in the days and weeks that followed, and Leela didn't dare to return to the house. The longer she spent in Delhi on her own, the more her thoughts took her round in circles.

She went through what had happened: reminding herself that the twins needed a loving family and the worst thing Leela could do was to come between their parents. In the end she decided that her father was right: and instead of going back to see her sister, she walked every morning to the school where she taught, and returned home to the empty house on Kasturba Gandhi Marg in the evening. She allowed herself to be courted by Hari Sharma, and to make plans for emigration. And it was only right at the end – in the very last days before leaving Delhi for New York – that she went back to see the twins: who would never know, or remember, or be able to tell Meera of the woman who had come to visit them on those two spring mornings.

Leela finished her shower, dressed and came out onto the veranda from the bedroom. Ram was sitting in the garden in Hari's planter chair, his legs tightly clad in a white churidar stretched out before him. He was smoking a cigarette.

'You missed the wedding lunch at IIC, Auntie. So did Uncle.'

'The wedding lunch?'

'Ash and Sunita's wedding lunch. Given by the Professor.' He smiled up at her.

'I forgot all about it,' she said. 'I was sleeping. Jet lag. Did it matter we weren't there?' Leaning over, she took a cigarette from him and lit it. Meera and she used to love shocking the aunties with their smoking; but it was a girlish thing, and she had dismissed it after marriage. Only since Hari had broken the news of their return to India had smoking become a habit.

'Yes,' he said. 'Nobody came from our side of the family except me.'

'Nobody?' Leela said; and wondered when she should explain that she was from both sides of the family.

He shook his head.

They smoked in silence, and after a while Ram said, 'My sister is lucky to have married into that family.' Then he asked: 'Do you like living here?'

'It has many memories,' she said. 'Do you?'

He shivered. 'Not at all.'

Despite herself she laughed at how emphatic he was. 'Why not?'

'See, I had a disagreement with Uncle Hari about it. I said, "This locality is not good, and the house is so gloomy."' Ram sighed. 'I actually found an architect who said he could make this place special: Rajasthani turquoise entrance hall' – he gesticulated – 'red Mughal drawing room, Hindu murals in the bathrooms . . . But Uncle Hari wanted this . . . plain, white, old-fashioned look everywhere.'

Leela gestured in her turn towards the house. 'Your uncle is trying to recapture the grandeur of the past.'

'He doesn't understand what matters today in India, Auntie!' Ram jumped to his feet enthusiastically, still holding the cigarette, and walked from the garden up the steps to the veranda. 'It is other places that matter now. He doesn't see the drug addicts in Connaught Place and the prostitutes outside the Hanuman Temple. He doesn't see all the rubbish thrown in the corners along with the paan stains and the needles. That's why all the families have moved away from this part of Delhi. The past is irrelevant. Why stay here because of it?'

'This whole area,' she said, 'reminds him of when he was taken as a boy to visit relatives in the government apartment blocks at Golmarket. He loved this place and what it stood for. He had a very modest upbringing, much more constrained than yours or mine.'

As she spoke, she thought to herself how strange it was that this brash young man should appear almost charming to her; twenty years ago she would have shunned a boy like this, of his culture and class and upbringing. And the thought of the years that had passed since then gave her a chill; an odd, echoing sense of time. She looked down at her hands, with their wrinkles of age. She suddenly felt old.

Ram left soon afterwards – he was going to a Diwali party somewhere on the edge of the city – and Leela sat on the veranda waiting for Hari to arrive, watching a crow as it strutted proprietorially on the parapet above, stopping every now and then to pick at something, its feathers oily, jabbing and pecking and hopping in ever tightening circles. Ram had asked her if she missed New York, and she had shaken her head and smiled. But she thought now of the wisteria on her roof terrace, the roses and jasmine she had planted. The distant sounds of taxis and sirens in the streets below. The wonderful silence. She shut her eyes and listened. This place had a quality of silence too.

She opened her eyes again. She had made the wrong decision as a twenty-two-year-old. She should have returned to Nizamuddin and demanded to see her sister. So much would have been different if she hadn't believed that sly old woman. Later, after Meera died, her father wrote to her about his sombre speculations concerning her sister's marriage. But it was too late now for such regrets. The question was how to make those mistakes better.

There was the sound of a key turning in the front door and Leela got to her feet so quickly that the crow took fright and lumbered into the air and flew away. She felt a sudden sharp feeling of relief. A quarter of a century keeping a secret: all about to end in a few brief words.

chapter 9

After Bharati stormed out of the flat to go to her brother's wedding lunch, Pablo had set about packing for his trip to Calcutta. Although he liked to think of himself as a pioneering environmental reporter – a tireless investigator of how India's new wealth was waging war on the natural environment – his editor liked to remind him, every now and again, that his strengths *actually* lay in literary features, svelte cultural analysis, and a certain way with words. That was his bread and butter, from the newspaper's perspective. And so he was being dispatched to Calcutta, to write a piece on the country's new archaeological acquisition.

The newspapers were calling it 'Museum Diplomacy'. India had relinquished to Pakistan three Savile Row suits belonging to Mr Jinnah, one in green Harris tweed, the other two in a fine off-white linen, as well as several silk ties and a pair of darned socks – which a faithful servant had taken from his house in Bombay at the time of Partition and stored, for the past fifty years, wrapped in tissue paper, dotted about with mothballs, at the bottom of a trunk beneath his own, and his wife's, much humbler articles of clothing. This trunk had accompanied the servant from Bombay to Calcutta in 1953, from Calcutta to his village three hours outside the city in 1967, and, in 1982, after he passed away, back to Calcutta again with his widow, to their only daughter's house, where it remained untouched until the day, fifty-two years after Partition, when his widow died, and their child went through her deceased parents' possessions and saw the note, in old-fashioned English script, explaining that the suits were to be returned to Mr Muhammad Ali Jinnah, the day he came back to India from Pakistan. There was a receipt in the pocket of the tweed suit from a bookshop in London's Charing Cross.

Since Mr Jinnah had died in 1948, however, and since his only child was a daughter – and not, therefore, likely to wear her father's clothing – the articles were donated to the nation during a reception for which the servant's daughter was brought from Calcutta to Delhi to meet the President. The story got into the Pakistani press; two museums, one in Karachi and one in Islamabad, immediately put in a bid for the items; and a clever civil servant at the Archaeological Survey of India in Delhi, reading this comment in the papers one morning, spotted a once-in-a-century chance for national glory and rapid personal promotion.

For the past fifty years, India had been agitating for the 'return' to India of a small Shiva lingam excavated during British times from a temple site on the far bank of the Indus and, since Partition, held in Pakistan. In 1948, following Gandhi's death, the first Prime Minister of Pakistan, who had scant time to interest himself in ancient relics, had granted permission for the lingam to be exported, in the wake of Pakistan's Hindu population, to India; but the official process for the migration of antiquities was considerably more lengthy and complicated than that of humans; and just before signing the final paperwork, he was assassinated. The new administration, cut from sterner and more modern cloth, saw no reason at all why they should continue negotiations on this trivial subject – especially when India was behaving with such intransigence over Kashmir.

Fifty years on, at the Archaeological Survey of India's prompting, the ruling party in India brought up the issue again with their counterparts over the border – and the current military dictator, a jovial, whisky-drinking man with a dog, who had enjoyed several sympathetic tête-à-têtes during his recent visit to India with that country's gracious, sari-clad Minister of Culture, proved sympathetic both to the plight of the Founder's clothes and to the 'Hindus' holy ding-dong' (as he called it in private with his generals and wife and lady friends in Lahore), and to the great delight of the Indian cultural establishment, its press and Hindu priests, the lingam and the suits were exchanged in a rare and much-hyped moment of understanding between the fractious neighbours.

Few in India mourned the departure of the suits. All attention was on the lingam, which had arrived that week in Delhi, flown first class by Pakistan International Airways to the Indira Gandhi airport, and thence by police escort to the Archaeological Survey of India at India Gate, and finally – after being subjected to a thorough examination by a team of respectful archaeologists – was packed up once more and dispatched to Calcutta, the city where Jinnah's servant had ended his days, where a brand-new case had been erected for it in the Indian Museum, in front of the entrance to the Archaeology Gallery.

That was the story, and it was Pablo's job to go to Calcutta, interview some passers-by about their feelings, and file a 'nice, upbeat, cultural piece' by the day after tomorrow at the latest.

As he sat on the terrace, waiting for the taxi he had ordered to arrive, Pablo thought about Bharati. He knew he had been insensitive for raising subjects as personal as her mother's poetry and her estranged aunt – and remarkably stupid for doing so within hours of achieving his teenage dream of getting Ash's sister into bed. Throughout their schooldays, Pablo and his friends had secretly pined for Ash's aloof and pretty twin. They had come to the house to play chess with Ash or to collect him for birdwatching, morosely hoping for some interaction with that lovely creature. But Bharati was oblivious to their pining. She breezed through the house, waving to them en masse as she went – as if Ash's entire social group was composed of another, less important species; as if she was the flame-feathered flamingo, and they were a flock of common starlings, or worse, something waddling and banal, a duck or a chicken. They persisted, however, coming round early on Sunday mornings, hoping to see her at family breakfasts – but already, by the age of thirteen, Bharati took extravagant lie-ins at the weekends, and emerged around midday, looking gorgeously dishevelled and dispensing tart little snatches of her moodiness. They brought offerings – slim editions of Keats, a battered *Anna Karenina*, a cloth-bound *Gitanjali* – but Bharati had always just come out of a Keats phase, or had grown exasperated with nineteenth-century literary heroines, or was terribly bored of the Indian obsession with the big-bearded laureate and his old-fashioned ideas of what constituted progress. She offered scorn or casual thanks, and only once in every twenty times did she bestow upon these tongue-tied young men anything more substantial than a quick word or a cool, appraising glance. Bharati, like the rare migratory bird that she was, disappeared along some more elevated flightpath.

A horn sounded in the street below, and Pablo slung the bag over his shoulder, locked his flat and walked downstairs, wondering if he had ruined his chances with Bharati. He had thought the mystery of the poem might intrigue her; he certainly didn't mean to upset her. But he had talked and talked this morning – it was as if a decade's worth of repressed conversation had come pouring out – as if they were fourteen years old again, and he was still trying to impress her. Perhaps when he got back from Calcutta he could try to make amends. He couldn't remember how long it was before she was due back in London – a week at the most. He could offer to take her birdwatching before that. He would tell her that he was no longer interested in the *Lalita* poems. But was it true? He had to admit that he had become a little obsessed by the idea of a collaboration between Meera and Leela. But if his guess was correct, then why hadn't Leela objected when the poems were published in Meera's name? And why had she had no contact with Meera's children? He remembered the woman he had met in the basti – so elegant and sad and intriguing all at the same time. Perhaps if Bharati had had a woman like that in her life, she would be happier.

Sitting in the departure lounge of the domestic airport, waiting for his flight to Calcutta to be called, Pablo pulled out a photocopy of the rediscovered *Lalita* poem and read it again and again, looking for clues.

'They say that this year the pollution is less,' said a talkative man to his left, 'because of this new compressed natural gas the taxis are running on, isn't it?' But although normally Pablo enjoyed interacting with strangers, and especially educating the ignorant about threats to the environment, on this occasion he ignored the opportunity. He had just noticed something about the poem – its date of composition, the place in which it was written: *Santiniketan, November 1979*. Twenty-two years ago. The year of Bharati's birth. The month the twins were born – Ash was celebrating his birthday on Thursday.

Pablo gave a cry. *Santiniketan* – it had been staring him in the face all along.

He arrived in Calcutta, went straight to his hotel and asked for the times of trains to Santiniketan. Rabindranath Tagore's university was on the outskirts of Bolpur, which was barely three hours away from Calcutta. The trains left Howrah station every morning at 6.05, and returned at four in the afternoon. He could get there and back tomorrow without anybody – the editor, the paper, the lingam – being any the wiser. This was an opportunity for him, a young reporter, to find out something, on his own, something real: not a regurgitated press release, or ministerial statement, or counter-claim from a non-governmental body, but something of true merit. He was supposed to return to the Indian Museum tomorrow and interview the Director. But he could do the interview on Wednesday, or on the telephone. He wasn't going to pass up a trip to Santiniketan for a repatriated lingam. No way.

The next morning, Pablo dozed off on the train, and when he woke, they were travelling through the open countryside. As far as the eye could see, there were date palms, ponds and fields dotted with peasants. Pablo, who had grown up in cities, had a fascination with the Indian countryside – he was pleased that it did not make him shudder – and he looked out at the women as they worked in the fields, carefully cutting, gathering, scraping the dry rice stalks into piles. The starch in their saris had long since worn away, but the women stood out in their splashes of yellow and orange, with their curved blouses, their collarbones and shoulder blades, even the occasional kneecap where the mud was deep, their hair knotted and oiled.

The train pulled in to Bolpur just after nine. There was one platform, and, at the exit, countless cycle rickshaws, and a noisy clamour. Pablo chose a bicycle with a smart yellow hood, whose driver was young and looked strong. 'Take me to the literature faculty,' Pablo told the man. They drove through the town, past shops selling things found the length of India: shelves of soap in luminous green and pink packets, kilos of sugar weighed out and tied up in thin plastic bags, hanging khadi cotton school satchels, folded flowery saris. There was a row of metal trunk shops, a television-selling centre, an Internet point, a guesthouse. After a while, the shops thinned out into stalls, the stalls into fields, and here the rickshaw turned left, towards a sprawl of trees and houses and, in the distance, spacious playing fields. The rickshaw driver's thick, muscular legs strained to reach them, over red, dusty paths, past yellowing hostels, under the branches of old, wide trees. 'University campus,' he explained, pointing right, and chanted: 'Rabindra Bhavan, Kala Bhavan, Sangeet Bhavan, Central Office, Central Library, Chinee Bhavan, Mandir.'

The driver stopped outside a large white building with a flight of wide steps, and Pablo, looking up, saw that he had been brought not to the literature faculty, but to the Central Library. Feeling in his pocket for his wallet, he opened it and took out the newspaper clipping of his article about the poem, with the picture of Meera Chaturvedi. Then he walked up the steps, pushed through the doors and presented himself to the two gentlemen at the desk.

But they shook their heads when they were shown the clipping. They were too young to have known her, Pablo thought; and he asked to be introduced to one of the older librarians. 'It's very important,' he said, pulling out his press card.

'We have reduced staff,' one of the men protested. 'It's still the Puja holiday.' But the other man got to his feet and moved off with some alacrity, and Pablo sat down to wait. He waited for a long time, and when the old librarian, a thin lady with glasses and a rough cotton sari, eventually arrived, she peered at the clipping and shook her head. 'What did the person study?'

'Literature,' said Pablo.

'Do you know who taught her?'

'Ved Vyasa Chaturvedi.'

'Oh, him.' The librarian sniffed. 'Wait a moment.'

She took out her keys and opened the door into her office. 'Come in,' she said, speaking over her shoulder as she shuffled towards a big metal cupboard at the back of the room. 'He had a year-photograph taken with all his students. It was a new fashion. For a while, all the teachers did it. I kept copies because the first year I was in it, too. He insisted.' She was looking through the shelves of files. 'Here it is.' She picked out a stiff cardboard print, flicked away the dust, and handed it to Pablo. 'I'm there at the bottom, on the far right.'

Pablo looked at the photograph. It was black and white, taken on some steps, probably of the library. The librarian sat a little away from the group on a chair, a smile of alarm on her face. Ved Vyasa Chaturvedi sat at the front, in the middle, his lips pursed slightly. Leela was at the very back, staring straight into the camera, absolutely solemn. She wore her sari with the pallu pulled tightly round her bosom and tucked primly in at the waist. Next to her, holding a flower in her hands, her face radiant, was a girl with a cascade of long hair. 'That's her,' Pablo said, pointing with his finger. 'Meera, the woman Vyasa Chaturvedi married—'

'If you say so.' The librarian took the photograph out of his hands, slipped it back into the cupboard and shut the doors with a clang. 'That's all I can help you with,' she said, ushering him out. 'Vyasa Chaturvedi was a very popular teacher, but he only worked here for a year.'

'Is there anybody else who might remember anything?' Pablo asked.

'Try the Public Relations Officer,' she said. 'Or go and ask at Vidya Bhavan, the humanities faculty. It's a five-minute walk away. The Puja holiday for the academics is still on but the admin are here.'

The Public Relations Officer was an affable man who worked in a building that resembled a cottage, with a gate and a flower garden and a desk with a large photograph of Gandhi and Tagore hanging above it. He ordered Pablo a fine Darjeeling tea, and spoke with enthusiasm of the university and its teachers and alumni but he had nothing to tell Pablo about Meera Bose. Twenty years ago was a very long time, he pointed out; the only people who might know were the academic staff. He doubted that there was anybody who had been here as long as twenty years. He opened his hands wide to show that he knew nothing and repeated what the library staff had said. 'But they won't return to full teaching until next week,' he sighed, 'after the last puja is over.'

Pablo, too, sighed as he walked outside, and down the lane that led into the middle of the campus, under Santiniketan's large peepul trees and into the pleasant, dappled shade. Vidya Bhavan was a long low yellow-painted building. By now it was nearing midday and most of the staff had left for the weekend. Pablo stood in the doorway, trying to explain his problem to the remaining Section Officer, holding up the clipping and feeling hopeless. 'What is her name?' the man asked. 'And her father's name?' But he shook his head when Pablo answered. 'Better that you come back the day after tomorrow,' the Section Officer said. 'Then we will allocate the concerned official to your problem. Actually,' he added, 'the day after is the Diwali holiday. Please return on Friday, when the clerical staff will be sure to see to your enquiry.'

Pablo was walking out to the road again, when the Section Officer cycled past. 'Go and ask at Central Office,' the man called. 'They stay till five on Tuesdays. Maybe they can pull out examination records for you.'

Pablo stood on the road where six workers with cloths wrapped around their heads were ladling red grit onto the path from a lorry. He felt annoyed with these people for not cooperating with his investigation. Not that they would be able to tell him anything useful

– for what was he looking for, anyway? That was the problem: he didn't really know. Yes, he could go to Central Office. He could also go and check for records of Meera at the girls' hostels; but perhaps what he needed most was some refreshment.

'Tea?' he said to the rickshaw driver, and the young man nodded. The student canteen was still closed for the holiday, but the rickshaw driver knew of a teashop nearby which was run by a Santiniketan old-timer: the same family, three generations since the era of Tagore.

It was lunchtime now, and the teashop, when they got to it, was almost empty. Pablo and the rickshaw driver sat down beside the window and gave their order to a waiter.

The waiter was an old man: thin and slow and haggard like so many working men in India. But he was of just the right age, Pablo reflected, and when he brought over their order, and put down the tray on the table, Pablo asked him, 'Have you always worked here?'

The man nodded, and asked, in his turn, 'Are you here on business of some kind?'

Pablo hesitated before answering, and it was the rickshaw driver who spoke, looking up from slurping his tea and saying something quickly in Bengali.

'So you are looking for somebody?' the waiter said, and Pablo nodded. 'For a woman?'

Pablo nodded again, and pulled out the clipping of Meera.

The man took it from him and studied it carefully. Pablo could tell nothing from the expression on his face but when he handed the clipping back, the waiter said, 'Never seen her before in my life.'

Pablo was beginning to feel very foolish. And what kind of scoop was this anyway? His editor wouldn't sanction yet another story on this twenty-year-dead poet, even if her daughter was a highly desirable individual whom the journalist in question was sleeping with. How was he going to explain himself back in Delhi? It was lack of sleep that gave him these pompous notions of himself; they always disappeared once he had some food inside him, leaving a faint, shameful residue in the mind. He took out his notebook, and with his pen, drew a dark, ominous line through the words that he had written at the top of a new page just this morning on the train: *Leela and Meera Bose. Mystery of the poet Lalita. Santiniketan?*

'I can help you,' said a voice, and Pablo looked up to see a chubby old man – or perhaps he was middle aged, it was difficult to tell – who was wearing a pair of glasses, an ingratiating grin and a long orange shirt, and carrying a newspaper, a banana, an umbrella, a notebook, a dictaphone and a pencil. Pablo could see at once that he was the neighbourhood busybody; Santiniketan must be full of them: people who hadn't quite made a career out of disseminating knowledge, and so dispensed it for free to any innocent visitor who was unlucky enough to be passing.

Before Pablo had time to shake him off, the man said, 'She hasn't been back here for over twenty years.' He smiled again at the look of surprise on Pablo's face, and then he said, 'I remember her *and* her sister.'

Pablo stared. Had he mentioned that he was looking for two sisters? He couldn't remember.

'They went to college here. They also spent some time at the Santhal Mission Hospital.'

'The mission hospital?' Pablo said, confused. 'Were they ill?'

'Oh no,' the man said, with a self-satisfied smirk, 'they weren't ill.' He looked towards the rickshaw driver and asked him something in Bengali. The young man grinned and said nothing.

Pablo felt annoyed at this collusion. 'What was wrong with them then?' he said.

The waiter picked up the empty tea glasses from the table and began to walk back towards the kitchen.

'Nothing was wrong with them,' said the man, jabbing his pencil in the air. 'They were both sweet girls. You can go there easily and see for yourself.'

'To the mission hospital?'

'Yes, yes,' the man said. 'It's easy to find. Even though it's no longer in use there's a chowkidar still and the chapel is kept clean for when the pastors are visiting. Take the road to Ilam Bazaar, three kilometres out, just before Sriniketan. It's a house down a lane to your left. You'll see the pond first, and then a grove of papaya trees. I'll tell the boy how to find it.'

'Will he manage, or should I call a taxi?' Pablo said, but the man shook his head.

'He'll be able to take you.' He gave the boy directions in Bengali. 'Good luck,' he said to Pablo as they left. 'Come back here if you don't find what you are looking for.'

What a nation of know-alls, Pablo thought ungratefully as they set off. The road to Ilam Bazaar was narrow and quiet and Pablo sat upright on his seat as the young man bent his head and peddled. He still didn't have a clear idea of what he would find at this hospital he was being taken to. He began to fret again about the wisdom of coming here in the first place. What if his editor wanted the finished lingam story by this evening? Meanwhile the rickshaw-wallah was swinging his vehicle left off the road, and glancing back, Pablo saw the pond the man had mentioned, and the papaya trees with their heavy green fruit. The path was very bumpy and Pablo soon called out to the man to stop peddling. He could see the iron gates of the hospital at the far end of the lane, which was shaded by large trees.

Pablo shivered as he walked up the avenue. When he got to the gate at the end, he stood with one hand on the latch, reading the faded sign:

Santhal Mission Hospital and Orphanage,
Est. 1968 by the Methodist Church of Bengal District Synod
(formerly Methodist Missionary Society of England).
Medical Superintendent: Revd. (Dr) D. Ganguli.

He pushed the gate open and walked up the red mud path. It had recently been swept and although the whitewash on the building was very old and stained by countless monsoons, and several of the windows were cracked and broken, the place hadn't been completely abandoned. Somebody had collected fruit from the papaya trees – there was a big pile of it on a sheet next to the path. Pablo walked up the steps and rapped on the door. But there was no answer, and the door was locked. He put his face to the dusty glass and found himself looking down a long tiled hallway which was reminiscent of the schoolrooms of his childhood. Three doors led off the hallway with signs above them but he couldn't make out the words.

Pablo came down the steps and walked around the building, across an overgrown garden, to the yard at the back. The chapel that the old man had mentioned was at a little distance down a path lined by red flowerpots with nothing in them. The chowkidar was clearly living at the back here, in what was probably the old kitchen of the hospital. Pablo rapped on the door.

The man opened it himself, stepping outside when he saw Pablo and closing the door behind him. Without speaking he led Pablo away from his private quarters – as if he was ashamed of them; or maybe he didn't want Pablo to see his wife – and down the path towards the chapel. It occurred to Pablo, as he followed him, that the man might think he had come here to pray.

'I don't want to go to the chapel,' Pablo said suddenly in Hindi.

The chowkidar stopped and looked back at him. He was wearing a long white shirt and a dhoti and his thick glasses had been mended with tape. 'Why are you here then?' he asked.

Pablo took out the clipping of Meera. 'I need to find out about this woman.'

The man took it and held it away from himself in his cracked and lined fingers. Then he handed it back, and said, 'Yes, she was here. She came at the end to be with her sister.'

'The end of what?' Pablo said.

The man looked away into the distance. 'She came here like all the rest,' he said. 'In those days the hospital had an orphanage. That was why she came here.'

'Ah, yes,' Pablo said. 'And what then?'

'Her sister had been here for a while and then, at the end, she came,' the man went on. 'And they both left soon afterwards.'

Pablo felt confused. He took out his notepad. 'Do you remember her name?' he asked, the detective in him being thorough and cross-checking.

The man seemed to consider the question for a very long time.

'Well?' Pablo asked at last.

'I'll ask my wife,' the man said. 'She worked with the nurses in those days. She will remember.'

The chowkidar walked back down the path towards his quarters, and Pablo followed him, feeling puzzled. But he waited as the chowkidar went inside his house to fetch his wife, and when the woman was brought out, and he saw that she was slow and arthritic and shy, in a worn cotton sari patterned with large flowers, he smiled at her as kindly as he could, and held out the newspaper clipping.

She barely glanced at it before handing it back. 'I can't remember her name,' she said, 'but her sister, who came here before that, she was called Leela. She stayed longer than the others and we all liked her best. This was a busy place then. But we never forgot Leela.'

'Are you sure?' Pablo said.

'Yes,' she said, 'Leela.' After a moment she asked, 'Is she all right? Has anything happened to her?'

'No,' Pablo said, 'everything is fine.' He pressed a hundred-rupee note into her husband's hand. 'I would like to see inside the hospital. Can you show me?'

The man hesitated a moment; but after fingering the note he disappeared it into one of the folds of cotton on his person, and without saying anything else, the husband and wife led Pablo round to the front of the hospital, under a big neem tree and up the steps to the door, where the man took out a key from somewhere and fitted it into the padlock. The door was pushed open and Pablo stepped in after him.

'They took the furniture and equipment away to the hospital at Bankura some years ago,' the man was saying as Pablo looked around the shadowy place with its cobwebs and broken chairs piled haphazardly together at the back of the hall. He tried to imagine it clean and full of sunlight with busy doctors and Christian nurses in their stiff white caps.

'Where did Leela sleep?' Pablo called after the chowkidar.

The old man stopped in front of one of the doors which led off the hall. 'The babies were put in the children's ward,' he said.

'But the unwed mothers,' said his wife, 'lived in a dormitory upstairs until their time came.' She pointed to the sign above the door and Pablo saw that it read, *Obstetrics*.

The chowkidar pushed the door open and Pablo and the woman followed him into a large empty room. 'There were thirty beds in here,' the man said. 'My wife did all the cleaning with one other woman.'

They walked across the room and their feet left marks in the dust. When they reached the high window at the end, Pablo looked up and saw the branches of the neem tree in the yard through the dirty glass.

The man turned to him as he spoke. 'We had a very good doctor, a Christian pastor, who delivered all the local women. Leela's sister had a boy—'

'She came here to give birth?' Pablo interrupted.

'Yes,' the husband said, and he and his wife looked at Pablo in surprise. 'That is why they came here.'

'I didn't know that,' Pablo said, feeling stupid in front of them.

'She had a boy,' the woman resumed.

'Twins,' Pablo said assertively, 'a boy and a girl.'

'No,' said the woman. 'The sister had a boy. Leela herself gave birth to a baby girl.'

Pablo looked between them. 'Leela had a baby?'

'A very pretty baby,' said her husband, and he glanced at his wife, and back again at Pablo. 'A lovely little girl.'

'But Leela stayed here alone,' his wife finished eagerly, 'and it was the sister who took both children back to Delhi.'

The rickshaw driver drove Pablo back in silence on the Bolpur road. At the station Pablo tipped him generously and bought a ticket to Calcutta. He sat on the platform as a succession of men with kettles of milk and pots of instant coffee came by and asked him, 'Kofe, kabe?' 'Cha?' 'Shonpapri?' 'Donation to Thalassaemia Genetic Blood Disorder?' As the train shunted back towards Calcutta, Pablo turned everything down. He didn't notice the fat man from the café, sitting a few seats away and regarding him with a look of satisfaction. He stared instead out of the window, and the hawkers learnt to ignore him, this man with the vacant eyes who didn't listen to a word they said. In fact, Pablo's eyes were registering every scene that passed: the neat squares of bright yellow and brown fields; a derobed statue of the goddess Durga, abandoned after her recent festival – sari, ornaments, even clay all washed away in the sacred immersion, and now only a naked straw figure left with a pike holding her onto her lion vahana. As the train passed over a deserted riverbed, he saw the sand patterned with a thousand anonymous bird prints. The shadows lengthened, the train drew near to Calcutta, and in the fields he saw men in white caps bending down to pray. And always one thought was going round and round in Pablo's head like an incantation: *Bharati is Leela's child.*

chapter 10

Urvashi discovered Aisha was missing the moment she came downstairs for breakfast. The guest room was empty. She must have had to go and meet her mother in a hurry, Urvashi thought, perhaps to buy some wedding clothes. They wouldn't take the train to Bihar without saying goodbye.

For the rest of the morning, Urvashi waited in the house. It was the day before Diwali, a festive time, and it was difficult enough spending it by herself; and then Feroze, when he called, refused to comment on the situation. Urvashi readily filled the silence with his likely reprimands: that she was in the wrong to involve herself in the family life of the servants, that she had interfered enough, that she was middle class and ignorant and muddled about social priorities.

Sitting there alone, Urvashi realised that she didn't even know where Aisha lived. Despite having been in this colony for almost a year, Urvashi shared with most of Nizamuddin West's inhabitants an abiding fear of visiting the basti. Feroze had taken her there once, to Karim's restaurant, and the things she had seen and smelt – the billowing smoke from the kebab vendors, the matted hair and cry of a female beggar, the crafty-eyed Muslim shopkeepers in their beards and white caps, the sickly sweet smell of a halal perfume shop opposite the restaurant – had filled her with revulsion. Until now she hadn't dared to venture to the slum where the servants lived.

But in the afternoon, Urvashi went upstairs, put on a simple salwar kameez and some flat shoes, and gathered her resolution around her like a big dupatta. Aisha's auntie, Humayun's mother, might know where Aisha lived. Humayun had pointed out his mother's tailor's shop to Urvashi once, as they drove down the Lodhi Road. It was on the lane at the far side of the shrine, and Urvashi walked there slowly, through the expensive part of the housing colony, into the place where Humayun and Aisha's families resided. She passed the police post where she had taken Aisha two days ago, and walked quickly through the streets towards the shrine itself, past a line of maimed beggars outside the mosque, past a madrassa. In the square outside the shrine, the food shops had sloshed down their doorsteps and the drains ran dirty with meat juices, blood and mud. Urvashi could smell something cloying and greasy. She asked directions from a fruitstall owner and he called to a small boy, his own son, and ordered him to lead her down an alley where there were stalls selling flowers, sugar sweets and religious texts. Hawkers of five-rupee meals for the poor called out to her as she passed. She ducked after the boy under an archway, into an even tinier street. They passed a barber's shop, a well, and another mosque. Two fat sheep bleated at her from a doorway. Urvashi was bewildered by the time they reached the small tailor's shop run by Humayun's mother.

Once Raziya had ascertained that Urvashi, too, knew nothing about the whereabouts of Humayun and Aisha, she refused to talk to her further. 'Haven't you done enough by allowing this to carry on in your own home?' she asked. 'Why didn't you tell me that girl was working for you? I would never have allowed my son near her.'

'I need to know where Aisha lives,' Urvashi told the boy after

Raziya had turned them away. They walked back along the street, and he stopped at the butcher's shop and asked. There was blood down the butcher's trousers; he had just strung up a sheep and was knifing through its innards. The guts spilt out onto the floor. 'Aisha, daughter of Tabasum?' he said, as he cut out the heart and liver and lungs and they plopped into a bowl. 'They don't live here any more, they moved out to the nala long ago.' He pointed out over the kabariwallah park, where children were sorting waste plastic and foil, and explained something to the boy.

Urvashi and the boy picked their way down the muddy street, past several charred houses. She felt the poverty and the malodorousness of this colony touching her hair and dirtying her skin. The rubbish-strewn wasteland was beyond the basti wall and she could smell the open sewer now. The boy beckoned to her impatiently and gestured to an opening. When Urvashi reached the entrance, she gasped at the scene that was laid before her. The stink was overwhelming. Nosing through the rubbish that lined the drain was a large black pig with a litter of piglets. The boy pointed across the concrete footbridge to the slope on the other side. 'The butcher says they live in the graveyard now,' he said. 'You can look for them there. But I have to go.'

After the boy left, Urvashi stood on the edge of this landscape, watching as the pig waded into the sewer water. She considered going home; but that would have been to neglect her responsibilities to Aisha. So she pulled her headscarf around her face in an attempt to keep out the smell, and walked down the path and across the plain of shit and rubbish, over the bridge, and climbed the bank on the other side. She couldn't face entering the graveyard alone. Hoping to find somebody to guide her, she approached the wispy huts made of plastic sheeting. Sullen-faced mothers were cooking over rubbish-fuelled fires; grubby children were playing barefoot in the dirt. 'Has anyone seen Tabasum and her daughter Aisha?' Urvashi asked cautiously. None of the parents answered, but several dirty little children came running up to her with outstretched hands, asking for money. Urvashi refused them, and walked on. 'Where is Tabasum and her daughter Aisha?' she asked. Still nobody answered. 'Please? Can somebody tell me?' Eventually a man looked up: 'We don't know anybody of that name here,' he said.

'And the entrance to the graveyard, where is that?' Urvashi asked, fearing very much to enter that place alone.

'The gate is over there,' he said, without offering to show her.

Urvashi walked carefully along the wall of the graveyard in the direction he had indicated, until she saw the green iron gate. A young Muslim man with a wispy beard was just coming out. 'Where does Tabasum live, and her daughter Aisha?' Urvashi asked him. The man looked at her in surprise, taking in her fine shawl and glossy hair. Urvashi clutched her handbag to her side, under her pashmina.

'Over there,' he said. 'Next to the watchman's hut. I've just been there myself. But how do you know Tabasum?'

'Her daughter works in my house,' said Urvashi.

'You are Mrs Ahmed?'

Urvashi nodded. 'I'm looking for Aisha.'

'Aisha has gone.'

'Where has she gone?'

'Humayun and she have disappeared,' the man said. 'They must have eloped.'

'Who are you?'

'Humayun's cousin, Iqbal. Salaam aleikum.'

'Waleikum salaam.'

'Come with me, I'll take you there myself.'

She followed him into the graveyard and he pointed to a whitewashed enclosure situated on a piece of high ground. There was a gate, and inside, Urvashi saw, a brick hut with a tent pitched against it. Next to it was a fire site. 'Aisha and her mother sleep in that tent,' the man said, and crouched down next to the fire. He pointed out a bundle of clothes, and a pan, in a recess of the wall. At the far end of the enclosure was a small room for washing in and a line where clothes were drying.

But the old chowkidar's wife came out of the hut to shoo them away. 'What are you doing here again?' she said to Iqbal, pulling her scarf over her head. 'You know we do purdah. My husband will be angry.'

'I am sorry, auntie,' he said, and stepped back behind the gate out of sight. 'This is Mrs Ahmed, her daughter's employer,' he called through to her.

'When she comes back,' Urvashi said to the old lady, 'please ask her to come and see me again. She knows where I live. I didn't understand before. I want to help her.'

She shut the gate behind her and walked down the slope to where Iqbal was waiting. She could scarcely believe that her own maid had lived all this time in this place, in this graveyard, crossing everyday over that hellish sewer. She began to cry. 'I want to help them,' she repeated.

He nodded. 'Of course,' he said, and his voice became squeaky with emotion and she realised how young he was and yet how solemn. 'You can help them by giving them work when they return to Delhi. But it is difficult for them now. His mother is angry. Be patient. It is the will of Allah and He does whatever He wills. We should go now.'

Iqbal and Urvashi walked in silence back through the graveyard, across the drain, and out to the road. 'Goodbye, Mrs Ahmed,' he said when they reached the kabariwallah settlement on the corner, and he said something in Arabic that resounded, complicated and unknowable, in Urvashi's ear.

She walked home, her mind moving slowly, as if coagulated into inertia. When she arrived she took off her clothes and soaked them in detergent to remove the smell of the nala. What she had seen today had shocked her, and that night, during dinner, when Feroze praised her cooking, Urvashi remained silent. She was thinking how negligent she had been, not to have enquired where Aisha and her mother lived, not to have understood their trials.

'Is anything wrong, Uzma?' he asked eventually.

'Do you know what *exactly* is DNA?' she replied.

'Yes,' he said in a surprised voice. 'It's the matter in our cells that contains our genes, where our hereditary information is encoded.'

'But what is it used for?'

'It tells us how humans are constituted. Scientists can tell things about disease from our genes. It is used to show who is the parent of a child.'

'But what do the police use it for?'

'Bodily tissue from a crime scene can be analysed and the suspect can be tested and if the two match then the police have their culprit.'

'For what kind of crimes?'

'Murders, theft, rape. You should ask Sunita's husband. He's a geneticist, isn't he?'

'Is he? I don't know.'

Feroze, reflecting that this esoteric and mystical branch of science had entered the public consciousness as thoroughly as sharbat stirred into a glass of water, and yet his own wife barely understood it, thought to himself as they walked upstairs to bed: *Now that Sunita is living in Nizamuddin we must overcome this family rift.* And he reached out a hand and rested it gently on his wife's taut belly, feeling soothed by the life that was growing inside her.

chapter 11

After his argument with Leela on the night of the wedding, Hari
Sharma had taken his car and driven it as far through the city as
he could go. It wasn't far enough. He wanted to surpass the city's
limits, to reach some wilderness, the mountains, a river – one
sublime piece of nature would have done just as well as another.
But it was night-time and nothing of that sort was visible; and
even in the daytime there was nothing like that near Delhi any
more. His headlights lit up the dusty road ahead of him, and all
he saw were empty plots of land and great tent cities, and people
– he couldn't get away from the people – more and more people
wherever he looked, walking through the dust or sleeping in the
dirt or squatting by the road staring aimlessly into the distance. In
the end, he parked the car next to a petrol station on the loneliest
stretch of road he could find, and sat in the darkness.

He telephoned the house before he started back again for home,
but there was no answer. An hour later, when he drew near to
Connaught Place, he tried Leela a second time but still there was
nothing. And then the anger which the drive had forced out of him
resurfaced, and instead of turning onto Kasturba Gandhi Marg he
drove up Janpath, pulled into the Imperial Hotel and asked for a
room and a bottle of whisky. He walked upstairs with the bottle

to sit in his room, motionless in a chair by the window, staring at the bunches of white, heavily perfumed tuberoses that a member of staff had come and arranged in coloured glass vases, and which reminded him so much of Leela. He wouldn't go home – not if she wasn't even there to assuage him with her contrition.

But as he sat in his chair he couldn't help remembering how, on Saturday evening, when she came back from her outing, she had smiled at him and said, 'The whole city smells of raat-ki-rani blossom, doesn't it?' And he had told himself: *Clever Hari, my queen of the night is putting down roots at last, she is coming home.*

He reached out for the bottle of whisky and poured himself a glass and remembered how harshly he had spoken to Leela when they got in from the wedding. Never before in their marriage had he raised his voice in anger. She had seemed to shrink a little in fear; or maybe, he thought, she had drawn herself back, away from him. Being a polite man, he had never questioned her in detail about her family. He knew that the past was painful for her; and he had respected her silence – considered her personal history irrelevant, even. He drank the whisky and poured himself another, and now tears of self-pity came into his eyes. What was it she was keeping from him? He began to weep for his ignorance, for the children they hadn't had together, for his stubbornness in bringing her back to India, for all that she hadn't told him.

He glanced up and caught a reflection of himself in the window: a small man, bald, with bags under his eyes. *Please don't leave me*, he suddenly begged, as if appealing to the city, the sky, the gods. He felt a kind of panic. *Please don't leave me, Leela*, he said, pressing his fingers against his face. And Hari, who had always spoken directly to Ganesh – for the god had guided his business transactions, his choice of a wife, his move to New York, his return to Delhi – implored him now: *Bring Leela home to me. Don't let her leave me.*

The next morning, after breakfast – after he realised that they had spent nine hours apart, and that they were the most awful nine hours of his existence – he went out walking in Connaught Place. He didn't want to ring her again – he didn't want to pursue her – but he hoped that she might call, or that he might bump into her. He watched women pass with their men, the young ones in crisply ironed bright cotton shirts, the married ones elegant in new saris for Diwali. He sat on a bench in a noisy ice-cream parlour filled with young people, slowly eating a mango kulfi, and watching. He wondered if he had ever done anything so simple and pleasurable with Leela. He would take her to a sweet shop like the ones she was used to from her Calcutta childhood – to buy her rose-flavoured chumchum and pistachio-flecked kulfi, to dress her in delicate cottons and kiss the back of her neck under the wave of her fragrant hair. Memories came to him of those first, early days of their marriage. In his innocence as a husband she had made him think of a woman from the epics, from a wondrous, pre-industrial age. He saw her wavy hair and long eyes reproduced from life a thousand years ago. She made love, he flattered himself, with that same mythical abandon. She would twist herself into any contortion for him; there was something divine about her bearing. But nothing would take root in her womb.

In the afternoon, when he couldn't bear the separation any longer, he called her and told her he was coming round. She was waiting for him when he arrived back at the house. Until the last minute – until he actually found himself walking down the path to his front door – Hari had hesitated about going home and executing the ultimatum he had given. He wasn't sure whether he really had it in him. But he found himself turning the key in the lock and pushing the door open – and there she was, standing at the end of the hallway, on the veranda, waiting for him. She was fiddling nervously with her packet of cigarettes and he knew that she was going to tell him something that might shatter them both, and he didn't know if he could bear it. But he had no time to stop her.

'Before we were married I had a child.' She spoke before he was even through the door.

There was a long silence during which he heard nothing but the blood pounding in his head.

'Who was the father?'

She didn't answer.

'*Who?*' he said, shutting the door and walking down the hall towards her.

'Vyasa.'

He couldn't help his sharp intake of breath. 'Ved Vyasa Chaturvedi?'

The news was so awful he didn't know what to say. All he could think of to ask was, 'Is the child alive?'

'Yes. She is Bharati, his daughter.'

He gave a long low moan.

'Hari?'

'Why didn't you tell me before?'

'I wanted to—' She stopped. 'I didn't want to betray you.'

Ved Vyasa Chaturvedi. It was worse than he had imagined. He looked at her – the expression of remorse perfectly arranged on her lovely face – and felt the first jolt of hatred. 'How can you have kept something like that from me? And I thought – I thought – you couldn't have children . . . Did you deceive me about that too?'

She shook her head. 'But at first I didn't want them.'

'You liar!' he shouted, clenching his fists. 'And this child. You must have been thinking of her all the time. All these years. When was she born?'

'November nineteen seventy-nine.'

'So her birthday is – when? Now?'

'In three days.'

He sat down on the veranda steps and put his head in his hands. 'All this time.' He looked up at her. 'Why?'

'I didn't tell anyone.'

'Vyasa?'

'No. He thinks she is Meera's child.'

'Your father?'

'Yes.'

'Your sister?'

'Yes.'

'Your daughter?'

'You're the first person I've told in twenty years.'

'You *gave birth to a child!*'

'Yes.'

'And then what?'

'And then I came to Delhi, and then I met you.'

He got to his feet again and paced up and down the veranda. He stood still and looked at her, his beautiful, perfect, paragon of a wife.

As dusk fell, Hari found himself asking questions – hurtful, damaging questions, to which he didn't need to know the answer – but they were questions which it was impossible to stop, and she sat there, her head bowed, and answered him as truthfully as she could. She told him how, right from the beginning, she had seen through Vyasa's cheap lines and easy charm; how she had despised the stories he told to Meera; how Vyasa had boasted of living all over India, of studying in Oxford, of trying this drink and that drug, of coming to Bengal as a man who has been out and seen the world. He had quoted from Darwin and Descartes, Kalidasa and the Kamasutra; had theories on everything from colonialism to economics to women's sexual emancipation. He had fought revolutions in rural places, he said, and had the scars to prove it, scattered across his skin like flowers. Meera drank in his stories as if they were divine revelations. Soon, she was talking to Leela at night (her hand in Leela's, her lips to Leela's cheek) of the old, false bourgeois codes of conduct, of embracing communal ideas of possession, of contravening the code of ethics they had been educated with. 'Look at the matriarchal clans of southern India,' Meera would say confusedly, half-echoing Vyasa's words; 'look at how we used to live. Why have we inherited this colonial construct, this monogamous two-parent family? Our bodies, our sexual freedoms, are enchained within the missionary model of our colonial masters!'

'Wait,' Hari interrupted. 'Your sister wanted you to sleep with her boyfriend?'

Leela shrugged. 'That's what she said.'

At first, Leela explained, she refused, and it was Meera who reacted like a spurned lover, pouting and sulking and throwing out cutting words whenever Leela came near her. Leela was distressed at the change that had come over her sister. But she thought that she had a choice. She told herself that she could watch Meera walk away with this man who had deluded her, or she could bring her to her senses by agreeing to the tryst that Meera and Vyasa both so wanted. It was only her body, and its functions, that they were talking about, after all. Not her mind, or her heart. And so, on a clear February day, as the scents of spring seeped mockingly out of the wet earth, Leela allowed Vyasa to touch her and kiss her, to untwist her from the cotton sari that Meera's mother had dressed her in. And then, when it was over, she found—

'What?' asked Hari, his head hammering with hatred for this man, Vyasa.

'That it wasn't what Meera had wanted, after all.'

She had felt clever, Leela said, until this moment; had thought that by agreeing to this thing she would make Meera realise what kind of man Vyasa really was. Now she didn't feel clever at all: she saw that it was Vyasa who was triumphant, and that it she who had been duped, and Meera who felt betrayed – and who would from now on be jealous of the sister she had loved. Something had gone wrong between them.

Soon after this, Meera moved out of the room she shared with Leela and began living with Vyasa in a house on the edge of campus. Leela learnt that her sister was pregnant. When the term ended, Vyasa and Meera left for Calcutta, where they were married, and travelled on to Delhi, where they were to live. Alone in Santiniketan, Leela found that she was pregnant, too. She waited, uncertain, and finally she wrote to her father.

'He didn't mind?' Hari asked, trying to conjure up an image of this father-in-law he had never met.

'He was a gentle, kind man,' Leela said. 'He loved us both.'

Her father wrote back, suggesting that she should continue with her MA, until her pregnancy began to show. Between then and now, he said, she must ring him every week, to let him know how she was doing; and it was during one of those phonecalls, as Leela stood in the phone booth telling him of her awful sickness, that he asked the question she hadn't yet been able to answer. 'What will you do with the baby?' Leela shook her head and said nothing. She still didn't know.

'So what did you do?' Hari asked.

'I went to the mission hospital near the university. That's what all girls in my position did. They gave you a place to hide your shame, they brought doctors to deliver your child, and then they took it and baptised it, and put it in their orphanage, and you were free to go, a new beginning . . .'

'So you were going to give the baby away?'

She glanced at him, and then quickly looked away. Instead of answering his question, she described the strange calm that descended on her in those days at the hospital. She could spend hours watching the clouds pass in the sky, or a yellow-striped squirrel climbing up and down a tree, or the sunshine moving across a patch of grass. After a while her stillness scared her.

Hari shifted uncomfortably. He hated this story – the way she was spinning it out, telling it so slowly. But then he didn't want her to rush these details. If she went too fast he demanded that she go back to the beginning; that she should tell him every last awful thing that had happened.

'Meera came to the mission hospital at the beginning of November. She had told Vyasa she was going to Calcutta to give birth in her family home. But when she reached our father's house he told her what had had happened to me. She hadn't known till then. So she came to Santiniketan to find me.'

The moment of Meera's return – Hari would never forget how Leela described it: two girls, mirror images of each other, walking slowly towards each other on the long avenue that led to the Santhal Mission, both their bellies hugely swollen.

'And then?' he said.

'And then—' Leela began, and stopped. And then. And then for two consecutive nights, Meera and she lay on adjacent beds in that high-ceilinged room at the hospital, dressed in identical cotton nightgowns made by the same hands in Calcutta, feeling their babies moving within them. Leela lay there in the half-darkness, listening to Meera's moans, glancing over at her pale and luminous face, the eyes dancing in pain like neem leaves in the wind, and as she watched the nurses moving briskly backwards and forwards across the room, a whisper came to her, a lilting intonation of long-forgotten village words: but before she had time to grasp their meaning, they had disappeared through the night under the whirring of the fan.

'What I remember most,' she said, 'is the sudden terrifying love I felt, a rush of love.'

There was a long silence. It was now too dark to see each other's faces. 'And what are you expecting now?' he said. 'Do you think she will ever be your daughter? After all this time?'

She answered back with a hard edge in her voice: 'Is Ram your son, really? Will he ever be? Does he actually think of himself as your son, or is it just you who thinks of it that way because you wanted a child so badly?'

He began to shout. He hated her anew, for this true and unfair comparison. He called her a whore and a liar. He shouted himself hoarse, until he was so worn out by his own emotion that he had to go and lie down on their bed and cry himself back to calmness.

Late that night, as they lay together, exhausted, he could sense the warmth of her body at the other side of the bed and he felt a constriction somewhere inside, an unknown tightness. Was it his heart?

He spoke through the darkness.

'Tomorrow you should go and see Bharati and tell her that you are her mother.'

Leela was silent. Then she put her hand in his. 'And what about us?'

'It was you who mentioned Ram,' he said. 'I have brought a son into our lives, why can't you bring a daughter?'

'I'm not sure her father will see it that way,' Leela said. 'And how can I go to her now, after all this time, and disrupt her life? She seems so confident.'

'Perhaps she's not as confident as you think,' said Hari. 'Imagine a life without a mother . . .'

'I don't dare, Hari. I just don't dare. Supposing she hates me. Supposing what I say does something to her—'

'What can it do?'

'It might make her sad. It might make her turn against her father. Any of these things. And who am I? I am nobody to her.'

To his shame Hari felt a pounding love for this woman whom, logic dictated, was a stranger to him.

But in the morning, when he woke, and saw her sleeping beside him, curled up on her side, he felt the enfeebling, sickening sense of injustice. The fresh sensation of having been wronged. The spouse he had boasted about to friends and acquaintance. *I could get addicted to it*, Hari realised with a shudder. *But if only she had told me: at least then I could say to people that I knew all along, that I wasn't deceived, that I married her anyway.* And looking down at her, he felt a germ of pity for everything she now represented.

chapter 12

He had slept on the train to Bombay with the money and jewellery in his arms, as if it was a baby he was carrying. She slept beside him. They shared a bunk, Aisha on the inside, her face pressed against the wall, Humayun on the outside, shielding both her and the money from the world. He woke throughout the night: every time somebody passed by, each time the train came to a creaking stop at a country station. He clutched her tightly to him, and in the morning when they sat up to wash their faces and drink some tea, she was refreshed and happy. He smiled to see her like that. For his part, he felt anxieties alighting heavily on his shoulders – like vultures hopping down to tear at a piece of meat.

During the day, as the train moved slowly through the country-side, through a monotonous open country of scrub and electricity pylons and distant villages, with only the occasional tree or pump gurgling water in the corner of a field to relieve the monotony, she looked out and was transfixed by what she saw. 'What is that?' she would ask, pointing at a banana tree; or 'Where are they going?' as a family of small children made their way along a fence leading infinitely away into the middle of nowhere. 'Why are we going to Bombay?' she whispered to him at dusk. 'Because that was the train which arrived,' he explained, only now beginning to feel exhausted by this new inquisitive trait he was discovering in her. 'It was our good luck.' He had passed a terrible, uncomfortable night in Hazrat Nizamuddin station, sore from the blows the police had given him, cold from the sudden drop in temperature, sad about leaving his mother. He added, in a sarcastic voice, 'Where would you rather go, to your village in Bihar?' She shrank back a little, and said nothing more for several hours – until a woman in a green and pink polyester sari climbed aboard with a basket of water chestnuts. And then she asked, 'Where does she get them from, Humayun?' The landscape grew darker, and finally, at his side, to his relief, Aisha fell asleep.

The train reached Bombay very early the following morning. He had been expecting a huge crowd and a rush at the station; imagined himself holding on to Aisha as the millions of people of that city pushed against them. But the station was quiet, and they followed the old man in a white skull cap whom Humayun had deliberately sought out for guidance – he was elderly with a black bruise on his forehead and a dull silver and enamel ring on almost every finger – down the platform and up some steps, from where the old man pointed out across the station. 'Take the C-train,' he said. 'Understand?' And Humayun nodded; yes, the C-train. 'Get off at the third stop,' the old man went on, 'Marine Lines. From there you walk east, past Vardhman Chowk, up Princess Street. The Jama Masjid is just there, next to Zaveri Bazaar.' He gave precise instructions and Humayun listened and tried to memorise the names of the nearby streets and the market where the best mosque of Bombay stood.

The man shook his head at them as he left. 'She is too young,' he said, gesturing to Aisha, and repeating what he had said on the train. 'There are many regulations in place nowadays.' And Humayun nodded equivocally, recognising that this was a problem, but knowing full well that the bride was always sixteen or under, for everybody knew that this was the very best age to get a girl married; and, anyway, Muslim law worked regardless of Indian law. Some qazi would agree to marry them under Muslim law; and he clutched the bag of money and jewellery to his side, and tried to feel again the determination that had brought him this far from Delhi.

The C-train came, almost empty of passengers, and Humayun and Aisha stepped onto it tentatively and sat together. 'The air smells of fish!' she said, as they reached the second station.

'It's the sea,' he said crossly, for he was concentrating on not getting down at the wrong stop.

'The sea!' she said; and, pointing through the bars of the window, asked, 'Is that the sea, Humayun?'

'Yes,' he said, glancing out at the greyish mass of water, uncertain whether it was indeed the sea or a lake or a river.

At the third stop they followed the few other passengers out of the station, and down to the road by a narrow metal bridge. Princess Street was lined by tall yellow and white houses with ornate painted balconies. Aisha and Humayun walked up the road towards the mosque, which was somewhere in the distance. He was apprehensive; she, excited by the city. 'Can we eat some fish for dinner, Humayun?' she whispered, as a gust of air from the sea brought a tingling taste of salt and sea life to their lips. He squeezed her hand. He would feed her fish, he would feed her sweets, he would feed her the best of everything that Bombay had to offer. He forced himself to shout these claims to the huge and uncaring city; and the city looked back at him and laughed at his ambition.

They walked on in silence, his eye noticing a courtyard with its stone statues of ladies in clinging dresses, and the large green trees with huge overlapping leaves as big as his head, and the bodies lying sleeping all along the pavement – but his mind was always thinking only of the mosque that lay ahead.

Eventually the white minarets came into view on the left, and he found that he had been expecting something austere and grand, made of red sandstone, inlaid with white, like the Jama Masjid in Delhi – but Bombay's central mosque struggled to rise above the tangle of shops and stalls at its base.

'Let's have some breakfast,' he whispered to her, afraid again, and they crossed the road to a teashop and ordered omelettes and tea and sat opposite each other in a booth, smiling at each other as he tried not to worry about the future. The first thing to do was find a qazi who could marry them. He sat facing the road, watching passers-by: taking in their clothes, and the way they walked, and how they spoke to each other. Tentatively, he allowed himself to feel pleased by what he saw. When a religious man passed, he ran outside and stopped him and asked respectfully, 'Please, what is the name of the qazi of the Jama Masjid?' The man looked at him, at Humayun's black eye and bruises, and said sternly, 'You should speak to the manager; he will call a qazi for you. It's the office on the right up the stairs past the library.'

When Humayun came back into the teashop, at first he couldn't see Aisha and the wild fear tore at his heart. But she was sitting out of sight, shrunk back against the wall. He slipped into the booth beside her and held her close to him for a moment, not caring who saw them. 'Never leave my sight again,' he breathed.

'But you went outside—' she began, and he shushed her.

'I know, it's my fault.' He stilled the sudden rush of anger inside himself, and said, 'Are you ready? Let's go.'

As he led her round to the mosque's eastern gate, through a narrow covered passageway of humdrum shops, he couldn't speak to her of the pang of longing he felt: for his mother, for his home, for Mrs Ahmed's car even, for the place he grew up in. What had Aisha done to him, to make him turn his back on all of this, to throw caution away, to come to Bombay with her, a penniless, fatherless girl? What dark magic was it she had worked on him? He listed the current insecurities of their life: how they would eat, where they would sleep tonight, how they would find work. What was he doing uniting himself with a girl of this fate and reputation? 'Stay behind me,' he said to Aisha sharply, as they reached the gates, and she stopped gazing around her and cast her eyes downwards, submissively.

He sighed to himself for his cruelty; and taking his shoes off at the entrance, left her fumbling with her slippers, and walked over to the huge sunken stone tank over which the mosque had been constructed. When he reached the steps, he turned to watch her: such a tiny, diminutive figure, the headscarf pulled up over her hair, helpless and vulnerable in this huge hallowed place. The love returned in a rush – he felt it flood back again to fill the space only recently echoing with resentment.

'Feel how cool the air is,' he said to her as she approached. They went right down to the water and splashed their faces and ran their fingers through their hair, shivering at the cold.

They were sitting on the steps of rough grey stone, wondering at this murky pool where real fishes swam, when there was an angry shout, and a young man – his lip shaved in the manner of Humayun's cousin – waved at them from the pathway: 'No women allowed at this hour.'

'But we have come to get married,' Humayun answered, affronted.

'Then,' the man replied, after the briefest of pauses, 'go and wait for the Nazir. He won't arrive till ten.' He pointed to a long white office building. 'Go over there and wait.'

By the time the manager arrived, there was a large group of men also waiting – older, senior to Humayun, more pushy – and even though he had been there since the beginning, he was forced to wait, and wait, and wait. Everybody was irritable and sanctimonious; and nobody wanted him to take his turn. After some hours the man with the shaved lip came back into the room, and seeing him sitting there, said, 'Hasn't he seen you yet?' He himself led Humayun into the manager's room and presented him to the man behind the desk.

There were three other men in the office, all of them serious-looking elders, and they listened as Humayun explained the situation, but it was the manager who spoke.

'Where is the girl's guardian?'

'Her father is dead,' said Humayun, which was the first lie. Nobody knew where Aisha's father was.

'And her mother?' said the manager.

'She is too ill to travel from Delhi,' Humayun said. 'We are poor people. The expense of bringing her is too much.'

'And why did you come from Delhi to get married?'

Again Humayun lied, explaining that he was here for work; he was a qualified driver, and the opportunities were better in a city like Bombay. But they did not believe him, for why would anybody leave their native place at the august and wonderful time of marriage, a time in one's life when the whole community joins together in celebration? They asked him about his own family, and why his mother and uncles hadn't arranged the marriage for them, and when his family planned to come from Bombay for the festivities. Eventually Humayun stumbled on his own lies, and they picked out the flaws in his story as easily as a woman sifting stones from daal. And so in the end he was forced to tell the truth: that his mother was against the union, that the girl had difficulties, that a match had

been arranged for her in Bihar with an old uncle, that he and she loved each other, that they wanted to spend their lives together.

After his speech the men tutted and hmmmed and spoke in low tones to each other. Eventually the manager said, 'My son, you are a smart young man. You have a future. The best thing for you is to return to Delhi and speak to your mother, and the girl's mother, and persuade them to let you get married openly, among your own people, with their blessing.'

'My mother,' he said, frantic now with the wait and the agony and the truth of everything they said, 'is against the marriage.'

'I will speak to the elder Mufti,' the manager said at last. 'Wait outside and I will come and let you know of his decision.'

So again Humayun waited. The next prayertime came, and they went downstairs to offer namaz with the rest of the congregation: Humayun anonymous in the main prayer hall with the thousands of other men, Aisha pushed up against the women in the discreet covered section. He returned alone to the manager's office to wait, and at last, when it was approaching dusk, the manager came out to speak to him.

'The elder Mufti counsels you to return to Delhi,' he said, and added kindly, looking at the expression on Humayun's face, 'Take the advice of your elders, young man. Anything different will lead to trouble.'

How much he hated these religious men, Humayun thought. If only Aisha and he weren't underage, he could have dispensed with maulvis and muftis and qazis, walked straight to a civil court and seen the wedding solemnised in Indian law; but the law said that the man must be twenty-one and the girl eighteen; and so it was by Muslim law that they would have to be married. Somewhere in this city of Bombay was a qazi who would marry them. But there was the night to get through first.

Following the recommendation of one of the shopkeepers, Humayun and Aisha looked for accommodation near the Mussafir Khana, at a hotel in a backstreet named after one of the holy places of Islam, where the man at the desk, his mouth smeared with paan, the clatter of cards being played in the room behind him, the smell of hooch lingering in the air, offered them a double room for eighty of their precious rupees. They ate downstairs, in one of the paupers' restaurants where the roti were made with poor quality flour, and the meat dish was hot and edible and cheap. Humayun, who had walked past restaurants such as this every day of his life in Delhi – they served the legions of beggars who queued up each evening, waiting for rich men to arrive with spare rupees – forced himself to finish everything on his plate. He forced himself not to cry.

That night, as Aisha and he lay together in their tiny room, she whispered to him through the dark. It was the question that neither of them had dared to address since coming here. 'Will we ever go back to Delhi, Humayun?'

'No,' he said, and his heart was full of longing. 'We will never go back to Delhi. This is where we live now.' And as they lay in the dark, listening to the moaning of their neighbour, to the noise of somebody hacking mucus from their lungs, to the distant thrum of cars, to the imagined sound of waves breaking in the distance, he willed his heart to harden, not to break, but to harden, so that there would always be a tiny, resilient piece of himself that no adversity could ever destroy.

The next morning they waited outside the home of a qazi Humayun had been told about at the Mussafir Khana, standing on the dirty stairs where other residents had thrown cigarette butts and shiny supari packets and fruit peelings. But they had come too early; at ten o'clock in the morning the qazi was still asleep. When he eventually appeared, they discovered that he was exceedingly frail and hard of hearing. He took them into his office where he sat and coughed and explained to Humayun why it was impossible for him to risk solemnising their marriage. Supposing her family in Delhi put out a police case for kidnap; supposing his parents appeared in Bombay accusing the girl of theft – for to escape their clutches she must have stolen some money, no? He looked at her briefly, and then looked away. No, absolutely not, it was not a thing for a man of his age to risk – police cases were for younger qazis than himself – qazis such as the man opposite, who was known to be accommodating about such matters (and known to provide well for his family as a result). No, if they insisted on being married here and now without the girl's parents and without their consent, they would have to provide proof of age; and if they had forgotten to bring her birth certificate or ration card or passport or school leaving certificate with them in their rush to leave Delhi – here he looked up and scrutinised Humayun's bruised face with a shake of the head – then they would have to go to the J.J. Hospital, it was not far, and ask for an age-verification certificate, for the staff were able to ascertain such things with blood tests and X-rays. Again he gazed at tiny Aisha, and for a second time shook his head, and said, slowly and regretfully: 'The girl is not looking fat and healthy.' Humayun looked out of the grimy window as the qazi spoke. Aisha didn't have any documents. She had barely gone to school. There was no such thing as a birth certificate in her family, given their upheavals and chaotic living conditions, and her absent father. He knew that it was the first thing he should have done for her, before finding her a job even. It was his fault they were in this difficult position. On the road below the window, men were building a flyover; there was a mess of swinging concrete structures and workmen in ill-fitting hats and sprouting metal where one day the cars would run through the air. When he looked round again, the qazi was still speaking. 'From the bones they would come to know,' he was saying, 'and with the ossification certificate you go to the Qila Court and take an affidavit from a lawyer that the girl is of correct age and enters willingly into the union and nobody has forced her and she has come here happily. Then we will see about the legal contract for your marriage.' And he got to his feet and said a polite salaam, and shuffled away to his room where his wife was waiting.

'Will he call the police?' Aisha whispered as they walked away downstairs. Humayun shushed her soothingly, although he didn't feel soothed himself.

'Nobody will call the police,' he said. But that morning he had counted their stash of money with another jab of fear and tied it in a handkerchief and pinned it deep into the pocket of his trousers.

They crossed the road, stepping through the dust of the construction site, and entered the building where the flexible qazi was said to reside. This building, too, was dark, and there were small guesthouses on each floor with venerable Islamic names, soiled and overused. The qazi's office was on the third floor, next to Ladoo Perfumers.

The office boy ushered them in and told them to wait on chairs beside a table with three newspapers neatly stacked upon it. The qazi would be back soon; he had gone out on urgent business. Humayun picked up a newspaper and let his eye run across the print as he turned the pages. A Muslim marriage took a matter of minutes, he knew; within seconds it could all be over. If this qazi married them, he would be united with this woman at his side for ever so that his ostracism was complete.

But though they waited all afternoon, the qazi did not return. When it was almost dusk, Humayun said to Aisha, 'Let's go downstairs for dinner.' He needed food inside him, and so he took out some rupees and led Aisha downstairs to the Shalimar Hotel where they ate kebabs – that were nothing like those of Nizamuddin but which filled their stomachs and soothed his mind nonetheless.

That evening, when he took Aisha back to the qazi's office, they sat as before and waited, and this time when the office boy went into an inner room, they heard a murmuring of voices, and when he came back it was to ask about the mehr, the marriage money due to Aisha in the event of a divorce. And so Humayun opened his precious cotton bag and took out his mother's heavy gold pendant – and with this proof, the affair took no time at all.

A young man with a beard and a cap appeared – a very young man, barely a decade older than Humayun himself. He was wearing a white salwar kameez, and Humayun looked up at him and judged from his humourless expression that this was the qazi himself, and that he was going to marry them (but with a small addition to the optional fee); and moreover that he was going to marry them now, without recourse to ossification certificates or affidavits from the Qila Court; and thus, if there was anything Humayun wished to say, he had only this moment in which to act.

Humayun said nothing – and barely twenty minutes later, they were married. The qazi did not raise any problems of age or witnesses or consent; he called his own father, and his brother and his brother's friend, and they acted as witnesses and wali. They crowded into the office, admiring the gold pendant, sneaking looks at Aisha, and then the qazi cleared his throat and told everyone to be quiet; and Humayun shut his eyes, and listened to the words the qazi spoke; and then he spoke in his turn. He heard Aisha give her consent to the marriage – and fear again entered his soul, enormous and unbiddable. She was now his wife.

The qazi wrote down their names in a register and wrote them out a certificate, and everybody appended their signatures, and

Humayun handed over two hundred rupees as voluntary contribution in lieu of fee. And that was it. The four men left them in the
room, and Humayun turned to Aisha. 'We should go now,' he said.
But where would they go? She smiled at him; and the bitter thought
entered his head that, for her, anything was better than sleeping
with her mother in a graveyard.

'You are tired, Humayun.' She sounded calm, and he nodded.
Yes, that was it; it was only that he was tired.

The following morning, the first thing Aisha did as a wife was
to pawn the Hindu pendant in a Marwari gold shop. There was a
room available in the long line of wooden huts near the Masjid
Bandar station, and the Hindu landlady wanted a deposit of a
thousand rupees. The room was painted turquoise and it had a
corrugated iron roof and wooden walls, with a drain in the corner
for washing pots and bathing in. The Marwari trader, a red tilak
on his forehead, sitting fat and content behind a glass-topped case
full of other people's jewellery, with his brother beside him as
security, counted out the notes; he was giving them seventy-five per
cent of the weight of the piece, at an annual interest of eighteen
per cent. Aisha knew that it was a bad deal, and that they might
well lose the pendant in the end, but she also knew that Humayun
needed to eat well; he needed three changes of clothes; he couldn't
work as a coolie, which was what the landlady's husband did, and
what she had suggested. He needed work that was worthy of his
upbringing and education.

Aisha's standards were lower; and with her fine Muslim name
and innocent face she at last found a job after three days' searching,
washing dishes every day for a family called Qureshi who lived
two blocks down from the Shalimar Hotel. 'I can make kofta and
paratha,' Aisha told the old lady who interviewed her; and remembering Humayun's boast to Mrs Ahmed in Delhi, she added, 'I can

even make shami kebabs.' The old lady laughed and pinched her chin and said, 'Very well; but first you must show that you can clean my sharbat glasses without breaking them like the last girl did.' But she implied that if Aisha proved herself trustworthy, the cousins next door might take her on, too.

Humayun, by contrast, did not take to Bombay. Every morning, as the light of day seeped slowly into their turquoise room and he began to see the outline of his wife lying beside him, he knew that very little time was left before he would have to get up and go out into the city to look for work. The thought made him feel nauseous. He had enquired about becoming a taxi driver – the rates were good – but he was warned that newcomers who spoke no Marathi might have difficulties finding work. He asked a few people at the mosque and in the surrounding areas about working as a driver, letting them know that he was qualified and licensed; but he hated to beg, and although his wife smiled at him when he came home, though she cooked carefully for him on the stove that he had bought with his stash of money (now half the size it had been), though he knew that she was good and faithful, nevertheless each evening when he returned home to the blue-painted hut, reached from the road by a little slippery ladder, he felt the resilience draining from him. As he lay next to her at night, listening to the strange noises of the city, he wondered what djinn had possessed him to come here. He refused to sleep with her, fearing that the rapist had made her pregnant, and the separation that this put between them in their exile made him bitter. Even that human comfort was denied him.

She had saved a plant thrown out by a neighbour – a little, useless, climbing plant with translucent leaves, which she watered every evening with dishwater. Humayun watched it warily, in the evenings, as he lay on his back in their tiny room, waiting for his dinner. It had no smell, put out no flowers, it had no use at all that he could see; and yet she tended it faithfully, and it grew, as if marking their time in Bombay. He felt that the plant and he were in competition.

Aisha, feeling that he was lost, took him to the sea to revive him; but he stared out at the waves, wondering what the policemen in Delhi had been trying to teach him. It was now the holy month of Ramzan, and she tried to persuade him to go to the mosque, thinking that he would find some community there. But he refused.

Then, one evening, when he got home, she told him that she had bled. Her monthly bleeding had come, taking that fear away, at least. It was a blessing. 'Mubarak,' he said, and smiled spontaneously for the first time in weeks.

That evening, in a spirit of thanksgiving, he went to the mosque for prayers. Muslims were pious during the month of fasting, and the crowd was huge in the Jama Masjid. As Humayun knelt before God, his forehead touching the mat in front of him, surrounded by his Muslim brothers, he prayed for Aisha, he prayed for his mother. Above all, he prayed for the return of that unthinking self-confidence, that unexamined contentedness, which was once the most secure and inviolable part of his being.

chapter 13

'Ash's schoolfriend telephoned for you,' said her grandmother, as Bharati let herself in through the front door the night before Diwali.

As a result of spending the day after the wedding lunch with Ash and Sunita, Bharati was now quite drunk. She had wanted to spend some time with her brother before leaving for London at the weekend, and before the newly-weds went on honeymoon on Friday, and because the twins' birthday on Thursday was being overshadowed by their father's Sanskrit lecture. But to recover from the prudish company of her sister-in-law, and her constant Hindi–English chatter, Bharati had gone to her friend Kavita's place in the evening, where she sat and laughed and talked and ate greasy kebabs from the market and drank too many beers – and, more to the point, smoked a lot of ganja, as she tended to in Delhi.

Bharati tiptoed with inebriated exaggeration into the front room where her grandmother was sitting by the window, a bowl of rasmalai on the table in front of her. 'He rang from Calcutta,' the old woman went on (as Bharati sidled up to her and ate two of the sweets, milk dripping from her fingers). 'Pablo. He says to call back whatever time you get in.' And she handed her granddaughter a piece of paper with Pablo's mobile number written on it in her spindly handwriting. 'Such a nice young man.'

'You liked him?' Bharati asked, grinning at the sweetness of what she was eating – her naughty Dadi was diabetic.

'I remember him from when you were at school.'

'Ah yes,' Bharati said. She kissed her grandmother goodnight, and was walking back through the hallway when the old black-and-white photograph on the stairs, of her mother at college in Calcutta caught her eye. 'Ma's sister whom nobody ever talks about,' she said. 'Did you notice that she actually came to Ash's wedding?'

Her grandmother's reply was sharp. 'That woman is nothing but trouble,' she said, and Bharati walked upstairs without asking anything further on the subject. But she thought to herself: *That's the third member of my family who doesn't want to talk about my mother's sister.* And she remembered her argument with Pablo, and how angry she had been with him for probing her mother's history, and wondered if his curiosity was justified after all.

Sitting in bed, Bharati dialled his number, and when he answered, she said, 'It seems you charmed the pants off my Dadi.'

He laughed, pleased with his success. 'Oh, good. Whatever it takes to please the venerable lady's beautiful descendant.'

'And what are you doing in Cal?' Bharati asked.

'A highly important lingam story,' Pablo said. 'My editor hates me. But today I went to Santiniketan.'

There was a pause.

'And?' Bharati said.

'And I found out something about your mother.'

'And?'

'And I can't tell you over the phone. But it's important. Very very important.'

'Oh *yeah?*'

'Promise me one thing.'

'What?'

'That you'll go and see Leela Sharma. Tomorrow.'

'Leela? Why?' She began to feel suspicious again.

'This is her number,' he said, ignoring her question. 'I got it for you from the office; Leela's husband is—'

'Yes, yes, I know.'

He read the number out. 'So promise.'

'Why the rush?' she said again.

'Because . . . because I want Leela to give you a crucial piece of information—'

Bharati laughed unsympathetically.

'Tell her I went to the Santhal Mission Hospital,' he said, a little defiantly.

'*What?*'

'Just tell her that. Promise me.'

'OK, I promise.'

'When can I see you?' he asked.

'When are you back?'

'Tomorrow evening.'

'So come by and get me,' she said, with cannabis-induced generosity.

'Really?'

'Don't take it personally.' She laughed. 'Anything to get away from Sunita.'

He laughed too, in disappointment. 'I'll be there by ten tomorrow evening.'

As she fell asleep she thought: *Why was he so insistent?* But when she woke the next morning, the first thing she did was to dial the number he had given her. It was the husband, Hari Sharma, who answered.

'I'm Sunita's sister-in-law,' Bharati explained: 'Ash Chaturvedi's sister—'

'Bharati.'

'Yes.' She was surprised he knew her name.

'Do you want to speak to my wife?'

'Please. Is she in?'

'Was she expecting your call?'

'No.'

'I'll go and get her,' he said.

'Thank you,' said Bharati. 'It's important. It concerns my mother Meera.'

'All right,' he said.

When Leela came to the phone she sounded a lot more reticent than her husband. At first she was reluctant to meet, but Bharati persuaded her that she only wanted to talk about Meera's poems. In the end they arranged to wait for each other at four o'clock that afternoon, outside the entrance to Humayun's tomb.

At half past three Bharati set out from home to walk to the tomb – it was barely ten minutes away from her house, up to the basti and across the main road next to the plant nursery – and the mild exercise did her good. She felt calm and prepared, ready to meet this sister of her mother's, even if it did go against both her father and grandmother's express wishes. Pablo's excited trepidation – his doggedness – kept buzzing in her head. She felt intoxicated all over again by the fuss he had made.

And yet, the longer she stood waiting in the cold, the more uneasy she felt. She wondered, for the first time, why siblings became estranged from each other. Bharati couldn't imagine ever wanting to cut Ash out of her life (even if he had married a woman she didn't care for). And what could *he* possibly ever do to *her* – what was he capable of doing? – that would warrant her saying: *I never want to see you again . . . ?* Such a thing was impossible.

Bharati had spent the morning rereading *The Lalita Series* – she couldn't find the copy she had brought from London, so she took one from her father's library – and had tried to locate within it hints of a joint authorship, or some presentiment of it at least. But there was nothing. Only in the new poem that Pablo had showed her did the poet allude to a creative association. *Sisterhood of blood and ink, proof of our collaboration.* And only in this poem, Bharati thought as she observed a white car pulling up to the entrance of the tomb, was Ved Vyasa mentioned in this sinister way. 'The Last Dictation' was written in November 1979. The month the twins were born. By then her mother was a married woman. Married to a man called Vyasa who taught the Mahabharata for a living.

A woman stepped out of the white car and Bharati knew it was her – the one from the wedding. Seeing her again like this, she realised: that was why she had seemed familiar at the wedding. Bharati must have seen her face in the background of one of those photographs that her father kept in boxes in his library.

Leela Sharma was wearing a cotton sari of a deep saffron-yellow, and a huge soft shawl. As she walked towards the gate where Bharati was waiting, she smiled, and her face, which had seemed so serious and intent a moment ago, looked momentarily happy.

'Hello, Bharati,' Leela said.

'Hello.'

They bought tickets from the booth. Bharati paid for them herself, talking to the ticket man in Hindi, and then, to get things going between her and Leela, just by way of conversation, and because she felt so tense, said to Leela, 'I'm writing a dissertation partly on *The Lalita Series*.'

'Are you?' Leela Sharma raised her eyebrows in surprise.

'I'm looking in particular at the thread of political disillusionment that runs through the poems, and the milieu in which they were written, the Writers' Workshops in Calcutta in the seventies, P. Lal's English translations of the Mahabharata . . . Do you think that was an influence? Do you think my mother went to one of his Sunday-afternoon recitations? I know that they are still going, twenty years later, I was thinking that I should go to Cal on this trip and go along to one of them myself. He might remember her, do you think?'

She knew she was gabbling.

Leela, meanwhile, reached into her bag and took out a copy of Bharati's mother's book. She held it in front of her and looked at it a little wonderingly. 'I think this must be yours. I borrowed it from your house.'

'It is mine,' Bharati said, annoyed, as the booth man handed her the change for the tickets. 'I looked for it this morning. When did you borrow it? I only brought it back with me from London on Sunday.'

'I came by on Sunday night after your brother's wedding. I had a long conversation with your grandmother. Didn't she tell you?'

'No,' Bharati said, 'she did not.'

'Well,' Leela answered.

'Well what?' Bharati gave Leela her ticket and walked ahead of her through the gate into the gardens.

'There was no reason for her to mention it,' Leela said when she reached Bharati, who was waiting for her on the path. 'I haven't seen her since I was a young woman. Or you since you were a baby. I'm not part of the family any more.'

They walked in silence after that, down the straight path that led up to the first of the two arched gateways that guarded the tomb. Visible from here in the distance, perfectly aligned with the top of the archway, was the pale marble dome of the tomb itself.

Leela had spoken calmly, but as they walked up the steps and through the gateway, Bharati realised her mother's sister was trembling. 'Are you cold?' she asked in surprise. And then, without waiting for Leela – perhaps because of that awkwardness she felt in her presence – she ran on down the steps and along the path to the second gateway, the red sandstone arch that led directly into the gardens of the tomb.

'So,' Bharati said to Leela, turning towards her as she approached, and trying to get back to the point of their meeting, 'you are my mother's long-lost sister.' They stood side by side, surveying the tomb and its gardens, which were criss-crossed by slender canals.

'Shall we go into the tomb?' Leela said in answer, and this time it was Bharati who followed her, along the canal and up the steps to where the graves of Emperor Humayun and his family and courtiers stood encased within the huge red sandstone shell, in a maze of darkened rooms joined and divided by stone lattice-screens, so that each vista was obscured by shadows and penetrated by stars.

'You were alienated from each other,' Bharati persisted, her voice echoing loudly in the stone chamber, not caring how many tourists and visitors heard her, caring only that her words sounded strained and unnatural. 'That's what everyone has told me.'

Still Leela didn't reply, and only after Bharati had followed her out into the garden again, where the green of the trees was dazzling, and down the steps to the lawns, did she say, 'There was certainly a month or two when we didn't speak. But by the time you and your brother were born it wasn't like that. However, because of something that happened, thereafter it became impossible for us to see each other again.'

'Because you moved to America with your husband,' Bharati pointed out. They sat next to each other on the grass beneath the shade of four large trees.

Leela didn't reply. Instead she handed Bharati the book of poems and said, 'Thank you for this.'

Bharati frowned at the dim sense she had of not quite understanding anything anymore. 'My friend Pablo thinks you wrote the poems together,' she said. 'He was the one who made me ring you.' And before Leela could reply, she said, 'But my father says that this unknown poem – you know the one that was published in the *Delhi Star*—'

'"The Last Dictation".'

'Yes, that it's a fake. That somebody was imitating Meera out of envy, or something.'

'Why would they do that?'

'I don't know.'

There was silence for a moment, and then Bharati asked, anxious now, 'So what do you think about the poem?'

'It isn't fake,' Leela said, looking straight at her, and Bharati was struck by her candid expression, by her long dark eyes. 'We wrote it together . . .'

'Right,' Bharati said. 'So you wrote all the poems together, or just that one?'

'All of them.'

'So . . .' Bharati began. So her mother wasn't the sole author of *The Lalita Series* after all; it was just as Pablo had said. 'Why did you do that?' she asked. 'And how come your poem is about Vyasa, when that's my father's name, and . . . ?' She didn't want to say it out loud: that the Vyasa of their poem was nasty and lecherous and egotistical. She didn't mean to ask the next question either, but something about Leela Sharma's whole demeanour put the worry in her head and the question came out without her being able to stop it: 'Did my mother *love* my father?'

As soon as she said it, she knew that it was a betrayal, and that if her father heard this conversation – or her grandmother – their dismay would shame her. For a moment the question hung there unanswered, and Bharati felt shocked by the thoughts that were veering into each other in her head, one interrupting another before she had time to unpick the meaning of the first. The question she had just asked made her think of her mother living in Delhi with her twins, away from her sister in New York and her father in Calcutta, and then the way she suddenly died, and the hints Bharati had gleaned during her childhood from people outside the family, which she had wilfully refused to explore, not even with Ash, about the nature of this sudden and tragic circumstance. And so, before Leela could answer the first question, Bharati asked another one. 'Did my mother mean to die the way she did? Was it deliberate?'

'Oh, Bharati.' A tear slid out of Leela Sharma's eye.

'Well?' Bharati said. 'Was it?'

Leela shook her head and brushed the tear away. 'I don't know,' she said. 'I was in New York by then. But my father told me – he said that she was—' She stopped and cleared her throat. 'Has Vyasa talked to you about this?'

Bharati shook her head.

'How can I talk to you about it then?' Leela said. 'We were so happy – she was so happy – when we were growing up. She was such a happy person.'

'And then she stopped being happy?'

Leela began to sob now, and Bharati, who hated crying, felt a tear run down her own cheek at the thought of her dead mother, and looked away from Leela in disgust. She stared instead at the archway they had just passed through, where two thin men – from the ticket booth, probably – were lounging, talking to each other, eyeing up all the pretty girls passing in and out of the gardens in their new Diwali clothes, and she thought of something her ayah had said to her once, about how difficult her mother had found it looking after twins.

'So what was it that made her sad? Was it being a mother?'

Leela turned to look at her. 'No, it wasn't that. You mustn't think it was that.' She wiped her face with the end of her sari. 'When I talked to Father about it later he thought it began after our mother died. I think so, too. While we were at university in Calcutta, our mother got cancer and it came on so very suddenly we didn't even know she was ill until afterwards. They didn't want to worry us and so she died like that' – Leela clicked her fingers – 'and of course we never had time to ask all the things you want to ask of your mother, which you would think of asking her if you knew she was dying. Meera resented our father for that. But we weren't children when it happened – we were students. It made us feel like children again, I suppose. Meera especially. From that time onwards there was a kind of sadness about her, not always, but every now and then.'

'My friend Pablo wanted me to speak to you,' Bharati said, 'because he said you needed to tell me something.'

'Is he the journalist? Pablo Fernandes? The one—'

'Who wrote about the poems, yes. He's in Calcutta. He went to Santiniketan yesterday. And he rang to tell me he had found out something important.'

'I see,' said Leela.

'He said he'd been to a hospital,' Bharati went on.

'Bharati.' Leela took a deep breath and knotted her fingers together. 'I didn't come here today to tell you this.'

'I need to know, don't I?' Bharati said, 'If Pablo knows, I need to know.'

'Oh, Bharati. I'm sorry. I hope you can forgive me.'

'Forgive you for what? Tell me what it is, quickly.'

'I haven't told you before, because I didn't want to upset you and the people around you. Meera knew, and our father knew, but nobody else did.'

'What is it?' Bharati said.

'I made Meera a promise when I left, and that's why I'm telling you this now. I hope you will forgive me—'

'For fuck's sake!'

'You see, the thing was, we both got pregnant at the same time. Your mother was married, and I wasn't—'

The expression on Leela's face as she made her confession was half-pleading, half-defiant.

'You haven't got any children.'

'I haven't got any now.'

'But you had some once?'

'I had a child.'

'And what happened?'

'Meera took her.'

'Her?' Bharati got to her feet, pushing at the air with her hands as if she was trying to make the words that Leela had just spoken disappear. 'No.' And then she screamed, so that pigeons flew up from the steps of the tomb. 'No! Don't come here like this, talking like this about me and my mother. Who are you?'

She walked away from Leela along the lawn and stood looking at the tomb, and then she looked back at her mother's sister, with her wavy hair so like her own, her eyes so like her own.

She walked back to where Leela was sitting. 'Why don't you just say it clearly?'

Leela looked up at her, her eyes full of tears.

'Say it!'

'You are my daughter, Bharati.'

'And who is my father supposed to be?'

'The same as Ash's father.'

'What? Both of you, with him?' She stared at Leela Sharma. 'All three of you, all at once?' The implications of what this woman was saying were disgusting: how could her father have sired children by two different women, by two *sisters*? It was too shocking to be real. 'I don't believe you,' Bharati cried.

'It wasn't like you think,' Leela Sharma interrupted.

'So how was it then?' Bharati said. 'You can't even say it out loud! You come to me after twenty years and you still can't say this thing clearly. Are you so ashamed?'

'I'm sorry,' Leela said, 'I'm sorry. I have always wanted it to be known and if I haven't told anyone it's because—'

'Because what?'

'Because I didn't want to make your life more difficult.'

'So instead you did – what? Gave me away and disappeared to America?'

'Yes,' Leela said, bowing her head.

Bharati stood looking down at her. 'How can you have deceived me so much? You *liar*.' She thought of her father. Her lovely father. Could he really have done a thing like that? It wasn't possible. But if it was true, and he hadn't known during all this time any more than she had, then he too had been tricked. 'You deceived Baba! Both of you lied to him, didn't you? Didn't you?'

Leela nodded. 'We didn't tell your father. But—'

'So you *abandoned* me,' Bharati said.

'I didn't.

'Why have you appeared now? What exactly do you want?'

'I didn't plan this,' Leela repeated. 'I didn't come here today—'

'Did you love my father?'

'No.'

'Yet he is my father. Something happened, didn't it?'

'It's difficult to explain,' Leela began. 'I would have done anything for Meera. I never loved your father, I never—'

'But you slept with my mother's lover—'

'It wasn't like that—'

'It was like in the poem, yes. Like in the epic.'

'But why didn't you come back and find me? She died when we were two years old. We were *babies* still.'

'Of course I longed to.' Leela put out a hand and touched her shoulder. 'Meera's death was very difficult for me. It made me see only bad in the world for a long time, and only sadness. I didn't think you would want a mother like that. And then my father died . . . all I had left was my husband Hari and I thought—'

'BUT YOU HAD ME!' Bharati shouted, pushing her hand off, and this time an old man who was passing with his stick and his old-man's thoughts looked round in surprise, and to her annoyance she recognised him as the retired judge who lived in the house that backed onto theirs and devoted his dotage to growing marigolds which he transplanted in springtime to the communal park.

'Yes, I had you,' Leela said, shrinking back, 'but I didn't want to inflict myself on you.'

'But you just have.'

Leela began to cry again, and Bharati listened to her sob, and did nothing to help her or comfort her. Gradually the crying stopped. They sat side by side, not looking at each other, in silence as the sun began to set, and one by one the picnicking families and romancing couples and exercising geriatrics started to leave the gardens.

'Do you mind if I smoke?' Leela asked, breaking the silence. 'It's such a bad habit, but . . .'.

Bharati shook her head. 'I'll have one too.'

Leela handed her a cigarette and the matches, and as soon as Bharati lit up she felt a wave of calm.

As she was finishing her cigarette, one of the men from the ticket booth came over to ask them to move towards the exit. Bharati got to her feet. She felt not just calm now but superior – numb, perhaps. 'I've got to go,' she said. 'I'm having dinner with my father. Ash has gone to celebrate Diwali with his marvellous new in-laws.'

'Will you tell Vyasa?' Leela asked.

'I'll have to, won't I?'

'This evening?'

'Probably.'

'When shall we speak again?'

'I'm going to London on Saturday.'

'Oh, Bharati.' Leela got to her feet too. 'Please don't leave like this. Can we meet again? I would love more than anything in the world to meet you again.'

Bharati held up her hands. 'Father's lecture at the old fort tomorrow.'

'Shall I see you there?'

Bharati shrugged. 'Goodbye, Leela,' she said, before the woman tried to hug her or extract any further promises. She began to walk away, but Leela called after her. 'It's your birthday tomorrow.'

'I *know* it is,' Bharati said, turning. 'At least, I've always believed I was born on that day. Maybe now you're going to tell me something different. That you gave birth to me in March, in a temple ashram, that my name was originally—' She broke off, disgusted with the way her words were coming out.

'You were born on November fifteenth, like your brother.'

'Right. Fine. Great. So. See you tomorrow then,' Bharati said, and before Leela could say anything else, she walked away towards the archway.

Only when she reached the steps did she feel the unfamiliar wrench of loneliness and fear, and turning again, she looked back at the woman who claimed to be her mother. Leela was still standing alone on the grass, gazing after Bharati – with that hair, and those long eyes, and those lips set in that way that seemed so much part of her, and that wrinkle of worry on her forehead. The strange unwanted ache of recognition made Bharati flinch as if in pain, and she hurried away to meet her father, thinking, *That woman is my mother.*

chapter 14

Ash Chaturvedi spent Diwali in his lab on Mall Road, at the edge of the university campus. This was, indisputably, the finest scientific institution in Delhi – one of the finest in India – a huge, imposing grey concrete structure, ultra-modern, the hallways haphazardly lined with red marble: a pristine bubble of progress set apart from the rest of the country. Wherever life took him in the future, Ash would always value the time he had spent here in this sequestered intellectual community. But he sighed as he walked down the corridor from the lab to his office. He had been on his feet from early that morning: collecting human gene samples from a doctor's surgery in Bhogal, taking them in a taxi all the way to CBT, processing them there alone in his lab – isolating the DNA, amplifying it, and then running it through the automated sequencer – and now that the data had been generated, transferring it onto the main server, where it would be slotted neatly in with the others in his gene library. And all this he had done at his sister-in-law's express request.

The telephone call he had received early in the morning was highly unexpected. He knew of Urvashi's existence, of course, and had long urged Sunita to introduce her sister to his family: after all, they were neighbours. But he was taken aback to find it was her when his grandmother called him to the phone before breakfast. 'It's Uzma Ahmed,' she said as he came downstairs. 'Please hurry. She has been waiting all this time just for you to finish flossing.' He had been in the bathroom when the phone rang and Sunita was still there, taking a bath. He took the phone from his grandmother, trying to remember if he had heard of someone called Uzma Ahmed. Maybe she was ringing from the travel agency with news of their honeymoon hotel in Goa? 'Hello?' he said.

There then ensued a very unexpected conversation. Uzma Ahmed was actually Urvashi Sharma, and she wished that Ash should analyse the DNA of the man who had raped her maid on the night of his wedding. 'I believe she is your maid, too?' Urvashi said as she finished her speech. She spoke politely but firmly. Her voice had cadences of her Hindi medium education and upbringing, as Sunita's did, but overlaid with something different and more recent and more urgent.

'You will have to collect the samples from the doctor,' Urvashi said. 'He won't give them to me.'

'No, of course not,' Ash said, and thought about it. 'I'll need permission from my head of lab. It might be difficult on Diwali. Isn't there a normal police procedure you can follow?'

'No,' Urvashi said firmly. 'The police are not motivated by the right considerations. You know they beat up Humayun and that now he's disappeared?'

'I didn't know that,' he said.

'Well,' she said, trying to sound understanding, 'you've had your wedding and all. You've been busy.'

'I'll speak to my head of lab,' Ash said. 'It shouldn't be too difficult. Each new sample is useful for my forensics identification protocol.' The constricted feeling he had woken up with – a whole day alone with Sunita on Diwali – disappeared. This gave him the perfect excuse to get out of the house. She would be fine on her own – she was using the time between now and Friday, when they left for their honeymoon, to train the cook up in all her favourite recipes, and to find a place in the house for each and every one of her brand-new possessions.

'Do you have the number of the doctor?' he asked Urvashi. 'I'll go round there right away.'

In his office, Ash brought up the details of the DNA analysis. For the purpose of his forensics chapter he looked at nine markers on the autosome, and every time he processed a new sample it gave him a little thrill. The doctor had provided him with an uncontaminated sample of the maid's DNA – a cheek swab – and with it a vaginal swab, which would presumably contain her DNA and that of the rapist. There were just three sets of coloured peaks on his chromatogram, including the control, and it would barely take thirty minutes or so for the software to remove the maid's verified genetic fingerprint from the tangle of DNA produced by the vaginal swab, and isolate the culprit's. This he would print out, and take straight over to Urvashi Ahmed's house, as proof that he had done what she had asked for. He had to hurry, because he was due home to Nizamuddin soon in order to pick up Sunita and drive her south to her parents' house for Diwali dinner.

Ash left the software running, and went downstairs to see if he could find a tea stall open on Diwali. Half an hour later, when he returned, he sat at his computer, brought up the Excel spreadsheet, and was about to press print, when he saw a message on his screen that made him push his glasses back onto his nose and peer in confusion at the computer.

The software had automatically searched for duplication between the new information he had added and data already on the system

– and it had found a match. Ash blinked and stared. He rubbed his eyes and looked again. He was confused. His computer was telling him something that couldn't possibly be true.

In his mind he went slowly and mechanically through every viable explanation for the result the computer had thrown up – that the doctor's samples were contaminated; that the software was malfunctioning; that his eyes weren't working properly. Then he shut down the program, restarted the computer, ran the software a second time and waited. Ten minutes later the match appeared as before, and at last Ash was forced to confront the possibility that . . . But he couldn't.

There was a telephone by the door and he walked to it slowly, steadying himself as he went. He dialled his sister-in-law's number.

She answered immediately and recognised his voice. 'You've done the test?'

'Yes.'

'Do you have anything?' She sounded excited.

Ash looked back across the room towards the computer. 'I think we should speak about it,' he said. 'I'll come round to your house. Don't mention this to anyone.'

Urvashi Ahmed was not alone when Ash arrived at the house in Nizamuddin. A tall man in a white shirt and jeans, whom she introduced to him as her husband, came to the door with her to greet him.

'So we are family,' the man, whose name was Feroze, said with a cautious smile, and put out a hand to Ash. 'Welcome.'

Ash crossed the threshold and stood in the hallway of his sister-in-law's house. He looked shyly at Urvashi. She seemed very different from her sister. She was wearing dangling seed-pearl earrings and a loose green printed salwar kameez. He looked at her huge swathes of hair, her healthy glow and happy plumpness. He felt a great relief to be meeting her at last.

'Can I get you a drink?' Feroze said, showing Ash to the seats under the window. Ash nodded and asked for a beer. As Feroze went out into the kitchen, his wife's sister smiled at him. So this was the woman her father had rejected.

'Does Sunita know you are here?' she said suddenly, as if she could see what he was thinking, and Ash shook his head.

'I will tell her, though, as soon as I get back. I am sorry—' he began, and stopped.

She looked at him questioningly.

'That you weren't able to come to the wedding reception,' he finished – and wished that he had stood up to Sunita's father on this issue too.

She shook her head and said nothing, and as soon as Feroze returned with the beer she got quickly to her feet and walked out of the room. She was clearly upset. Ash sighed, and looked around him. The house was very large for such a young couple; her husband's business must be doing well. Or maybe there were other family members living here too. He took the beer from Feroze and asked him, 'Do you live here alone?'

'For the moment,' Feroze said, and a smile appeared on his face. 'But as of next year, in May . . .' He paused, waiting for Ash to finish his sentence for him.

'Is she expecting?'

'Yes!' Feroze said. 'Sunita hasn't told you? She will become a mother in under six months.'

'I didn't know.' Ash shook his head. Sunita had never mentioned it.

When Urvashi returned, carrying some snacks on a tray, she had recovered her composure, and Ash was able to congratulate her on her forthcoming joy without the tears springing into her eyes again. He felt glad to be sitting with his wife's sister and her husband, and again he wished that he had done something more about the family divisions before he married Sunita . . . But he couldn't bring himself to examine the damage he himself was inflicting on Sunita through his secret relationship with her brother, let alone the traumatic revelation that he held in his pocket in the form of his DNA analysis.

He took a sip of beer and said nothing for a moment, unable to think how to describe his confusion about what he had discovered.

'You are a geneticist?'

Ash looked up. It was Feroze who had spoken.

'Yes,' Ash said, 'that is why I am here. It's to do with the rape of the maid.' He put down the beer bottle on the table.

He realised that an awkward silence had developed in the room. They were waiting for him to speak. He sighed, and said to Urvashi, 'Please. I have something very difficult to tell you. Should I say it here, or is there somewhere we can go in private?'

She cast an anxious glance at her husband, but he merely nodded. 'Why don't you have your conversation in my study?'

Urvashi nodded, and Ash followed her into the room next door. There were books on the shelves, and a computer on the desk, and next to it a large colour wedding photograph of Urvashi, dressed in red silk with a heavy gold tikka in her hair, and standing behind her, one hand resting on her shoulder, Feroze, a serious expression on his face, dressed in a dark sherwani.

Ash and Urvashi sat opposite each other across the desk. 'Well,' she said at last, 'what have you discovered?'

Ash unfolded the print-outs and offered them to her. She took them from him and studied them for a moment in silence.

'The first thing to say,' he began by way of disclaimer, 'is that the PCR I did to get the STRs is only a rough analysis. It proves something is true but it has no legal application. CBT is not a forensic institute and to check that you will have to—'

'I don't understand,' she interrupted. 'What do they show? What is PCR? STR?'

Ash sighed. 'Polymerase Chain Reaction. Short Tandem Repeats. It's a way of—' But he broke off when he saw the blank look on her face. He took his glasses off and rubbed his eyes. Then he put them back on again, smiled understandingly at his sister-in-law and spoke as clearly and simply as he could.

'The sample the doctor gave me contained the DNA not of two people as I expected – the victim and the rapist – but of three people. That is what is shown up on the gel matrix.' He pointed to the relevant portion. 'By chance, one of those people had a match with another in my . . . gene database. I had already tested certain people in your family . . . I had already tested your father.'

'My father?'

'Yes,' he said, and went on bravely, 'He wanted me to prove the existence of an Aryan gene in him. That's why he is in my database. So what my analysis showed up was Aisha's DNA, as expected. There was a second anonymous person, who by statistical probability, seems to be her relative. And there was a third person, who, as I explained, was in my database already.' He locked his eyes to Urvashi's as he spoke, determined to say it out loud: to be clear and unequivocal and unflinching. 'Your father was in my database already—'

But she interrupted. 'My father? You're not trying to tell me that my father . . . ?'

He nodded.

'What do you mean?'

'I need to know whether your father has been at the house recently. Has he slept in your house, used a bathroom that Aisha may have cleaned, met her at any time? Could there have been any inadvertent contamination of the sample taken by the doctor?'

'My father has never been here. He hasn't spoken to me or seen me since I left to get married.'

'I see,' Ash said slowly. Instead of thinking of the heinous crime that Sunita's father had quite possibly committed, however, he thought of the shame that such a revelation would unleash – not just on Sunita's family but on his.

'There's another thing,' he said. 'The DNA of the second person, Aisha's relative. Can you think of a reason why that would be?'

'Yes,' said Urvashi. 'Aisha was having a . . . thing with her cousin, our driver.' It was as his mother had said: they had deceived her with their clandestine romance.

'And Humayun and Aisha are definitely related to each other?' Ash went on, not wishing to acknowledge that, secretly, this is what he had hoped: that somebody else other than Shiva Prasad had raped his grandmother's young Muslim maid.

'They are cousins,' Urvashi said.

There was a silence. 'Of course,' she added, 'that doesn't mean he raped her.'

'No,' Ash said, 'except that – you said that she's a minor.'

'But it was Humayun's intention to marry Aisha.'

'Was it?'

'And,' Urvashi said, in a small voice, 'she told me that the rapist was an old Hindu man.'

Ash glanced at Urvashi, who was sitting with her eyes cast down, fiddling with a gold Islamic pendant round her neck. He knew that he ought to submit the results of the sample he had analysed to the police. What he wasn't clear about was whether he was legally obliged to draw their attention to the genetic match he had discovered (quite by chance, after all). Without this coincidence there was very little likelihood that Shiva Prasad's supposed crime would ever be discovered. Indeed, the police would be more likely to deduce that Aisha had been raped by a relative and would pursue that line of prosecution instead.

'Nothing is ever one hundred per cent certain in genetics but assuming neither of the samples was contaminated . . .' Ash began. He got to his feet suddenly. 'But it may easily have been contaminated! I tested Shiva Prasad's DNA in my lab. There could easily have been cross-contamination there.'

Urvashi looked up at him in relief. 'Yes,' she said, 'it could easily have been contaminated. Have you told Sunita yet?'

'No.'

'That's good. It would have been very difficult for her. She loves her father.'

He sat down again, and finally he said, 'But I must tell the police that the sample has been analysed. That is my duty.'

She picked up the telephone on the desk, consulted an address book and dialled. Then she held the receiver out to him. Ash spoke to the policeman in Hindi, trying to sound authoritative. He threw in some words of English, to show that he meant business. But the policeman wasn't getting it. 'Put me through to your superior,' Ash said at last, growing annoyed.

The superior took a long time to come to the phone. This time, Ash explained that he was the son of Professor Chaturvedi from Nizamuddin West, G-block.

'Professor who?' This man wasn't getting it either.

Ash explained the story all over again – of the rape, the samples of bodily fluids taken by the doctor, the fact that he himself had analysed them.

'But, sir,' the superior officer said, 'the girl in question came in yesterday. She withdrew the rape allegation and we let the boy go.'

Ash put his hand over the receiver and consulted with Urvashi.

'It's true,' she said, 'they've disappeared – they've eloped.'

The policeman heard her answer. 'Now that the charges have been dropped and the girl has absconded, we cannot mount an investigation. The case is a dead end, sir.'

'What if my work shows who the rapist is?' Ash asked.

'Very helpful, sir, thank you. But first bring the girl back to Delhi. Till then, let me assure you, there is nothing we can do.'

In the room next door, Ram, who had rung his sister half an hour ago on his new mobile to ask if he could come over for a chat, and had been told that she was expecting Ash Chaturvedi any moment, gloomily accepted a beer from Feroze and lapsed into a self-pitying silence.

'What are they discussing in there?' he asked Feroze at last. They had met only a few times but he found his sister's Muslim husband to be a sympathetic, straightforward person. Normally they liked to talk business but not today.

Feroze shrugged in answer to Ram's question – as if to imply that life was full of benign and mildly intriguing mysteries, which was not at all Ram's take on the issue. 'Something to do with Ash Chaturvedi's genetics work. Do you want another drink?'

Ram shook his head. For a few moments the only sound was the murmuring of voices – those of Urvashi and Ash – that came from behind the door of the study. Ram got up and walked towards the front door. 'I'll wait in the garden,' he said. 'I need to smoke a cigarette.'

Feroze nodded and picked up the book he had been reading. 'She's made haleem. This time you should stay for dinner.'

'OK,' Ram said, fleeing into the garden.

He knew that Ash had been avoiding him since the night they

spent together. During the wedding lunch he wouldn't even look him in the eye or make any special sign of recognition. He no longer came online at midnight, he didn't come to the phone when Ram called the house – or worse, sent Sunita to talk in his place. The most terrible thing was that Ram now felt jealous almost all the time. Until the wedding, he was certain that nothing carnal had yet occurred between Ash and Sunita, but every night that had passed since then had been a torment. Late at night he woke up sweating, imagining his lover locked in the most disgusting of embraces with his sister; and since all of this was quite disturbing, and knowing that he needed someone to talk to about what was happening in his head, he had rung Urvashi to ask her to meet him and listen to his problems. Yesterday he had considered telling Auntie Leela, but decided against it at the last minute – and now, he found that Ash had beaten him to it and was confiding in Urvashi himself.

Could Ash really be telling Urvashi what had happened? And if so, what would she say? And the notion suddenly entered Ram's head that Urvashi herself might well consider that her brother was guilty of interfering in the special pact of marriage.

He sat down on the bench next to his sister's ferns, and dismissed the thought impatiently. He was angered by the complacency of these married people, who always assumed that their way was right. He had known Ash for just as long as Sunita had. Simply because one relationship was legitimate in the eyes of the world, and the other was not, did not make it better.

But he wondered about Ash, nevertheless: about what would really make him happy. On the wedding night, Ram had bragged to Ash of how they could go travelling together, to London and Paris and New York. He had depicted them walking through Leicester Square, spending Uncle Hari's money in bars and nightclubs, climbing the Eiffel Tower, swimming in the skin-shrivellingly cold European seas, eating aphrodisiacal oysters and millionaire's caviar. But now, as he smoked, a second vision came to Ram, of Ash in his other, more conventional avatar: as a husband, boating with Sunita through the verdant backwaters of Kerala; wearing baggy shorts as he played with her in the surf on a Goan beach; shopping for the things that husbands and wives liked to buy – curtains, he supposed, for the bedroom, vegetables for dinner, garments for their children.

He placed these competing visions side by side, knowing full well that they could not co-exist. Ash was too shy to be deceptive – and he would always fear opprobrium. Ram himself had got used to the secrecy that was required in India; he didn't mind it; as long as one didn't say it out loud it was even possible to be open, demonstrative, loving. But Ash would never behave like that. He would cower in the shadows; he would play the faithful husband; and as soon as he could manage it he would become – actually become – a doting father.

Meanwhile, there was the question of keeping the relationship secret from Uncle Hari. And for the first time, Ram wondered whether it was the kind of offence that warranted a family rift – disinheritance, even.

Ram lit another cigarette and drew the smoke deep into his lungs, willing it to calm the anger he felt at the injustice. He breathed it in and out, reminding himself that nothing could be improved on in his life; he knew that, truly he did. He thought of all the smart places he would visit on his travels, all the money that was his to spend, and all the gorgeous men that he would meet. Ash was just one tree in the forest – a particularly touching, lost and lovely tree, it was true – but just one, nevertheless. And Ram forced himself to see the forest of his life stretching away, through London to New York, into the green misty distance.

And yet, even as he sat in the dark, he wondered how soon he could persuade Ash to spend another night with him – at least one before he left on honeymoon – *just one more tryst before everything ended.*

Inside the house he heard voices, and Ram knew that Urvashi's meeting with Ash had ended. In a minute, they would come face-to-face. He stubbed out the cigarette, stood up and walked over to the front door. 'I have to get home,' Ram heard Ash say to Urvashi – he was declining some invitation – 'Sunita is waiting for me. We're going to her parents' . . . to your parents', for Diwali dinner.'

'You must come round for a meal when you get back from your honeymoon,' said Feroze to Ash. 'When are you leaving?'

'Friday,' Ash said. 'We're back in two weeks' time.'

'We'll make a plan with Sunita as soon as you return,' Feroze said, and then the door opened, light from the house spilt out into the garden, and suddenly Ash was standing there before him. Ram looked up and saw the man he had spent the night with, the man he had chatted with twice a week for the past twelve months, the man who blinked at him now through his glasses and smiled so suddenly that Ram flinched. Then the smile disappeared from Ash's face, he pushed his glasses back onto his nose, said goodbye to Urvashi and Feroze, and without a word to Ram, almost ran away down the path to the gate.

'You can eat Diwali dinner with us instead then,' Feroze said to his brother-in-law. Ram barely noticed that this invitation directly contravened his father's edict. He was staring up at his sister.

'What was Ash Chaturvedi doing here?' he asked her.

A fearful expression came over her face, and she half turned away to go into the house.

'Tell me what he was saying,' Ram insisted.

'He analysed the DNA of the man who raped our maid,' Feroze said soothingly. 'Come inside. I'll get you another beer.'

'What was he saying to you?' Ram almost shouted at Urvashi.

'He did a DNA test,' she said, looking back at him at last. 'But the results were contaminated,' she went on, and her voice grew in confidence the more she spoke, 'and the police aren't interested, and the maid has run away, so there is nothing we can do at all tonight, except celebrate Diwali together. Come inside and have dinner with us, just like Feroze said.'

And before Ram could follow Sunita's husband down the path to wherever he was going in the world, she pulled him into the house and shut the door behind him.

chapter 15

All the way home from the restaurant in the car, Vyasa and Bharati drove in silence.

'You'll have to get a test done, to prove it,' he said suddenly as they turned into Nizamuddin West.

Bharati glanced over at him and said, in a tone of voice far too jaded for a twenty-two-year-old (even she felt that): 'We look the same, Baba, stop being a dickhead.'

He began to interrupt her ('Don't you dare talk to your—') but the look she gave him was so withering that the phrase dried up in his mouth.

'You did sleep with her like she claims, right?' she said.

'Once.'

'Once is enough, Baba, to get a female pregnant. Is there anyone else out there, do you think, reeling from your failure to contracept them?'

By now they had reached the house. Bharati got out of the car, slammed the door behind her and ran up the steps – to find Pablo in the sitting-room, drinking beer with Ash, who had returned from an excruciating dinner at his in-laws.

Bharati frowned at Pablo most severely once she'd got him out of the house. He had arrived this evening on the night flight from

Calcutta and come straight over. They stood in the garden and had a whispered conversation.

'I saw Leela today. I've told my father. I don't want to stay here tonight. Can I stay at yours?'

'Yes, of course.'

He bent down and kissed her but she shook him off.

'Listen, if you write a story about the things you found out at Santiniketan I'll kill you.'

'I was thinking, if I discussed it with my editor—'

'No!'

'It's an important story, the story of the poetry – this dual authorship, their shared creativity—'

'It's my life, you bastard. You'll disgrace my family.'

'But if—'

'And anyway,' she went on before he could reply, 'they'll never print something unflattering about Hari's wife; and really, Pablo, it's not the kind of story that a journalist should be investigating, quite frankly. You did your lingam story, didn't you?'

'That thing!'

'I'm so sorry,' she said, laughing at him unkindly, 'did I mess up your scoop? Did I . . . ?'

'Yes,' he said, placing as much pathos as he could on that one word, 'but you're right. I won't mention it to anyone.'

'Thank you,' she said, and bestowed a commiserating kiss upon him.

It was only much later that night, as they lay in bed together listening to Diwali fireworks exploding all over the city, that Pablo dared to ask, 'So what did he say when you told him?'

'Who?'

'Your father.'

Bharati thought of how he had denied at first that such a thing was possible, and how she had had to spell it out. She considered how best to reply to Pablo. 'He fucked up,' she said flippantly.

'What?'

'In the epic, Ved Vyasa gets three women pregnant, two sisters and—'

'The servant.'

She laughed. 'You know everything.' Then she said, in a more serious voice, 'I think my father is in shock. But really – what was wrong with him? Indira Gandhi was sterilising the villages, and there he was, out there in the sticks, reproducing. Who did he think he was?'

'And Ash, what does he think?'

'I haven't told him yet.'

'Don't you—' he began.

But she turned round and put a finger to his lips. 'Not yet, no.'

And then one more: 'What did you think of her?'

There was a long silence.

'I'm not sure. She gave me up.'

'Presumably she thought it was for the best.'

'Maybe.'

'Did you like her? I liked her.'

'Maybe. I don't know. Let's see.'

Next morning it was still dark when she woke – and her first thought was: *I do like her after all.* She was too proud to admit this to anyone, of course; and she felt a lonely pang for Ash, whose own mother remained in a state of deadness.

She turned over restlessly in bed and Pablo whispered, 'Are you awake?'

'Yes.'

'So, let's get dressed. I'll take you somewhere special.'

'Where?'

But he wouldn't say.

He insisted that she dress up warm: a hat to go below the motor-cycle helmet, two pairs of socks, his jumper, her shawl. Only once they were out on the road, with her huddled behind him on the bike, did he tell her that they were going to see the birds of Delhi.

'No!' she shouted at him through the rushing wind, feeling scandalised. 'You're not serious?'

'Yes I am,' he shouted back, sounding amused at her tone. 'I know it's what you've always wanted.'

'Haven't all the birds been scared away by the fireworks?' she asked.

But the birds hadn't gone; and nor did the fog that wreathed the city at that hour diminish his enthusiasm. 'There are flamingos on the river,' he yelled as they drove south down an almost empty road towards the Okhla barrage.

'We're not going to the *Yamuna*?' she asked, dread in her voice at the cold and the distance and the endeavour.

'Of course we are,' he answered, his voice happy. 'Like Radha and Krishna. We'll be there in twenty minutes.'

Half an hour later he parked the bike on the edge of a mud track, paused briefly to show her the river from this perspective – misty, green with water hyacinths, the hum of the city disturbingly far-off in the distance – and then he led her down to the river, into the reed-beds.

As Bharati shivered with cold, Pablo showed her how to look through his binoculars at a green bee-eater and then a blue-throat and finally a purple swamp hen: 'The lipstick bird!' He explained about local migrants, and those birds that arrived at this time of year from the other side of the world. 'What migrations!' he said. 'What odysseys.'

'What's that awful shriek?' she asked. There was a high-pitched cry coming from somewhere in the heavens. 'Is it a kite?'

'Better than that. It's an osprey,' he said, gazing upwards, and pointed out the gliding shape far above them. 'They sound like women grieving.'

'Do they?' she said, and clung onto him ever tighter.

As the sun rose he showed her the quick, blurred forms of other birds through his binoculars, the names of which she immediately forgot, and as they drove back towards Nizamuddin, he wanted to take her on to the Lodhi Gardens, to look for a smiling or laughing or something dove, but she refused on point of principle, which was that human beings should not be exposed to such cold, at such an hour, for so long, for such frivolous reasons. Her fingers were icy, her nose and cheeks windblown, and even her internal organs felt as if they were being slowly frozen. When they reached Nizamuddin, she insisted on being taken straight to her father's house where there was a guaranteed supply of constant hot water, as well as the cook's famously unhealthy fried breakfast, washed down with lots of her father's coffee. 'Baba will have left for the fort by now,' she added quickly, as he turned off the main road into Nizamuddin West, 'but my grandmother will be there. You can meet her. And I have to go and wish Ash happy birthday.'

When they reached the gate, however, and as he was locking the bike, he said, 'I can't just turn up here like this with you and surprise your family without warning them first.'

'Because you've pointed out in print that our mother wasn't the only author of *The Lalita Series*?'

'Because you spent the night with me, Bharati.'

'Oh, I wouldn't worry about that. Anyway, Ash and Sunita won't be awake yet. We'll go and see my Dadi first. We'll take her some breakfast.'

'Won't she disapprove just as much?'

'I don't have to tell her where I spent the night,' Bharati said. 'And anyway, she remembers you from our schooldays. You came to the house all the time as a sweet little twelve-year-old.' She laughed at him. 'With your chessboard and your bird books and your expensive binoculars.'

'It'll be obvious.'

'Too bad. Father did the same in his time. I probably get it from him.'

She turned and led him into the house and he followed her upstairs to meet her beloved Dadi. The old woman, despite both their apprehensions, was on her best behaviour. She sat up in bed, wrapped in a soft shawl, and instead of asking about Pablo's parentage and prospects, as Bharati had feared, she quizzed him on the birds: 'Where are the white-rumped vultures?' she said, as if their decline was his fault. 'Where have the carrion birds disappeared to? They used to gather in flocks – but they're nowhere to be seen. And the waterbirds on the nala? And the sparrows?'

'Oh!' said Pablo, and the two of them entered an avian realm of superlatives and sorrow, leaving Bharati standing at the window, drinking her third coffee, feeling thoroughly earthbound.

The telephone rang and Bharati ran downstairs to answer it.

'Bharati,' said a woman's voice, which at first she was unable to place. 'It's Linda,' the voice said, and then Bharati remembered.

'Linda, how are you?' She smiled at the thought of her scruffy and inelegant English friend. 'Why are you ringing? What's happened? Isn't it the middle of the night in England?'

'I'm in Delhi,' Linda said. 'My paper was accepted by the Living Sanskrit Akademi. I sent you an email. I assumed you already knew. I arrived last night and I'm giving my lecture at eleven this morning. Will you come? Can we meet?'

'You're here for my father's lecture-series?'

'Yes. He is opening the proceedings, and then I am giving my paper, and then it's lunch, and then there's one other speaker in the afternoon.'

'Excellent,' Bharati said, not knowing what else to say. 'How long are you here for?'

'Oh, a week,' Linda said. 'There's something else, too, but I can't tell you over the phone.'

'What is it?'

'I'll explain when we meet. It's very confusing, I don't quite know if I believe it.'

'Believe what?'

'The taxi's arrived to take me to the old fort,' Linda said. 'I've got to go. And by the way – happy birthday.'

chapter 16

'It's almost time,' Feroze called through to Urvashi in the kitchen. 'Hurry up with the tea. We should leave soon.'

They were due at Uncle Hari's place at ten. He had rung the night before, soon after Ram left, to wish them happy Diwali, and to invite them over for a family meeting. 'A reconciliation,' he had said in his urgent way. 'I want to make things good between my brother and you. The sooner he comes face to face with your husband, and sees what a wonderful man he is, the sooner he'll learn.'

'What will he learn, Uncle Hari?' Urvashi had asked, thinking of the discussion she had just had with Feroze about Ash Chaturvedi's DNA analysis.

'How foolish he is not to have seen you all this time,' Uncle Hari said with a laugh. 'Don't worry, Pinki. I have everything under control. We'll expect you here at ten?'

'Yes, Uncle Hari,' Urvashi had answered. But this morning, she could barely think straight for the tension.

'Should I veil my hair from now on?' she said, looking anxiously at her husband as she brought the tea over to the table.

'Absolutely not,' Feroze said. 'What gave you that idea? I love your hair.'

'And you don't mind that other people see it?' She poured some more tea for him, and waited for his answer.

He glanced at her. 'You think I'm a Taliban or something?'

'No, it's just,' she began, and stopped. 'I thought it was written like that in the holy book.'

'It's an extremely oblique reference,' Feroze said, spreading bright-red jam on his toast. 'And we are living fourteen hundred years after the time of the Prophet. And clothing is the least important aspect of our religion, in my opinion. Stop worrying about these things. Think about what you are going to say to your father.'

She sat down at the table. 'I don't want to see him,' she said in a whisper. 'How can I when I know that . . . ?'

'Look,' he said, putting up his hands in resignation, 'it's for you to decide. He's your father. Aisha has disappeared and we'll probably never see her again. If you want to pursue the course of justice with this DNA proof, I will support you one hundred per cent in that. If you decide not to, that is also your decision. I thought you said that the sample may have been contaminated.'

'Allah will guide me,' Urvashi said piously, thinking of the peaceful feeling she had got kneeling in prayer last night and pressing her face to the mat and uttering the words her mother-in-law had taught her.

'No he won't,' Feroze said. 'You have to think for yourself about what is best.'

'Oh my God,' Urvashi burst out again. She felt such a clutching and twisting inside her at the thought of seeing her father that she got to her feet and came and put her arms around Feroze, pressing her face into his chest, grabbing at his shirt. As he held her, she tried to breathe deeply, smelling her husband's scent, his clean kurta, the smell of the freshly ironed khadi cotton, but the sickening inside went on and on. She wanted to weep and scream but the tears wouldn't come. She felt as if she was falling and the noise that came out of her throat was strangled. *I want my father to love me again.*

On the drive north to Connaught Place she was glad, at least, that they weren't meeting at her parents' place. She had longed so much, during the early months of her marriage, to return to the house where she grew up. She had cried to herself at night, as she lay beside her husband in their stuffy bedroom in his parents' claustrophobic house, wanting to return to that tiny, familiar flat with its smells of turmeric and asafoetida, once the only smells of home that she knew. She hadn't been back since the day she eloped, and from then on she and Feroze had avoided the southern swathe of the city. They never went further south than Lajpat Nagar if they could help it; they drove the extra distance to the cinema complex in the far south-west rather than go to the nicer one in Saket. Her parents still lived in the same small flat where she had grown up, and it was as if there was now an invisible wall cutting through Delhi along the ring road, between Defence Colony and Greater Kailash, Sarojini Nagar and Safdarjung, separating their two worlds.

She stared out at the endless stream of cars, with their windows tightly closed because of the air-conditioning, at the breezy, cranky buses. They passed the old fort with its moat and boating teenage lovers. The city as a whole felt remote and shadowy and insular to her now that she lived in the tightly circumscribed circle of Nizamuddin-Khan Market-Defence Colony. She realised that the little community she had built up since they moved there – Humayun the driver, Aisha the maid, the tailor in the market – was a precious thing. She prayed again, to Allah, that Humayun and Aisha would be all right. And as they drove onwards she saw India – its huge expanse, stretching all the way from the mountains to the sea – and Humayun and Aisha within it, tiny specks, wandering down a road in a part of India that Urvashi herself had never seen, Kerala or Karnataka or Tamil Nadu, their possessions bound up in a cloth on Humayun's back.

The car stopped at a red light and a beggar, a woman with a baby, rapped on the glass. Feroze reached down to a pocket by the gear stick and picked up a handful of coins. He opened the window and handed the coins to the woman, and her whining voice filled the car. 'Ten rupees more,' she said. 'My baby is sick; God will bless you with children.' But the lights turned green, Feroze put the car into gear, and as the beggar moved back onto the kerb, she made a small gesture of irritation.

'Do you always give them money?' Urvashi asked, surprised. She didn't remember him doing so in the days before they were married, during their long drives out of Delhi.

'Yes.' He glanced at her and looked back at the road.

'But they are fakes,' she said.

He was silent for a moment, and then, as they reached India Gate, he said, 'I feel sorry for the babies.' And with one hand he reached out and felt for her belly and kept it there until they arrived on Kasturba Gandhi Marg.

Uncle Hari's house was set back from the road slightly, one of those colonial-era properties that Urvashi had glimpsed from the outside many times but had never viewed at close quarters before. She felt strangely excited. This was the place where her brother was living now.

The front door was opened by Uncle Hari, who smiled at them both and shook Feroze's hand and hugged Urvashi for a long moment, then stood back and looked at her. 'When is it due?' he asked.

'In April,' she whispered, and he gave her one of those big smiles she remembered.

'Are you scared about seeing your father?' he said, and when she nodded he answered, in a voice of supreme confidence, 'You'll be fine,' and led them without any further ado across the cavernous hallway, and into a huge drawing room with windows at each end, where her family was assembled. Delicate glass chandeliers hung down from the far-away ceilings. Urvashi saw four faces turned towards them. Her little sister Sunita was perched on a chair in the middle of the room, looking prim and pleased with herself, holding a glass of juice. Her handsome brother, Ram, was sprawled across a chair. Her mother was on a settee, the ample and once-familiar curves of her body wrapped in a mauve cotton sari. And there, beside her, the man Urvashi had doted on: her father.

He was speaking to the room at large, loudly and forcefully, when they entered, and he didn't stop talking even when Hari led his estranged daughter into the room with her Muslim husband. 'How anyone can bear to live here I just don't know,' he said. 'It's amazing there are still families in the area when there is so little in the way of amenities and communal facilities. No vegetable hawkers, no residents' association.'

'Nothing is lacking here. We love it,' Hari answered, and began to say something else, but Shiva Prasad interrupted.

'Connaught Place itself has changed a lot,' he said. 'When I first came to Delhi it was all clean and tidy. Where there's now that tower block behind, the neighbourhood boys played cricket. During wedding season women would come on tongas to buy saris from Glamour on Saturday afternoons.'

'Tongas!' interjected Sunita, presumably amazed at a world without motorised vehicles. Urvashi averted her eyes from her mother's gaze and sat down on the couch next to Feroze, one hand protectively over her womb. She ran her tongue over her lips and breathed slowly through her nose, trying to calm the fear she felt.

'Sunita,' her uncle said, 'can you pour the lemonade for your sister and Feroze?'

As Sunita brought over two tall glasses filled with the fizzy drink, the ice cracking within them, Urvashi's father continued talking. 'There was a bookshop selling all the best things available in Hindi,' he said, looking around for agreement from his offspring.

But Ram interrupted: 'And now there's a McDonald's and a Benetton, and all those other lovely foreign shops.'

'Professor Chaturvedi,' piped up Sunita, 'says that globalisation is a danger to Indian culture.'

Ram turned to his father: 'So the Professor and you agree on one thing at least.'

Urvashi could see that her brother was showing off in a way he never used to at home. 'Did you confront him on the night of the wedding as you planned?' Ram went on. 'Amma says you left early to make him recant his anti-national theories.'

The siblings' mother made a ssshing sound. 'Beta, your father is a very civilised person. He went to see the Professor to discuss certain ideological questions. Please don't bring up this thing in front of Sunita.'

'And did the Professor agree with you?' Ram persisted, his eyes shining with the novelty he felt at presiding over his father in argument.

Shiva Prasad waved his hand dismissively. 'He wasn't in. Only the maid was there.'

Uncle Hari got to his feet at this moment and raised a hand to call for silence. 'I have asked you all here today,' he began, 'because

I want our family to be whole again. We are all guilty of encouraging division. I have been away too long –'

But Urvashi could barely hear the words her uncle was saying. A coldness had entered her. *Only the maid was there.*

Hari bowed his head, '– away from India, and my family, and my loved ones –'

Only the maid was there.

'My brother Shiva has cast his daughter out—' And now all eyes turned to Urvashi. 'But the moment has come for the pain of the past to be set aside.'

Only the maid was there.

Urvashi's mother suddenly began to wail in the hysterical, forced way, which was familiar from funerals. 'My daughter, my daughter. We never disallowed our daughter's marriage to this Muslim gentleman,' she said, gesturing in the direction of Feroze. '*She* ran away from her family. *She* should be asking her parents for forgiveness.'

'Ma!' said Ram, 'she didn't run away. What are you saying? Pita-ji forbade it and so did you.'

Their mother had obviously been expecting this outburst from her son. She looked over at Urvashi, waiting for her to speak. *You were always your father's favourite,* Urvashi could hear her mother saying through the silence. *You were the one he loved best. Show that you are the faithful and respectful daughter we always knew you to be, until you married this Muslim. Redeem yourself.*

But before Urvashi could answer, her father got to his feet and crossed the room towards her, a look of forgiveness composed upon on his face; her beloved father whom she missed so much; and when he reached her side, and put out a hand and actually touched the bump of the baby inside her, in a gesture both of humility but also of possession, Urvashi looked up at him.

'Only the maid was in. What do you mean, Only the maid was in?'

A look of affront passed over her father's face. Urvashi pushed his hand away and got slowly to her feet.

'My maid – who is also Professor Chaturvedi's maid – was raped on the night of Sunita's wedding.' It was her voice that was speaking. 'When everybody was away at the wedding, father went to the house, and only the maid was there.'

She regarded each of them in turn, imagining the effect of the words she had to say.

'It was father's DNA that was inside the girl.'

There was a long moment of silence – and then her mother started screaming. Uncle Hari turned to face her, his arms flailing, 'What are you saying? What are you accusing him of?' Ram – or was it Sunita? – was yelling that Urvashi had had her head turned by Muslim propaganda. 'I invited everybody here today to make peace, not to start new battles,' Uncle Hari shouted.

But Urvashi continued talking. She turned to Sunita, and explained that a doctor examined the girl, and because of Ash Chaturvedi's Arya Gene Project, this linked their father to the crime, but that the maid had absconded, and the police would do nothing.

'Ash's gene work?' somebody said – possibly Ram.

'Ash wouldn't do that!' Sunita gasped, and Urvashi knew that it was her little sister who would take the news the hardest – she, the youngest and most innocent of the three.

Urvashi heard her mother hurl abuse at her, then saw her lunge towards her. She felt Feroze and Hari both move forward to shield her from her mother's grasp. She saw Ram take his mother by the shoulders; allowed herself to be led by Feroze to the door; and the very last thing she saw as they left was her father, standing alone in the middle of the room, his head bowed, his hands clasped together, his mouth open as if beseeching; and she never knew (and in the weeks after nobody could tell her) whether or not he was begging her forgiveness.

Urvashi Ahmed only saw Humayun's mother once more that winter. She came to call one evening towards the end of Ramzan, to ask if Urvashi had heard anything about her son. But of course, Urvashi had heard nothing, and she had to turn the woman away.

Raziya walked from Urvashi's house back along the drain road to where the Professor lived. She had taken to coming to the Chaturvedis' house every week, after closing up the shop, and before cooking dinner, to stand at the front door and ask if there had been a phonecall, if anybody had heard anything at all. Every time the Professor's mother gave the same answer: nothing yet but we will let you know as soon as we hear.

At first, Raziya felt sure that her son would return. She had read his note, and knew what an obedient boy he was – how faithfully he had always performed the tasks she required of him, how he attended school right through until Class Ten, how he brought home his salary every month and gave it to her. As the days passed following his disappearance, she thought about him all the time. She thought about him as she took orders from customers – in one month's time it would be Eid and every lady in the colony was thinking of the new clothes she would wear, and all of them wished to discuss the virtues of bell sleeves versus three-quarter-length, boat or sweetheart neckline, piping, or a special hand embroidery for which Raziya's shop charged twenty rupees per square inch. Always she wondered where he was, and what he was doing. She thought of him as she lay in bed at night, worrying about how he was living and whether he was safe. She thought of him as she closed up the shop, and counted her earnings, and put half of it in a new locked box in her bedroom and then walked with the other half to the bank. After three days passed, she forgave him for eloping without her permission. Five days went by, and she excused him for taking the gold and her money. After a week, she even ceased to curse his sweetheart. She began to wish that she herself had not been so hasty in denouncing their union.

One afternoon, at the bank in the market, Raziya asked for her account balance and saw that in addition to the black money that she, like everybody else in the country, kept in the house or about their person, she had saved twenty thousand rupees in the past ten years. Part of that was contributions from Humayun's salary. And she had been saving it – for what? For her son and his wife and their future offspring, Raziya's own grandchildren, those little unborn angels whom she would clothe and nurture and educate to a life of happiness and plenty.

The following Sunday, after shutting the shop early, Raziya took a bus to Lajpat Nagar central market, walked up the road with five hundred rupees in her handbag, and chose, one hour later, a pale green baby's jumpsuit, embroidered with small red flowers on the chest from a shop in the covered market. Before turning for home, she also entered the first bangle shop she came across, where she picked out a box of twelve pretty red glass bangles for Aisha.

Back in Nizamuddin, Raziya looked around her small house, and tried to imagine a daughter-in-law within it. She considered whether they would stay here in this room, with her – she could easily sew a good thick curtain dividing the sleeping space in two – or whether she could sleep in the passage leading to the kitchen. Then there was the question of where their babies would go.

In the end she decided that she could have a partition built down the middle of the bedroom, and she called a man from the market who came with his tape-measure, wearing a grubby brown shirt that needed a wash – he was a Hindu – and took off his shoes and looked respectfully around the space she presented for his inspection and asked, after taking some measurements and walking up and down and thinking about it, 'Do you have access to the roof?' She nodded: of course, the roof. There was nothing much up there – only a few pots of tulsi and coriander, and a little chilli plant, and the water tank.

They went up onto the roof together, and the man explained how he could build a large bedroom with an insulated tin roof and concrete block walls in no time at all and for only ten thousand rupees. Raziya thought about it, and bargained him down to five thousand by opting for concrete sheets lined with polystyrene. The man returned the next morning with his men and started work; and Raziya began to furnish the space in her mind, filling it with things appropriate to a bridal chamber.

By now it was the second week of Ramzan, and all her staff were fasting and the small room where the tailors worked (behind the space where Raziya received her customers) was full of irritation – they all complained about the dust that the Hindu builder caused to fly around as his men tramped upstairs, and the noise of sawing planks, and, above all, about the smell of drifting cigarette smoke from the roof, and the delicious aroma of Hindu tiffins at lunchtime.

But the man was prompt, and the room was ready within the week. Once he had finished, Raziya called in another man – from the basti, this time – and paid him three hundred rupees for paint (from Bhogal) and two hundred rupees labour charge, and long before Eid the room was white and shining and smelling of the gloss paint that had been used on the woodwork.

Raziya had in the meantime visited the carpenter on the edge of the basti market, and ordered a double bed, for which she paid nine hundred rupees. The carpenter had made it from solid Indian ply with a slatted hardwood base that smelt faintly sweet and sickly, as if it had been dragged from a rubbish tip, and the next day Raziya came home from Bhogal on a cycle rickshaw, balancing a new foam mattress, plus two double sheets, a thick green and pink blanket still in its transparent plastic case, and some red fabric roses with drops of dew pasted all the way down the petals, which she bought from the greeting card and gift shop next to the chemist.

Finally, when the bed was assembled and spread with the sheet and the roses placed in a vase on the window sill, she took down from the row of hangers in her shop the garments that she herself had stitched: a white khadi cotton kurta and pyjama for her son, and a simple but well-cut thick cotton suit made from a red and purple print with a matching diaphanous dupatta for his wife, and she carried them upstairs to the roof, unlocked the padlock to the room, laid them next to the baby suit on the double bed, spread with its new sheets and patterned blanket. She sat down at the foot of the bed, and put her head back and listened, imagining her son in this place with his wife and child. She could hear nothing, only the cars on Lodhi Road and the crows on the electricity lines and the birds of prey swooping through the sky, far above her head.

chapter 17

Linda walked over to the lectern and looked around her at Emperor Humayun's fort – with its proper medieval battlements and pink, octagonal sandstone library (like in the history books), its huge elephant-procession gateway and daunting views over the city. She stood in the midst of it all, facing the audience seated in packed rows on the concrete steps of what passed for the fort's open-air auditorium – on the very place where refugees bound for Pakistan, and Emperor Humayun's courtiers, and the Pandava brothers, had all stood in their turn – and she couldn't believe it: that she was finally in India, in this hallowed place she had thought about so often in the past, giving a lecture about the Mahabharata, on her birthday. Ever since she had walked out of the airport and smelt the warm, tangy air, she had thought how strange it was. She remembered her mother here before her – younger than Linda was now, heading off into the eastern part of the country – and the idea exacerbated her slightly exhausting sense of continual amazement. She thought of her mother as she took a taxi into the centre of the city, as she stepped out of her hotel and looked at the streets around her, as she stared and listened and soaked in the reds and oranges and greens, like her dumbstruck yokel self, aged thirteen, in Leicester Square.

And beneath her lecture notes, neatly typed out, was the so-called 'novel' that the mysterious Indian customer had asked her to transcribe. The neatness of the typing belied the chaos. Linda was a staunch supporter of the imaginative process, but there were things asserted within which she knew to be *factually impossible*. Either that, or it was an elaborate prank mocking her own Ph.D. thesis. There was, however, a lot that made sense.

Linda placed her notes on the lectern and gazed across the crowd of expectant faces. Professor Chaturvedi had just given the keynote speech – all the usual stuff about the god Ganesh, mixed in with some political statements about the present government, as well as obsequious thanks to the Akademi's funders, and a rather dry and curt manifesto for what this new body hoped to achieve in India and beyond.

It was Linda's turn now. Of course she felt nervous. She hoped she wouldn't blush too much. She prayed her voice wouldn't dry up, that her hands wouldn't shake, that the pages of her lecture wouldn't blow away into the audience. She had watched the professor as he spoke. During her research, she had read almost everything he had published. She was familiar with his frequently pleasing turn of phrase, his gift, rare amongst academics, for illuminating entire ages in broad, clear strokes of colour. She had realised this morning, as soon as they were introduced, that his ability to make antiquity feel *real* lay, in part, in his own demeanour: open, attractive, accessible. And then, his attitudes were voguish: sexual politics was his calling card, gender relations, *women*. Judging by the number of young women in the audience, his female students found it shocking and stimulating in equal measure. As a teacher, he was clearly much admired. Linda wondered how she was going to tell Bharati what she had come to know about Professor Chaturvedi.

'The legend of Ganesh as the Mahabharata's scribe,' Linda began, 'has not fared well with scholars. Even though Ganesh is a popular god, ubiquitous in folklore, these very words – *popular, folklore* – are anathema to Sanskrit scholars. They have generally treated Ganesh's literary credentials with contempt, denouncing him as anachronistic, and editing him out of their editions. Today, I wish to reinstate the god Ganesh at the heart of India's literary canon.'

And catching her friend Bharati's eye – she was sitting three rows from the front, next to a man with curly hair, whom Linda guessed was the latest boyfriend – she smiled.

'The description of Ganesh's role as scribe frames the epic – and yet it has been in jeopardy ever since the late nineteenth century when the idea that Ganesh was a spurious, later addition to the epic became current. Indeed, the late-twentieth-century Chicago translation of the Mahabharata excised the Ganesh episode altogether.'

Linda knew that Professor Chaturvedi had made this notion – of Ganesh as a late interpolation – the basis for his much-quoted thesis about the god, and that the theory she was to lay before her audience, and his audience too, posed a subtle challenge to his scholarship. This was not an auspicious basis for a future relationship. However, there was nothing to be done. She took a sip of water. She felt very calm.

'Where did this idea come from? The first person to raise it was one of the fathers of Sanskrit studies in Europe, the famous nineteenth-century scholar Moriz Winternitz. Winternitz noted that there were crucial differences between the various versions of the Mahabharata, which was not surprising given its length and antiquity, and because of the original oral transmission of this text.'

She glanced over at Professor Chaturvedi. He was listening to her words with great attention.

'The main disparity scholars found when they consulted these different editions was the South Indian text's "remarkable" omission of the Ganesh legend. Winternitz therefore proposed the formation of a Sanskrit Epic Text Society, the explicit aim of which would be to publish a critical edition of the Mahabharata that reconciled the differences. It was this suggestion that led to the Bhandarkar edition, and, in turn, to the marginalisation of the Ganesh legend.'

Linda was enjoying herself now. She scanned the crowd for the Dictator's characters with whom she had recently become so familiar. Maybe that was 'Pablo the Protector' sitting next to Bharati. And was that anxious-looking boy on her other side 'Ash the Genealogist'? Had shy and retiring Sunita come to the lecture? Was 'Urvashi the Truthteller' here?

'It is understandable why Winternitz and his followers drew the conclusions they did. Other than in the dictation scene, Ganesh is not mentioned elsewhere in the Mahabharata, nor in the Ramayana nor the Vedas, and given that the first verified textual appearance he makes elsewhere in Sanskrit literature is in the comparatively recent Puranas – around the fifth century AD, possibly a millennium after the initial composition of the Mahabharata – scholars have till now had good reason to assume that the dictation legend cannot have existed within the epic before that date.'

Linda saw Professor Chaturvedi nodding in agreement.

'Furthermore, in the more easily authenticated and historical Puranic cult of Ganesh, there is no mention of the elephant god as *scribe*. As one twentieth-century scholar noted, "No ancient Indian frescoes or sculptures depict him in this role." Another has reflected that the "late interpolation" probably represented a pragmatic and belated attempt "to get Ganesh into the epic of which it is said that anything which is not included within it does not exist". And yet, there *are* certain features of the Puranas which may be connected to the dictation legend of the Mahabharata. Indeed, I believe these reveal that the Ganesh legend was present in the Mahabharata from early on, and was there for a specific historical reason.'

Professor Chaturvedi was by now looking distinctly wary. Linda couldn't help feeling pleased. In the process of transcribing the Dictator's pages she had at first been infected by the narrator's derogatory view of the Mahabharata's Vyasa – which was complicated, given the position she then found herself in vis-à-vis the Professor.

'In the Puranas,' she continued, 'Ganesh is given wives (or attributes), variously known as Buddhi and Siddhi, or Buddhi and Riddhi. Academics have long argued' – and here, she knew, she was indirectly criticising Professor Chaturvedi himself – 'that the association of Ganesh with script arose through a confusion of the name of his wife Siddhi (the word *siddhi* means success) with *siddham* (a term for the Hindu alphabet from ancient times). But scholars have not examined the possibility that the name of Buddhi could actually be taken to refer to the Buddha.'

A woman a few rows back from Bharati looked up sharply at this. Linda had noticed her already, pen in hand, taking notes, and she glanced now between the woman and Bharati. They looked alike. Could she be the famous Leela?

'I would like to argue that Ganesh's role in the Mahabharata is a response to the competition Buddhism posed to the oral hegemony of the Vedas, from the sixth century BC onwards. Remember that while the Vedic tradition was predicated on *oral* transmission through the "perfect" and elite vehicle of Sanskrit, Buddhism made a merit of disseminating its message in as many dialects, languages and scripts as the faith came into contact with. Also, while the Vedic priests stressed *veda* (to announce or proclaim), the Buddha's own focus was on *budh* (to understand, to awake) – that is, on actually *understanding* rather than simply *repeating* the scriptures.'

The Leela woman was certainly lovely. She had wavy dark hair like Bharati, and the longest, biggest eyes that Linda had ever seen. Linda thought of the way the Dictator had described Leela in his book – with her 'cow-lash eyes' – and thought that on balance the phrase didn't do her justice. On the whole, she wasn't sure she'd liked the Dictator's cast of women. She had doubts about their over-lofty stature, their lustrous skin, their dark, flowing, Ganges-glossy hair. She was dubious about their breasts, those annoyingly perfect rotundas, as big and smooth as supermarket melons.

'In the Puranas, Ganesh's marriage to Buddhi stakes Hinduism's claim of authority over the scriptures. Similarly, one could argue that he was placed in the Mahabharata in an attempt by Hindus to co-opt the new and previously shunned medium of script, which, thanks to the Buddhists, was becoming increasingly popular in India.'

This Leela lady was the only true exception. Though the Dictator was apt to lose himself in his story (as Linda found through the ache in her fingers when she typed up his ramblings), and although she was bemused by his supernatural tales of Leela's exploits, she couldn't help feeling admiration. As she listened to the gentle Indian voice enlarging on Leela's various incarnations, she even felt a pang of envy. *She* wanted to be a woman like that. To have somebody describe *her* as a brave and undaunted firebrand kind of person.

'We can see this in how the Ganesh dictation episode is described in the North Indian edition of the epic. Here the act of writing protects "divine words in the language of truth". For the first time in recorded history, script becomes integral to the fabric of Vedic-Hinduism.'

The more she followed Leela's story – and that of Meera, her playmate, supporter and associate – the more Linda began to wish herself into the book too. She wanted to be one of Leela's followers. She wanted to sit in those cool clay courtyards, under the shade of those tamarisk trees, by chill mountain rivers. Before long, every Leela-episode the Dictator invented underwent the same metamorphosis in her imagination.

'But the question still remains,' Linda said, 'if Vedic-Hinduism used Ganesh as a means of answering those challenges from Buddhism that were seen as most dangerous – "understanding" and script – then how does one explain the concurrent prominence of Ganesh-worship within Buddhism? Where does Ganesh come from?

'All the evidence I have looked at points to the simultaneous and independent existence of Ganesh-worship within Buddhism. Emperor Ashoka's daughter took Ganesh-worship to Nepal. The Buddha himself disclosed a mantra in praise of Ganesh to his companions. There has been a very wide dissemination of Ganesh-worship via Buddhism, beyond the borders of India – to Buddhist Nepal, China and Tibet, as well as to Burma and Indonesia. Indeed, Chinese-Buddhist paintings and sculptures of Ganesh are earlier than any Ganesh image in India. If Buddhism took Ganesh-worship to China as early as this, logically it must have existed in India before that.'

It wasn't until she was at the end of the Dictator's tapes, however, that she saw how closely his story was related to Bharati's. Why had this strange man felt compelled to speak a magical tale about Bharati's father Vyasa into a dictaphone and given it to her to transcribe? Should she warn Bharati? She was about to ring her mum – who had been so against her doing the Indian man's typing in the first place – and ask her advice, when she got an email: her paper had been accepted by the Living Sanskrit Akademi. She was on her way to Delhi!

'Ganesh himself,' Linda said, 'probably represents a pan-Indian deity, older even than the Vedas, worshipped by people from pre-Aryan times, and later standing for the overthrow of elite Sanskrit hierarchy and mindless repetition in favour of true understanding through writing.'

And so when she rang her mother, instead of expressing her anxiety about the typing, she was instead full of excitement and talk about the Indian trip and how she would read her paper in front of Professor Ved Vyasa Chaturvedi—

'Oh, Linda!' her mother blurted out. 'If you go to Delhi and give that lecture, you will come face-to-face with your father!'

'What are you talking about, Mum?' Linda asked. And then it all came out: that the man who got her mother pregnant in 1979 was a Sanskrit academic; that though she knew his name, he had no way of knowing where she disappeared to or that she had a child; and this was why baby Linda was brought up as an English girl, the daughter of the childhood sweetheart her mother had hastily married upon her return from India.

'Mum! Why didn't you tell me before?'

'I wanted to, Linda,' her mother said, 'and after I saw you getting interested in India, I came to London that time to tell you. But I couldn't. Supposing your father didn't want to know you, after all these years?'

And mother and daughter wept down the phone to each other, overcome at last.

'What this suppressed history illustrates,' Linda said in conclusion, 'is that Ganesh the scribe was there to pull things together. The Mahabharata – so gargantuan, so all-encompassing – is the work of numerous minds over many hundreds of years. A communally owned text, an expression of countless histories, court chronicles, beliefs, practices and religions, the work of many minds over a long and diverse epoch of Indian history, written over hundreds of years, the epic has such a great diversity of character, place and action, is such a mixture of traditions, orthodox and unorthodox – that it is impossible to fathom in one sitting. Ganesh and his pen make sense of it. By writing the Mahabharata down, Ganesh ushers a new age into existence.'

chapter 18

My aim has been to reunite siblings, to bring together mothers and daughters – to remove from my characters' lives the obstacles that impinge on their happiness – and to expose Vyasa's wrongdoing. I couldn't help congratulating myself as I stood in the fort, looking at my characters gathered together in Indraprastha. I surveyed the scene, with its exquisite torrents of emotion, and recalled, in a pleasurable aside, all those grandiose phrases, which, in his over-weening pride, Vyasa had forced me to inscribe in the epic about the Pandavas' palace. (The flowers that rained from heaven; the trees made of gold; the jewels brought here from a mountain north of Kailash to adorn the walls.) I relished how effectively the words of Linda had upstaged Vyasa – how cleverly she had reinstated me, under Vyasa's unknowing auspices, into the heart of Indian history and tradition. I saw from a distance Bharati introducing Linda to her brother, and then I saw Leela walk towards them. An expression of doubt crossed Bharati's face, a hint of fear lit up Leela's – and at last, to my eternal joy and unending satisfaction, Bharati held out her arms to her mother. I would savour that sight for aeons to come. For a moment Pablo, Linda and Ash watched, breathless, as the two women embraced, and then Bharati abruptly freed herself, glanced round at everybody with a defiant expression, and started gesticulating as she untangled from her sister the complicated story of a newly discovered English sibling and a strange Indian author's dictaphone. And I stood and watched them, safe in the knowledge that the story she was describing was mine.

The last words I spoke into the dictaphone were: *This story is for Leela.* And so, as Linda obediently handed over the typescript to my heroine, I rejoiced in how completely my characters had done what I had planned for them. If there was one anxiety left it was poor Ash, caught between Sunita and Ram, unable to unite these two sides of himself. But I trusted that Leela would befriend him and help him find his way. It was about time he had a mother too. My only task now was the book itself.

Lost as I was in these glorious meditations, I didn't forget to disguise myself for my final meeting with Leela. Walking after her across the lawns of the fort, I wrapped my head in a muffler, took up a large outdoor brush, and began to sweep the leaves from the path, in the thoughtful (some would say ponderous) fashion of India's government-employed gardeners. That way, I surmised that, even though I was a little too chubby for the job, she wouldn't even notice my existence.

I was right. After speaking with her daughter, and collecting the manuscript from my little English typist, she headed away from the crowd, straight for Emperor Humayun's octagonal stone library – a smile that I hadn't seen for many centuries lighting up her face. Leela sat down on the top step of the library, and gazed out over the green tree canopy of this capacious fort, the book on her lap. I looked at the library's solid outline, built by the usurped and usurping Afghan king, with its white marble stars inlaid into the red sandstone; and I thought of my cast, scattered through time like the stars in heaven, and now fixed forever upon the pages of my book.

Then Leela began reading Linda's typescript, and I watched in pleasure as a look of bemusement, then wonder, displaced her smile. She turned over page after page that I had scripted in my wisdom, and when she finished reading, she looked up and frowned very hard into the distance. Finally, she tidied the sheets together and put them back in the envelope. Then, taking out a pad of paper, she bent her head, and didn't look up, even as I approached. I saw that she was writing – writing and crossing out and writing again.

But somebody was interrupting this tranquil scene of mutual creation. Twirling my brush with grandiloquent strokes, I stepped into the wings as Vyasa came striding across the lawns to where Leela was sitting. He cleared his throat, and when she didn't respond, he addressed her in his most tentative tone, 'Leela?' She looked up and I could see in one instant from the expression on her face, that though she was open to the world of books and monuments and elephant-scribes and daughters, she would always keep him at a distance. I was glad of that.

'Hello, Vyasa,' she said.

'I hope I'm not disturbing you,' he said. (I was delighted to see how nervously he was disporting himself.) 'It's so nice of you to have come to the lecture.'

Leela paused a moment before answering, and then she said, 'That last paper was very interesting. The speaker is at university with Bharati, is she?'

'Is she?' Vyasa said, but it seemed that another subject weighed more heavily on his mind. 'Bharati told me about . . . about . . .' He seemed unable to say it. 'I wanted to say that I am very sorry,' he said at last.

'Sorry about . . . ?'

'Everything that happened,' he said, trying to keep his voice under control. 'I had no idea that you had a child. That Meera knew.' His hand stroked his beard. 'And then the poetry.'

'The poetry doesn't matter,' she said. 'It's juvenilia.' Her voice was wonderfully clear and calm.

She looked down again at the words she was writing, but still he stood there. She looked up again and sighed. 'Is there anything else, Vyasa?'

'No,' he said. 'Yes. Well, the fact that you are . . .' He looked at her pleadingly. '. . . Bharati's mother . . .' He was behaving, I was delighted to observe, like a tongue-tied teenager.

He clearly wished that she would say something conciliatory. But she did not speak; and so he said (wise now, to the fact that he might not get another chance like this, to be alone with her): 'Why did she take the child?'

'Why? Because she was my sister. Because she felt responsible. But I don't think there's any need to speak about the past.'

'No, of course not,' he said hastily, although it was evident he felt the exact opposite. 'But, Leela? I do hope that you and I can be . . . friends?'

'Let's see,' said Leela, getting briskly to her feet and walking down the steps.

'Can you lend me one?' she called out. I looked up. She was talking to me. She was holding out a cigarette.

By now I had swept the leaves and grass cuttings into a huge pile in one corner of the path that ran right round the eight sides of the library. During their conversation I had gone backwards and forwards, up and down, in and out of character. I had even broken into a sweat. It was only when I crouched down before my pile, staring at it for quite a long time – as if it were deeply fascinating, as if perhaps it held the answer to the secrets of the universe – and finally took out a match, that she addressed me. Listening to her voice, I felt my love for her swelling like the throat of a songbird.

'You need a light?' I said.

'Please,' she replied. She came towards me, the book under her arm, and standing beside my pile of leaves, took the match and lit her cigarette. Then she glanced one final time at Vyasa. 'We should talk about these things another time,' she said, not unkindly, 'but not now. Look.' She pointed over to the lawns, where Bharati was standing with Ash and Linda. 'Your children have something important to say to you. Goodbye, Vyasa.'

She waited calmly until Vyasa had walked away across the lawns, and then she turned her eyes to me.

'If you light that now,' she said, pointing to the pile of leaves, 'won't it create a lot of smoke?'

'It's a delicious smell,' I ventured; and added poetically, 'The smell of so many autumns in Delhi.'

'And how many autumns have you known?' she asked, looking at me in that sideways fashion which I loved, as she smoked.

I paused, as if I was counting in my head. 'Hard to say,' I said at last.

'That many?' She raised an eyebrow. 'Were you born here?'

'No, madam,' I said, and added, bravely, 'I was born somewhere very far away.'

'And will you return there soon?'

'Oh no!' I looked at her, horrified. Return to Kailash? What a thought.

'So you will end your days here?' she asked.

'Madam, I try not to think about my death. It is, after all, what we do between the time of birth and the certain end that matters.'

'Are you saying the end is final?'

'I am saying that the interim is important.'

'Indeed,' she said, 'the interim is of supreme importance.'

As she spoke these words, I knew that she was speaking directly to me, in my godly capacity. She was letting me know that I had done what I could for her; I had been the cause of meetings and revelations. I had tried to reconcile her to the part she played. I had indeed removed many obstacles.

'There's no time to waste,' she added.

'No time at all,' I agreed, a little chastened.

'Goodbye,' she said to me politely, and I blinked up at her, thinking, Is this it? Is this the moment? Is this the end of our mortal acquaintance? Am I to say farewell to her so quickly? The space between us – the air itself, the sunlight, the solid warmth of the sandstone library, the very being of Delhi – tingled with unsung potential.

'Wait,' I called after her as she began to walk away. 'What have you been writing?'

She turned back, and a frown appeared on her brow as she contemplated the figure of her creator. 'I am writing a book for Bharati,' she said at last.

'The Mahabharata?' I cried, scarcely able to suppress my delight. 'That text with a million voices?'

'No!' she laughed. 'A book for Bharati. But yes, it will have many voices.'

'Passed from one hand to the other,' I dared to say.

'If you like,' she said, with the sweetest of smiles.

And then she walked away down the path I had swept, across the lawns of Humayun's fort, and back to the daughter she had found.

Acknowledgements

Thank you to Tristram Stuart (who nurtured this book from the beginning), and to Shuddhabrata Sengupta and S. Gautham for years of friendship and wise counsel. Funding from the Arts and Humanities Research Board enabled my enquiry into the Ganesh legends; meanwhile, the specific issue of Ved Vyasa's reputation in the Indian tradition was elucidated by Bruce M. Sullivan's book *Kṛṣṇa Dvaipāyana Vyāsa and the Mahābhārata: a new interpretation* (Leiden, 1989). Nandini Mehta, Dr Arijit Mukhopadhyay, Dr Bhaswar Maity, Taran Khan, Ananda Bannerjee and Nikhat, Ashraf, Yusuf and Sulaiman Mohamedy gave their time, ideas and corrections. Tahmima Anam and Roland Lamb were generous readers; Ellie Steel from Harvill Secker worked hard on the final version; Ben Madden was noble; Jin Auh, Charles Buchan and all at the Wylie Agency made things happen in between. Finally, thank you to three people in particular: Sarah Chalfant, my amazing agent; the formidable Chiki Sarkar of Random House India; and Rebecca Carter, who edited this novel with such divine dexterity.

LEELA'S BOOK

Alice Albinia

LEELA'S BOOK

Alice Albinia

Alice Albinia on writing her novel, *Leela's Book*

Ten years ago, when I was living in Delhi, I had the idea to write two books. Both of them were shaped by the heat of a Delhi summer. The first was about a chubby Hindu god; the second about a cool mountain river. The river idea slipped into my mind while I was reading a translation of India's most ancient and sacred Sanskrit text, the Rig-Veda. In my notebook, I wrote down 'Indus', 'Aryans' and 'Alexander'. Those three words led to journeys through Pakistan, India, Afghanistan and Tibet, and archival investigations into the history of the Indus valley, once the celebrated territory of the Rig-Veda, now the backbone of Pakistan. This was how I came to write my first book, *Empires of the Indus: The Story of a River*.

The other idea I had that summer also emerged from a reading of a Sanskrit text: the Mahabharata, India's devastating, adventurous epic about a warring family. I noticed something very simple and seemingly overlooked. While popular versions of the Mahabharata included the framing narrative about how the author, Vyasa, called on the elephant god, Ganesh, to be his scribe, scholarly versions of the epic always excised this section. I began to wonder why. These thoughts led to my novel, *Leela's Book*.

I began to collect translations of the epic. At the Sahitya Akademi in Delhi I photocopied reams of text in the translations by Kisari Mohan Ganguli and M.N. Dutt. On a visit home to London I bought all three volumes of the unfinished Chicago translation. On a journey to Calcutta I visited the publisher P. Lal and brought a stack of his brightly coloured, cloth-bound 'transcreations' of the epic back with me to Nizamuddin. I thought a lot about the recording of texts in ancient times, about cultural inheritance and tradition, about the retelling of well-loved stories.

Above all, I began to think about Ganesh himself, and how he might have responded to the task of writing down this massive book. Did he even like Vyasa's story? Did he find the assignment daunting, or exciting, or thankless? The shelves of my flat filled up with the Mahabharata in its variant translations, but none of those volumes would yield up any answer.

Instead, a story about Ganesh, creation and subterfuge began to take shape in my mind. Every afternoon when I arrived home from the literary magazine where I worked as an editor, I sat down at the desk under my window and wrote out the section of the book called 'Ganesh's Narration'. The heat of that summer was crucial; it kept me there, under the ceiling fan, with just my imagination to distract me.

Since Delhi was built around Indraprastha, the city and its mythologies became central to my story, as did the idea of womanhood in this culture where the Mahabharata's proud women, fierce goddesses and ancient matriarchies compete with other more generally pervasive notions of feminine submission and piety. By the autumn of that year I knew two things: that I would have to leave Delhi for the Indus valley, and that in the meantime I would wind around Ganesh's narration a modern-day story of the characters he had invented in a spirit of mischief and retribution.

Now that both books are written, I can see how much they fed into each other during the years I was travelling and researching. The very last journey I made for *Empires of the Indus* was to the source of the Indus in Tibet, a week-long walk north of Mount Kailash. I remember standing in the snow after the journey was over, looking at the stark outline of the sacred mountain and thinking how strange it was to know the Mahabharata better than the English epics *Beowulf* or *Paradise Lost*, and southern Pakistan better than northern England. My stranger's gaze was useful, but it also gave me a sense of dislocation. Then I remembered the significance of the mountain I was looking at: it was here that Ganesh wrote down the Mahabharata. It was time to return home and finish my novel.

DISCUSSION QUESTIONS

1.   There are many parallels between the lives of the characters in the Mahabharata and those in *Leela's Book*. What connections can you find? How are these episodes altered in the modern world?

2.   Many of the book's dramas come from the clash between two separate people or ideas: between Ganesh and Vyasa, between Hindu and Islam, etc. Can you identify other such dichotomies?

3.   The Mahabharata is a huge epic covering generations of Indian history and myth. By contrast, the majority of the action in *Leela's Book* takes place in a mere few weeks. How does the abbreviated scale of *Leela's Book* affect its impact?

4.   There are many groups of siblings in this book, some estranged, some close: Hari and Shiva; Meera and Leela; Bharati and Ash; Urvashi, Sunita, and Ram. What is the importance of the sibling relationship in the book?

5.   Why do you think Ganesh has such an attachment to Leela? Why is it that he is concerned about her above all others?

6.   The book presents two different explanations for Leela's fainting at the wedding: seeing Bharati, or seeing Ganesh. Which do you think is right? Could they both be possible?

7.   What is Ganesh's relationship to *Leela's Book*? Is the book he has Linda transcribe the very book that we are reading? If so, do you think Ganesh is a reliable narrator?

8.   What do you think of Vyasa? Does your opinion of him change over the course of the story, and if so, how?

9. Why do you think Leela hides the secrets of her past from Hari? Why did she marry him in the first place?

10. Why does Shiva Prasad harbor political ambitions? Do you think his reputation will improve when he follows Dharma and retires to the forest?

11. One theme of the book is reconciliation, and by the end of the book there have been several notable reconciliations. However, there are notable conflicts and dilemmas that have not been resolved: the relationship between Aisha, Humayan, and his mother; the relationship between Ash and Ram. What do you think the future has in store for them?

12. The book ends with Leela's promise that she will write a book for Bharati. Why do you think Leela is doing it, and what do you think its contents will be?

*Available only on the Norton Web site: www.wwnorton.com/guides